Susan Wittig Albert

FORGET
ME NEVER

Persevero
Press

Forget Me Never
Copyright © 2024 by Susan Wittig Albert

This is a work of fiction. Names, characters, places, and incidents are the product of the author's imagination or, in the case of historical persons, are used fictitiously.

Publisher's Cataloging-in-Publication data
Names: Albert, Susan Wittig, author.
Title: Forget me never / by Susan Wittig Albert.
Description: Bertram, TX: Persevero Press, 2024.
Identifiers: ISBN: 978-1-952558-23-8 (hardcover) |
978-1-952558-24-5 (paperback) | 978-1-952558-26-9 (paperback)|
978-1-952558-25-2 (ebook)
Subjects: LCSH Bayles, China (Fictitious character)—Fiction. | Murder—Fiction. | Sisters—Fiction. | Texas—Fiction. | Mystery fiction. | BISAC FICTION / Mystery & Detective / General | FICTION / Mystery & Detective / Women Sleuths | FICTION / Mystery & Detective | FICTION / Mystery & Detective / Cozy
Classification: PS3551.L2637 F67 2024 | DDC 813.54--dc23

If you didn't remember something happening,
was it because it never had happened?
Or because you wished it hadn't?
Jodi Picoult, *Plain Truth*

You have not forgotten to remember;
You have remembered to forget.
But people can forget to forget.
That is just as important as remembering to remember—
and generally more practical.
Idries Shah, *Reflections*

Before

Olivia isn't crazy about getting up before sunrise every morning.

But it makes her feel virtuous to be out of bed and into her jogging shorts and T-shirt while her neighbors are still sleeping and it is black as the pit outside and cool. Well, cooler, anyway. It may be spring, but this is Texas. March brought a couple of ninety-degree days and April is off to a blazing start. If you're going to run, you'd better do it in the cool, dark hours before dawn.

Dressed, she laces her Adidas, puts on her headlamp, plugs in her earbuds, and adds the neon-green reflective ankle bands she wears because Zelda (who never hesitates to tell her younger sister what she should do) is forever nagging about the dangers of running in the dark. Zelda has given her an expensive reflective vest, too, with rechargeable LED lights and clever zippered pockets. But it's scratchy and her running shorts have pockets for her cell and house key. Her Fitbit registers her heart rate and—important—counts her steps. It also has a GPS that tells her where on earth she is.

Which she doesn't need because she runs the same out-and-back route every morning. From the end of the driveway, left on Harper Drive, a tenth of a mile to Purgatory Bend Road, a mile west on Purgatory, a mile back east to Harper and home. There's never any traffic on Purgatory at this early hour, so it's just Olivia and her thoughts and her playlist for 6,250 steps, a few more or less. It isn't always easy to be out the door at five in the morning, but her predawn run gets her blood pumping and her brain working and keeps her weight down, which is a challenge now that she's crossed into the never-never land of past-forty.

As Olivia turns out the lights, locks the door, and begins her stretching routine, she's thinking of her plans for the day. A quick shower and breakfast after her run, the morning at the insurance office where she works half-days, and the evening on her laptop, answering email and finishing the weekly post for her true-crime blog and the new podcast she is planning. This post is about the 1885 axe murders of seven servant girls in nearby Austin—gruesome serial slayings that Olivia thinks may have inspired Jack the Ripper. No actual evidence of a connection, of course, but it's interesting to speculate that the Ripper's grisly killings might have been inspired by newspaper coverage of the American murders. Olivia posts one or two historical crimes every month. These allow her to showcase her research interests. And the history gives her blog a little class, she thinks—sets it apart from other true-crime blogs that do nothing but cover the same bloody territory day after boring day.

She drops to one knee and begins flexing her hips. Her blog—and the new podcast—focuses on Texas crime, the more sensational the better, like those gruesome axe murders. She knows that her readers have an insatiable taste for blood, and there's no shortage of raw material. Texas logged over two thousand homicides the previous year. Most killers used guns, of course, but they also employed knives, machetes, blunt objects, narcotics, poison, vehicles, explosives, and (among the less creative) plain old fists and feet. There's no end to the ways people find to kill other people.

Olivia stands, drops to the other knee, and repeats the flexing. After she finishes her blog post, she'll start on the script for the new podcast and then on the plans for the monthly Crime Club book group she manages for Darla McDaniel at Bluebonnet Books. Next week, she and China Bayles will be co-leading the discussion of *Furious Hours: Murder, Fraud, and the Last Trial of Harper Lee*, by Casey Cep. A former criminal defense attorney, China has a somewhat cynical view of the criminal justice system and always raises good questions about a true-crime book. *Furious Hours* will spark a lively discussion.

She stands again and begins a right quad stretch. Maybe she'll even manage to sell a few copies of her own recent book, about the teenage beauty queen from San Antonio who was convicted of poisoning her mother with something she stole from her high school chem lab. The girl might have gotten away with it if she hadn't told her boyfriend what she'd done. "A nearly perfect crime," the Bexar County DA called it. Olivia had snatched that phrase for the title. She'd been so sure it would finally be her breakout book, but it wasn't.

Left quad stretch, then right and left hamstrings. Yes, *A Nearly Perfect Crime* hadn't quite done it. But Olivia never gives up. In fact, she's already moved on to her next project, a winner this time for sure: a story that's powerful enough for *I (Almost) Got Away with It* or even *Dateline*. This killer—Kelly, his name is, or was—really *did* get away with it for nearly twenty years. And now he lives right here in Pecan Springs, under another name, of course. He has become successful and admired, someone everybody looks up to. Well, people won't admire him when they learn who he was and how he managed to finagle a free ride for the last quarter-century, while his crime and his innocent victim have been buried in the past, forgotten by everybody, including the law. She is about to fix that.

Olivia gets back to her feet for a few wall pushes, then turns on her music and begins to jog up Harper, a quiet suburban street on the far southwestern edge of Pecan Springs. It has rained in the night and the air is clean, sweetened with the pleasant scent of damp grass. If she weren't listening to the urgent beat of Journey's "Don't Stop Believin'" in her earbuds, she might have heard the early-morning sounds of the Texas Hill Country: the nearby call of a poor-will, the distant yelp of a coyote on a dawn prowl, a faraway train whistle, the nearer sound of a pickup's ignition—someone else getting an early start on the day. But Olivia hears only the music when she runs, just clears her mind of everything else and lets the rhythmic beat pull her along, powering her stride and feeding its electric energies into her muscles and bones.

This morning, clearing her mind isn't easy. She is thinking—to be honest, she is worrying—about her afternoon meeting with her lawyer, Charlie Lipman. It won't be pleasant, because Charlie wants to talk about the defense he's working on for the trial, which begins in three weeks. Darwin Neely took offense at a few things she wrote in her blog last year and is suing her for defamation, invasion of privacy, and intentional infliction of emotional distress—even though she had written true things about the Adams County murder investigation that Darwin had bungled. Even the sheriff had admitted to mistakes.

Well, being honest again, maybe not everything she wrote about that clown of a sheriff's deputy was *strictly* true. She might have exaggerated a bit here and there, especially when it came to his use of marijuana. If she could do a rewrite of that part she would, but she can't. And Charlie Lipman is warning that the deputy has a pretty strong case now that the judge (probably one of Neely's poker pals) seems likely to rule that, as a freelance blogger and soon-to-be podcaster, she isn't a journalist and is therefore not entitled to protect the anonymity of her sources. It's beginning to look like she will actually have to come clean and admit that she has no sources for a few of the things she's written. Depending on the jury, Charlie says, Neely could win big, both in general damages for pain and suffering and reputational injury and his medical expenses. She should consider settling, Charlie says— that's what he wants to talk about this afternoon. But where would she get the money? And there's Charlie's legal fees, too. He doesn't work for peanuts. Where's that coming from, huh? And what if Jeremy Kellogg decides to make good on his threats and sue for what she had written about *him*?

Olivia reaches the corner where Harper dead-ends at Purgatory Bend Road and runs in place for a moment, looking in both directions, checking for traffic. She doesn't look back over her shoulder. If she had, she might have wondered why the pickup truck a block or so behind her was driving, slowly, with its lights off.

There never is any traffic at this early hour, so she picks up the pace and turns left onto Purgatory, a winding, two-lane road with plenty of ups and downs to test her stamina. The waning moon casts flickering shadows but her headlamp produces a strong cone of light on the shoulder ahead, so she steps it up on this first downhill stretch. For the next quarter mile, she runs on the shoulder of the eastbound lane. She's facing traffic, so if there is a vehicle coming, she'll see it. Past the next snaky curve in the road, however, the left side drops off steeply down to Possum Creek, and a thigh-high metal guardrail lines the road. That's where she always crosses to the westbound side for another three hundred yards or so. It's a downhill stretch where she has to run *with* the traffic. Which she doesn't like, but there's no shoulder at all on the eastbound side, so she has no choice. It's a short stretch and at this time of the morning there is rarely any traffic. She'll be fine.

Delta Rae's "Run" comes up next on her playlist and Olivia matches her rhythm to its insistent bass. It's her favorite piece, not just the beat but the lyrics, especially the line about loving the roads that can't be tamed. That's how she thinks about her life: roads that go somewhere, everywhere, who knows where? Inbound roads that take you into settled places, outbound roads that draw you into wilderness. Usually she loses herself in the song's crashing urgency—*I want to run I want to I want to run run run.* But this morning, the worry about Neely's lawsuit overrides the music. What's on her mind is *money money money.* How much will she need? Where is it coming from? How is she going to get it?

Olivia has reached the top of the downhill stretch toward Possum Creek. When Charlie told her that it seemed likely the judge would rule that she wasn't a journalist, she'd been compelled to do something she'd sworn she wouldn't. A few days ago, she went to the *Enterprise* and begged Hark Hibler, the editor, for her old job as a reporter. She had even given him a few juicy details of the Kelly story, tempting him with hints about how big it will be once she gets her teeth into it. She had told him it didn't matter what kind of job she had—maybe "special assignment" or even as a general assignment reporter—just something, *anything*, that would allow her to claim that she was employed as a journalist. She didn't need a desk or a computer, she didn't even need a press pass. All she really needed was some legal cover. And once she was on board, she would give him Kelly's full story, the *real* story—who he had been, what he had done, who he was now. It was a bombshell.

Unfortunately, the interview hadn't gone as well as she'd hoped. Hark reminded her that he had fired her several years ago, after she had misstated those sources. Worse, he had brought up the Neely lawsuit and remarked—more forcefully than necessary—that a reporter who couldn't stick with the facts was a liability, not an asset. But she could tell that he was tempted by the Kelly story. He had agreed to think about her pitch and get back to her. Maybe she will hear from him today.

She picks up the pace. Charlie has pointed out that whether she settles or Neely wins his suit, it's going to signal her vulnerability to anybody else who thinks he—or she—has a cause of action against her. This afternoon, the lawyer is going to ask her about those potential liabilities. He'll want to know the names of everyone who might not like what she wrote about them. Who might have a grudge against her. Who might come forward with a hand out, demanding money.

If Olivia weren't so fully engrossed in these troubling thoughts or if her playlist hadn't swung into the loud, hard, pulsing beat of "Bad Moon Rising," she might have heard the vehicle accelerating on the downhill slope behind her.

But she doesn't.

And then, quite suddenly, the music stops.

Forever.

Chapter One

Forget-me-not, the memorable folk name of the lovely *Myosotis scorpioides,* has a story behind it. A medieval knight and his lady were walking beside a river. The knight bent to pick a handful of flowers but slipped and fell into the swift-moving water. Before he was carried off and drowned (no doubt weighed down by all that chain mail he wore), he tossed the flowers to his lady, crying "Forget me not!"

China Bayles
"What Am I Forgetting? Herbs to Improve Your Memory"
Pecan Springs Enterprise

Got a minute, China?"

I looked up from the calendar on my laptop to see Ruby in the door between our two shops. She was a costume-drama queen in an ankle-length red bandanna-print caftan, dressed up with gold three-inch hoop earrings, a rainbow of bangle bracelets, and cork-soled wedges that boosted her height to six-feet-plus, all of it topped with crazy-kinky red curls.

"Take all the minutes you want," I said. "It's Monday, so they're free." I smiled indulgently. "To you, anyway, babe. Love that caftan."

But she wasn't smiling. She had her iPad in her hand and something on her mind.

Ruby Wilcox has been my best friend and business partner since I came to Pecan Springs, and the years have eased us into a comfortable routine. Our shops—her Crystal Cave, my Thyme and Seasons—are closed on Mondays, so that's the day we make a little extra time to connect. Early in the morning, we catch up on our weekends, share our to-do lists for the coming week, and remind ourselves (gently) of the problems we have to solve. From the frown on Ruby's face, I guessed that—on this particular June morning—she was dealing with a difficult problem. I was right.

"See this?" She put her iPad on the counter, opened a web page, and turned the tablet around to face me.

I peered at the screen. A lavender-and-gold banner across the top of the page read "The Psychic Sisters of Texas. Seers of the Lone Star State."

Beneath that, another banner: *Choose the psychic that suits your needs and get your first five minutes free!*

Beneath that were displayed photos of four attractive women of various ages. Beneath every photo was a name—obviously a stage name—and a description of the services, with per-minute cost ranging from 99 cents to $3.99. The first one, Mystic Sense, was an intuitive in "mysteries of the heart." Dnalea, a beautiful blonde, was a "psychic empath" who used pendulums and other magical tools to identify "imbalances in your chakra system and auric field." Gaia Gem had stunning silver hair and offered astrological readings, with a "focus on your unique future."

That was the first three. When I got to the fourth, I blinked. She was billing herself as Ashling, an Irish name that means *dreamer.* According to the website, Ashling was an expert in dream analysis, a dream coach, and an "intuitive who specializes in major life decisions." But her real name is Ramona. She is short and plump as a dumpling where Ruby is tall and willowy, but she has Ruby's frizzy red hair and freckles and high-voltage personality. She is Ruby's younger sister. Or, as I've been known to call her in my more exasperated moments, Ruby's evil twin.

"Uh-oh," I said quietly. "Ramona's gone rogue again."

"This is on Facebook, too," Ruby said grimly, jabbing at the screen. "With a prominent link back to the Crystal Cave. In fact, Ramona is asking me to feature this . . . this business of hers. On *our* website. Where she knows she'll get lots of traffic."

"*Our* website? Yours and mine?"

Ruby and I have spent a fair amount of time and money on a website that features both our shops as well as Lori Lowry's weaving studio, the tearoom, our catering service, and Cass Wilde's personal chef business, the Thymely Gourmet. These are all parts of a whole that Ruby and I are involved with and committed to. Adding the Psychic Sisters of Texas would *not* be a good plan.

I opened my mouth, but Ruby beat me to it. "I've already told Ramona it's not going to happen," she said firmly. She gave a resigned sigh. "But you know my sister. When she gets an answer she doesn't want to hear, she just keeps asking."

Which is true. Ramona is a woman with a little too much money (she was bought out by a guilty ex-husband) and a lot of squirrely ideas. In one recent three-month period, she announced that she was buying the Crystal Cave, launching an advertising agency, and purchasing the children's bookstore next door. When all three of these schemes fell through, she bought a controlling interest in the Comanche Creek Brewing Company, even though she doesn't drink beer and knows next to nada about brewing. And not only was she buying the company, she declared, she was engaged to marry the owner as soon as he got a divorce from his wife.

But that plan flopped too. The beer guy made other arrangements, and Ramona pitched her next scheme to Ruby. They would create a website. Ruby would offer psychic consulting. Ramona would do her dream-coach thing. They would go into business as the Psychic Sisters of the Crystal Cave. Brilliant idea. Sure-fire hit. They would make a ton of money.

Now, I have to admit that—from Ramona's point of view, anyway—this team project makes a certain kind of sense. As you may know, Ruby Wilcox is psychic. She inherited this gift (which she privately calls a curse) from her grandmother and great-grandmother. There is nothing made-up or silly or hocus-pocus about it. It may sometimes be weird and occasionally even scary, but it is every bit as real as the red curls and freckles that are coded into her Irish family's DNA. Ruby really *is* psychic. Really.

But I don't expect you to take my word for it. Unless you know somebody like Ruby, you're probably in the same place I was before I met her. I am a logical, rational, skeptical, cut-to-the-chase kind of person, and my native skepticism has been sharpened to a point by years of legal training. I enjoy rational argument. I am curious about the causes of things. I prefer to think there's a reasonable explanation for every event. In short, I am a left-brain thinker.

But Ruby is a quintessential right-brain intuitive who has shown me that there are things in our universe that are simply inexplicable. I am not likely to buy this when it comes to UFOs, visitors from another dimension, and other people who think they're psychic. But I am no longer a skeptic when it comes to Ruby. Her gift is truly magical. And inarguably genuine.

Ramona has inherited a strong dose of the family gift, too, especially when it comes to dreams. She managed to apply herself long enough to earn a degree in transpersonal psychology and a certificate in dream studies. But she somehow missed out on the sense to know when it's appropriate to use her gift and when it's time to unplug. She can tune in to what other people are feeling or thinking, but she usually gets a garbled version. She can sometimes see the future, but never clearly enough to be reliable. And when she gets frustrated or spooked, her inner poltergeist comes out. Weirdness happens. So when I heard about her harebrained scheme for an internet-based psychic consulting service, I thought it was just another very good example of her very bad ideas.*

Ruby thought so too, and said a firm no, not just once but several times. At the Crystal Cave, she teaches classes in the use of divining tools. She loves to show people how to use astrological charts and develop their own psychic abilities with runes, the I Ching, and tarot cards. But she never *sells* her gift and she rarely gives it away, either. She goes out of her way to avoid knowing what's in her friends' minds, especially mine. And she's always apprehensive when she gets a glimpse of the future. She wasn't about to become one of the Psychic Sisters, and she turned Ramona down flat. But looking at Ramona's website on Ruby's iPad, I could see that the refusal hadn't quite done the trick.

Ruby shook her head glumly. "I thought I'd managed to talk Mona out of it altogether, but it looks like I've failed." She turned the iPad around for another look. "I have no idea who these women are and what kind of skills they have. I don't think they're from around here, or I would have heard of them." She paused, her head on one side, considering. "But they're attractive, don't you think? All of them have pretty smiles. They look like they like to talk to people."

"Yes, but the photos could be phony." I pointed to a paragraph

---

* For more about Ramona, read *Blood Orange* (China Bayles #24) and *NoBody*, book 1 in the Crystal Cave trilogy.

titled "Your Choice of Format." "See that? It says I can consult with one of these psychics either by phone or online chat. I can't talk to her via video, so I don't know if I'm talking to the woman in the photograph. In fact, I'd have no idea *who's* on the other end of the line. For all we know, Ramona may be the only real person in this quartet."

Ruby stared at me. "You're saying that these three women are *fictional*? That Mona has made them up? But that's . . . that's cheating, China!"

"More like false advertising. You know as well as I do that anything's possible when it comes to the internet." I frowned. "And especially when it comes to Ramona on the internet." The thought of it was . . . well, unthinkable.

Ruby pressed her lips together. "Do you suppose she's going to get into trouble?" she asked. "Legal trouble, I mean."

"I doubt it," I said. "It's pretty hard to prosecute even the worst of these things."

This is true. Even if Ruby's sister were running an out-and-out scam, she probably wouldn't get nailed for it. I recently read about a woman—a corporate executive with a law degree—who was forced to sell her house to pay a $66,000 bill from her online psychic after the local district attorney told her she didn't have a prosecutable case against him. And the dentist who is still trying to retrieve the $47,000 he paid to a "psychic counselor" who operated out of his laptop. Psychic fraud is one of the fastest-growing web scams, perhaps because lots of people are looking for a little help from the Universe and hope they can get it via the nearest uplink. But there are some ninety-five thousand psychic websites and no easy way to tell which are the scams. So the fraud goes unpunished. Or the fraudster gets off with a baby fine, probation, and time served.

Ruby sighed, and I knew why. Even if Ramona's new project didn't get her crosswise of the law, it posed another danger. She might be hiding behind a stage name, but she's a resident of Pecan Springs and a regular at the Crystal Cave. Ruby's customers are bound to recognize her from her online photo. And, with the help of Facebook and the town's time-tested grapevine, word will get around fast. If they're not for real, the Psychic Sisters have the potential to compromise Ruby's reputation and that of her shop. And by association, perhaps that of Thyme and Seasons; our tearoom, Thyme for Tea; our catering service, Party Thyme; and the Thymely Gourmet. If that happens—

But before we get to the play-by-play, maybe I'd better take a time out and give you a quick overview of our little team. In case this is your first visit to our enterprise, my name is China Bayles. A dozen years or so ago, I left my practice as an attorney in a Houston big-law firm, trading my skyscraper chrome-and-glass office for a very old stone building on Crockett Street in the smallish town of Pecan Springs, halfway between Austin and San Antonio. When I bought it, an architect had converted the front rooms of the building to office and studio space, with a small apartment in the rear where I lived until McQuaid and I married. Now, it's home to my herb shop and Ruby's Crystal Cave.

Each part of our joint enterprise wears the stamp of our individual interests. Ruby's New Age shop invites you to stock up on the magical stuff you need for your extended explorations of inner and outer space: rune stones, astrological charts, crystal balls, magic wands, dream catchers, sage bundles, incense, candles, and so on. In Pecan Springs, the Cave is *the* place to go if you're looking for books on astrology, crystals for divination, or a class in how to read the I Ching. And if you can't decode your tarot card layout or your Ouija board clams up and won't answer your questions, Ruby will be delighted to help. She likes to play cosmic music, and the air is always filled with the soft scent of sandalwood incense.

Plants are my personal passion, and Thyme and Seasons offers everything herbal: racks of dried culinary and medicinal herbs, extracts, and tinctures; herbal vinegars, oils, jellies, and teas; bath herbs, herbal soaps and shampoos; and fragrances, potpourris, and massage oils. I like to support local crafters, so many of the products I offer are made right here in Pecan Springs. There are shelves of books, too, and wreaths and swag on the wall, and racks of potted plants just outside the door. The air smells like dried rosemary and lavender, and there's always a plate of cookies and a sampler of herb teas for customers who care to loiter.

Lori's weaving loft is a recent addition to our little collection of businesses and required some remodeling. Building inspectors are fussy about things like fire exits, so the old wooden staircase had to be brought up to code. The extra air conditioning required rewiring, and windows had to be replaced. But when we took out the existing interior partitions, we discovered that we had a spacious room with an original pine floor and cypress rafters, illuminated by the new skylights and track lighting. Lori has added built-in shelves, worktables, and several looms. She sells yarn and supplies and teaches classes in all things fiber: weaving, spinning, knitting, felting. She also invites the local knitting and quilting groups to meet there, so people are always coming and going.

The tearoom is behind the shops. Ruby came up with the idea and chose its décor: hunter green wainscoting on the old stone walls, green-painted tables and chairs with floral chintz napkins, terracotta pots of herbs on the tables, larger pots of cactus here and there, and a longhorn cow's skull over the door, its horns draped with ivy. The menu is simple and healthy: sandwiches, salads, and quiche, with a sweets tray for afternoon tea parties. The teashop provides an alternative to the usual burger-and-bun fast lunch, gives small groups a place to hold private lunches and teas, and attracts people to the shops.

Cassandra Wilde manages the culinary end of our enterprise. She and her little team use our kitchen—a small-space marvel of food-service engineering—to produce lunches for the tearoom, goodies for Party Thyme (our catering service), and heat-and-eat meals for subscribers to the Thymely Gourmet. Cass, who is certified by the American Culinary Foundation, has worked in the food industry for more than a decade. She's a creative cook with enormous energy and strong marketing skills, a reservoir of cheerfulness that never seems to run dry, and the ability to do what has to be done without a lot of drama.

The limestone building that houses this entrepreneurial crew was built in 1882 by the Duncan family. Once, it sat in the middle of an expansive green lawn. Now, it's surrounded by a half-dozen or so herbal theme gardens, linked by meandering stone paths. Cass's favorite is the Kitchen Garden, with the usual culinary mix of parsley, sage, thyme, mint, basil, savory, rosemary, and more—all featured daily in her menu. Ruby often directs people to the Zodiac Garden, a large circle sliced into twelve pie-shaped wedges: the houses of the zodiac, with the herbs traditionally associated with each. Lori sends her students to gather plants in the Dyer's Garden—coreopsis, tansy, Turk's cap, yarrow, prickly pear cactus. And when I have a quiet moment (not often enough, I'm afraid), I love to sit on the bench beside the Fragrance Garden, which is filled with roses, nicotiana, sweet peas, lavender, and pineapple sage. And on the alley, behind the gardens, is

Thyme Cottage, once a stone stable, now a rustic cottage that I rent as a bed-and-breakfast when it's not scheduled for a class or a workshop.

There you have it: what Ruby laughingly calls our three-ring circus. She and Cass and Lori and I are the ringmasters, jugglers, tumblers, high-fliers, stilt-walkers, fire-eaters, and lion-and-tiger tamers. We are the lions and tigers, too, and the tightrope walkers and the tightrope and sometimes the clowns—*especially* the clowns. Ruby is right. Running a small business is very like living in the middle of a circus act. And when you have several circus acts under one big top, it's even . . . well, more so. We have learned that if we want to stay in business in this challenging economy, we'd better have more up our collective sleeves than a single quick trick.

But we do *not* need to add Ramona's Psychic Sisters fortune-telling act to our already crowded circus. And Ruby didn't need me to tell her so.

With another sigh, she said, "Okay. I'll tell Mona we've talked about this. We're not putting it on our website." She turned off her iPad, hesitated, then—sounding more cheerful—added. "Do you have lunch plans? How about Dos Amigas at noon?"

"Sounds great," I said. Most days, we have lunch in our tearoom. But Dos Amigas is just across the street, which is handy on Mondays when the tearoom is closed. I'm especially fond of their avocado, orange, and jicama salad, which comes with just the right amount of fresh feta cheese and a basket of blue corn tortilla chips, homemade by Maria Lopez in the Dos Amigas kitchen.

Ruby picked up her tablet. "Well, I'd better go back next door. My wand-crafter sent me some awesome new magic wands and I'm rearranging the display to make room for them. They're lovely. I've already picked out the one I want for myself."

I'll bet you don't have many friends who spend their mornings rearranging their magic wands. But I only said, "Hang on a sec." I pulled my laptop around so she could see the screen. "Before you go, here's what we have on our June calendar. Check it over and tell me what I've forgotten."

Propping her elbows on the counter, Ruby scanned the screen. For the next few minutes, we talked about the schedule: a mini-class on yaupon holly, plus two classes and two guest workshops in the cottage; the weaving guild show Lori was hosting in the loft; three private teas in the tearoom, including one for the Pecan Springs Alzheimer's group; and Party Thyme was catering a private party for the Warrens out at their Blind Penny Ranch, out on Remington Road. I had also included the talk I was giving at the Native Plant Society over in Fredericksburg in a few days. June was going to be hectic.

Ruby finished reading and straightened. "Looks right to me," she said. "But busy. Maybe we shouldn't try to do so much."

"Fine," I said. "Which events would you like to cancel?"

Ruby lifted her shoulders and let them drop.

"My feeling exactly." I turned the laptop around. "The calendar will go on the website today and the newsletter will go as soon as it's finished. This afternoon unless something gets in the way."

Ruby patted me on the arm. "I'm glad you can manage that computer stuff. I'm such a dunce at it."

"We all have our gifts," I said. "I'm such a dunce when it comes to that psychic stuff."

She stuck out her tongue at me and left.

Chapter Two

What does our blue flower badge represent? The flower is a forget-me-not, a small blue flower that represents remembrance and is long associated with dementia. People with dementia may experience memory loss, among other symptoms. This makes the forget-me-not the perfect flower to represent our cause. The blue flower pin is a symbol for anyone who wants to unite against dementia, raise awareness and support people affected by the condition.

Alzheimer's Society: United Against Dementia
https://www.alzheimers.org.uk/

I went back to work, but not for long. Khat, our imperious shop Siamese, bounced downstairs from the loft and announced that he had been busy with other matters this morning and had missed breakfast. I told him that I was gainfully occupied at the computer and he could wait until lunch.

But Khat likes to make his wishes known—loudly, repeatedly, endlessly. If I didn't feed him I'd never get any peace. So we went to the kitchen where, a few minutes later, he was addressing himself to a bowl of the chopped liver (slightly warmed) that Cass keeps in the fridge for him. Khat's official name, Khat K'o Kung, was chosen by Ruby in honor of Kao K'o Kung, Qwilleran's talented Siamese in the famous Cat Who series. Khat, of course, insists that this is a mistake. Kao K'o Kung is named after *him*. He would appreciate it if you would correct the oversight.

I glanced at the clock over the fridge. If I intended to post the new inventory items on the website, I'd better get on with the job. I left Khat tucking into his liver and went back to my laptop. I had just uploaded the calendar to the website and was getting started on the newsletter file when I heard a sharp rap on the front door. I had made sure that the CLOSED sign was prominently displayed, so I ignored the rap, thinking the rapper would quit.

She—or he—didn't.

"Go away," I growled, and kept on ignoring until I couldn't. Finally, forcing myself to sound cheerful, I shouted, "Closed today. Open tomorrow, ten until five. Come back then."

"I can't come back." The voice belonged to a woman. "I'm flying to Dallas this afternoon. And London tomorrow. Please—I need to talk to China Bayles *today*."

No, she didn't. I raised my voice again. "Everything we have in the shop is available on the website. And we're always happy to ship. Plants, too."

Well, plants not so much, maybe. And definitely *not* to London. But I'm happier to pack and ship than to interrupt a perfectly good Monday morning to wait on an impatient customer who doesn't understand the word *CLOSED*.

But the woman wasn't taking *happy to ship* for an answer. She rapped again, more urgently now. "If you're China Bayles, please listen, please! I am not a customer. Charlie Lipman sent me. About an important matter. A personal matter." More rapping, even more urgently. "Please!"

A personal matter? Charlie Lipman?

Charlie is a friend and one of Pecan Springs' best lawyers. What's more, McQuaid—my husband, Mike McQuaid—handles many of Charlie's investigations. In fact, McQuaid was down in Brownsville today, doing predeposition interviews in the discovery phase of one of those cases. Was there a problem? A sudden emergency? Had Charlie sent this woman with news about McQuaid?

My belly muscles clenched and I froze for a moment. Then I hit Save, went to the door, and peeked through the glass.

The woman standing outside was tall and slim with a diamond-shaped face and intelligent blue eyes behind squarish tortoiseshell glasses. Her long dark hair was parted in the center and curled on her shoulders. She was dressed in trim-fitting ivory slacks and blazer over a red silk scoop shell. Gold hoop earrings, no other jewelry. I put her in her late forties. She was carrying a black leather briefcase—a lawyer's briefcase.

The bell over the door tinkled when I opened it a crack. "Yes?" I asked apprehensively. Was there something wrong in Brownsville?

"I'm Zelda Andrews." She thrust a business card through the crack. "Mr. Lipman has been handling my sister's legal affairs. He says you knew her—that you were friends. Olivia Andrews."

I glanced at the card. Zelda Andrews, Vice President, Human Resources, Robertson Energy Ltd., Dallas, London. She had her sister's determined chin and confident voice.

And with that, a wave of sharp regret rushed through me. Olivia had been killed in a hit-and-run jogging accident in the spring. I was in North Carolina looking for a missing antique herbal when it happened, so I only knew what I'd read in the *Enterprise* and what I'd heard afterward, from Darla McDaniel at Bluebonnet Books, where Olivia and I facilitated the monthly Crime Club readers' group. It had happened in the very early morning, I remembered, before dawn. A narrow road, running with the traffic. The police had never found the driver who hit her.*

"Olivia and I were friends," I said slowly, looking at the card again. Olivia had usually spoken of her older sister in critical terms, and I had the idea that they weren't close. Zelda's high-powered career kept her busy and she didn't get in touch as often as Olivia thought she should. So what did Zelda want with me? Why had Charlie sent her? And why did this have to happen *today*?

I took a deep breath. The only way I was going to get any answers was to let the woman in and hear what she had to say. I unlocked the door and held it open. "Sorry if I was rude, Ms. Andrews. I'm always a couple of weeks behind on everything and Mondays I play catch-up. Come in."

"Zelda, please," she said, stepping in. "And I'm sorry, too. I just"— she straightened her shoulders with an Olivia-like gesture—"I won't take more than twenty or thirty minutes of your time."

Twenty or thirty minutes. Well, there went the rest of the morning. Resigned, I locked the door again. "If we're going to talk, let's sit down. And do it over iced tea."

I led the way through the door at the back of the shop and into the tearoom. The morning sunlight flooded through the French doors and across the tables, brightening the old stone walls and beamed ceiling. I gestured. "Sit anywhere you like."

"Thank you." Zelda pulled out a chair at one of the tables and put her briefcase on the floor. She glanced around. "What a lovely space. The building looks quite old."

"It is," I said. "Maybe you saw the plaque by the front door. This

---

* The story of China's search for Elizabeth Blackwell's rare and valuable book, *A Curious Herbal*, is told in *Hemlock* (China Bayles #28).

was once a house, built in the 1880s. It has an interesting past—and a lot of character." I nodded at a group of photographs on the wall. "That's the family who lived here, for over sixty years." I might have pointed out that Annie, our resident ghost and the woman for whom the house had been built, was the lovely woman in the white Gibson girl blouse in the larger photo. But Zelda was opening her briefcase and taking out a Redweld expandable file. Whatever this was about, she was not in the mood for history.

A few moments later, I had fetched glasses, ice, and a pitcher of the ruby-red hibiscus tea Cass keeps in the fridge. But no cookies. I wasn't feeling that hospitable.

Zelda began the conversation without preamble. "I think you know that my sister was killed." She said this in a businesslike tone, but the intensity I read in her eyes belied any neutrality. "Early one morning, while she was running."

"Yes," I said, and matched her tone. "I was out of town when it happened, so I didn't learn about it until I got back." I'd read about it in the *Enterprise*, where it was covered by my friend Jessica Nelson. "I am really very sorry," I added. "Your sister and I were coleaders of a book group and we both did trail runs over at Bastrop State Park. She was a strong runner—and a good writer, too. She was quite . . ." I hesitated. "Quite well known in Pecan Springs. She won't be forgotten."

Which is true, of course, in more ways than Zelda Andrews might guess. But I didn't want to go further until I understood where this was going. Was Olivia's sister looking for compassion? Confirmation? Correction? What?

"I miss her too," Zelda said matter-of-factly. "More than I expected, actually. I travel quite a bit for my work and we didn't see one another all that much. She kept saying I'd forgotten her. It wasn't true, but . . . well, life has a habit of getting in the way. I wish now I hadn't let that happen. We could have been closer."

I could understand that feeling, and the guilt that likely came with it. I don't have a sister, but Leatha—my mother—and I had problems when I was growing up. When I left for college and law school, I stayed away. And felt abysmally guilty about it. I was glad those years were over and the two of us had mended our relationship. But I still feel guilty. Maybe that just comes with being a daughter. Or a sister.

Zelda took a deep breath. "I was able to get here the week Olivia was killed, but only for a couple of days. I'm the executor of her estate—simple as it is—so I locked up her house, turned the probate over to Charlie, and let everything wait until I could get back again. This is the first chance I've had. I've been staying there at her house, selling furniture and getting the place ready to go on the market. Last week, I moved the stuff I want to keep to Olivia's storage unit, on King Road. It's only ten by twelve and she'd already stored some furniture there, so it's pretty crowded." She sighed. "It's been quite a job, believe me."

I remembered Olivia's house, in a new development on the west side of town. "The house ought to sell pretty quickly," I said. "I hear that the market is hot just now."

This is true. There's far more new-home development in the area around Pecan Springs than is good for the fragile ecologies of the Hill Country, and existing homes are in great demand. I read recently that the shelf-life of a residential sale property is less than two weeks. Zelda ought to be looking at an offer in a few days.

"The realtor is optimistic," Zelda said, and went on with her narrative. "Long story short, as I was packing up papers and stuff from Olivia's home office, I discovered some notes she was making on a new project. A big one." She pushed her hair back. "I guess you know she was a blogger. True crime. And that she was planning to start a podcast." Her mouth turned down at the corners, giving me the idea that she wasn't exactly enthusiastic about her sister's side hustle.

"Yes, I know," I said. "I was one of her followers. I read every post as soon as I got an email saying it was up." It was true. I'm a fan of true crime, in books, blogs, whatever—probably a holdover from my legal career. And while Olivia sometimes sensationalized the facts, her posts were always a good read. I was genuinely looking forward to her podcasts. I added, "The last time I looked, your sister's blog was still there. Have you taken it down?"

She shook her head. "I've run into a few problems. For one thing, I haven't been able to find her laptop. I have her password but all her online credentials—Facebook, Twitter, her blog—are on the computer. Which is nowhere."

That was strange. Olivia was addicted to her devices. But I was more interested in the project Zelda had mentioned. "She was working on something new?"

"Well, new to her. But it's an old case—twenty years old. The killer was already convicted and sentenced." Behind her glasses, Zelda's eyes were fixed on my face. "As I said, I just discovered this project material of hers, and now I have to leave again. I won't be back here for two or three months, maybe longer. So I thought I should talk to somebody about what Olivia was up to. Somebody who might . . . well, might be able to help."

Help how, I wondered. I wasn't sure I wanted to know. I sidestepped. "So that's why you went to see Charlie Lipman?"

She nodded. "I thought he might know what she was up to. He didn't. But he told me to talk to you. He said you knew Olivia well.

You'd know something about the projects she got involved in. The way some people felt about . . . well, about what she wrote."

The way people felt. That might sound a bit strange, but I understood what Zelda was saying. As a blogger, her sister had built a dedicated coalition of enthusiastic readers who followed every story and commented on her posts. I knew from reading her Facebook page that they genuinely missed her. And yes, she had a lot of followers—but they weren't all friends and fans. How to say this? I took a breath.

"It's complicated," I said. "Your sister had strong ideas and a big voice that she knew how to use. That bothered some people, but it was what I liked about her." I was choosing my words carefully, threading through a maze of difficult truths about a difficult woman. But Zelda was nodding as if she understood and agreed. Or at least accepted.

Olivia Andrews had made a name for herself as a local writer. She got her start as a reporter for the *Pecan Springs Enterprise* when it was still owned and managed by the Seidensticker family. She covered accidents, the weekly jail log, and crime, but when Hark Hibler took over the editor's desk, he brought in a couple of new people and let her go. She got a part-time job with Carter's Insurance, over on Nueces Street, and with the rest of her time, she sat down at the computer and wrote a true-crime book about the infamous 1884–85 Austin axe murderer. The killer attacked sixteen people and killed eight of them—seven servant girls and one man—predating Jack the Ripper by only a couple of years. In fact, Olivia argues in her book that the Austin killer pulled up stakes, moved to London, and *became* the Ripper. Unfortunately, she wasn't able to summon any credible evidence to back up her assertion, other than the fact that both killers targeted servant girls and liked to work at night. It was vintage Olivia: interesting ideas, long on sensational claims but short on evidence.

A couple of years later, she wrote a second true crime, a dramatic account of a teenage beauty queen who was convicted of poisoning her mother with something toxic she stole from her high school chemistry lab. It attracted so much attention that Olivia even began hoping for a movie deal. At one point, she told me that Matthew McConaughey (remember him from *The Lincoln Lawyer?*) was about to make an offer for the film rights. She was bitterly disappointed when it didn't happen.

But if neither of her books attracted the national or even the state-wide attention she hoped for, Olivia's blog, called *Forget Me Not: A Crime Victim's Storyboard*, was an entirely different matter. It started off slowly when she launched it three or four years ago, but by the time she died, it boasted nearly twenty thousand followers and was frequently featured in the *Austin American-Statesman* and the *San Antonio Express-News*. She chose her crimes carefully, always looking for the most sensational, but always paying more attention to the victim's story than the criminal's. She tracked every case from the earliest report of the crime through the police investigation to the arrest and indictment and then the trial and sentencing, which she defined as the final achievement of justice for the victim. She squeezed dramatic, out-of-the-ordinary details out of the cops, the DA's office, the local newspaper, and of course the victim's family and friends. At the trial, she claimed a prominent place in the journalists' pew, eyes on the jury and notebook in hand. And after the verdict was rendered, she interviewed everybody she could catch up with, making her own cellphone videos of the interviews and posting them on her blog.

She also posted her favorite theories of the crime, along with freely expressed criticisms of the perpetrator, the cops, the prosecutors and defense attorneys, the judge, the jury, and any politicians who got involved in the case. Olivia was an equal-opportunity blogger, taking potshots (cheap shots, some called them) at everybody except the victim, which is not exactly the best way to earn friends and influence people. It's fair to say that while many readers mourned the untimely death of *Forget Me Not*, there were those who celebrated its passing and hoped it would be quickly forgotten.

Don't get me wrong. I might not have appreciated everything Olivia wrote, but I admired her unerring sense of what was important, her fearless curiosity, and the bulldog way she sank her teeth into her stories. She might sensationalize the crimes themselves and the criminals, but—unlike many true-crime bloggers—she focused on the victims. She posted their photographs, interviewed their families and friends, researched their backstories in depth and told those stories in moving, deeply felt detail. I appreciated the respectful effort she put into keeping them front and center, neatly symbolized by the stylized blue forget-me-not that was her blog's logo. "Let's not forget," she wrote often. "Please, let's not forget." Her readers loved it.

But while Olivia's blog made her something of a local celebrity, it also brought her plenty of unwelcome trouble. True-crime junkies who got obsessed with her work. Paranoid crazies who thought she was writing about *them*. And there was the legal trouble. Serious legal trouble.

Which was where Charlie Lipman came into the picture. She had hired him to defend her when a couple of the people she wrote about in her blog took serious offense and filed defamation lawsuits. Charlie had gotten the flimsiest suit dismissed, but I knew of one—brought by Adams County deputy Darwin Neely—that was still alive when Olivia died. And I had heard of another, this one threatened by Jeremy Kellogg, a televangelist who got into some trouble at a megachurch in Dallas and had to step down from the pulpit. Olivia had told me that

Charlie was advising her to settle, but she was afraid that settling might attract other suits.

The way people felt about what she wrote. Yes, it was complicated.

Zelda took a sip of her tea, set her glass down with a clunk, and looked squarely at me. "Anybody who knew my sister knows that she had her share of enemies. I know it. I think you know it, too." She took a breath. "And if you ask me, whoever hit Olivia did it on purpose. Her death was no accident. It was *murder*."

That stopped me cold. "I agree about the enemies," I said slowly, "but what makes you think it wasn't an accident? Olivia was running in the early morning, when it was still pitch black, on a narrow shoulder, on the wrong side of the road." I could hear myself being critical, but every runner knows that's a dangerous practice. "The newspaper said she was struck from behind, probably by a vehicle's passenger-side mirror. You know, one of those long-armed towing mirrors you have on your car or truck if you're pulling a trailer."

"It was a hit-and-run." Zelda met my eyes. "The driver left the scene. He was never caught."

"Leaving the scene makes it criminal." I shook my head. "Doesn't make it murder."

"This does." Zelda reached for the file folder she had taken out of her briefcase and eyed me with something like her sister's bulldog determination. "What I have here is the motive. I want you to read it."

I pressed my lips together. I had admired Olivia—admired her style, her doggedness, her insistence on having her say. I thought of her often, missed our trail runs, missed reading her blog posts and discussing books. But I had plenty else on my plate. Too much.

"I'm sorry, Zelda," I said, trying to soften my refusal. "Early summer is our busy season. I have a ton of garden work to do, plus catering events to manage. I don't have time for extra reading right now."

"Some of my sister's stories got her sued." Zelda tapped the folder. "This one got her killed. It contains the stuff I found in her office, in her old rolltop desk. It's mostly drafts of the blog entries she planned to post. There are missing details and blanks to be filled in, so you need to think of it as a work in progress."

"Now, wait a minute, Zelda," I began, but she was going on.

"Other notes are there, too—where she thought the story was headed, the research she was planning, the people she intended to talk to. There's even a note about an exchange of texts she had with this guy, when he threatened her."

"He . . . threatened her?"

"Read it and see what you think. Her note about that is pretty cryptic and she doesn't name names. But he was trying to shut her up, get her to drop the story." She became more intense. "I hate to say it but I'm not surprised, really. I've never pretended to know what compelled my sister to do what she did. We grew up together. You'd think I'd have some idea what made her tick. But this part of her life—the blogging part—was a mystery to me. All I know is that she had a habit of making enemies. Like that lawsuit."

"Oh, come on," I replied lightly. "If you're thinking of Darwin Neely, think again. Neely was never a threat to your sister's life. Why would he kill her? She had no factual basis for the exaggerated claims she made in her blog, and he was going to win his suit. If she had lived, she'd have owed him money. He had no reason to want her dead."

"I agree," Zelda said flatly. "Neely didn't kill her." She tapped the folder. "This guy—the guy she's writing about here—had a different reason to do it. She hadn't written about him yet. He had to stop her."

"Really?" I refrained from rolling my eyes.

Zelda leaned forward, focused, intent. "Why are you surprised? Charlie Lipman says you used to be a criminal lawyer, so you surely know the risks she was running. I told her time and again that her habit of naming names and pointing fingers was going to get her killed. I wasn't trying to be clever or funny or anything else. I just wanted to *scare* her." Her voice grew more urgent. "I wanted her to think about the people she was writing about, some of them criminal, some of them powerful, all of them with something to hide. But she didn't listen." There were tears in Zelda's eyes. "She never listened," she said in despair. "Olivia *never* listened to anybody, especially not to me."

We both fell silent. I couldn't help feeling that Zelda was exaggerating this whole thing. But Olivia was undeniably dead.

"And that's what you think happened?" I asked slowly. "Your sister uncovered an old murder and intended to out the killer—but he killed her before she could reveal who he was?"

"Yes, that's exactly what I think." Zelda dropped her hand on the file folder. "Look, China. All I'm asking you to do is read this. I didn't have time to dig out all the notes, and there may be more in Olivia's storage unit, where I stashed the stuff from her office." She was hurrying on, anxious to get it all out. "What's here is what I could put together quickly, mostly about the case in River Oaks, the arson murder. What *isn't* here is the name of the convicted killer. But he's obviously of some importance in Pecan Springs or maybe in a nearby town. Charlie Lipman says you know everybody. You'll be able to figure out who he is. Once you've done that, you can use the information to—"

"Whoa, Zelda. Hang on a sec." River Oaks? That was the affluent neighborhood in Houston where I grew up. But that wasn't what had caught my attention. Very serious now, I raised a hand.

31

"Charlie Lipman should have told you to tell this to the police. They've got access to all the information they need—databases, DNA records, fingerprints, all that high-powered forensic stuff. What's more, they don't like it when somebody who isn't a cop starts poking her nose into cop business. They call it obstruction of justice."

"I looked that up." Zelda was brisk. "It's only obstruction when there's an active investigation. Olivia's case is closed. It's been ruled a hit-and-run. There's nothing to obstruct."

"Nope, not true. In Texas, there is no statute of limitations on a hit-and-run that results in a fatality. The police may not be pursuing your sister's case as actively as you'd like, but it's still open. Whatever's involved here, you should take it to the cops."

She wasn't daunted. "Actually, I have *been* to the cops, for all the good it did. I spoke to the investigating officer on Saturday, right after I found Olivia's notes. A woman named Kidder."

Rita Kidder. I knew her. She was fairly new, but a good cop. "What did she say?"

"She listened politely, but that was as far as it went. They're done. They've got other things to keep them busy." She leaned forward. "Look, China. If my sister was right, this thing goes back to a murder twenty-some years ago. This guy killed his wife and was tried, convicted, and then released. But the connection between that and Olivia's death is . . . well, it isn't the kind of thing the cops are set up to handle easily, even if they wanted to, which they don't. And of course I'm not asking you to do this as a favor. I'm glad to pay you for your time."

She pushed the file folder toward me, speaking fast. "Here it is, everything I could put together on short notice. There are two codes written inside the folder's front cover. One is the seven-digit code you need to get through the gate at the storage place. The other is the code to the lock on the storage unit door. Take a left when you get in. Unit 126 is one of the smaller ones, all the way to the back. It's a bit crowded with some family antiques Olivia was storing there—a china cabinet and a vintage table, plus the things I've stashed because I might want them. The desk, for instance. Olivia loved it so I'm keeping it for now. I put all the files you'll want to look at in the boxes stacked just to the right as you go in the door. There are five of them, all marked office."

"Wait." Something had snagged my attention. "You said this man—what's his name?"

"James Kelly."

"You said Kelly killed his wife, was tried and convicted and *released*. Because he was exonerated?"

"There was no exoneration. The sentence was just . . . vacated." Zelda pulled her heavy brows together. "*Vacated*. That was the word Charlie used. When I asked him to explain, he laughed and said it was a slick defense attorney's trick that you would know about." She paused. "He also said that you're probably acquainted with the lawyer who made it happen, because he was a partner in the law firm where you used to work." Her mouth grew tight. "To tell the truth, that made me more than a little curious. Did a clever defense lawyer enable a convicted killer to go free? To get away with murder—so he could murder somebody else?"

You might have heard of a vacated sentence. It happens when an appellate court sets aside the judgment of a lower court. It means that the appellate court must have found a significant error in the lower court's trial process. Somebody—usually the prosecutor or the judge—is found to have made a mistake, or there was juror misconduct or even witness tampering. Whatever the reason, the vacatur simply means that the conviction was legally voided and the case was sent back to the trial court. Had it been retried? If so, what was the verdict? If not, why not?

And who was the slick defense lawyer who got this guy off? Did I know him? I had to admit that my curiosity was piqued—at least about this part of the story. And I was beginning to see what Zelda was getting at.

"So you're saying that your sister dug up an old story about a guy who got away with murder a couple of decades ago. She intended to update it and publish the results. He found out what she was doing and killed her to keep her from doing it."

"Arson murder," Zelda said. "And yes, that's it. That's what I'm saying."

I shook my head. "The theory sounds plausible enough, I grant you. But it's got a built-in fatal flaw. Kelly's murder conviction was *vacated*. The case may even have been dismissed. There's no statute of limitations on murder, but I can double-damn guarantee you that the Harris County DA's desk is stacked to the ceiling with hundreds of current and recent cases, all of which have a higher priority. The DA isn't going to waste valuable prosecutorial resources investigating a twenty-year-old vacated case that a previous DA apparently didn't retry, probably because he decided he couldn't win it. Bottom line: this whole business has been forgotten. Olivia was no threat to this man. So he was no threat to her. Period. Paragraph. End of story."

"But Olivia didn't just dig up the old case." Zelda was emphatic. "She connected it to the killer, to Kelly. He's assumed a new identity. He's living here in Pecan Springs. And he's important. He's somebody who can't afford to have his cover blown."

"Oh, yeah?" I asked skeptically. "Who is he?"

"I told you, China, I don't know. But from Olivia's notes, he's somebody with a lot to lose if the old story ever comes out. So you see? It wouldn't matter whether the sentence was vacated or not. This man was convicted of murder. He wasn't exonerated. He could still be retried. And he attempted to escape his past by taking on a new identity. He isn't James Kelly any longer. He's somebody else."

"Ah," I said. It was true. If Olivia had her facts straight—which might be a pretty big *if*—she could pose a serious threat to somebody who had gone to a lot of trouble to ensure that his past was forgotten. "And you have no idea who?"

Zelda shook her head. "No clue. There's a note in that folder suggesting that Olivia was going to interview a cousin of the murder victim in Fredericksburg. The woman apparently remembered the crime and might be willing to talk about it." She paused and her eyes grew brighter. "Why, of course! I should have thought of that. The cousin might even know who he is. Who he is *now*, I mean. Maybe that's where Olivia got her information."

Well, now. I was giving that talk in Fredericksburg in a few days. If Olivia had made a note of the name and address, I could maybe check out the cousin. I looked down at the folder.

"So you want me to review Olivia's notes and try to identify this man she was planning to write about. What else?"

"I really don't know," Zelda said slowly. "Maybe you could talk to Officer Kidder and get her to take another look at what happened to Olivia?" She paused. "And as I said, I haven't been able to find Olivia's Lenovo. She used that laptop for all her writing, her notes and interviews, all that stuff. It wasn't in the house or in her car. I called all the repair shops in town, but nobody seems to have it. Her cellphone, too. I'm sure she'd never go running without it, but Officer Kidder said it wasn't on her when she was found." She flashed me an eager glance.

"Then you'll do it, China? You'll see if you can find out what happened to Olivia?"

"No," I said emphatically. "I'll read her notes. That's as far as I'll go right now. You said you're headed back to England tomorrow?"

She nodded. "I wish I could be here to help. But I'm available by phone and text, if there's anything I can do." She took out a business card and scribbled something on the back. "Chloe McDermott is the name of the listing agent for Olivia's house. If you want to get into it for any reason, just call her. There's my personal cell number. And an address where you can send me the bill."

"I'll invoice Charlie Lipman," I said drily. "He's the one who got me into this."

"No, don't." Zelda stood, all business now. "I'm *your* client, not his. Invoice me."

"Hey, that was a joke," I said, getting hastily to my feet. "You're not a client. And I don't have an investigator's license."

The corners of her mouth turned up in what might have been meant as a smile. "You're a lawyer, aren't you? I'm sure you'll think of something."

A figure shadowed the doorway and I turned to see Ruby. "Gosh," I said, startled. "Is it lunchtime already? Hang on, Ruby—I'll be with you in just a moment."

"And I'll get out of your way," Zelda said. Leaving the folder on the table, she picked up her briefcase. "I'm anxious to hear what you find out. Do keep me posted. And *bill me*." She was gone before I could say "Don't hold your breath."

"Bill her?" Ruby followed Zelda's exit with an inquiring look. "What's that about?"

"Long story," I said, as the bell over the front door tinkled, announcing Zelda's departure. "I'll tell you after lunch."

Ruby gave me a rueful glance. "Sorry, but I have to cancel. The nursing home just called. Doris has escaped again."

"Escaped? Oh, no! Has she been gone long?"

"A half hour. The police have put out a Silver Alert. Amy and I are going to look for her."

You may remember Doris, Ruby and Ramona's mother. Back in the day, she was one of those women who like to call the shots. She was the head honcho, the big boss, in charge of everything, at home and at Perkins Used Car Dealership, where she worked as the company bookkeeper for nearly four decades.

But a couple of years ago, Doris stopped calling the shots. She was still working and living independently when Ruby noticed that her mother was forgetting appointments, forgetting her keys and her credit cards, even (as time went on) forgetting the names of her daughters. But it was when she morphed into a kleptomaniac with a passion for scarves that Ruby had to take command. They weren't your everyday, dinky dime store scarves, either. A security guard at Neiman Marcus in San Antonio once nabbed Doris as she was leaving with a three-hundred-dollar bag stuffed full of sixty-dollar hand-painted silk scarves—and no cash register receipts. And when Ruby started snooping around her mother's apartment, she found scarves hidden in the closet, in drawers, in the refrigerator, in the oven.*

There was only one conclusion: Doris was losing her marbles. Or as her granddaughter Amy put it with a sad affection, she was two tacos

---

* For Doris' story: *Spanish Dagger* (China Bayles #15).

short of a combo plate. Or, repeating the food metaphor, "Gramma Doris has been out to lunch for the past year or so."

Doris now lives in the Alzheimer's wing at the Castle Oaks Nursing Home. To see that somebody brings her back if she goes AWOL, Ruby found some help-cards that have a drawing of a little blue forget-me-not, a flower that has long been associated with remembrance. The cards have her mother's name and address and an emergency contact number. They're useful––when Doris remembers to put them in her pocket.

She also has a forget-me-not pin with a one-word legend: *Alzheimer's*. But she wears it upside-down. When Ruby asks her why, she says she likes to be able to read it and remember why she keeps forgetting that word. "It's the *z*," she explains. "I can't remember words that have a *z* in them. They ought to do away with that letter. Nobody can remember it."

This may all sound very funny, and in a way, I suppose it is. Ruby and I are often moved to laugh at the genuinely comic things her mother says and does. "I am nuttier than a pecan pie," Doris once remarked in frustration. But we can't help feeling guilty when we laugh. After all, there's nothing even remotely funny about forgetting—especially when it's your name you can't remember. Still, what else can we do but shake our heads and smile at the sad comedy of being human and growing older and losing our death-grip on the dailiness of life? If we can't laugh, we have to cry, and as Doris says, "Nobody wants to be a crybaby when they grow up."

When it became clear to her daughters that she could no longer live alone, Doris came to stay with Ruby—until she began wandering the neighborhood, hardly a safe pastime for a senior citizen who may or may not remember where home is. Ruby and Ramona found her a place at Castle Oaks, about ten minutes from Ruby's house. The home is comfortable, the nurses are caring and compassionate, and the facility promises to keep its residents under lock and key.

The trouble is that Doris isn't fond of staying put, and when she wants to wander, she can be wily. One chilly morning, she filched a nurse's coat, slipped out the front door with a group of visitors, and hiked to Cavette's Market, some six blocks away. There, she liberated a bottle of apple juice and a dozen Hershey's bars. When Junior Cavette confronted her on her way out and asked her for money, she looked at him cheerfully. "I have twenty-three million bucks in the bank," she said, "but I forgot to bring my checkbook."

Junior took in the situation (Doris was wearing bedroom slippers and a nightie under the coat) and politely confiscated eleven of the Hershey's bars before he phoned the cops. To Doris' delight, the call was answered by a handsome young officer who was happy to put on his flasher and siren for the trip back to Castle Oaks. She has forgotten now why she went to Cavette's but remembers that the officer invited her to ride home in the front seat of his squad car. "Right beside him!" she crows. "And he was a *hunk*."

And today she was off again. Ruby, Amy, and I got in our cars and fanned out, going to places that Doris had visited on earlier expeditions. Amy headed for the campus, where her grandmother had once been discovered in the art museum, gazing raptly at a painting of a nude male. Ruby drove to Pedernales Park, and I went to Cavette's Grocery, thinking that she might be shopping for more Hershey's.

It was Ruby who found her. Doris was sliding down the sliding board at the park, her legs sticking out like a scarecrow, her dress hitched up around her waist. As she reached the bottom, Ruby held out a hand and said gently, "We need to get you home, sweetie. Everybody's looking for you."

Doris was ready to bargain. "I'll come if you promise not to tell Mom. That woman is as mean as the Wicked Witch of the West. She never lets me go *anywhere*."

"Of course I won't tell her, dear," Ruby assured her. "It'll just be between you and me."

"Thank you," Doris said with a sigh, obviously relieved. "I know I can trust you. You are such a wonderful sister."

Chapter Three

Of all the many things humans rely on plants for—sustenance, beauty, medicine, fragrance, flavor, fiber—surely the most curious is our use of them to change consciousness: to stimulate or calm, to fiddle with or completely alter, the qualities of our mental experience. Like most people, I use a couple of plants this way on a daily basis. Every morning without fail I begin my day by preparing a hot-water infusion of one of two plants that I depend on (and dependent I am) to clear the mental fog, sharpen my focus, and prepare myself for the day ahead.

Michael Pollan
This Is Your Mind on Plants

Upstairs in the bedroom that night, McQuaid pulled off his polo shirt. Quite seriously, he said, "Honestly, China, if you're going to look into Olivia Andrews' death, I think you should bill her sister for it. Everybody deserves to be paid for the work they do. And if you're nervous about it, you can work under my license and *I'll* bill."

Brownsville-to-Pecan-Springs is a five-hour drive, and McQuaid had gotten home late. But there was time to share a companionable bottle of red wine, a plate of cheese and crackers, his recap of his trip, and my report of Zelda Andrews' theory about her sister's death—and her billing instructions.

"What would you charge her?" I asked, after we had gone upstairs to the bedroom. McQuaid has always liked to joke about hiring me as an investigator, but while I enjoy resolving the occasional puzzle—like that intriguing business with the vanilla orchids last year—I don't have a burning desire to be on my husband's payroll. Still, it would be interesting to know the going rate.*

"We bill a flat three hundred for a full criminal records search, like that twenty-year-old murder case," he said over his shoulder as he headed for the bathroom. "Interviews, accident reconstruction, undercover if necessary—that's all field work, one-fifty an hour. Plus travel and expenses." He turned at the door. "Plus clerical, too, if the client wants a written report instead of a phone update."

Surprised, I sat down on the bed. "Three hundred for a criminal history search? Why, that's highway robbery! Somebody who knows what he's doing probably wouldn't spend more than twenty minutes lookup time on the internet." I raised my voice over the sound of running water. "Really, McQuaid, I had no idea. You and Blackie don't come cheap, do you?"

My husband's reply was somewhat blurred by the buzz of the electric toothbrush, but I was able to make it out. "That's what pays the bills around this place, honeybunch."

"The shop does its share, too," I countered, as Winchester, our basset hound and successor to our still-missed and long-lamented Howard Cosell, lumbered into the bedroom and came over to lean against my knee. I bent over to fondle his droopy ears. "Your humans work hard to pay for your puppy biscuits," I reminded him affectionately. "We promise you'll never run out."

I don't think Winnie believes me. Not quite four yet, he is still young and gullible enough to be lured into an ear-flapping,

---

* The orchids were part of the plot of *A Plain Vanilla Murder* (China Bayles #27).

jowl-swinging, stubby-legged gallop by an insolent squirrel or a blundering armadillo. But he is by nature a mistrustful old soul who has already seen enough of the betrayals of this world to be profoundly pessimistic about its long-term prospects, especially when it comes to issues of food security. Winchester is a gloomy fellow for whom happiness is always just out of reach—unless it is dinnertime. Or breakfast. Or lunch or snacks. In those moments, with actual food within sight, he is as close to blissful as a basset can get.

But he licked my nose anyway, heaved a melancholy sigh, and plopped sixty pounds of dog across my feet. I retrieved them and began pulling off my sandals.

"You're saying the sister thinks somebody ran into Olivia Andrews *intentionally*?" McQuaid came back into the bedroom with toothpaste at one corner of his mouth. "That hit-and-run on Purgatory Bend a few months ago—she claims it wasn't an accident?"

My husband is athletically built, six feet two and broad-shouldered, with dark hair, intent pale blue eyes in a craggy face, a once-broken nose and a knife scar across his forehead. A former homicide detective, he currently holds two jobs. He's an adjunct professor of Criminal Justice at Central Texas State University and a private investigator with his own firm: McQuaid, Blackwell, and Associates. Blackwell is Blackie Blackwell, previously sheriff of Adams County, now married to my friend Sheila, the Pecan Springs chief of police. Associates are freelancers hired to do surveillance, financial asset searches, witness interviews, and the like. Every once in a while, McQuaid has asked me to help out on a case when they need someone with legal experience. I'm always willing to put in my two cents on an informal basis, but that's as far as I go. I have plenty to do at Thyme and Seasons.

"Right.," I said. "Zelda is convinced that it wasn't an accident." I stood, unzipped my shorts, and stepped out of them. "I've read enough of Olivia's notes to think that she might be onto something. If the guy driving the vehicle that killed her was the person whose past criminal life Olivia was threatening to reveal, he could have had a pretty strong motive." I gestured toward the manila folder on the table at my side of the bed. "I'll have a better idea after I finish going through the notes."

"That's research," McQuaid said. He had stripped to his jockey shorts. "Sure we can't hire you? Seventy an hour to you. More if you take good notes."

"*Seventy* an hour?" I said, my eyes on him. "You're making that up." He's all muscle, flat belly, slim hips, lean thighs, not an extra ounce. I pulled off my T-shirt.

"Am not," he replied firmly. "With your trained legal mind and years of experience, you should definitely get paid."

"I don't have a license." I unhooked my bra.

"I do. Like I said, you can work under mine." Head cocked to one side, not quite smiling, he was watching me. "Very nice," he said appreciatively. "Spectacular, even. Let's make that eighty an hour."

"Ninety," I said. I appreciated his appreciation. Since I started trail running last fall, I'm leaner. And stronger. And feel much better.

He stepped out of his jockeys and came toward me, eyes glinting. "What else do you have there, wife?"

"What you see is what you get." I slipped out of my panties, stood, and held out my arms. His kiss tasted like toothpaste. "Don't step on Winchester," I murmured against his bare shoulder. His skin was salty.

"Out of the way, dog," he growled. He kissed me again, then lifted me onto our bed and leaned over me, bending his head to my breast. I arched against him, replying to his urgency, responding to my own. He had been out of town for the past five or six days. Before that, our adopted daughter Caitie and I had spent a long weekend at my mother's ranch in South Texas, where Caitie was now. Before that, he'd been in Dallas on an investigation for a new client. We had missed each other. We were hungry.

So for the next little while, as Winchester snored companionably beside the bed, McQuaid and I did what two people do when they're in love and have a healthy appetite for sex and have been apart for too long. It was an enjoyable and deeply satisfying few moments. When we were finished, he rolled over onto his back.

"Why?" he asked, his eyes still closed.

I grabbed a breath, and then another. My heart was pounding as if I'd just run up and down the stairs a half-dozen times. "Why what?"

"Why don't we do that more often?"

"Because we aren't together that often. I've been gone. You've been gone. We'll have to synchronize our calendars."

"I was thinking of something more immediate." He opened his eyes, turned his head toward me, and reached for my breast. "How about tonight? We could read for a while and see if the spirit moves us again."

"Greedy fellow." I rose on my elbow and dropped a kiss on his nose. "I'll pencil it in."

"That's my girl." McQuaid picked up his iPad and opened John Sandford's latest Lucas Davenport thriller. McQuaid sometimes imagines himself as Davenport. I tell him it's not much of a stretch, actually. There are a great many similarities, if you disregard Davenport's fondness for expensive suits and bespoke shoes from Cleverley of London. McQuaid is a jeans-and-sneakers guy.

I put on my reading glasses, adjusted the pillow at my back, and reopened the folder. As Zelda had said, there were two codes written inside the front cover, with the address of the storage unit—Store-It-Rite, on the east side of I-35. I pulled out the loose pages, mostly printouts of computer files with some handwritten annotations and a few marginal notes, and began reading. It didn't take long.

"Interesting," I said, taking my glasses off.

No, not just interesting. It was fascinating, with all the appeal of a classic true crime. The facts were still cloudy, but that's often the case when it comes to facts, at least when you first start looking at them. People like to say that facts don't lie, but that's not quite true. Facts can lie, and can be used to lie. Facts are often vague, unclear, ambiguous. Resolving their ambiguities can take a while. And even then, there's the question of who assembled this particular set of facts and why and on what principles and from what sources. And so on.

McQuaid glanced at the bedside clock. "Twenty-two minutes. We bill in fifteen-minute increments. The client could already owe you thirty-five dollars." He chuckled. "See how easy it is? And when you clear the case, you'll be eligible for a bonus."

"Imagine that." I made a wry face, remembering how good it had felt when I left the law firm and was no longer required to turn in two thousand billable hours, parceled out in six-minute increments.

"Just teasing," McQuaid said, patting my bare thigh. He turned off his iPad and put it on the table. "Anyway, I suppose you've already figured out who dunnit. Killed your blogger friend, I mean."

"There's nothing in these notes about Olivia's death," I said. "This is about the case she was working on, the *original* crime. It's an entirely separate matter." Except, of course, that the notes in this folder might provide a motive for what happened on Purgatory Bend. "It's a murder in River Oaks a couple of decades ago. A man was convicted of killing his wife, appealed, and was released when his sentence was vacated.

He seems to have dropped out of sight for a while. Then he came back with a whole new identity and has gone on to bigger and better things—in Pecan Springs. At least, that's what Olivia seemed to think."

"A new identity, huh?" McQuaid glanced at me, eyebrows raised, interested. His firm does its share of identity tracing. "Who is he now? Somebody we know?"

"Olivia doesn't say. And her notes—at least, the ones I have here—are a little scrambled." That was an understatement. The pages Zelda had gathered and stuffed into this folder were a *lot* scrambled. I had found myself wondering if there was more in Olivia's laptop and wishing I had it. "Apparently he went abroad somewhere after his conviction was vacated. He came back with a new identity. That's it."

"Can be done." McQuaid pursed his lips. "A couple of years ago, I worked on a case where a guy bailed out of a bad relationship and took off for Costa Rica, where he committed pseudocide."

"Pseudocide?" I frowned, puzzled. Then I got it. "Oh. Pseudo-cide. He faked his own death."

"Exactly. Went on a seashore hike and just didn't come back—supposedly fell off a cliff into the ocean. But he didn't leave much behind except some bad feelings. No wife or parents to mourn him, no unfinished business, no significant debts, no insurance claim. And faking your death isn't a crime."

"That depends," I reminded him. "Packing your wheelie and boarding a plane may be perfectly legal. It's the ancillary stuff that can get you in trouble. Tax fraud, insurance fraud, obstruction of justice. Not to mention the Texas law against using or possessing a fake ID."

"Yeah," McQuaid conceded. "There's that. Well, anyway, a few years later, my guy came back to the states with a shiny new identity, launched a start-up, and made himself a brand-new life. Got away with it too, for over a decade." He paused. "Of course, that kind of thing was easier when you could still get a Social Security card with a fake birth certificate and a plausible story. And it worked best if you had a wad of cash. Margaritaville doesn't come cheap."

"Pseudocide," I said again, trying it out. "It was probably easier before social media, Google, and facial recognition software. That's when Olivia's guy did it—before the internet." I corrected myself. "*Allegedly* did it."

"Definitely easier before the internet," McQuaid agreed. "If you planned your exit and reentry right, even the best skip tracer in the business could come up empty."

I thought about that for a moment. "Well, if Olivia was right about this guy being an upstanding citizen *now*, he probably had something to lose if his friends and fans found out who he was back *then*." Something big to lose. Maybe even something worth killing for.

"You haven't figured out who he is?"

I shook my head. "What's here is mostly about the River Oaks murder case—the original crime." I flipped through the pages. "Maybe you'll recognize it." McQuaid had been a detective at Houston Homicide, and the Houston PD would have investigated this murder.

"Could be. When was it?"

I found the date, and he did a quick calculation. "Nope. I was still in the police academy that year. Where were you?"

"In my first year at the law firm, working seventy-hour weeks. No time for newspapers or TV news."

He nodded. "Let's hear the short version. It might jog my memory."

I pulled out a page of Olivia's notes. "We're talking about a man named James Q. Kelly—Q for Quincy. He was young, good-looking, a successful real estate agent. The story begins when he sold a River

Oaks mansion to a wealthy widow, Eleanor Blakely." In the margin, in pencil, Olivia had written "Cousin, Margaret Greer, Fredericksburg." There was a phone number. I reached for the pad of sticky notes I keep on the bedside table and jotted it down.

"River Oaks." McQuaid stretched out his legs and wiggled his toes "Most affluent section of town. Where you grew up."

"Right," I said with a sigh. My father had been a workaholic lawyer, my mother an alcoholic. It wasn't a recipe for a happy family, even in a place that seemed to have everything going for it.

River Oaks. Tucked neatly between Uptown and Downtown Houston, with Buffalo Bayou on the north and the Southwest Freeway on the south, it was and still is an opulent enclave of sprawling estates and azalea-lined avenues. It grew up around the River Oaks Country Club in the mid-1920s and quickly became home to Houston's most prominent residents: Ima Hogg, whose laugh-out-loud name was bestowed on that poor lady by wealthy but linguistically impaired parents; Oveta Culp Hobby, editor and publisher of the *Houston Chronicle*; and John Connelly, the former Texas governor who was in the front seat of the car in which JFK was murdered. Deed restrictions barred Blacks and Jews. But Jeffrey Skilling, the disgraced CEO of the Enron Corporation, lived in River Oaks until he was hauled off to an Alabama federal prison camp to serve a fourteen-year sentence for securities fraud, insider trading, making false statements to auditors, and conspiracy. Senator Ted Cruz also lives there when he's not vacationing in Cancún.

And that was where Eleanor Blakely Kelly was found dead after a fire half-destroyed the palatial Ironwood Drive mansion she had bought the year before. Some seven or eight months later, her husband,

James Kelly, was charged with her murder. The two had been married just six months. She was fifty. He was twenty-five.

"Hey. I remember that part of it," McQuaid remarked with interest. "Quite an age gap, wouldn't you say?"

"I would, yes. She was a widow with a sizable fortune inherited from her first husband. According to the early newspaper reports, she was smoking in bed when she fell asleep. The fire destroyed her bedroom and several adjacent rooms on the upper floor. The husband, who got out unscathed, said he was downstairs watching *The Tonight Show* when he began to smell smoke and discovered the fire—too late to save his wife."

"Autopsy?"

"Smoke inhalation, Quaaludes, alcohol, other pills—which he bought for her, from his friendly neighborhood dealer. An expert witness would testify to arson. That was all the prosecution had, apparently, until somebody phoned in a tip about a longtime relationship Kelly had with a male dancer at a Houston gay strip club. The two were seen together frequently after Eleanor's death. The prosecution called it a homosexual relationship."

"And Kelly hit the jackpot with her will. Do I remember that right?"

"Yes. There were no children from the first marriage. A cousin— Eleanor's only family—got some mineral rights. The rest of the estate went to Kelly. Since his conviction was vacated, he kept it. Score that one to the appellate lawyer."

Inheritance law—the slayer rule—prohibits a murderer from inheriting or collecting his victim's life insurance. But the vacatur meant that Kelly was no longer a murderer. Of course, maybe the cousin (apparently she was Eleanor Kelly's closest kin) sued Kelly in civil court, where she might have prevailed, making him ineligible to inherit and handing the estate to her. If so, Olivia hadn't yet dug that up.

"Sounds like the case was mostly circumstantial," McQuaid said.

"Top to bottom. I suppose that's why it took a while to bring the indictment. There was no physical proof connecting Kelly to his wife's death or to the fire, and no witnesses. Even so, the lack of evidence doesn't seem to have made much difference. The arson expert was persuasive, and so was the money motive. The male stripper proved to be a high school buddy but the friendship offered just enough titillation to appeal to a jury's prurient imagination. They were out for only four hours. Guilty. Life without parole." Better known in Texas as death by incarceration.

"Well, of course." McQuaid chuckled. "What do you expect, Counselor? Especially with that jackpot on the line and the male stripper lurking in the wings." He paused. "I think I might know the lead detective on that case—an older guy I partnered with when I first got into Homicide. Loomis, Chuck Loomis. He's retired by now, I'm sure. I could call him—see what he remembers about the case. You said the sentence was vacated?"

"Yes, and that's where the story gets interesting. Kelly had served just a few months when Johnnie Carlson filed the appeal."

"Johnnie Carlson." McQuaid tapped a finger against his lips. "Wasn't he the one who—"

"That's him. At one time, he was a partner in the firm where I used to work. He and Aaron Brooks went into practice together." Sweet, hunky Aaron, with whom I had had a wild and wonderful fling back in the days when both of us were young and foolish. While I'm happily out of the law now, Aaron's still in, with a thriving criminal practice and a top-notch reputation. If I ever find myself in legal trouble, he's the attorney I'll call. Immediately.

But for sheer star power, Johnnie Carlson was the more impressive. Most criminal defense lawyers don't have an active appellate practice and even fewer are certified in both criminal trial law and criminal appeals. Johnnie was, and he was *good*—especially when he got his teeth into a case in which there had been any kind of misconduct. Investigative, prosecutorial, judicial misconduct—Johnnie had a nose for it. He's dead now, but in his life, he loved it all. If you aimed to win your appeal, he was your go-to guy.

McQuaid was following my train of thought, as he often did. "What were the grounds for the appeal?"

"Prosecutorial misconduct."

McQuaid grunted. "Chuck would've been pissed about that. There's nothing a cop hates worse than an incompetent prosecutor who screws up his case."

"Olivia is skimpy on that part of the story, so I'll have to do a little research. It sounds like slipshod lawyering. Or maybe the prosecutor got careless in his closing and said something he shouldn't. The First Court of Appeals vacated the conviction and sent it back to the trial court."

"What happened there? An appellate reversal doesn't mean the defendant gets a free pass."

"If there was a retrial, Olivia doesn't mention it. Arson is a hard case to make. It's possible that the DA simply decided to cut his losses. The bottom line: Kelly went free."

McQuaid chewed on that. After a moment, he asked, "You really think your friend's hit-and-run could have been murder?" His tone was skeptical.

Murder. My stomach clenched at the word and I forced myself to step back, be objective. Could Olivia have been killed deliberately?

"I suppose it's possible," I said slowly. "You could set your watch by her regular early-morning runs along Purgatory Bend. Somebody could park on her street and keep an eye on her for a few days, then follow her and pick the right place along that narrow road. There can't be that much predawn traffic out there, and wooded stretches with no houses. No worries about being spotted." I paused. "Yeah. It's . . . possible."

"I see." McQuaid gave me a raised-eyebrow look. "So what are you going to do?"

I took a deep breath. "Get Charlie's take on the situation," I heard myself saying, even though I hadn't consciously made any such plans. "Talk to Sheila—see what the police turned up in their investigation. Also, I want to take a look at the accident site. And there's a cousin over in Fredericksburg. I've got to go over there in a couple of days. I could talk to her."

"You're going to Fredericksburg?" He frowned in pretended irritation. "Hey. I thought we were staying home. Spending more time together."

"It's been on the calendar for a while. I'm scheduled to give a talk to the Native Plant Society there. But it's an afternoon talk. I won't be staying overnight." I grinned teasingly. "Anyway, if I did stay over, you wouldn't have to sleep alone. Winchester will be glad to share the bed."

He reached for me. "Personally, I think we should maybe stock up. Just in case you or I have to be gone longer than a night or two. Doesn't that sound like a good idea?"

It did. A *very* good idea.

Chapter Four

Coffee can help you remember? That's what the scientists say.

The herb (yes, coffee *is* an herb!) has long been known to increase energy, improve mood, and make people feel more productive. But now there's more. A 2013 study at Johns Hopkins University focused directly on caffeine's effect on long-term memory. The researchers found that caffeine not only powers a short-term energy boost, it acts on the brain to improve the accuracy and duration of both short- and long-term memory—something most of us are looking for.

And other research suggests that two or three daily cups of your usual Joe could have an even more beneficial effect: lowering the risk of developing dementia or Alzheimer's disease in your senior years. In a twenty-one-year study, people drinking three to five cups of coffee a day at midlife demonstrated a 65 percent lower incidence of late-life dementia. Good news for coffee drinkers!

China Bayles
"What Am I Forgetting? Herbs to Improve Your Memory"
Pecan Springs Enterprise

McQuaid was sleeping in, but I got up at my usual early hour, put on my running shorts and shoes and a cool mesh tank, and groped my way downstairs to the kitchen, where I started the espresso machine that McQuaid and the kids gave me for Christmas. My morning run goes better when I have my caffeine fix first thing. My current favorite: a hazelnut latte with a darker roast so there's less acidity and lower risk of stomach upset. There's about four times more caffeine in espresso than there is in regularly brewed coffee. It's in your bloodstream within five to ten minutes of that first sip, peaks in sixty minutes, and hangs around for three to five hours. If you're otherwise healthy and caffeine jitters don't trouble you, an espresso may give you the boost you're after. The great gift of the coffee bean.

Caffeine aside, I feel much more energetic since I started doing a 2K morning run, up our lane to Limekiln Road and back again. I have the gravel two-track all to myself in the predawn stillness, when the cool air is resinous with cedar and sweet with the scent of damp grass. When I first began running this distance a couple of months ago, my best time was eighteen minutes. I'm down to fourteen minutes now, working on thirteen, but it's not the time, it's the persistence that counts. Knowing I can do this every day makes me feel good about myself.

Back home, I settled down with my laptop to finish my weekly herb and garden column for the *Pecan Springs Enterprise*. June is Alzheimer's and Brain Awareness Month, so I focused the first column of the month—titled "What Am I Forgetting?"—on herbal memory boosters. I had been reading *Remember: The Science of Memory and the Art of Forgetting* by Lisa Genova. And yesterday's tragicomic pursuit of Doris was a painful reminder that we all need to protect and defend our memories.

Hearing me rustling around, Winchester had abandoned the bedroom and come downstairs. Bassets are long and low-slung so they don't do stairs gracefully. Winnie, however, has perfected the complex canine art of going downstairs—backward. He starts with an intricate little sidewise hop, then takes it slow, one deliberate paw at a time, yipping triumphantly as he negotiates each stair tread to announce that he has conquered one more. Arriving at last downstairs, he stations himself beside his bowl, making it clear that it's time for breakfast.

The dog was tucking enthusiastically into his kibble when the cat (Mr. P, aka Pumpkin because he's that color) sauntered into the room. Caitie (who is also my niece) fell in love with this war-torn old tomcat when he showed up at our back door one stormy night, sopping and starved. I tried to suggest that a kitten might be more lovable, but she was determined.*

"He's just like me when I first came to live here," she said, clutching him tight. "He needs somebody to adopt him. He needs *me*." When he heard this, the cunning old reprobate licked her cheek and turned up the volume on his purr. As McQuaid said later, Mr. P had been on the lam long enough to know that he had lucked into the deal of nine lifetimes.

Since Winchester was eating, Mr. P demanded his breakfast, too. And when Spock, our parrot, heard that a party was afoot, he announced that he was awake and would like to join us. His sleeping cage stands in the corner of the kitchen, beside the pantry door. I took the cover off, told him good morning, and gave him a small carrot with the leafy green top attached, the way he likes it. He greeted it with an affectionate, "Bacon. Oh, boy!" and went to work.

If you have animal companions at your house, you know that their personalities are all quite different. Winchester is gloomy in the morning—well, all day, actually. He is emotionally prepared for the sky to fall and resigned to the fact that today is very likely to be his last. Mr. P, on the other hand, is a born cynic, and a survivor. He fully expects somebody to knock the props out from under the sky so it has to fall.

---

* Caitlin, the daughter of China's dead half-brother, comes into China's life in *Nightshade* (China Bayles #16).

But he has his safe place picked out. When the sky comes down, as he knows it will, Mr. P will be the last cat standing.

In contrast to both, Spock—an Eclectus parrot with stunning green feathers, splashes of blue and red under his wings, and a bright orange beak—is unfailingly cheerful. If the sky should threaten to fall, he will meet it with a commanding "Beam me up, Scotty!" His first owner was a Trekkie who taught him to speak Klingon. McQuaid's son Brian, also a Trekkie, discovered this intriguing talent when Caitie was making a list of the parrot's vocabulary words for a school project. Brian heard Spock counting from one to nine in Klingon—*wa', cha', wej, loS, vagh, jav, soch, chorg, hut.* Turns out that Spock can swear in Klingon, too. His favorite: *veQDujn' oH Dujllj'e',* which translates to *Your ship is a damned garbage scow.* (You can't prove this by me. I'm only reporting the kids' research.)

Fully caffeinated and energized by my run, I finished my column and got ready to email it to Hark Hibler—ahead of my deadline, for a change. I had been thinking of Olivia, who had once worked at the *Enterprise*, and wondered whether she might have talked to Hark recently about any of her projects. So I attached the column to an email saying that I'd like to stop in and see him for a few minutes sometime during the week. I had a question for him about somebody we both knew.

Then I popped three breakfast tacos into the microwave and went upstairs. I met McQuaid coming out of the bedroom dressed in his usual polo shirt and khakis. We traded a good-morning kiss flavored with the sexy memory of the night before and I pointed him in the direction of the microwave and the espresso machine. I showered, got into jeans, my green Thyme and Seasons T-shirt, and sneakers—my usual work outfit for the shop—and headed downstairs.

McQuaid had finished his taco and was heading out to his truck. He opened the kitchen door. And stopped.

"Hey," he said, and bent over. "It's vinegar." He picked it up and squinted at the label. "Why is a bottle of vinegar sitting in the middle of the doorway?"

"It's for me," I said, snatching it. "I put it there to remind myself that Mrs. Graeber called last night. She wants to pick up a dozen two-inch pots of thyme this morning. I'd just potted up the plants and needed to remember to take them to the shop with me."

"Oh." McQuaid gave me a quizzical look. "But I don't get it. What's the connection between Mrs. Graeber and a bottle of vinegar?"

"Because she's the most *acidic* woman I know," I explained. "I didn't have a pencil handy, and the vinegar was on the counter in front of me when she called. I've been reading Genova's book about how to improve your memory, and this is one of her tricks. It's called associative memory. Like tying a string around your finger."

"You could have put a clock on the doorstep." McQuaid chuckled, pleased with himself. "Time, thyme. Get it?" In case I didn't, he spelled it out. "T-i-m-e. T-h-y-m-e. Time. Thyme." He chuckled again. "Memorable, huh?"

I gave him a look and went to fetch the plants.

THYME AND SEASONS IS MY second home. I love it best in the mornings, when the sun slants across the worn pine boards of the floor and blesses the old limestone walls with an almost magical light. There are bowls of fragrant potpourri on the shelves, baskets of dried yarrow, sweet Annie, larkspur, and tansy on the floor, and wreaths and swags on the walls. There are cards and gift baskets and stationery and books, of course.

And something new. Under a sign that reads Banned Book Nook. Borrow and Share! I had installed several new shelves displaying a few of the nearly eight hundred books that have been banned from a Texas library in the past couple of years. There's one of these little guerrilla libraries in most Crockett Street shops now. The books in this one have been donated by visitors to the shop. On the top shelf, I was glad to see that Toni Morrison's *The Bluest Eye* had been returned. It goes out and comes back at least once a week. *Nineteen Minutes*, by Jodi Picoult, had come back, but *The Handmaid's Tale* and *The 1619 Project* were both out again. And somebody had just brought in a copy of *Itty-Bitty Kitty-Corn*, by Shannon Hale. It won both the Caldecott and Newbury awards but is being banned by a Texas school district because it features a pink kitten who wants to be a unicorn—and gender-neutral pronouns.

The children's bookstore next door also has a free shelf, the Crystal Cave has two shelves, and there are shelves in every shop in the Craft Emporium next door—our local counter-offensive in the battle against the hysterical mania of book banning that's sweeping the country.

And since this is an herb shop, there are of course herbs, as many as I can find room for. I've stocked an antique hutch and wooden shelves with herbal vinegars, oils, jellies, and teas. The corner pine cupboard displays my curated collection of personal care products crafted by local artisans: herbal soaps, shampoos, massage oils, tooth powders, cleansers, lotions, and bath herbs. Gleaming glass jars of dried culinary and medicinal herbs and bottles of extracts and tinctures fill a wooden rack in the middle of the room.

Some of the most interesting research in herbs these days is focused on the nootropics—plants that boost mental energies or calm jittery nerves—and I've reserved a prominent display shelf just for them. There is ginkgo, ginseng, gotu kola (*Centella asiatica*, an herb in the parsley family), and ashwagandha (a nightshade), all of which are used in traditional Chinese and Ayurvedic medicine. There are also the more familiar herbs: rosemary, lemon balm, turmeric, and holy basil (*Tulsi*, that is, not the basil you grow to make pesto). Caffeine is the most commonly used nootropic, so I've included caffeine-rich herbs: a small jar of coffee beans, black tea and green tea, yerba mate (the South American holly that is brewed as a tea), and some yaupon holly leaves I gathered from the shrubby tree outside the shop window. There's a sign with information about each herb. I had even come up with what I thought was a cute tagline for the sign: *Worried about losing your marbles? These herbs might help you remember where you put them.*

The morning started off slowly, which gave me time to sit at the counter with my laptop and look into the story behind the Kelly case— proving once again that nothing can hide from Google. I found several old newspaper articles describing the fire, Eleanor Kelly's death, and the trial of James Kelly, his sentence, and his appeal. I was hoping to find a photo, to see if he resembled anybody I know in Pecan Springs. No luck.

But I fared better on FindLaw.com, where I read the appellate court's ruling that vacated Kelly's conviction. In his closing, the prosecutor had made several apparently careless references to the defendant as the "only person" who could answer certain questions about his wife's death—and that he had left these questions unanswered. The court ruled that those references reminded the jury that Kelly had declined to testify, thereby violating his Fifth Amendment rights. Kelly's lawyer had failed to object and preserve the error for appellate review, which amounted to ineffective assistance of counsel. It was no surprise that the conviction got tossed.

And I could see—or thought I could—why the DA hadn't moved for an immediate retrial. The arson evidence was weak and the rest of the case was circumstantial. I could also see why Olivia thought this was such a strong story. It was perfect for a show like *Dateline*, which usually includes a dramatic courtroom scene or two, with a twisty outcome the audience doesn't anticipate. Vacatur fit that bill, since it's logical to expect that once a man is convicted of his wife's murder, he'll stay convicted.

But if Olivia got her teeth into the story and brought it some national attention, there might even be another twist. With no statute of limitations on murder, the prosecutor's office might be prompted to take a second look at the case. Of course, twenty years is a long time. Leaving a case open indefinitely would raise concerns about the defendant's right to a speedy trial, and most prosecutors would keep that in mind. So I had to wonder whether the charges might have been dropped or the case dismissed at some point in the past, and Olivia just hadn't scoped out that detail. Or maybe she thought it didn't matter. For her, what mattered was the shock value of the original conviction.

Bottom line: James Kelly—or whoever he was now—could have something to fear. Or he *thought* he did, which amounts to the same thing, when push comes to shove.

I glanced back at the history of my Google search and took a few minutes to copy the URLs of the newspaper stories and the FindLaw report and email them to myself. If I wanted to review those web pages, I'd know where to find them. But now I was wondering what Charlie Lipman knew about this case—and what he might be willing to tell me. I phoned his office and asked Rosie, his secretary, if I could drop in on him today. She could squeeze me in for a few minutes after lunch, she said.

"As long as you don't linger," she added sternly. "He has to be in court by two-thirty." Rosie is a straitlaced lady of fifty-something, married to the principal of Pecan Springs High School. She runs Charlie's office the way her husband runs the high school—by the bell. She takes every opportunity to make it clear that she's the Boss of the Office.

There was more research to be done on the Kelly case, but it would have to wait. Jennifer Wilson, a regular customer who loves to bake, had come in asking for whole vanilla beans. Lenore Pickens was looking for turmeric powder to add to veggies, rice, and greens as an anti-inflammatory that might ease her arthritis pain. She had read that the body absorbs turmeric better when it's combined with freshly ground black pepper and wondered about the proportions. We looked it up online and found a recommendation for a quarter teaspoon of fresh-ground black pepper to a quarter cup of turmeric. Lenore went away with both peppercorns and turmeric.

And then Gini Potter and Linda Dunn, teachers at the Montessori school down the street, brought their group of kid-sized gardeners to water, pull weeds, and inspect the plants in their "Peter Rabbit" children's garden. I had given Gini and Linda a plot in the garden and some starter pots of mint, parsley, lavender, basil, chives, and lamb's ears, along with seeds for lettuce, marigold, and nasturtium. The children had collaborated on an attractive garden sculpture made of stacked clay pots filled with cascading herbs: creeping thyme, prostrate rosemary, dittany, pineapple mint, and a trailing peppermint geranium. It was a lovely little project.

The kids were still working enthusiastically when Mrs. Graeber came in to pick up her flat of thyme. She gave the plants a suspicious glance and remarked, "I don't suppose you have anything better?"

I was tempted to fire back, but I held my tongue. "They're the very last, I'm afraid," I said mildly. "It's a little late in the season. Most people plant perennial herbs in early April, while the weather is still cool. Or they wait until October. That's plenty of time for the plants to get their roots into the ground before January's cold snaps." I paused and gave in to temptation. "Of course, if these don't suit you, Walmart might still have a few."

"I suppose they'll have to do," she muttered sourly, and left with them.

The usual mid-morning trickle of customers grew into a stream when the tearoom opened. It was my turn to seat people and help with the serving while Ruby took her lunch hour to run errands. When she returned, I left her in charge of both shops and took my own hour. Charlie Lipman's law office is only four blocks away, so I walked.

Lipman Law is located in the middle of a block of small frame houses that have been converted to professional offices, their manicured lawns replaced by native shrubs, grasses, and wildflowers that tolerate heat and don't need much water—an imperative in Texas, where we are learning to live with the extended droughts and blazing summers of climate change. Charlie's is the neat gray house with blue shutters, set well back from the street under a couple of large live oak trees, with a graveled parking area off to one side. His banged-up F-150 pickup was parked in the lot, so I knew he was there. And I knew he wasn't going to Austin or San Antonio today, or he'd be driving his Lexus LC 500.

Charlie and I had been friends long enough to know what's good and what's bad about the other. He knows that I'm apt to be impatient, pigheaded, and hypercritical, and that I am not the most tactful person alive. I know that he has two separate personas and inhabits whichever one he thinks will get him what he wants. Around Pecan Springs folk, he's just another good old boy, like Spencer Tracy in *Inherit the Wind*—hair uncombed, sleeves rolled, tie loose, with a vocabulary shared by the other good old boys at Bean's Bar and Grill and Lila's Diner.

But while Charlie talks down-home Texan here in Pecan Springs, elsewhere and otherwise, he is an urbane, well-spoken fellow who wears three-piece suits, tosses off five-syllable words, and regularly argues cases before the Supreme Court of Texas. He has his battles with the bottle, and some weeks it looks like the bottle is winning. But he's still the best and the busiest of a growing cadre of Pecan Springs lawyers who hover, like MacBeth's witches, over a steaming cauldron of local disputes.

And while we may be a small town, there's always something cooking. Zoning issues, a suit over water management, accusations of cop misconduct and hiring discrimination, as well as the many legal knots people tie themselves into. Everybody who is anybody in Pecan Springs wants Charlie Lipman on their side when they find themselves in front of a judge. He is everybody's lawyer and knows everybody's secrets, which has sometimes resulted in interesting conflicts. Charlie and I are friends, yes, but I often feel he's not giving me the full story. McQuaid does investigative work for him but isn't always sure which side the boss is on. We're both fond of Charlie, but we sometimes wonder how far he can be trusted.

Rosie was at her secretary's desk, dressed in her usual law-office costume, a polyester pantsuit (this one maroon) and tailored white blouse. She frowned and nodded shortly in the direction of Charlie's office.

"You'll have to wait. He's with a client. And don't forget that he has—"

"A court date," I said sweetly. "Thanks, Rosie. I won't."

I took a chair, pulled out my phone, and checked messages. I was answering an urgent text from Caitie (Mom, can I stay at the ranch an extra week? I have a new HORSE to ride!!!) when the door to Charlie's office opened and Cassidy Pennington Warren stepped out.

Cassidy is one of those women you have to look at when they come into a room. She's statuesque and shapely and her golden-blond hair is trendily streaked and tousled. She was dressed fit to kill in an elegant white summer suit and four-inch white heels that made my toes curl just to look at them. I caught a quick whiff of some sophisticated perfume and was suddenly conscious of my down-to-earth work uniform: jeans and sneakers and Thyme and Seasons T-shirt, sweaty across the back from my four-block walk in the early summer heat.

For decades, the Pennington family has been as close to royalty as we get in Pecan Springs: old Texas ranching and cattle money, bank ownership, and a family seat in the state senate. Now in her late forties and the lone survivor of this stately clan, Cassidy is president of Pennington Philanthropies, in charge of doling out her inherited Pennington dollars to deserving charities. Her husband Palmer manages oil and gas leases and has served a couple of terms on the city council. You'll find one or both featured in almost every issue of the *Enterprise*. Palmer and Cassidy Pennington Warren. The town's preeminent power couple.

But there is more to Cassidy than meets the eye, for beneath that highly polished high-fashion exterior is a champion barrel racer who grew up on horseback and is more at home in jeans, a plaid cowboy shirt, and an old pair of scuffed boots. If you know anything about that insanely demanding sport, you know that Cassidy is the kind of woman who can sit tight, hold on, ride hard, and move fast, all of which no doubt helps her to manage the quarter horses she breeds, rides, and trains and the philanthropies her parents—gone now—created and left to her to manage. The Penningtons were legendary in the Hill Country, famous for the quarter horses they had bred for nearly a century and for their generous support of local and state charities. I didn't know Cassidy Pennington Warren well, but well enough to respect her tenacity and tough-minded grip on the Pennington reputation. The family legacy mattered to her. It *mattered*.

Charlie followed Cassidy to his office door, a jovial smile pasted across his face. "Next time you come, better bring a wheelbarrow and a couple of buckets," he called after her. "You'd maybe leave with a little more loot."

Cassidy tossed a firm "I'll do it, Charlie," over her shoulder. She stopped when she saw me and registered who I was—helped, no doubt, by the Thyme and Seasons logo on my T-shirt.

"China Bayles, isn't it?" Without waiting for my reply, she went on. "I was so pleased with that birthday party you and Cass and Ruby put together for Palmer back in February. He was surprised, and all our friends had such a great time. I'm glad that you guys can handle our barbeque out at the ranch. A few more than we had for Palmer's birthday party, but it will still be small. We'll have horses for those who want to ride, and there's tennis and fishing and swimming and dancing and horseshoes and archery—all kinds of exciting things for people to do."

She didn't wait to find out if I thought this was exciting, although of course I did. "Please tell Ruby that we've lined up the Devil's Rib bluegrass boys. Cass will need to include the six of them—the boys, I mean—in the headcount for the meal. Oh, and let Ruby know that I'm making separate arrangements for the bar, so you girls won't have to worry about that. And we'll need somebody to come out to the ranch ahead of time, so you're aware of our layout."

"I'll tell them," I replied, my sincere enthusiasm brightened by the recollection of Cassidy's recent "little" birthday party at the Warrens' town home. It had grown to two dozen couples, stretching us to the limits of our resources. But the Warrens paid on time, tipped generously, and the gig would have been worth it for the advertising alone. Palmer is one of Pecan Springs' major influencers and Cassidy has recommended us to their many friends. And if I needed more reasons to be enthusiastic about our next event with them, the historic Blind Penny (the vast Pennington ranch is named for a much-loved and long-gone horse) is said to offer remarkably beautiful vistas of the Hill Country. And maybe best of all, the Devil's Rib is my favorite local band. I could dance all night to their "Cotton-Eye Joe."

Cassidy gave me one of her forthright smiles. "Looking forward to working with you and Ruby again." She turned and raised a hand to Rosie. "Bye, now, Rosie. And for a switch, your boss is paying me, instead of the other way around. You can send his check to the post office box." With that, she was gone.

Rosie gave an audible, almost involuntary sigh. "What I would give for a peek in her closet." She remembered that I was there and frowned. "What? We shouldn't admire a nicely dressed woman? Especially when she is such a terrific rider?"

"Of course we should," I replied, suppressing my smile. I got up and went into Charlie's office. "How much did she hit you up for?"

Charlie's pasted-on smile was gone. "A grand," he grumped. "Golf tournament. Prize money for Back the Blue on the Green." He shook his head. "It's hard to say no to that woman when she starts flexing her Pennington muscle. She might look like Miss Texas—talk like her, too.

But she has a spine of steel and the teeth of a piranha, especially when it comes to anything having to do with the Pennington family. Believe me. You don't want her for a client. That husband of hers, either. Two of a kind."

So the Warrens were Charlie's clients. I hadn't known that, but I wasn't surprised. The Pecan Springs movers and shakers tend to end up in his office. He is a man of secrets. He knows where all the skeletons in town are buried.

He dropped into the chair behind his untidy desk. Unlike other lawyers of my acquaintance, Charlie claims to work best when he has to dig for the files he wants. Rosie is forbidden to touch his desk, and the top is perpetually buried beneath a litter of papers, folders, briefs, books, a few open bags of chips, and a couple of empty takeout cartons.

Rosie had followed the two of us and now stood in the doorway, pointing sternly at her wristwatch. "Mr. Lipman, you mustn't forget that you have a court date at two-thirty. Judge Lyons gets all bent out of shape when anybody's late. And you asked me to remind you to pick up your suit at the cleaners on your way home."

"Thanks, Rosie. Glad you're minding the clock."

When she had closed the door, I said, "So she talks like that to you, too. I thought maybe it was just us Muggles who get her orders."

Charlie grunted. "Don't badmouth her. She takes dictation."

"So do dictation apps," I said. "I'm sure you can find one that doesn't snarl."

"Maybe. But it won't deliver lunch." He gestured toward a Big Mac box on top of a stack of trial transcripts.

Charlie Lipman is big and balding, with pouches that sag under his eyes and a belly that sags over his belt. Today was a Spencer Tracy day, and he was suitably uncombed and rumpled. He pointed to two client chairs, both piled high with briefs. "Move that crap and have a seat. Am I supposed to know what's on your mind?"

I transferred a stack of files from one chair to another and sat down. "Olivia Andrews. And her sister Zelda. Whom you sicced on me yesterday."

"Ah, yes." A look of something like disquiet flickered briefly across Charlie's face, then disappeared. "Dear, departed Olivia," he said. "Gone but not forgotten." He pushed the Big Mac box aside, rooted around under some papers, and pulled out his pipe. "Especially by her fan club. Darwin Neely is still looking for his pound of flesh. And the Reverend Jeremy Kellogg deeply regrets that he didn't sue when she was alive."

"Somebody else had it in for her," I said, noticing that Charlie had not replied to my mention of Zelda. "At least, that's what the sister thinks. She has the idea that Olivia was murdered. Did she share that interesting speculation with you?"

"Something like that, maybe." He pulled out a desk drawer, rummaged through it, closed it, and rummaged through another. "Ah, there you are," he said triumphantly, tossing a tobacco pouch on top of the litter. He pulled out a third drawer, leaned back, propped his feet on it, and began filling his pipe. It took a while.

Stalling for time, I thought. *What's this about?* After a moment, I said, "Well? What do you think? About Zelda's theory, I mean."

It took a few moments of searching his pockets before he found his lighter. He leaned back, lit his pipe, and drew on it. Finally, he said, "Didn't give too much thought to it, actually. But now that you ask, I think she's way off the mark."

Didn't give too much thought to it? That wasn't Charlie. The suggestion that a client of his had been murdered should have merited his full

69

attention. So I had to ask myself why he wasn't answering my question. Why he was disclaiming any interest.

He drew on his pipe again. "When it happened, you know— when Olivia got killed—my honest-to-God first thought was that the woman was asking for it. Any damned fool with half a brain could figure that running on Purgatory Bend in the dark is a suicide mission. From what I read in the paper, the cops thought so, too. It was a simple hit-and-run. And I haven't seen a good reason to change my mind." He puffed on his pipe. "McQuaid get back okay last night?"

He was prevaricating and I ignored the question. "Did you talk to Sheila about it?" Sheila is well known to both of us, although the town's top cop and top defense attorney often find themselves on opposite sides of the legal fence. "When it happened, I mean. After all, Olivia was your client. I have to believe you had at least some interest in the way she died. And who killed her—accident or not."

Charlie lifted a shoulder and let it drop. "I closed the pending court case. The accident itself seemed pretty straightforward to me." He puffed on his pipe and squinted at me through a cloud of blue smoke. "Did *you*? Talk to the police about it?"

"I was out of town when it happened. I didn't know about it until I got back. And at the time, what I read seemed straightforward to me, too." I paused. "Until I talked to Zelda."

And now I had to wonder why Charlie had sent Zelda to me. And why he was attempting to deflect my questions about her.

"Yeah, well, sounds like you and I saw it pretty much the same way, China. Straightforward accident." He went on grudgingly, as if he might be willing to concede a point or two, "But the sister is right when she says that Olivia had a passel of enemies. It's a stretch, but I suppose it's conceivable that one of them didn't like what she was posting on that blog of hers, happened to see her all by her lonesome that morning, and couldn't resist the opportunity to whack her with his passenger-side mirror. That's what killed her, according to the write-up in the paper." A pause, a puff on the pipe, more Spencer Tracy. "Could've been any one of a half-dozen folks, I reckon. As I say, there was a right sizable crowd that wa'n't any too fond of that lady and her blog."

Charlie's Texan talk is one of his tells. He is always at his most duplicitous when he wants you to think he's just a simple country lawyer. I could see there was no point in pursuing this, so I changed tacks.

"The project Olivia was working on—the twenty-year-old murder." I phrased my question carefully. "James Kelly's conviction was wiped out with a vacatur. Did Olivia mention that case to you? Had you heard about it before Zelda came to see you?"

He took out his pipe and regarded it thoughtfully. After a moment, he said, "Olivia was kinda paranoid about what she was working on, you know. Never shared it with anybody until it showed up in her blog. Said she liked to surprise folks." He gave me a lopsided smile. "Anyway, you've been to law school. You know all about attorney-client privilege. Olivia may be dead, but what we talked about still stays between the two of us."

He was right, of course. Privilege persists after the client's death. But he was using that fact to avoid answering. "True enough," I said. "But Zelda isn't your client. You talked to her about it. You sent her to see me. And you mentioned the name of Johnnie Carlson. So you obviously knew about it before Zelda darkened your door. Come clean, Charlie."

Puffing on his pipe, Charlie swiveled to look out the window. "Point taken," he said finally, swiveling back to me. "A while back, Olivia said she'd dug up a story about somebody who got himself convicted for killing his wife a couple of decades ago. He was sentenced to life but the appellate court gave him a get-out-of-jail card and the DA didn't retry. Olivia happened to mention the name of the lawyer who argued that appeal. When I heard it was Johnnie Carlson, I remembered that you two had been in the same firm back in Houston. So when Zelda showed up with that folder full of her sister's writing, wondering what she should do with it, I thought of you." He gave me a rueful look and his Texan became exaggerated. "I sincerely apologize. But hell, China, I didn't think you'd bite. Figured you'd send her packing and she'd be out of our hair."

So that was it. Charlie had dumped her on me, thinking I would dump her too—which would totally discourage her. I chuckled agreeably and brought us back to my topic.

"So what do you think of Zelda's theory that James Kelly is here in Pecan Springs?" In a conversational tone, I added. "And her notion that Kelly—or whatever name he's going by now—killed her sister to keep her from outing him. Interesting?"

"Not much." Charlie shrugged dismissively. "Good as any theory, I reckon—works until it butts up against a hard fact or two." He regarded me, one eyebrow raised. "What do you think?"

"I'm curious," I admitted. "I did a little quick research this morning and found out how Carlson got Kelly's conviction vacated. It was a prosecutor's terminally stupid mistake." I waited for Charlie to ask me what the mistake might have been. He was too busy fussing with his pipe. After a moment, I went on, "So what do you suppose happened to Kelly after that? Where'd he disappear to for a couple of decades? Did he really end up in Pecan Springs? Sounds to me like Olivia was cooking up a pretty strong story."

Charlie shook his head, scowling. "You know as well as I do what kind of trouble that blogger lady's overactive imagination could get her into. Like as not, Olivia made it all up—the Pecan Springs end of it, I mean. She did that before, you know. If she didn't like a set of facts, she dug around until she found some that suited her better. Maybe stretched 'em a little, too. That's why Darwin Neely was suing. And while she didn't go that far with Kellogg, he would have had a halfway decent case, especially after the judge ruled that she had to reveal her sources. I told her, if we had to go to trial, Neely would win. And when he did, Kellogg would join the hunt."

More diversions. Neely and Kellogg were history. And beside the point. "But Zelda has—"

"Has only those scrappy notes of her sister's to go on. And plenty of guesswork." Charlie gave me a hard-eyed look and his voice was firm. "And Kelly, well, that case is a couple of decades old and not worth getting all excited about. The fella likely ended up in Mexico. That's a good place for people who have a reason to disappear. If he was smart and took a few bucks with him, he's still there. Or he's dead. Sorry I inflicted that Zelda woman on you, China. But as I said, I didn't think you'd take her seriously. You've got better things to do."

He was digging around for an ashtray in the litter on his desk. When he found it, he knocked the tobacco out of his pipe into it and glanced pointedly at his watch. "Hate to cut this short, but Rosie's gonna be on my tail if I don't hustle on over to the courthouse." He stood and began rolling down his sleeves, jovial once again. "McQuaid get back from Brownsville last night, huh? Interesting case he's working on down there. I'm glad to have that man of yours on the job, China. He's damned good."

And that was the end of that. Pretty much the waste of a good

73

lunch hour, I thought, as I walked back to the shop. But I believed him when he said he was sorry he'd sent Zelda to see me. That had obviously been a mistake. And it seemed pretty clear that he was uneasy with my questions. He'd as much as told me to butt out. And when somebody tells me *that* . . . well, I quite naturally want to butt right in.

And the time hadn't been a waste. I had learned that the Devil's Rib was playing for the party that Party Thyme was catering at the Blind Penny Ranch.

Which, all by itself, was probably worth the trip.

Chapter Five

An illicit drug is whatever a government decides it is. It can be no accident that these are almost exclusively the [plants] with the power to change consciousness. Or, perhaps I should say, with the power to change consciousness in ways that run counter to the smooth operations of society and the interests of the powers that be. As an example, coffee and tea, which have amply demonstrated their value to capitalism in many ways, not least by making us more efficient workers, are in no danger of prohibition, while psychedelics—which are no more toxic than caffeine and considerably less addictive—have been regarded, at least in the West since the mid-1960s, as a threat to social norms and institutions.

Michael Pollan
This Is Your Mind on Plants

I had planned to stop at the police department and have a chat with Sheila after I closed the shop that afternoon. I wanted to get a fix on what she knew about Olivia's death. But McQuaid called and said that Brian would be driving down around suppertime. Did I want him to bring anything from Austin?

"Besides his laundry, you mean?" I asked dryly. The washing machine in Brian's rental unit has been out of operation for a while.

McQuaid chuckled. "He's thinking of a pizza or something. Casey isn't coming. She's visiting her parents in Baton Rouge."

Casey Galbraith is Brian's live-in girlfriend.

I did a quick mental inventory of supper possibilities. "We had pizza the last time he was with us. There's a rosemary chicken casserole in the freezer—it'll defrost fast and be easy to heat up. I'll stop at Cavette's and get salad fixings and some fresh strawberries. Brian loves strawberry shortcake." I'd have to call Sheila's office and reschedule my drop-in visit. And ask Connie Page, her assistant, for a copy of the police report on Olivia's death.

"That ought to be a winner." McQuaid hesitated. "The kid sounded like he's got something serious on his mind. I wonder if—" He hesitated. "He made a point of saying that Casey wasn't coming."

"Ah," I said regretfully. "Maybe they've split again."

I like Brian's girlfriend and admire her commitment to what she's chosen to do. She's pre-med and going to school on a tennis scholarship, not an easy combination. She is as striking as a fashion model, with satiny dark skin, close-cut black hair that accentuates the angular African American contours of her face, and a lean, athletic figure. They're an attractive couple.

But Brian is carrying a full load in his environmental science major and working part time at John Dromgoole's organic nursery, the Natural Gardener. Casey is carrying a full load and is active in campus politics. The two lived together last year, but they found it difficult to fit a relationship into their schedules. So Casey moved back to the dorm and Brian located another roommate—a guy, this time—to share his rent. That hadn't lasted long, though. About midway through the spring semester, Brian told us that Casey was moving in again.

"I don't know how that pair manages everything," McQuaid said. "They must live in a constant state of overwhelm."

"They're young," I reminded him. "Don't you remember? When we were twenty, we could do anything. Plus, you and I actually had to go to class. Brian and Casey have all that cyber technology. They just log on and they're there. And with Google, they have the library in their laptops. It's not like the old days, when we lived in the stacks."

"Yeah, you're right." He chuckled. "If we'd had the internet, school would've been an entirely different story." Another chuckle. "Listen, if you're stopping at the market on your way home, would you pick up a six-pack of Hans' Pilz. If they don't have that, see if they've got Fireman's Four."

This is not Greek to me. These beers have been on my shopping list before. Hans' Pilz is an old-country German-style artisanal beer that is brewed by some friends of McQuaid's over in Blanco County and named for the brewer's dog, Hans. It is hoppier (as beer fanciers put it) than most beers, crisp and a little fruity. Fireman's Four is a pale ale that goes well with the spicy stuff McQuaid loves.

"Brian's driving," I reminded him.

"I think he's old enough to remember that," McQuaid said. "If he isn't, I'll be glad to remind him."

CAVETTE'S MARKET MAY BE A holdover from the previous century, but it has a large cadre of dedicated customers who'd rather shop there than at Safeway or Randalls. Tucked away in the shadow of the Sophie Briggs Historical Museum, it is a small, family-owned grocery with baskets of fresh fruit and veggies on the sidewalk outdoors, old-fashioned shelves and wood floors and pressed-tin ceilings indoors, and the smell of fresh melons and warm cinnamon buns throughout. At the bakery counter, you can buy Maria Lopez' blue corn or flour tortillas and crisp taco shells, homemade in the Dos Amigas kitchen. And if you want something that isn't on the shelf, just ask Old Mr. Cavette, Young Mr. Cavette, or Young Mr. Cavette's son Junior. (I agree with

Sheila, who once remarked that the shop and all three generations of Cavettes ought to be registered as historical landmarks.)

"Good afternoon, Miz Bayles." It was Old Mr. Cavette on his stool behind the counter, stooped and shaky but keeping a watchful eye on a kid studying the candy rack. With a smile, he gave me the rest of the Cavettes' ritual greeting. "You havin' a good day today, ma'am?"

I gave him my own little ritual—"Always, thank you, sir"—and pulled a cart out of the rack. I had added a bunch of fresh baby spinach from the produce counter and was reaching into the adjacent bin for a perfectly ripe and absolutely gorgeous avocado, when somebody elbowed past me and snatched it.

I straightened up with a jerk, turned, and came face-to-face with the Reverend Jeremy Kellogg, dressed in jeans, a black jacket, and a black T-shirt that said *Jesus, Family, Guns, & Freedom.*

"Oh, pardon *me*," he said insincerely, dropping the avocado into his basket. "That wasn't the very one *you* wanted, was it?"

It was. But I wasn't going to arm-wrestle the man for a ripe avocado. That would be humiliating.

"Thank you, no," I said.

He turned away. "God bless," he tossed over his shoulder.

I stifled a snarl and chose a couple of others, almost as nice and without any accompanying trauma.

I owed what I knew about the flamboyant Jeremy Kellogg to Olivia's blog posts. Before he showed up in Pecan Springs, he had been a television personality and the pastor of a Dallas megachurch called the United Souls Ministry. But scandal had caught up with him, according to Olivia, who had summed up the backstory in one of her blog posts the year before. He was forced to leave his pulpit after he publicly confessed to an "improper" relationship with a married member of his flock—a young woman of nineteen—amid an ugly swirl of rumors of other dalliances as well as funds "borrowed" from the church's fundraising program. There was a flurry of charges filed, then dropped, and Kellogg flew under the radar for a couple of years. He'd resurfaced in Pecan Springs, raising money for a new church with a new name—Truth Seekers—and new hopes of scoring big. He preached the prosperity gospel: "Give your money to me and God will make you rich." Well, I had just given him my avocado. Maybe I would be blessed with an avocado tree, but I somehow doubted it.

A few moments later I was taking a pack of Hans' Pilz from a shelf of artisanal beers when someone stepped up beside me. "You should have slugged Jeremy Q. right in the kisser," Jessica Nelson said in an exaggeratedly gangsterish voice. "That was *your* avocado."

Jessica is an energetic young woman with a sprinkle of sandy freckles across her nose, boy-cut blond hair, and steady gray eyes. She wears one of those cheerful girl-next-door smiles and an optimistic air, but behind her easy, breezy manner is a savvy newspaper reporter with keen observation skills, a quick brain, and plenty of street smarts. The crime reporter for the *Enterprise*, she looked the part in a cobalt blue blazer over a white top with a chunky red necklace, neat-fitting black slacks, and her favorite red heels. She was carrying a grocery basket over one arm.

"I'm waiting for Kellogg to show up in one of your crime stories," I said. "It shouldn't take too much ingenuity for you to nail that man for something the DA can charge him with. Stealing from widows and orphans, maybe? Mutilating a puppy? Assaulting a Sunday School teacher?"

"I'm keeping my eye on him," Jessica said. "Didn't Olivia Andrews blog about him? Something about some dirty work in his former church, as I recall."

"She did." I saw a six-pack of Fireman's Four bottles and added that to my cart, too. McQuaid would be pleased. "Interesting that you should mention Olivia. Her sister Zelda stopped in to see me yesterday."

I could see Jessica's reporter-antennae go up. "Small world," she said. "I happened to be at the police station on Saturday, interviewing Rita Kidder about those thefts at Ryans' Sport Shop. Zelda Andrews came in to talk to Rita about her sister's accident."

I wasn't surprised. Pecan Springs *is* a small world, and Jessica knows most of its corners and cubbyholes. "Zelda mentioned talking to Rita," I said. "She didn't mention you."

Jessica shrugged. "No reason she should. She was focused on Rita and I was just sort of hanging out. I'm planning to give her a call, though. She's got the idea that whoever killed her sister did it on purpose. But Rita had other things on her mind. Their conversation didn't go very far." One eyebrow went up and she cocked her head. "So what's going on, China? Why did Zelda Andrews come to see *you*?"

That's Jessica for you—always *why*, followed closely by *what, when, where, how,* and *how much.* That's what makes her a good reporter.

"She wanted to try out her idea on me," I said. "The one Rita wasn't interested in. You might have trouble reaching her, though. She's on her way to London." I hesitated, remembering that Jessica had covered Olivia's death for the newspaper. An idea was beginning to take shape in the back of my head, but I needed more time to think about it. "I have to get home and make supper for Brian and McQuaid, Jess. Are you going to be around tonight? I could give you a call—maybe share some of Zelda's story with you. If you're interested."

Jessica brightened. "Do call, please. I *am* interested." She reached into her grocery basket and pulled something out. "This is for you."

"Is that my avocado!" I stared at it. "How'd you get it?"

"Your avocado." Jessica grinned. "Snitched it out of that jerk's cart while he was looking for the cheapest toilet paper. I thought you should have it."

"You won't get any argument from me," I said, putting the avocado in my cart. "Call you tonight."

HOME IS A TWO-STORY VICTORIAN on Limekiln Road, some twelve miles west of town. The house is white with green shutters, with a porch on three sides and a turret in the front corner. It's set back a half mile from the highway behind a thick woods of hackberry, cedar, and oak and a grassy meadow that, in the spring, is gloriously carpeted with bluebonnets, paintbrush, and wine-cups. Behind the house, there's a vegetable-and-herb garden and a clear, spring-fed creek that's cool and fresh on a hot summer day. It was the creek and the woods and the meadow that sold us on the place, along with all the extra room the big house offered. There are bedrooms for the kids—Caitie has claimed the round turret room and Brian uses his old bedroom when he's home for a few days. There's a craft room for me, a study for McQuaid, and a roomy family-size kitchen with a pleasant view of the garden and Caitie's chicken coop.

A half hour after saying goodbye to Jessica, I was in the kitchen with McQuaid. I tied an apron over my jeans and shifted into full domestic goddess mode, moving the chicken casserole and the shortcake from the freezer to the microwave and putting the dinner rolls in the oven. McQuaid halved the fresh strawberries and whipped the cream with some peppermint syrup I had made a few days before. I got out a carton of cottage cheese and mixed it with some chopped chives, fresh minced dill, celery seed, and chopped cherry tomatoes—early ones from the garden, still a little warm from their day in the sun. I topped the chicken casserole with some leftover cooked wild rice mixed with a half-cup of grated Swiss and popped it under the broiler, then assembled the salad. By the time Brian got there, the table was set and the casserole was waiting.

McQuaid's son is a good eight inches taller now than I am, almost as tall as his dad and with the same dark hair falling across his forehead, the same pale blue eyes, the same deep voice and level head. I first met him when he was seven, when McQuaid and I started seeing one another. The memory is sweet, in spite of the multitude of escaped lizards, free-range frogs, and itinerant tarantulas that have come between us. Being a young boy's mother had not been part of my plan for an ideal life. But Brian stole my heart—just as Caitie did, when she came along a few years later.

We traded quick hugs and Winchester greeted Brian with his usual lugubrious passion, then took up his station under the table, readying himself for bits of whatever might fall between his paws. But before we sat down, I took Brian's duffle bag to the laundry room and sorted quickly, whites in one pile, colors in another. I have never understood how a simple washing machine could defeat such a smart kid, especially one who's been playing with computers since before he could read. I often suggest that he sign up for Laundry 101, which is a skillset every bit as useful as typing and driving a car. I'm sure he could master it easily.

But as I picked up his favorite black Mountain Goats T-shirt, I wrinkled my nose. Smoked cannabis has a potent, unmistakable scent.

Once you've smelled its skunky, burned-rope odor, your nose will never let you forget it. Weed, pot, grass—whatever you want to call it, that's what I was smelling on Brian's shirt.

There's a story here, of course. Medical marijuana was legalized in Texas several years ago. Not long after that, voters in Austin (where Brian goes to school) approved a local ballot initiative effectively decriminalizing weed. At the next election, a half-dozen home-rule cities, including Pecan Springs, followed suit, putting a stop to arrests for possession of less than four ounces of marijuana. And recently, the Texas House of Representatives voted to decriminalize low-level possession and expand access to marijuana for medical purposes. The bill wasn't brought to a vote in the senate but will likely be back next year. There's a lot of money at stake here, and plenty of people want a piece of this market.

But as Michael Pollan says, an illicit plant is whatever a government decides it is, whether it's cannabis, the opium poppy, coca, or peyote. Here in Texas, pot is still illicit—and will be, for the foreseeable future.

I held my son's T-shirt to my nose again. What should I do? Speak to him about it? Remind him that while Austin and Pecan Springs police won't arrest you for a few ounces of this particular illicit plant, the state troopers who patrol the interstate will? Point out that cannabis is still a Schedule I drug on the feds' no-no list, right there beside heroin, LSD, and Ecstasy? Bring up the research suggesting that too much grass for too long can have a negative effect on cognition?

But too much alcohol and too many cigarettes for too long can have a very similar effect—a fatal effect, even—and booze and tobacco are both legal. There hasn't been enough reliable science to say how much cannabis is too much and how long is too long. And the evidence I held in my hand, while compelling, was only circumstantial. I

83

had seen Casey wearing Brian's T-shirts. Maybe the pot was hers, not his. Or maybe he had worn it to a party where joints were making the rounds and there was enough smoke in the air to get everybody high.

And there was that collection of nootropic herbs on the display shelf in my shop, plants that are used by people all around the world to make themselves feel better, boost their energy, calm jittery nerves. How different, really, is cannabis from caffeine? From tobacco, with its load of nicotine? Come to that, I've read that people are using nicotine in gum or patches as a nootropic.

So maybe I should just keep my mouth shut about my inadvertent discovery. I've watched the boy grow into a thoughtful young man. He has good sense. I can trust him to make reasonable choices—at least, that's what I told myself as I dropped his aromatic shirt into the washing machine.

But the shirt wasn't the biggest surprise of the evening. That came after we had done justice to the casserole, the salad, and the dinner rolls, to the accompaniment of Spock's chatter and with Winchester begging a sample of every dish. I left the table briefly to put the colored clothes into the dryer and load the whites and again to put the whites in the dryer. I returned to pour coffee while McQuaid spooned strawberries over the shortcake and passed the peppermint-flavored whipping cream. We were just settling into dessert when Brian put down his fork, looked from his father to me, and delivered some startling news.

"Casey and I have decided to get married."

It was a showstopper. Followed by a long moment's silence.

"Wow." McQuaid said finally. "But what about—?" He swallowed and looked at me.

I thought for a fleeting moment that he might be going to bring up the guess-who's-coming-for-dinner question we confronted last year when we learned that Brian and Casey had moved in together. As you might expect, the boy's choice of a live-in girlfriend had given both of us something to think about. Something that caused us to take a close look at where we stood on interracial marriage.

It turned out that we were okay on the subject. You love whom you love, and we both understood that our son's choice of a partner was entirely his choice. Whether it's Casey or somebody else, all he needs from us is the assurance that his family loves and trusts him and is firmly in his corner. With us behind him, he can work out the rest, whatever that might be.

And Casey is a lovely young woman and smart as the dickens. "I don't blame Brian for being smitten," McQuaid had admitted after we met her. "It just takes some getting used to, that's all. And it certainly makes me feel old. My little kid with a live-in, when he's barely old enough to vote." He had given me a worried look. "I just hope they're being . . . well, careful, you know. About sex. Taking precautions, I mean."

I had pointed out that both Brian and Casey were serious about school and that Casey was pre-med. Which meant, I supposed, that she knew how to keep from getting pregnant—which presents a special problem now that the legislature has decided to draw the line at an impossibly early six weeks. I was hoping that marriage wasn't going to come up any time soon.

But it had. Tonight. Just now.

McQuaid cleared his throat and tried again. "But what about *school*? You haven't finished your undergrad work and you're planning a graduate degree. Casey's pre-med. She could have another ten years or so, depending on her residency. Those are some pretty big commitments." Helplessly, he appealed to me. "What do you think, China?"

85

What I thought was that a little cannabis might go a long way toward mellowing out a tense moment. But I heard myself saying, "Congratulations, Brian. Casey is a wonderful girl with a bright future. We're so glad for you!" And then, "Have you guys set a date? Are you thinking like maybe right away, or after you finish school or . . ."

I let my voice trail off but Brian saw through my awkward, unfinished question. He gave me a crooked grin. "If you mean, do we have to get married right away because we're pregnant, the answer is no. But if we wait until we've both finished school, we'll be waiting for a decade. That's too long." His grin faded. "Both of us are ready *now*. We're only waiting because . . . well, because her parents aren't totally on board." He swallowed and his voice dropped. "The Galbraiths aren't on board at all. In fact, they're opposed. Majorly."

"Opposed?" I let my breath out and waited a beat. "Why?"

"Money, probably." McQuaid spooned more cream onto his shortcake. "If that's it, Brian, I understand their position. China and I can't realistically chip in more than we're currently doing. And I doubt that Sally can, either."

Sally—Brian's birth mother and McQuaid's ditzy first wife—is perennially underemployed and financially overcommitted. She pays her share, although she isn't as regular as she's supposed to be and she isn't in touch with her son very often. I didn't think she had met Casey yet.

Brian nodded earnestly. "I appreciate all the help I'm getting, Dad. I'm planning to keep my job at the Natural Gardener. My grades are high enough to keep my scholarship. Casey is giving up her athletic scholarship but has already qualified for an equal amount of aid. When it comes to grad school and med school, of course, student debt will be an issue that we'll both have to figure into our planning. But we can live together cheaper than we can live apart. And we don't want to wait any longer than we have to." He became emphatic. "Anything could happen, you know."

It might be easy to brush this off as the impatience of the young, but Brian is right. For all of us, for a lot of reasons, the path ahead looks riskier than ever before, and the people we love—the people with whom we share all these risks—are somehow dearer than ever. It shouldn't come as a surprise that two young people in love wanted to face an uncertain world together.

But he hadn't answered my question, so I asked it again. "Why are the Galbraiths opposed?"

Casey's family lives in Baton Rouge, where her father is a pediatrician and her mother teaches high school English. We haven't met, but from things Casey has said, they seem to be a very close family.

Brian looked down at his plate. "Because they don't want their daughter to marry a white guy."

McQuaid and I exchanged glances, sharing the same question: *It's a razor that cuts both ways, isn't it?*

"Is that what they said?" McQuaid asked at last.

"Not exactly." Brian poked at his shortcake. "Not in so many words, I mean. But that's what Casey thinks. They had her paired off with the son of a Black family friend in law school at Tulane." He looked up with an engaging laugh. "Her father told her he hoped I'd be doing better things with my environmental science degree than pushing a wheelbarrow loaded with dirt. But don't worry. Casey says they're really liberal at heart. They'll let me into the family."

"Well, I should hope so," McQuaid said. "After all, you're a pretty cool kid. We think so, anyway."

And that broke the tension. We wouldn't need the cannabis after all.

The rest of the strawberry-shortcake conversation was about Brian's plan to take Casey to meet his mother sometime in the next few weeks. He was a little nervous about it, which I could understand. McQuaid offered to go with them but Brian shook his head. "I think this is something I have to do myself." He gave his father a look that let me know that he didn't want Casey to get caught in the crossfire between his parents—which is what would likely happen if McQuaid went along. He and Sally don't see eye to eye on *anything*.

We would have talked longer, but Brian's workday at the Natural Gardener started early the next morning. While I packed some leftovers that he could take back home with him, he went into the laundry room, folded his dried clothes, and put them in his duffle. Back in the kitchen, he turned to me.

"Thanks for the laundry, Mom. Oh, in case you caught a whiff of weed on my Mountain Goats shirt, it's because Casey and I went to a block party last night. We didn't stay long after the joints started coming around, but the smell kinda stuck to my shirt." He made a face. "Sorry. I meant to mention it, so you wouldn't think I had taken up pot-smoking in my spare time."

"Oh, really?" I said innocently. "I didn't notice."

He smiled at his dad, then at me. "And thanks for understanding about Casey and me, you guys. Means a lot—more than I can say. We love you. Both of us." He gave us a hug and a quick kiss, added, "We'll be in touch about the wedding," and was gone.

In touch about the wedding. McQuaid and I put the dishes into the dishwasher, more silently than usual. Both of us, I think, were feeling just a little ancient. And more than a little sad. My mind was full of images of Brian as a scrawny, dark-haired kid who was crazy about iguanas and tarantulas, loved codes and cryptograms and his computer, and always slept with his socks on. It's one thing to have a son in college and we'd pretty much gotten used to that. After all, we could still think of him as a college boy. It's quite another thing to have a son who is a married man. It might take a while longer to get used to that.

The kitchen cleanup finished, McQuaid retreated to his study to compile his Brownsville notes for Charlie. I had told Jessica I would call her, so I sat down with my phone in the living room and spent the next few minutes giving her a condensed version of Zelda's theory of her sister's vehicular homicide—the vehicle driven by a man whose past life included a conviction for his wealthy wife's murder. After all, Jessica had already written several newspaper stories about the accident and likely knew the details of Olivia's death better than I did. What's more, she is an investigative reporter who is professionally acquainted with many of Pecan Springs' prominent citizens. And while Pecan Springs is growing fast, it's still a small town. One way or another, between the two of us, we know pretty much everybody. If Olivia's murderer lives here—if there *is* a murderer, that is, not a careless driver—one of us is probably acquainted with him. The thought of that sent a quick shiver down my spine.

My tale was followed by a moment's silence. When Jessica spoke, I could hear the skepticism in her voice. Which is okay. She's a reporter. That's her job: to be skeptical.

"So Zelda believes that her sister was killed to keep her from telling people that somebody was *exonerated* from a murder charge twenty years ago. You've been around the courthouse more than I have. As a motive, doesn't that sound a little far-fetched?"

"Not exonerated," I corrected her. "The sentence was vacated. There's no statute of limitations on murder, which means that if the current DA decided to reopen the case, he could. There could be issues around the right to a speedy trial, yes, but Kelly might not be aware of that. It's possible that Olivia did some digging and found something new and plausible, a material issue of fact that she thought would interest the DA. Or this guy thought she had." Or even that Olivia *told* him she had, just to get his full attention. Several possibilities here.

Another silence. Then: "What have you done so far? Anything?" There was less skepticism now.

"I looked up the newspaper reports of Eleanor Kelly's death and James Kelly's trial. And read the appeal and the appellate court's ruling. I also talked to Charlie Lipman, who was defending Olivia in the Neely defamation suit. Zelda had told her story to him. He says he doubts it." But if Charlie *really* doubted it, why had he sent her to me? He'd have to figure I'd be interested.

"Give me those names again," Jessica said. "I'll do some digging too. When did you say this murder happened? Where?"

"James Q-for-Quincy Kelly," I said. "The dead woman was Eleanor Blakely Kelly." I gave her the location and date of Eleanor's death and the trial and appeal dates. "I'm going to ask Rita Kidder to show me the spot where Olivia died, but I need to clear it with Sheila first. I'm seeing her in the morning. If the chief says okay, do you want to go with us?"

Jessica didn't hesitate. "Of course. But don't be surprised if the trip doesn't pay off. I arrived at the scene an hour or so after Andrews was killed. There wasn't much to see then—there'll be even less to see now." She paused. "But Zelda's theory is . . . interesting. You say that she's gone back to London?" I could hear the keys clicking. Jessica was at her computer, making notes on a possible interview. That young woman has a nose for news. Even if an investigation went nowhere, the theory itself could be a story.

"Yes, back to London, but I can give you her contact information.

And I'll call you after I've talked to Sheila. You're available to go see the accident site with Rita and me as soon as tomorrow, if we can set it up?"

"Absolutely," Jessica said. "Email the contact info. And thanks for looping me into this, China. I appreciate it."

I clicked off. I was the one who appreciated it. For a small-town reporter, Jessica is top-notch. And the deeper the story is hidden and the more complicated it is, the better she likes it. I was willing to bet that the minute we were off our phones, she was headed straight for Google. By midnight, she would have her arms around the entire James Q. Kelly story, start to finish.

McQuaid came into the living room with Winchester at his heels and a can of Hans' Pilz in his hand. "Want a beer?"

I stood. "I'm thinking wine. Meet me on the back deck for the magic hour?"

"Sounds right," he said. In the kitchen, I poured a glass of white wine and went out to join McQuaid and Winchester. We love to watch full darkness fall across the Hill Country and listen as the creatures of the night begin to pursue their dark-side affairs. We'll sit for a half hour or more, saying nothing, just listening.

Winchester gets bored easily and never sits with us that long. To-night, he got a whiff of something he couldn't resist—an armadillo, a possum, perhaps a skunk. (Please, God, not another skunk. The potent memory of the last one will be eternally with me.) He bumped down the steps and blundered away into the dark. Mr. P, who had been on an evening excursion of his own, jumped up on the deck to join us, bring-ing his purr. He shared my lap while we admired the full moon that flooded the grass and trees with silver—a Strawberry Moon, named for the June strawberry harvest.

McQuaid and I often say that we love living in the country because it's so quiet out here. But it isn't, really—and especially not at night. A welcome shower had briefly cooled the afternoon, and the male green tree frogs were honking their loud nasal courting entreaties. The thrum of the cicadas was punctuated by the crickets' metallic chirping, while from somewhere on the other side of the stone fence that separates our yard from our neighbors' woods, I could hear the wheezy *who-who-whooo* of a great horned owl. If I sat there long enough, I would likely hear, too, the haunting yips and yodels of a family of coyotes.

I hugged Mr. P, enjoying his throaty purr and thinking of Brian and Casey. My mom-self couldn't help wishing the kids would put off a major commitment. But I knew that they had to make their own choices and that my job, my *only* job, was simply to stand beside them, whatever those choices were.

Somewhere in the dark woods, I heard Winchester's deep, melodic basset bark, letting us know that he was doing his job to warn off some trespassing creature. From the direction of the creek came the loud, raspy *awk!* of a great blue heron. And then my lawyer-self piped up, reminding me of my unsatisfactory conversation with Charlie Lipman that afternoon. He hadn't even tried to answer my questions about Johnnie Carlson's appeal or the DA's decision not to retry. And when I'd wondered out loud where Kelly had gone, he dismissed my question. "The fella likely ended up in Mexico," he'd said.

Mexico. A good place to disappear and entirely probable, since Kelly likely had a substantial war chest. But Olivia had believed that he had eventually shown up in Pecan Springs. Was she right? How much of her research had she shared with Charlie? How much did *he* know about what she'd found out? Why didn't he want to share it with me?

Good questions. Now, if I only had a few answers . . .

Chapter Six

Finding yourself habitually forgetful during the day? Perhaps it's because you didn't get enough sleep the night before—or because you're suffering (as many of us do) from several days of sleep deficit. In her book *Remember: The Science of Memory and the Art of Forgetting*, Lisa Genova writes that sleep is essential to the memory-coding process. "After a miserable night's sleep," she adds, "you'll probably go through the next day experiencing a form of retrograde amnesia." According to Genova, recall can be enhanced by 20 to 40 percent after a period of sleep, compared with recall after the same amount of time awake.

And there's help. Five familiar nootropic herbs—lavender, chamomile, valerian, passionflower, and lemon balm—have been used for centuries to promote a naturally restful sleep. You can choose to sip a warm tea, scent your bath with an essential oil, massage an oil on your body, add essential oil to your bedside aroma diffuser or your handheld inhaler, or take a capsule of the herbal extract. Try several strategies, to see what works for you.

China Bayles
"What Am I Forgetting? Herbs to Improve Your Memory"
Pecan Springs Enterprise

When I rescheduled my drop-in at Sheila's office for early morning, I promised to bring breakfast. So I filled an insulated lunch bag with bananas, pecan muffins, frozen spinach-feta-basil tortilla wraps (we could heat them in the cops' breakroom microwave), and hazelnut lattes for three, then blew a kiss to McQuaid and headed for my Toyota.

November and December had been nicely rainy, and the April and May wildflowers—especially the bluebonnets—had run riot along the Hill Country roadsides. It was June and the bluebonnets were gone, but Limekiln Road was still alive with a patchwork quilt of colors. Swaths of vivid red paintbrush were laced with ribbons of pink evening primrose and bright yellow Engelmann's daisies and coreopsis. Splashes of orange gaillardia—blanket flower—were punctuated by impressive spires of purple horsemint and brightened by scattered mounds of white blackfoot daisy, purple prairie verbena, and winecup.

With so much brilliant color spilling onto the shoulders, it was hard to keep my eyes on the road. But I had to watch, because the Hill Country is full of white-tailed deer with the reckless habit of dashing across the road in front of oncoming cars. The last thing you want first thing in the morning is a shattered windshield and a dead deer in your lap.

Or a dead bicyclist. At the top of Crazy Joe Hill, Limekiln Road is just two narrow lanes with a deep ravine dropping off to the right, down to Crazy Joe Creek. As I crested the hill, eastbound, I saw a guy on a road bike directly in front of me, in my lane. There wasn't even time to jam on my brakes. The only thing I could do was swerve sharply into the lane to my left. If a westbound car had been coming up the hill, it would have hit me head-on. Or I would have hit the cyclist. But it wasn't and I didn't. We were safe, the cyclist and I.

As I caught my breath after this close call, I thought of Olivia. Something very similar had happened to her, hadn't it? According to the reports, she was running in the predawn dark, with the traffic. It could have been an accident just like the one that hadn't happened a moment ago. I didn't need Occam's razor to tell me that the most likely answer to the question of her death was the simplest: it was just another accident on a dark and narrow road. The stories of Eleanor Kelly's murder and her murderer were interesting. But irrelevant.

I was still thinking about this as I drove down the eastern rim of the Edwards Plateau, across the Pecan River, and into Pecan Springs. From a distance, the town looks peaceful and cozy, the dream of every chamber of commerce. Still bearing the distinctive mark of its settlement by German immigrants in the late 1840s, it is built around a courthouse square, where the original public buildings were located. One of these was the police department, which until a few years ago shared an old stone building with the jail, the Tourist and Information Center, and a sizable nursery colony of Mexican free-tailed bats, which swarm out at sunset on their overnight mosquito patrol. Known as guano bats for the impressive amount of droppings they produce, they are also known for their contribution to the Civil War. The local Confederates built a guano kiln on Crazy Joe Creek for the making of gunpowder—until one memorable night in 1863 when the place blew itself to smithereens. Also irrelevant but interesting.

Then the police department was moved out of the bat building to a nifty new brick-and-glass affair on West San Marcos Street that is shared with the municipal court, the mayor's office, and the city council. I parked in the lot behind it and went in through the back entrance and down a short hall lined with photographs of cops and first responders receiving medals for doing good things in bad situations. I stopped at the information desk in the lobby and said good morning to Dale, the uniformed officer on duty.

"Breakfast," I said, unzipping my lunch bag for his inspection. "With the chief."

He stamped my pass. "Maybe it will improve the mood back there."

"Bad day already?" I asked sympathetically.

"No worse than usual." Dale was matter-of-fact. "Five a.m. T-bone at San Jacinto and Durango. One fatality. Armed robbery at the Valero station on the interstate. Plus the usual drunk-and-disorderly, auto theft, and"—he handed me my pass—"possession of a controlled substance, criminal trespass, evading arrest, felony possession of a fire-arm." He lifted one eyebrow. "Not to mention—"

"I get the picture." I clipped the pass to my T-shirt and headed for the chief's office. Pecan Springs only looks peaceful and cozy on the surface. Beneath, we are just as criminally inclined as any other town.

Connie Page glanced up from her computer with a brisk "Good morning, China." Sheila's indispensable assistant looked efficient as always in a white blouse, her dark hair cut short, wearing a minimum of makeup. She had been McQuaid's assistant when he served as acting chief before Sheila came on the job, so I've known Connie for a while. She's only recently back from an extended leave of absence, dealing with her mom's and sister's health issues in Dallas.

"I understand it isn't," I said sympathetically. "A good morning, I mean."

"Sort of normal, actually," Connie replied. "We'd get along better, though, if we didn't have three patrol officers and a dispatcher out sick. Plus two cars in the shop for repair." If you want to know what's going on at the PSPD, Sheila can give you the big picture, but Connie is your go-to person for nuts-and-bolts details. She knows how it all fits together.

I unzipped my lunch bag and took out one of the lattes. "Maybe this will help."

"For me?" Connie asked gleefully. "Blessings on thee!" The coffee in the breakroom is notoriously bad, and both cops and staffers reg-ularly trek the half-block to Lila's Diner. Lila's coffee stays with you.

I took out three tortilla wraps, tidily bundled in waxed paper. "Could you put these in the microwave, please? One for the boss, one for you, one for me." I pulled out a muffin and a banana. "These are for you, too."

"Oh, goodie!" Connie sounded positively exultant. "I'm still catching up after Dallas, so I skipped breakfast and came in early. Thank you." She stood, reaching for a folder on her desk. "The chief is expecting you. And Rita dropped off the accident report you asked for." She looked at me curiously. "It's several months old. I was wondering why you're interested."

I learned long ago that nothing gets past Connie, so I told the truth. "Because I wasn't here when Olivia was killed. And because her sister asked me to have a look."

"Oh, *Zelda*," she said. "She got to you, too, did she? She was here for more than an hour last week, talking to Rita." She handed me the folder. "You can keep this copy." Lowering her voice, she added, "Go easy on the chief, China. She hasn't been getting enough sleep. Noah's giving her a hard time."

Sheila Dawson, Smart Cookie to her friends, is one of those enviable women who look terrific in anything, even in a dark blue cop uniform. In fact, if you didn't know that she has almost two decades of police work under her belt and can outshoot most of the men in her department, you might expect to encounter her on a movie set or a fashion photo shoot. Shiny blond hair, high cheekbones, deep-set blue eyes, a creamy complexion. But this morning, Connie was right. Sheila was clearly tired: dark circles under her eyes, skin pale and shadowed, mouth tight, shoulders slumped.

"Tough day already?" I asked sympathetically, unzipping my lunch bag.

"Tough night." Her voice was thin. "Noah's teething. He's fussy." She sagged back into her leather desk chair. "For the past week, he's been getting us up three or four times a night."

On the shelf behind her was a silver-framed photograph of Blackie Blackwell, her husband (also McQuaid's PI partner), proudly holding the new member of their family, who was wearing the dark blue baby cop's cap that Connie had crocheted for him. Eagerly anticipated, Noah had been born the previous November, further complicating his mom's already complicated life. Blackie was a great deal of help—experienced help. He'd already raised two boys, so a baby in the house was not a new thing to him, as it was to Sheila. There was joy, yes. But getting up three or four times a night couldn't be a piece of cake.

"Poor you." I put the lunch bag on a chair. "When I get to the shop, I'll put together a get-some-sleep rescue kit for you. I'll add something for Noah's gums, too. If he sleeps better, so will you."

Sheila covered a yawn with her hand. "I was going to ask you about clove oil. I've read about people using it for toothache. Could I use that for Noah?"

"Clove oil is great for grownups," I said, "not so great for kids under two. Lavender and ginger oils are better. I'll put some in the kit for the baby." I reached into the lunch bag and took out the remaining lattes, muffins, and bananas, plus plastic plates and napkins. "Meanwhile, here's something that will keep you going while Connie is heating our tortilla wraps. Spinach and feta cheese with fresh basil."

"Oh, *coffee*!" Sheila exclaimed. She seized the latte with both hands, sipped, and closed her eyes reverently. "And wraps. China, you are a lifesaver."

"Caffeine will do it every time," I said, as Connie brought in our warm breakfast wraps and then went back to her desk.

Sheila made a face. "Not the caffeine in the breakroom. And of course I can only have a couple of cups. I'm still breastfeeding." She sipped again. "So what's going on with you?"

Ten minutes later, we had finished eating and caught up on our family news: Brian's announcement. (Sheila: "They'll probably change their minds a dozen times.") Noah's new backward crawl. (Me: "Do babies *really* do that?"). Our husbands' latest case: an independent West Texas oil company with an employee embezzlement situation that the manager didn't want to share with the police. That part of the conversation was interrupted by a call from the mayor's office that Sheila had to take. While she was on the phone, I took the opportunity to scan the two-page report of Olivia's death.

The time-and-place information was neatly filled in: 5:30 a.m. April 3, on the westbound side of Purgatory Bend Road just past mile marker 10 and twenty yards east of the Possum Creek bridge. The driver and accident vehicle sections contained only the words UN-IDENTIFIED and VIZPLUS MIRROR, whatever that meant. Gloria Tanner, neighbor, was listed as a witness, with a phone number and an address on Purgatory Bend. Printed below Tanner's name: WITNESS HEARD VEHICLE COMING DOWNHILL. HEARD A THUMP, VEHICLE STOPPED, THEN STARTED AGAIN SEVERAL MOMENTS LATER. SAW A WHITE PICKUP, HORIZONTAL SCRAPE ON THE PASSENGER DOOR, NO MAKE/MODEL/YEAR. DIDN'T NOTICE DAMAGE. CAN'T ID THE DRIVER, MALE-FEMALE.

I sighed. Since there are over four million pickups in Texas and almost 60 percent of them are white, that means there are something like two million needles in this particular haystack. And even if you get lucky and locate the vehicle (fat chance), you don't have much of a case if the witness can't even identify the driver's gender.

On page two, the section marked "Disposition of injured/killed" was filled out with Olivia's name and address and the word "killed" was circled. Below that, the words DRIVER FLED SCENE appeared in the "Charges filed" section. And below *that*, the investigating officer had penciled in three factors that contributed to the incident: JOGGER MOVING WEST WITH WESTBOUND TRAFFIC; NARROW SHOULDER; INADEQUATE REFLECTIVE GEAR. In the "Field Diagram" box was a sketch of the road, the point of impact, and the location of the body, twelve feet from the road. In the narrative box: DECEASED SPOTTED BY PASSING MOTORIST PAUL DUNCAN @ 6:15, with Duncan's address and phone number. The box for "Evidence Collected" was checked, along with the number of the evidence bag. At the bottom, the investigating officer had signed her name: Rita Kidder.

I frowned at the sketch. There was something missing, wasn't there? Had it been overlooked? I made a mental note to ask Rita about it.

Sheila put down the phone, hard. "Friggin' golf tournament," she muttered. "As if I didn't have *enough* to do."

I looked up from the report. "Let me guess. Back the Blue on the Green?"

"That's the one," Sheila growled. "Sponsored by the Pennington Foundation. Palmer Warren is in the mayor's office right now, setting things up. I'm supposed to hand out some special awards at the banquet. Warren will be here in a few minutes to give me the details."

"I saw his wife yesterday. Cassidy was hitting up Charlie Lipman for prize money." I shook my head. "You'd think they'd give the chief of police a pass on community service. Especially if she's a new mom."

"Are you kidding?" Sheila rolled her eyes. "They're doubling down with this stuff *because* I'm a new mom. The mayor is besties with Palmer Warren, you know. The two of them want Blackie and me to bring Noah to the banquet—wearing the cute little cop cap Connie crocheted for him. It's the 'people side' of policing. Goes along with fixing an air conditioner for a senior citizen or pushing kids on the merry-go-round at the park." She became cynical. "Oh, and it wouldn't hurt to be sure there's a photographer around to get your picture while you're doing something nice for somebody—like giving Ruby's mom a lift back to the nursing home. It's all about public relations these days." She nodded at the report I was holding. "So tell me. What's your interest in Andrews' accident?"

A straight-up question, so it got a straight-up answer. "Her sister Zelda says the accident wasn't accidental. Somebody deliberately took Olivia out."

"Mmm," Sheila said, in a neutral tone. "Ms. Andrews tried out that theory on the investigating officer last week too. Something about a guy killing her sister because she was about to write a blog post that would tell everybody he was somebody else. Is that it?"

I chuckled. "Lacking in detail but it pretty well gives the general picture."

"Rita said the whole thing sounded far-fetched and she doesn't have much of a place to start—especially since all she's got is a truck but no license plate, no make-model, no driver ID. Plus, she's working a couple of ongoing investigations that are more likely to produce results."

Results. I knew that Sheila's success in her job was measured by her officers' clearance rate. It's all about the bottom line. When I didn't answer, Sheila frowned.

"So this Zelda woman took her story to you?"

"She dropped in on Charlie Lipman first—Olivia's lawyer. He sent her to me."

"Oh, Charlie," Sheila said wearily. "A thorn in my side." She finished her breakfast wrap, balled up the waxed paper, and tossed it in the waste basket beside her desk. "Why'd he unload her on you? You do something to piss him off?"

"He knew I was a friend of Olivia's. And one of the characters in the backstory was a defense lawyer I used to work with." I chuckled, making light of it. "Also, he wanted to get Zelda out of his hair and my name came to mind."

She grinned. "That's Charlie—especially if he didn't think the sister was going to turn into a paying client." The grin disappeared. "But you know where we are on this, China. Everybody hates hit-and-runs. They're the devil to resolve, and even when we have a suspect, the devil to prosecute successfully. Every jurisdiction has way too many of these fatalities on the books, some a couple of decades old. We cleared only fifteen percent of ours last year, but even at that, we're doing better than some departments." She drained her latte. "But if you come across anything interesting or useful in the Andrews case, I'm sure Rita will be happy to listen." She made a face. "Well, maybe not happy, but she'll listen. A hit-and-run is open until it's closed."

"So you don't mind if I do a little digging?"

"Not as long as you keep Rita in the loop—let her know what you're up to."

"Thank you," I said. Striking while the iron was hot, I added. "With that in mind, okay if I borrow her today? I'd like to take a look at the scene. We could do it at the end of her shift."

"Be my guest." Sheila cocked her head. "Rita said the sister's story is based on some decades-old murder case. What do you know about it?"

"Not much yet." I sketched out a tweet-length version.

Sheila looked interested. "A vacated conviction that wasn't retried? The prosecution must not have had much to start with."

"Yeah. Could be all kinds of reasons for that, I guess, but it means that the case could still be open, which could be a threat to Kelly. Zelda believes that her sister identified him, probably even got in touch with him. He's supposedly living here in Pecan Springs under another name—which doesn't show up in the notes I've read so far. Olivia intended to blog and podcast his story, but he got to her first. That's Zelda's theory, anyway."

Sheila frowned. "Wait a minute. I'm remembering—didn't Olivia Andrews get sued for doing something like this previously? Publishing things about people? Including claims she couldn't back up?"

"You're remembering right. There was one defamation suit pending when she died—Darwin Neely. Another one, from Jeremy Kellogg, was threatened. Charlie Lipman says that Neely was likely to prevail. If he did, Kellogg was next in line."

"Huh." Sheila sat forward, elbows on her desk. "If they were going to win their lawsuits, it would be counterproductive for either one to kill her."

"That was my thought, too," I remarked. "Unless one of them is Kelly in disguise."

"Well, Neely isn't your man," Sheila said with a little laugh. "Darwin was a deputy back when Blackie was county sheriff. He grew up in Adams County. His family has been here forever." She pulled her brows together. "Jeremy Kellogg, now—well, he's another matter. He's one of those holier-than-thou types that nobody likes. Some of my people have raised questions about his fundraising tactics, but nobody's found anything specific enough to warrant an investigation. And I hear rumors that he's been in trouble with the law before he got to Pecan Springs."

"It would be fun to nail that guy for something," I said, thinking of the encounter over the avocado. "He's about the right age, too. What do you know about him?"

"Only that he had a church up in Dallas or Fort Worth—somewhere up there. I think I heard that he was a missionary before that."

"A missionary? Where?"

"I don't know. Mexico, South America, maybe? If you find out anything about him, let me know. I'm curious." She shook her head. "I'm still not quite sure why you're interested in that hit-and-run, China. I'm okay with your having a look, and talking to Rita, too. I just don't understand what you expect to find."

"I'm don't either," I confessed. "But if there's something behind it, I'd like to know. Olivia had her enemies, I'm sure. Still, I've always had the sense that for all her brashness and exaggeration, she genuinely cared for the victims of the crimes she covered. She wanted to tell their stories, to make sure they wouldn't be forgotten—something that lots of people lose sight of. She had her faults, yes. But she *cared*, and that was important." I paused, thinking about my conversation with Charlie. "And also because I still can't figure out why Charlie sent Zelda to see me. He made a point of telling me to butt out when he knows full well that when somebody tells me that—"

"You want to butt in," Sheila said.

I was about to say that she knew me too well, too, but there was a tap on the door and it opened. "Mr. Warren is here from the mayor's office," Connie said.

Sheila turned to me. "Are we mostly done?" When I nodded, she raised her voice. "Come on in, Palmer."

If Cassidy Pennington Warren is queen of Pecan Springs, that makes her husband king—right? Well, he is, and looks it, too. He's what Ruby calls a George Clooney hottie. His distinguished salt-and-pepper hair and close-clipped gray beard are awesomely styled, his blue sport jacket and designer jeans are impeccably tailored, and his alligator Lucchese boots are immaculately polished. Together, he and Cassidy make an impressive couple. Apart . . . well, I wouldn't be surprised to learn that Palmer Warren inspires the erotic daydreams of quite a few Pecan Springs matrons. His oil and gas leases made him rich in his own right before he married Pennington money, but for all that, he's probably the more civic minded of the pair and definitely more hands-on. He's president of the hospital board, sponsors minority scholarships at CTSU, and is involved with a half-dozen annual charity events as well as various projects for kids. And even though he holds no elected office, he and the mayor are buddies, which affords him plenty of local political clout.

"Good morning, Chief." Warren put a large envelope on the desk. "Just wanted to be sure you got the list—and to personally thank you for agreeing to hand out the awards at the banquet. We couldn't do things like this if it weren't for our volunteers."

"My pleasure," Sheila said staunchly. She gestured at me. "Do you know China Bayles?"

He thrust out his hand. "Oh, China—sure. Hello again. I understand from Cassidy that you and Ruby are catering our little get-together. This coming weekend, is it?"

"Next," I said. "I'm looking forward to it."

"So are we." He glanced at Sheila. "Cassidy called you? Hope you and Blackie can make it."

"Wouldn't miss it for the world," Sheila said heartily.

"Good. Wonderful." He turned back to me. "Oh, and tell McQuaid I'll be calling him to see if he's available to judge the Pennington Bass Fishing Tourney again. He's a first-rate judge. Uncovered a cheater at last fall's tournament. Guy loaded his fish with lead weights."

"Thank you. Yes, I'll tell him," I said.

"What happened with the cheater?" Sheila asked curiously. "And how come I don't remember that?"

"It happened the week you had Noah," I said. "The angler got off with a warning when he could have been hit with a felony." McQuaid, the judge on that round, had noticed the disparity between the normal-sized bass and its outsized weight. When he cut it open, the lead spilled out of the felonious fish. The prize was fifteen hundred dollars, which could have made it attempted grand theft, a third-degree felony, worth up to ten years and a ten thousand–dollar fine.

"Letting him off was my wife's idea," Warren said. "I would have thrown the book at the guy. But we settled for a lifetime disqualification, thanks to McQuaid." He tapped the envelope. "Let me know if you have any questions. And now I'll get out of y'all's hair. Thanks again, Chief."

"Be still my heart," Sheila said, when he was gone. "I love Blackie, but that guy . . ." She let it hang.

"He's plenty easy on the eyes," I agreed. "And nice, to boot." I gathered up the breakfast things and put them into the lunch bag. "I'll see if Rita is available to go out to the scene this afternoon. Jessica Nelson wants to have another look, too. Oh, and something else. Zelda says that her sister's cellphone is missing. I was thinking it might be in your evidence locker. Do you happen to know—" I stopped when I saw the blank look on Sheila's face. "Never mind. I'll ask Rita."

"Do that," Sheila said. "And please don't forget that . . . what was it? Some sort of stuff to put on the baby's gums?"

"Lavender and ginger oils," I said. "I'll remember."

"Good." Sheila waved a weary hand. "Because I won't. These days, I would forget my head if it wasn't screwed on."

Chapter Seven

What do peppermint and sage have in common? Besides the fact that they are cousins (both belong to the Lamiaceae family) and likely share the same shelf in your kitchen pantry, both have been scientifically demonstrated to improve memory and mental alertness, thereby affirming their traditional use as memory enhancers.

- Researchers at Northumbria University in England found that study participants who drank peppermint tea reported improved long-term memory. The menthol in peppermint stimulates the hippocampus area of the brain, which controls memory and learning.
- Published research studies present evidence that sage provides memory improvement both in Alzheimer's patients and in young and old healthy persons. The results may be due to the flavone known as apigenin, which is reported to stimulate adult neurogenesis—the generation of neuronal cells in the adult brain.

In some studies, adults over the age of sixty-five appeared to benefit the most from these memory-boosting herbs. But you don't have to be a senior citizen to enjoy the brisk taste of peppermint tea or the familiar flavor of sage. And both are available as powdered extracts, in capsule form.

China Bayles
"What Am I Forgetting? Herbs to Improve Your Memory"
Pecan Springs Enterprise

It didn't take long to assemble the sleep kit for Sheila—a pillow filled with dried lavender blossoms, hops, and mugwort; a selection of essential oils (chamomile, jasmine, rose); a luscious body oil made of lavender, chamomile, and bergamot mixed with grapeseed and jojoba oils; and a tin of bedtime tea made from passionflower, skullcap, and chamomile. She was breastfeeding, so I didn't include any of the nootropic herbal supplements that might help—ashwagandha, for instance. But she could use the body oil for both herself and Noah. And with Noah's ginger and lavender oils, I included instructions for using them on his gums. I had to search the storeroom shelves for some ribbon and the right-sized basket, but I finally found what I was looking for behind a stack of toilet paper. I had arranged everything in it and was tying on a ribbon when Ruby came into the shop.

"That's pretty," she said, eyeing the basket. "For somebody special?"

"Sheila and baby Noah. He's teething and neither of them are sleeping." And then, because I had been thinking about it while I was putting the basket together, I told her about Brian's news.

"They're great together," I said, "but I'm afraid they're too young. Brian's got to finish his undergrad work and then there's grad school. And Casey—" I shook my head. "If she stays on her med track, it will be even longer for her."

Ruby said the same thing Sheila had said. "They'll probably change their minds. And if they don't, there's not much a mom can do. You might tell them that marrying before they're twenty-five means that divorce is a lot more likely. But they'll just say that people get married and divorced at all ages, and they'd be right. I know somebody who got married at sixty and was divorced by the time she was sixty-two. There's no magic age. In the end, we just have to trust them. I didn't have a lot of confidence in Amy and Kate making a go of it, and I'm happy to say I was wrong."

"True," I said. "I need to stop worrying about it." I picked up Sheila's basket. "Oh, I don't think I told you. I ran into Cassidy Warren yesterday. She says we won't have to handle the bar for their barbeque. And she's booked the Devil's Rib, so we need to tell Cass to add the band to her head count. There are six."

"I'll do it," Ruby said. "Looks like we're going to need a tent and tables for about fifty."

"Fifty?" I yelped. "I thought this was a *small* group of friends!"

Ruby laughed. "Fifty is her idea of small, I guess. I emailed her a menu and she's supposed to get back to me tomorrow. I've talked to Janie and Janet at Dos Amigas, and they'll lend us a couple of their wait people to help. Cass and I will be there, too, of course. How about you?"

"I wouldn't miss it," I said. "That ranch is spectacular, and I'm a fan of the Devil's Rib. Sounds like you have everything under control."

"More or less, I guess." Ruby made a face. "I wish I could say the same about Ramona."

"Uh-oh," I said. "Trouble?"

Ruby sighed heavily. "I love my sister, but she is *such* a pain. I told her to forget about putting a link to her Psychic Sisters on our website. She wasn't happy, of course, until she came up with an idea she likes better. She wants to use the garden and the tearoom for a psychic fair. She's thinking about the last weekend of June. What do you think?"

What did I think? I thought it would probably be next to impossible to work with Ramona, who at best is a tricky personality and at worst . . . I shuddered.

"That was my first response, too," Ruby said with a wry smile. "But the more I think about it, the more it seems like an interesting idea. Ramona says that she and the Psychic Sisters have started a podcast series and are already creating a following. They're real, by the way. The psychics, I mean. Dnalea and Mystic Sense and Gaia Gem—those are their professional names, of course. But the women themselves are real. That's their actual pictures we saw. And I met Dnalea face-to-face, over at Ramona's house. Of course, I have no idea how authentic her gift is, but she's a very nice person."

"Good to know," I muttered.

Ruby went on brightly. "Ramona—Ashling, that is—says she'll offer a free talk on dreamwork, which should attract a sizable audience. We could put her in Thyme Cottage and do RSVPs. She's located a guy who does aura photography, which would be something different. And I'm sure she'll be able to sign up at least a dozen people who would be happy to offer readings of various kinds."

"Readings?" I asked suspiciously. "As in tarot readings?"

"Exactly!" Ruby was enthusiastic. "Tarot, astrological readings, I Ching, runes, past lives, dreamwork." She furrowed her brow, thinking. "Ramona can do her thing on dreams, and I'm sure we can find psychics who do palm readings or skrying. We could feature it as a family event, with an astrology game for the kids and other children's features. I'm sure Ramona can come up with some creative kids' activities. We could also have astral music—I have a half-dozen CDs that would be perfect. And we could encourage everyone to come in costume, to give the event a little more pizzazz."

More pizzazz? I rolled my eyes. Didn't we have enough pizzazz already? How much more pizzazz did we need?

Ruby gave me a measuring look. "Don't be too quick to dismiss this, China. I know it's hard to work with Ramona, but she may have come up with a very smart idea—something we could do a couple of times a year. It could bring in some new customers to both our shops. People who haven't heard of us, I mean."

"Sure it could," I said. "New customers from the outer reaches of our local lunatic fringe. People who want to get their dreams analyzed and—"

"We can sell sandwiches," Ruby said, ignoring me. "We could have the tearoom open for snacks and drinks. I'm sure Cass can whip up something easy and cosmic-themed. And in the shops, we could put out some sale items. I have some dream catchers that would be perfect. I could mark them down by twenty-five percent, just for the event." She looked around. "You probably have a few things, don't you? Sage bundles? Dream pillows, herbs that are good for dreaming? Books on magical herbs?"

Sandwiches, music, markdowns, aural photography. This was beginning to sound like an epic production, worthy of George Lucas or Steven Spielberg. But it looked like Ruby was already sold on the idea, so I might as well go along with it. And yes, I did have a few books that I could put on a special display.

But I didn't want to go overboard on this thing. "Well, we don't want people tramping through the herb beds," I cautioned. "If we're going to do this, the tables ought to be set up at the back of the gardens, on the cottage lawn. But not too many. Maybe limit the vendors to a dozen?"

Ruby nodded emphatically. "We could put the CD player and the speakers for the music on the cottage deck. It could be plugged into the cottage's electrical system."

"That would work." I frowned. "We'll have to keep the volume down, though. You know how Mr. Cowan feels about noise." Mr. Cowan is the elderly man who lives across the alley. His yappy Peke, Miss Lula, takes it as her personal responsibility to alert everyone within earshot to every trespassing cat, dog, and bird. A psychic fair was likely to send her into hysterics.

I added, "I'm afraid somebody will have to explain astral music to me, though."

"Oh, you know," Ruby said with a careless wave of her hand. "Trance music. Body experience music. Music for out-of-body journeys." She noticed the expression on my face and patted my shoulder soothingly. "It'll be okay, dear. Really."

"As long as we don't have people floating off into space," I said. "We don't want to lose any of our customers." I paused, considering. "I suppose this could attract a few new people, if it's done right. Tell Ramona to check with Mrs. Baggett in the city planning department about the permit. She should be sure to have all the details in mind. Mrs. Baggett can be a dragon about times and dates and payment—especially payment."

Ruby made a face. "Oh, yes. Mrs. Baggett. I remember her. She gave our quilt guild a hard time over a permit for our exhibit."

"Yes, and she has the final word about everything, I'm afraid. She's never very easy to work with. Ramona should also tell the vendors that they need to bring their Texas sales tax permits. We won't have to get a food-service permit since the food will come from our kitchen. But maybe you should take a look at our insurance policy to make sure we're covered in case somebody gets so enlightened she floats off into space."

Ruby frowned. "You're thinking like a lawyer."

"Well, somebody ought to," I said. "I would feel a lot better if this were anybody but Ramona. I'm sorry," I added hastily. "I know she's your sister, but—"

I left it hanging. It might not be so bad if Ramona would develop enough discipline to manage the weird poltergeisty thing that takes over when she gets stressed or annoyed or frightened. But she doesn't. Which leads to . . . well, bizarre events.

I'm not kidding. Like the evening the three of us were having dinner at Ruby's house and Ramona—steaming from a confrontation with a neighbor—walked into the kitchen. The pot rack crashed to the floor, a blind snapped up, a flowerpot jumped off the windowsill and into the sink, and cupboard doors flew open. Or the time she came to my house excited about her plan to buy the Comanche Creek Brewery and marry the brewmaster, prompting the microwave to chirp like crazy, the kitchen lights to blink off and on, and our antique cuckoo clock—a McQuaid family heirloom that sprung its mainspring decades ago—suddenly start shouting *Cuckoo! Cuckoo!* I don't understand Ramona. I don't want to.*

But Ruby does, and is personally familiar with her sister's weirdness. She studied me for a moment, then gave a resigned nod.

"I get it, China. I know this isn't really your thing. So I'll be responsible for dealing with Ramona. The two of us will get everything set up, including the permits. If you want to, you can show the vendors where you want them to put their tables. Or manage the tearoom. Or just enjoy seeing everybody having a good time. Maybe even have one yourself."

I sighed. If Ramona was involved, there was no possibility that I would have a good time.

IT WAS AN ORDINARY WEDNESDAY at the shop: slow in the morning; busy around noon, when the Friends of the Library came in for their

---

* The details: *Blood Orange* (China Bayles #24).

monthly lunch; and slow again in the afternoon. I took advantage of the lulls to post a couple of sale items—some potpourri and some unscented massage oil base—on the bulletin board behind the counter and do a little work on the website. I even made a colorful ad for the psychic fair and put it across the bottom of the front page. When Ramona came up with a list of vendors, I would include that, with photos and short paragraphs about each one. Then I went over to our Facebook page and posted a heads-up about the fair. Once the details were finally settled, I would include the fair in our *Enterprise* ad. I wasn't hugely enthusiastic, but it looked like we were going to do this thing, so we might as well do it right.

I was just finishing on Facebook when I got a call from McQuaid. "There's been a development in that case I was working on last week," he said. "I'm heading out to Midland. I'm leaving right now, could be gone several days." Midland is an oil and gas town some four hundred miles west of Pecan Springs, in the middle of the Permian Basin. McQuaid and Blackie were working on an employee embezzlement case for an oil company there. "Just letting you know I won't be home for supper."

"Well, phooey," I said. "Not to complain, but what about staying home for a change? Remember? We were going to spend more time together."

"Duty calls, sweet." He chuckled. "And we'll enjoy each other even more when we get back together again."

I sighed. "You'll be careful, I hope."

"Of course. I'm always careful."

Which was true, I knew, although that fact doesn't alleviate all my fears. McQuaid's investigative work offers fewer opportunities for getting shot or knifed or otherwise physically damaged, but it isn't hazard-free. He's not out on the mean streets every day, the way he was when he was in law enforcement. But things happen. When he's gone, I tend to dwell on the dark side.

"Be *more* careful," I said.

His voice softened. "I will. Take care of yourself and don't go getting into trouble." This is something he always says. I think he worries about me as much as I worry about him. "I'll see you in a few days. I'm booked at a motel close to the company headquarters. I'll call when I get checked in."

The rest of the afternoon went by fast. Polly Frame brought several volunteers from the herb guild to do some garden cleanup, and I went out to show them the areas that needed attention—the Zodiac Garden, especially, and the Kitchen Garden, which Cass raids at least once a day and is always untidy. Between customers, I answered a couple of texts from Caitie, who was entranced with her new horse, and one from my mother, confirming that it was okay with me if Caitie stayed for an extra week or so.

And then it was four o'clock and Rita Kidder came in, still in uniform at the end of her shift. "Ready to drive out to the accident scene?" she asked.

Things were pretty quiet and Ruby was available to close both shops. So I followed Rita to her squad car, where I phoned Jessica to tell her that we were on our way to the site where Olivia had been killed.

"Oh, sorry," she said regretfully. "I'm covering a crash on the interstate and then I have to get back to the office for an editorial meeting. I'm afraid you and Rita will have to do this without me today. But call me later, please. Let me know if you two uncover anything interesting."

"I'll do that," I said.

I've known Rita—a single mom with a six-year-old boy—since

she joined the force a couple of years ago. Between her son and the police department, she doesn't have time for a social life. She is barely regulation height and her bouncy chestnut ponytail makes her look younger than her thirty years. She's strong and wiry and while she might not have as much muscle as her male patrol partners, I'll bet she has a lot more stamina.

Rita is usually as friendly as a puppy, with lots of smiling energy. Today, though, she seemed wary about our outing. When I called her to set up our trip to Purgatory Bend Road, I said only that Olivia Andrews had been a personal friend and that the chief had okayed my request to take a look at the spot where she died. Could she show me where it was? I added that I'd also like to take a quick peek into the evidence bag. Her "okay" seemed to come a little slowly.

Now, as she drove south on Cesar Chavez, she let me know why she seemed guarded. "Ms. Andrews' sister Zelda came by the station on Saturday and we had ourselves a little talk. The chief tell you that?"

"Yes," I said. "And Zelda mentioned it to me when she came to see me."

There was a silence while Rita considered this. "So she floated her theory past you, too." She didn't say *that cockamamie theory of hers*, but her tone implied it, along with an unspoken reproach for wasting our time on this fruitless errand.

"She did," I said. "I know it sounds a little far-fetched, but you never can tell, can you? Stranger things have happened, I suppose." Brightly, I added, "Anyway, it reminded me that I had intended to have a look for myself. I was out of town when Olivia was killed, so all I know is what I read in the newspaper. Thanks for taking the time to show me where it happened." I put some extra oomph in my voice. "I know how busy you are, Rita. So I *really* appreciate it."

"No problem," Rita said in an off-hand tone, but this time she smiled and changed the subject. "Have you seen the chief's baby? Isn't he a stunner?" Which led to a spirited exchange about children and how hard it is for working moms to balance everything they have to do. We were friends again.

It was a pleasant early summer afternoon, with puffy white clouds in a wide, sun-blessed Texas Hill Country sky. Purgatory Bend Road strikes west off the Hunter Road a few miles south of Purgatory Natural Area. The eastern edge of the Edwards Plateau is a region of upland meadows cut by rugged limestone canyons and rolling hills. Ashe juniper, hackberry, and live oaks blanket the ridges, with an understory of yaupon holly, redbud, and dogwood. Purgatory Creek is home to white-bark sycamores and towering bald cypress with their knees in the water. Most of the Hill Country is a karst landscape where rainwater and runoff have eaten into the soluble limestone. It's known for its deep, water-filled sinkholes—like Blue Hole and Jacob's Well, west of Wimberley—and bubbling springs, shady canyons, and caves hidden away in the limestone bluffs. The hills and stream bottoms belong to white-tailed deer, coyotes, foxes, possums, and raccoons, and the trees are a birdwatcher's paradise of resident and migratory birds. Some, like the golden-cheeked warbler and the black-capped vireo, are shy and hard to spot. Others, like the painted bunting and the vermilion flycatcher, are so gorgeous they'll take your breath away.

Purgatory Bend Road is a narrow two-lane asphalt with challenging ups and downs, snaky curves, trees growing close on either side, and minimal shoulders—obviously dangerous for cyclists and joggers. It runs past the Hill Country subdivision where Olivia lived, heading west toward Canyon Lake and the dinosaur trackway at the Heritage Museum, where you can gawk at the immense footprints left in the

117

mud by massive creatures who claimed this landscape for much longer than we humans.

Rita began to slow as we came up on mile marker 10, on a fairly steep downhill stretch on the westbound side of the road. She pulled off as far as she could on the narrow shoulder and turned on her flasher and warning blinkers so the car wouldn't be rear-ended by a careless motorist barreling over the crest of the hill.

"That's where it all went down," she said, pointing toward a spot on the shoulder about ten yards ahead, close to the bottom of the long downhill slope, near the concrete bridge over Possum Creek. On the eastbound side of the road, a thigh-high metal guardrail ran along the edge of the eastbound lane, above a steep limestone cliff.

"So how do you think it happened?" I asked as we got out of the car and began walking down the hill.

"I figure that she's been doing the smart thing, running against the traffic on the shoulder of the eastbound lane," Rita said. She pointed to the other side of the road. "Until she gets to that guardrail. There's no more shoulder, so she crosses the road, intending to run on this wider shoulder until she gets over the bridge and the guardrail section ends. That's where she'll cross back to the eastbound side and be safe." Her voice matter-of-fact, she looked down, where she was standing. "But she doesn't get that far. She's whacked from behind right about *here*, where we found her shoe." Rita pointed to a spot just ahead, a jagged gray limestone outcrop about three or four yards up the hill. "She was flung up there, against that ledge. She was wearing just one shoe."

I looked toward the outcrop. A white wood cross with a spray of bright blue plastic flowers—forget-me-nots, I thought—was staked beside it. Olivia's name and the word *Remember* were painted neatly on the cross. Somebody hadn't forgotten.

"No drag marks?" I asked. "Like somebody pulling her?"

"Nope. And there's plenty of loose gravel. If the body was moved, we would have seen it. We see these crosses a lot," Rita added. "Families put them out. Her sister, probably."

I pressed my lips together, trying to recreate what had happened that morning. This was a dangerous stretch of road, even in daylight. In the predawn dark, it had been deadly. "As I remember, Olivia ran to music. She had different playlists for different runs so she could time herself. Was she wearing earbuds?"

"She was," Rita replied. "We found both of them—the kind that hook over the ear—along with that loose shoe and a piece of the mirror that hit her. I'm guessing she never even heard the vehicle as it came up behind her." She blew out a long breath. "One of those tragically unlucky things, you know? This is just about the only section of this road where it might have happened—where she had to run where she couldn't see the traffic coming up behind her."

"That mirror," I said. "On the accident report, I saw that you were able to identify the brand. Vizplus, was that it?"

"Yes, that's right," Rita said, sounding pleased that I had noticed. "It's one of those towing mirrors that extend almost two feet from the side of the vehicle. The bottom section of the mirror apparently popped out of the frame. That's the part we found. It had the Vizplus logo on it—an off-brand, as it turns out, no longer available. A few prints, but nothing clear enough to read. It's in the evidence bag, along with the earbuds."

"I checked the accident report for the skid mark measurement. It wasn't there." That was the missing information I had spotted and meant to ask her about.

She gave me a look. "No skid marks to measure."

119

I raised my eyebrows. "Does that suggest that there might be something to Zelda's theory?"

Rita shrugged. "Could be the driver didn't see her. Didn't have time to hit the brakes before he hit her."

I thought of what had happened that morning when I came over the crest of Crazy Joe Hill. I hadn't hit my brakes, either. So yes, that's how it could have happened—except that this was on the downhill side. Why didn't the driver see her?

"Anyway," she added, "we don't see skid marks all the time. Newer tires often don't leave skid marks. Antilock braking systems are designed to keep the wheels from locking up—so no skid marks, even during hard braking."

I nodded. No skid marks. I got that. But there was something else. "Cellphone?"

Rita shook her head. "We didn't find one. The sister asked me about that, too. The victim was wearing a pair of compression running shorts with zip pockets for a cellphone, plus a waistband pocket for a key. The shorts and her other clothes, along with her shoes and the Fitbit she was wearing, are in the evidence bag. But no cellphone, no house key." She eyed me. "I did think that was a little strange. I never run without both. Stan Drexell was partnered with me that morning. The two of us spent extra time searching. Came up empty."

No cellphone, no house key. Yes, more than a little strange. Like Rita, I don't go out the door to run without my cellphone. Twist an ankle or worse and you're on your own until somebody happens along to help. I walked toward the spot where it happened, imagining how Olivia had run along this shoulder, music loud in her ears, the cool morning air sharp with the scent of juniper, maybe a little ground fog ahead, along Possum Creek. Running easily, rhythmically, thinking of . . . of what?

Perhaps of her sister, away in London or wherever. Or the legal mess she was in with the Neely lawsuit, another one threatened. Or maybe the project she was working on—the man who had been convicted of murder twenty years before and was now living the good life in Pecan Springs. Or just thinking of nothing until it happened, and then a bone-shattering impact and after that, no more thought. No thought. No thought at all.

I shuddered and took a deep breath. "Olivia's Fitbit. Is that where you got the time of death?"

"Yes. At five-thirty a.m. it recorded a massive spike in the heart rate, then a sudden crash. Then nothing."

"So the evidence bag has only the popped-out mirror section, the earbuds, and the clothing and shoes, plus the Fitbit?" If that's all there was, I didn't need to have a look, at least, not right away.

"That's it. Stan contacted all the local windshield repair shops—asked for a follow-up, too. Nobody brought in a white or light-colored truck with a damaged windshield."

"What about replacing that mirror?"

"You can buy them at Home Depot. He could install it himself."

I nodded. "The report listed a witness—Gloria Tanner, a neighbor. Where does she live?"

"Up there." Rita pointed to a bluff on the other side of Possum Creek. "Tanner wasn't a witness, actually. That is, she didn't see the accident itself. She was standing at the end of her driveway, down by the highway, when the accident vehicle left the scene."

"Standing in her driveway? At five-thirty in the morning?"

"She was taking the trash to her can on the highway. She heard the vehicle coming down the hill and then a thump. A couple of minutes later, she saw a light-colored pickup with a long, horizontal scrape low

121

on the passenger door driving past her, fast. She didn't get a glimpse of the driver. No make or model year on the truck. The scrape on the door probably wasn't related to the accident. It was too low."

"A couple of minutes later?" I frowned. "You mean, *after* she heard the thump?" That detail hadn't been in the report.

Rita nodded. "She figured that somebody had hit a deer and stopped to drag it off the road. That happens around here, you know. Deer are bad to jump out in front of you. No time to brake. Anyway, she went back home and didn't think anything more about it until she heard the sirens and looked out her window to see the EMS ambulance and the squad cars parked along the road. She realized then what she'd heard and came down to tell us what she'd seen. Her report of the time was corroborated by the time on Andrews' Fitbit."

"There was somebody else, wasn't there? The guy who saw the body and called it in. What does he drive?"

"That would be Paul Duncan. He drives a red Ford Focus. He's a nighttime security guard on the CTSU campus. He was on his way home and happened to glance up toward that limestone outcropping and thought he saw somebody on the ground. He stopped to render aid, but she was dead. He called 9-1-1."

"You cleared him?"

"Yeah. We verified with his supervisor that he was at work until five-forty-five." She made a wry face. "God, I hate hit-and-runs. You know? It's always so random—wrong time, wrong place. The description of the vehicle is usually vague or there isn't one, especially at night on low-traffic roads. And even when you track a damaged vehicle to a repair shop, it can be hard to nail the driver. The vehicle could have been stolen. Or loaned, or borrowed without permission. It's frustrating. Somebody's dead and the killer is out there, living his life." She glanced at me. "Most of them turn out to be young guys with a history of DWI and license suspensions. Accidents waiting to happen. Which is what we've got here, in my opinion. A kid driving a pickup. Maybe even his dad's pickup."

There was something of defiance in the look she gave me, and I knew she was thinking of Zelda's story. I could see her point, too. The scene offered nothing to distinguish Olivia's death from any of the other vehicle-pedestrian incidents Rita had investigated in her time on the force, and she had been thorough. If this was something more ugly and deliberately evil than a careless hit-and-run, I wasn't likely to learn about it from this end.

But I wasn't quite ready to throw in the towel. I turned back to Rita. "Since we've come all this way, how about stopping at Tanner's house? It must be after five now. Maybe she's home from work."

"She works remotely—a web designer or something like that," Rita said. "She also takes care of her father. She's probably home."

Back in the squad car, we turned at the road on the other side of the creek and climbed uphill. The frame cottage, likely once a vacation home, was painted a rustic red with a sky-blue door, blue steps, and a blue porch railing. Tucked under a clump of large live oak trees, it was perched on the bluff over Possum Creek, with an enticing view of cedar-clad hills lying warm and still under the late afternoon sun. Several pots of bright red geraniums splashed color on the porch, and a marmalade cat darted inside the front door when Gloria Tanner opened it to our knock. She was in her forties, attractive, with dimples in a pleasantly round face framed by a tumble of dark curls. She was wearing white shorts and a loose white tank top over a blue sports bra.

"Oh, hi," she said, recognizing Rita. "You're the cop who was on the accident this spring, aren't you?"

"That's me." Rita reintroduced herself, explained that I was a friend of the woman who had been killed, and said that we would like to talk about the accident with her.

Gloria—we were all three on first names before we sat down with cups of peppermint-and-lemon tea—had been about to make an early supper for herself and her elderly father, who watched us without curiosity from a wheelchair parked by a wide window that looked out over the creek. Overhead, a ceiling fan stirred the warm air. There was an old-fashioned woodstove in one corner of the rustic room, a couple of colorful braided rugs on the floor, and a dozen pairs of deer antlers studding the walls, along with several stuffed deer heads. The orange cat, purring loudly, was now draped across the old man's knees.

"Dad has dementia," Gloria said matter-of-factly. The two of them traded affectionate smiles. "He never forgets my birthday. Mom's been dead for eleven years and he never forgets hers, either. But three minutes after you're out the door, he won't remember that you were here. Isn't that right, Dad?"

"That's right," her father agreed cheerfully. "'Getting' old ain't for sissies."

Gloria hadn't forgotten Olivia's death. "I think about it every time I go out on that road," she said with a shiver. "It was terrible, what happened. I still can't imagine somebody doing that and then just driving off, like it was just a roadkill." She shook her head. "That's why I put that cross there, and those blue flowers, and her name. So people who use this road will remember she died there."

"Oh, so that's *your* cross," Rita said. "That's very thoughtful of you."

"It was the least I could do," Gloria said firmly. "Somebody robbed that poor woman of the only life she had. That shouldn't be forgotten." She paused. "Olivia. An old-fashioned name, don't you think? Pretty."

"She liked to run along this road every morning, very early," I said. "Had you seen her before?"

Gloria shook her head. "No. But we're up here on this hill. Anyway, if she always ran while it was still dark, it was before I start my day."

"But you were up early that morning?" I asked.

"Yeah." She gestured toward a computer workstation under another window. "Like I told Officer Kidder, I was on deadline that week and I got up at five to work on the project. We're on the early end of the trash pickup and I'd forgotten it the week before. So the minute I remembered, I figured I'd better take it down. It was still black as midnight so I took a flashlight. When I got down there, I saw that dogs or coyotes had knocked the can over and there was trash scattered all around. I was picking it up when I heard a vehicle coming down the hill lickety-split. And then this loud thump, really solid, I mean. No scream or anything, just the thump, and I thought, 'Oh, shit, somebody's hit another deer.'"

"You'd heard that sound before?"

"Yeah. Happens a lot right along here, you know. Deer come down to the creek to drink and get out on the road and get hit. Sometimes they don't die right away. When Dad was younger and able, he used to take his gun down there and put the poor things out of their misery. Then he'd call Smoky Michelson—he's our game warden—and tell him what happened, so Smoky could come out and pick up the carcass." She glanced at Rita. "That's how Dad got some of those racks on the wall," she added in an explanatory tone. "Smoky let him take them."

"I was wondering," Rita said blandly. It's illegal to pick up roadkill, but people do it anyway. They take the antlers, too, especially if the animal is a buck with a big rack.

Gloria went back to her story. "Anyway, I heard the thump and then the truck stopped and—"

"Hang on," I said. "Before you heard the thump, did you hear anything else?"

She shook her head. "Just the truck. The engine, I mean."

"No brakes screeching? No tires skidding?"

"Nothing." She said it emphatically. "The driver probably didn't see a thing until he hit her. He stopped right after that, though."

"He stopped?"

"Yeah. My first thought was that he wanted to be sure the deer was dead and maybe drag it off on the shoulder. You can't just leave a big animal lying on the road. It'll cause a wreck, sure. Or I thought maybe he was taking the rack. This was before I knew he'd hit somebody. A *person*."

"He stopped. For how long?"

"Oh, gosh, I don't know. A few minutes. Long enough to . . ." She swallowed. "To drag her off the road, I guess."

But that wasn't what happened. There'd been no drag marks, Rita said. Olivia had been *flung* off the road, not dragged. Had the driver stopped to make sure she was dead? Or—

Rita's eyes were fixed on Gloria and I knew she was remembering the same thing I was. That missing cellphone. And if Zelda were here, she would insist that her sister's killer had stopped to steal her sister's house key and cellphone. Then he had driven to her house, let himself in, and taken her laptop. Because there were messages on it from him. And texts on her cell.

Gloria was going on with the rest of the story. "I was still picking up the garbage—there was a lot of it scattered around—when I heard the truck. I turned around real quick and saw it coming across the bridge, fast. It scared me and I jumped back. I thought he might hit *me*, like he'd hit the deer." She shook her head. "The woman, I mean. But I thought it was a deer, then."

"The vehicle's headlights were on?" I asked. "Did you notice anything about them?"

She squeezed her eyes shut, as if she were replaying the scene in her memory. After a moment, eyes still closed, she said, "Regular headlights. And there were these amber-colored lights across the roof of the cab. Five of them. No, only four. One in the middle wasn't working. Or it was gone, or something. I just saw four, with a gap." She opened her eyes. "And then I jumped back and it went roaring past me and I saw that it was a pickup. Pretty big, but not one of those where you can load the kids into the back seat."

"It was a two-door model?" I asked, making sure. "A regular cab?"

"Right. Two-door. Light-colored, white or maybe a real light gray, with a long scratch in the passenger door, a foot or so up from the bottom. The door had mud on it, so I don't think the scratch was fresh." She stopped, thought a moment, and frowned. "Wait a minute. You were asking about brakes and tire sounds and stopping. Are you saying this guy maybe intentionally—"

I held up my hand. "I'm not saying anything. Just asking." I didn't want to be accused of prompting a particular memory. "But take a minute to think back on what you might have heard that morning, out there in the dark. What sounds do you remember?"

Gloria stared at me. In the room, the silence deepened. The cat was still purring. Beside the window, the old man coughed. Her voice low and intense, she said, "What I remember is that the driver actually *gunned* it. He gunned it before he—"

She gulped, shaking her head. "Oh, sweet Jesus. All these weeks, and I totally forgot that sound until just now."

"That's okay," I said. "It was a stressful moment. It's easy to forget details."

"But that's *important,* isn't it?" She looked at Rita, pleading. "I remember now. There weren't any brake noises or tires screeching or anything like that. That driver wasn't trying to stop. Instead, he was actually *gunning* it before I heard the thump. The impact, I mean."

"Hey." Rita was taking out a notebook and pen. "This stuff—the acceleration, the cab roof lights—those things weren't in the report you gave us. Why didn't you mention it at the time?"

"I don't know." Gloria twisted her hands. "I definitely wasn't keeping any secrets. I guess I was pretty shook up when I found out that it was a woman who got killed, instead of a deer. I remember somebody—you, or maybe your partner—asking me what kind of truck it was, what color and what year, that kind of stuff. I think I must have been concentrating on what I saw while it was going past me." She shook her head, chagrined. "I am really sorry. I just didn't think about *before.* The way the engine revved up just before the impact, I mean. And those cab lights, if they mean anything." She swallowed. "Can I maybe change my statement?"

I understood. In my former life, I had questioned plenty of witnesses who later recalled things—even crucial things—that they had forgotten to mention the first time they were questioned. Or forgot a detail they had vividly remembered earlier. Or conflated two things or reversed their order. Memory is a tricky thing. That's why you question your witnesses more than once, on the record, even before depositions and again before they go into the courtroom. And why careful, detailed police reports are useful.

I gave Rita a quick glance, and she flipped her notebook open and began to write. I went back to Gloria. "We've been saying 'he,' but the report says you couldn't tell whether it was a man or a woman behind the wheel. Is that right?"

She shut her eyes for a moment, then opened them. "Yes, that's right. It was just too dark. The windows were maybe tinted. And the truck was going too fast."

"How about physical damage, maybe to the windshield or the right front fender?" She hadn't been in a position to see the glass in the towing mirror, which had been broken in the impact.

"I was asked about that." She shook her head regretfully. "If there was any other damage, I didn't see it."

"A moment ago, you said you jumped back to avoid getting hit. At that point, were you still pretty close to the edge of the road?"

"Well, yes. I guess I was."

"How close, would you say?"

She wrinkled her nose, estimating. "Oh, about as far as from me to you, maybe."

I was on the sofa. Her chair was about a yard away. "Three feet?"

"Yeah. Three feet. The garbage guys like it when the can is where they don't have to take extra steps." She looked puzzled. "What are you getting at?"

I held her gaze. "If you were that close to the road, you were likely standing in the range of the driver's headlights. Do you think he saw you?"

"Uh-oh." Her eyes grew round. "Oh, lordy sakes. I didn't think of *that.*" Her hand went to her mouth. "Well, yes, now that you mention it, yes, he must have seen me. I mean, I was wearing gray sweatpants and a sweatshirt and his headlights shone right on me. So . . ." She swallowed. "So he knows I live here. He might—"

"I don't think so, Gloria," I said, wanting to reassure her. "It's been a couple of months. If that driver was going to come looking for you, he would've come by now."

She sat back in her chair. "I suppose you're right." She gave me an uncertain look. "But maybe I ought to . . ." Her voice trailed off.

Rita looked up from her notetaking. "Have you seen that truck on this road? Since that morning, I mean."

Gloria was emphatic. "No, I haven't. And it's not for want of looking. I actually think about it whenever I see a white truck anywhere. I ask myself, 'Is that the one I saw? The one that killed that poor woman?' Once, I saw one parked in front of the bookstore on the square. I drove around the block and parked and got out so I could look for that long scrape on the door." She sighed. "I didn't see it. So it wasn't the right one."

There wasn't any point in telling her that a scrape can be fixed. A truck can be repainted. And a driver who saw a witness who might identify his truck would do just that. Repair the scrape and repaint the truck.

Rita closed her notebook and stuck it in her breast pocket. She gave me an inquiring look and I nodded briefly. We'd gotten all we were going to get, at least for now. The information about the sound of acceleration just before impact certainly suggested intent. And those cab lights might help to identify the truck, if we could find it. But even then, it would be impossible to tie it to the scene without some sort of significant physical evidence of some kind.

We thanked Gloria for her help—genuine thanks from me,

because she had told me several things I hadn't known. Outside, in the car, Rita gave me a long look.

"You went at that like you had her on the stand, Counselor." It was an observation, not an accusation.

I gave her a rueful smile. "Old habits die hard. Anyway, she didn't change her testimony. She just added to it."

Testimony. Gloria Tanner hadn't been on the stand, and never would be—unless we could find that truck and the physical evidence necessary to link it to the crime. And the driver. Which was a very long shot.

"You'll amend your police report to include what she heard?" I asked. "And make a note of those roof lights?"

"Yeah." Rita turned the key in the ignition. "You know, based on what I just heard, I'm beginning to think there might be something to Zelda's idea."

"Yes," I agreed thoughtfully. "Might be."

We pulled onto Purgatory Bend and headed back toward town. After a moment, Rita spoke again. "I'm taking the car back to the cop lot and then I have to pick up my kid at my mom's. Is your car at your shop or do you want me to drop you somewhere else?"

"The shop, please. I'm looking forward to getting home, taking off my shoes, and sitting down with a Chardonnay."

But given what I had learned in the last hour or two, there was something I ought to do first. And I didn't want to share it with anyone else, including the police.

Not just yet, anyway.

Chapter Eight

Eastern medicine has long relied on herbs to promote mental health and balance and to improve memory. Ashwagandha (*Withania somnifera*, also known as Indian ginseng and winter cherry) is an evergreen shrub in the nightshade family. A powerful antioxidant that also helps the body fight inflammation and resist stress, it has been used to treat a range of conditions, such as rheumatism and insomnia (hence the species name *somnifera*).

A recent study found that ashwagandha significantly improved participants' reaction times and attention spans across a variety of tests, as well as their immediate and general memory. This outcome may be the product of the herb's anti-inflammatory properties: it can reduce the brain inflammation that inhibits the growth and functioning of neurons, especially in the area of the brain (the hippocampus) where learning and memory occur.

China Bayles
"What Am I Forgetting? Herbs to Improve Your Memory"
Pecan Springs Enterprise

Most afternoons after work, I head straight home to make supper for the family. But Caitie was at the ranch with her new horse and McQuaid was on his way to West Texas. I had the rest of the day to myself, which was a good thing. I had something else to do.

It was after six by the time I pulled my Toyota out of the parking area behind the shops, and the afternoon traffic—always heavy with homebound university faculty and staff—had mostly cleared. My route tonight took me east instead of the usual west, across I-35 on King Road, past the Sonora Garden Center.

When I first moved to Pecan Springs, King Road was a narrow two-lane asphalt and Sonora was called Wanda's Wonderful Acres, a sprawling plant paradise hedged in by truck farms and wide green pastures dotted with dairy cows. The cows and the truck farms are a thing of the past. Sonora (now owned by my friend Maggie Walker) is the largest and busiest garden center between Austin and San Antonio. And King Road is a six-lane east–west highway slicing through a busy shopping and office district, with vast vistas of condos and tract homes sprawling north and south on either side. The chamber of commerce views this as progress. I miss the cows.

But it is what it is and I was on a mission. I was looking for Store-It-Rite—the storage place where Zelda had stashed the boxes of her sister's files—a couple of miles past Sonora, on the right. Store-It-Rite proved to be three rows of adjoining metal units with bright blue doors, surrounded by a head-high chain-link fence with a prominent sign: GATE MUST BE CLOSED AND LOCKED AT ALL TIMES. In case you didn't read English, this was repeated in Spanish: PUERTA DEBE PERMANECER CERRADA EN TODO MOMENTO. Zelda had given me the seven-digit secret code, so I punched it into the keypad and when the heavy gate obediently swung open, I drove through, made a left, navigated almost all the way to the end of a gravel aisle about fifty yards long, and parked in front of unit 126.

The Texas sun had been shining on that metal roof all day, and the searing heat slapped me in the face as I lifted the blue roll-up door. The unit was dark, musty-smelling, and crowded with stuff both Olivia and Zelda had stashed there. As the pale overhead fluorescents flickered on, I saw that the contents had been organized on either side of a narrow center aisle. There were moving boxes marked BOOKS and LINENS and several large pieces of what looked like antique furniture: a mahogany gate-leg table and a tall china cabinet with arched glass doors; a handsome vintage walnut rolltop desk, a couple of side tables, a brown velvet loveseat, and an ornately framed round mirror. And of course more boxes, plus a couple of plastic laundry baskets full of bedding and a jumble of household goods that Zelda hadn't had time to take to the thrift shop.

The boxes she had told me about, though, were stacked just inside the door on the right, as she'd said. I counted five of them, all taped shut and marked OFFICE with a black Sharpie.

What I really wanted, of course, was Olivia's laptop, where she did most of her work and undoubtedly kept her records. But that, like her cellphone, had yet to be found. There might be something important in one of the boxes, but it was a needle-in-a-haystack search (especially tough since I didn't know what the needle looked like) and I wasn't going to hang around in this heat. It took less than ten minutes to load the boxes into my car, but by the time I was finished, my T-shirt was soaked with sweat. I was definitely ready for that glass of Chardonnay.

But lunch was a distant memory and I was hungry. With nobody to cook for at home, I could treat myself to barbequed brisket and a side of German potato salad at Bean's Bar and Grill or a bowl of split pea soup and a grilled chicken wrap at Lila's Diner. But the shop was on my way home and I was remembering what had been on the Thyme for Tea menu that day. I parked in the alley, let myself into the tearoom through the French doors, and raided the refrigerator. I found a container of leftover cold cucumber soup with sour cream, yogurt, and dill; a large cup of chicken salad with basil and mint; and some strawberries and watermelon cubes with lavender flowers and mint.

McQuaid is a meat-and-potatoes guy so we usually have a hearty supper, but this deliciously light meal was perfect for me. I packed my lucky finds into a takeout box along with a couple of croissants and several nice bunches of green and purple grapes, and carried it out to the car. Next stop: Sheila's house, to drop off that basket of herbal items I'd put together for her.

And to update her on what had transpired that afternoon on Purgatory Bend Road. This was tricky. I know Rita Kidder to be a conscientious, competent police officer, but she might have her own agenda on this case. It probably wasn't smart to count on her to keep the chief clued in to all developments. But the PSPD is Sheila's responsibility and I was involving myself—meddling, some might say—in her law enforcement business. This had the potential to turn into one of those high-visibility cases that could rise up and bite us—one or two or all three of us—in the butt when we weren't expecting it.

I didn't want to take that risk without keeping Sheila fully in the loop.

SHEILA AND BLACKIE HAVE REMODELED an older home on Hickory Street, in a neighborhood of well-kept Victorians with spacious backyards, not far from Ruby's house. Parked in their driveway: the chief's black Impala and Blackie's big red F-150, which had a couple of square bales of hay and a bag of alfalfa cubes in the back. Blackie owns a house with a barn, a trio of horses, and thirty-five Hill Country acres west of town, and both he and Sheila would prefer to live out there. But it's a forty-minute drive and Sheila's job means that she's on call twenty-four-seven, so Blackie rents the house to a CTSU faculty member and keeps the barn and pastures for his horses. He and Sheila get out there whenever they can, although that probably doesn't happen as often as it used to now that they have Noah.

Sheila's little sleep-basket over my arm, I was greeted at the backyard gate by a fearsome-looking Rottweiler, who dashed up to welcome me with an enthusiastic volley of woofs. Rambo is a dual-purpose police dog, a valuable member of the force who is trained both in narcotics sniffing and suspect apprehension. He works the day shift in the PSPD's K-9 unit (nights, too, when there's an emergency). With bad guys, Rambo can be a junkyard dog, all snapping teeth and vicious snarls, but with friends, he's a sweetie with exquisite manners. We're pals, so he escorted me courteously up the steps to the back door. While he has many impressive physical skills—he's been clocked at twenty-five miles an hour and I've seen him clamber up and over a six-foot chain-link fence—he can't manage a latched door. So I rang the bell for both of us and we waited until Blackie opened it.

"Hey, China. Good to see you," he said heartily. "Come in, come in." He pushed the screen door open. "You too, Rambo. Sorry, fella," he added apologetically, as the Rottie gave him a reproachful look. "I guess we got busy and left you outside."

Blackie Blackwell may no longer be a county sheriff, but he'll always wear that quintessential cop-look: square jaw, square chin, square shoulders, military posture, sandy hair cut in regulation style. He comes from a long line of cops: his grandfather Digger Blackwell was a Texas Ranger in the early days of the force, his father Corky was reelected to multiple terms as an Adams County sheriff, and his mother Reba ran the county jail. Blackie himself did a great job as sheriff, enjoyed what he did, and was well liked by the people he served. Even those who aren't terribly crazy about cops (and there are plenty of them in the distant reaches of the Hill Country) have to admit that he's one of the good guys.

But when he and Sheila got serious about marriage and kids, they decided that two law enforcement officers in one family might be pushing their luck. The trouble was that they couldn't decide which of them should bow out: Blackie the sheriff or Sheila the chief of police. After months of discussion of this unsettling but crucial question, they did what any normal people would do. They tossed a coin.

Blackie takes it philosophically. "Lost a job, gained a wife," he says with a grin. "Fair trade." And to all appearances, he means it.

Today, the former sheriff was wearing a faded orange T-shirt and ragged cutoffs—not exactly regulation garb—and held a large spoon in one hand. A lot of his investigative work is done from home these days, so Blackie usually manages the weekday evening meals as well as the baby's daytime care. When he has to be on the road, Noah goes to daycare.

Blackie brandished his spoon. "McQuaid's on his way to Midland so you don't have to feed him. We're having ham and beans with corn-bread for supper. Join us, why don't you?"

"Is that China?" Sheila called from the kitchen, then came padding into the hall, barefoot and in shorts. Her blouse was open and she was holding Noah, nursing, at her bare breast. "We're just about to start dinner," she said. "Come and eat with us." She wrinkled her nose. "Blackie's pot of beans will feed the entire force."

"My mother taught me how to make ham and beans," Blackie retorted. "And she always cooked enough to feed everybody in the jail."

I chuckled, nodding at the baby. "Looks like Noah is already tanking up."

Sheila smiled down at her son. "He's always hungry." She smoothed his cheek with her finger. "I get no peace."

"A growing kid," Blackie said proudly. "Got an arm on him, too. He'll be playing quarterback for the Cowboys before we know it." To me, he added, "Apple pie for dessert." At Sheila's quizzical glance, he shrugged. "Sarah Lee. I was pushed for time."

"Thanks for the invitation," I said. "Nothing against ham and beans or Sarah Lee, but I'd better get home and feed the animals." I held out the basket. "I just stopped by to bring a few things that might help Sheila and Noah sleep a little better." To Sheila, I said, "I tucked in a few how-to notes."

"Oh, wonderful," Sheila said, as Blackie took the basket. "I'll let you know how it turns out." She paused. "Rita said you two were driving out to Purgatory Bend this afternoon. Did you make it?"

"We did," I said. "We also had a conversation with the witness, Gloria Tanner. Some new information emerged. Based on that, Rita says she intends to amend her report."

"Really?" Sheila studied me, pursing her lips. "So you're thinking it *wasn't* an accident?"

There was a sharp *ding* from the kitchen. "Cornbread wants to come out of the oven," Blackie said. He turned and went down the hall, Rambo at his heels.

"I have my suspicions," I said, and gave her a quick sketch of what we'd seen and what Tanner had told us. "Based on what I saw and heard, I'm guessing that the driver of the truck hit Olivia intentionally, then took her cellphone off the body because it could provide incriminating evidence—and maybe let himself into her house and took her laptop. But it's Rita's scene and I don't want to get too far ahead of her, so let's wait and see how she amends her accident report. I think she's planning to do that tomorrow."

"And in the meantime?" Noah pulled away from his mother's breast and hiccupped. Still holding him, she fastened her bra and fumbled with the buttons on her blouse. "What are you planning?"

Sheila knows me too well, I thought ruefully. "In the meantime, I'm going to look through Olivia's papers. That's what her sister asked me to do." I tilted my head. "Do you see any problems with that?" I wasn't challenging her, exactly. But since she'd asked, it would be nice if she'd go on the record.

She was still fumbling. "I don't see any problems. What are you looking for?"

If we couldn't get at Olivia's killer from this end—that is, from the crime scene itself or from Gloria Tanner's testimony—maybe we could get at him from the other. Assuming, that is, that Zelda's theory holds water.

"Well, first off, I'd like to find information that could identify the latest incarnation of James Kelly. Something that might show us who Olivia was targeting for this project of hers and how she got that lead." I held out my arms. "Here, give me that baby. You need both hands."

"Thank you." She began buttoning. "Okay with me."

Noah smelled of baby oil with rich overtones of yucky diaper. He turned his face to my breast and nuzzled me hopefully.

"Okay what? Do you mean, it's okay with you if I go ahead and dig into this?"

"I'm not stopping you," she said—a non-answer answer, but probably the best I was going to get. Gripping my finger surprisingly hard with his plump little hand, Noah began to nip at my T-shirt.

"I think he's still hungry," I said. When I hold a baby, there's always a part of me that turns all soft and squishy and wishes I hadn't chosen to ignore my maternal instincts. I could feel that impulse again, but I have learned to be stoic about it. My biological clock says that babies are out for me. Anyway, for all I know, this time next year I might be a *grandmother.* I bent over Noah and whispered, "Sorry to disappoint you, kid, but you're not going to get any supper from me. I don't have what you want, but your mama is right here and she's got plenty."

Sheila laughed and reached for him. "We started him on strained peas and carrots last week, and he's scarfing it up. Tonight he gets sweet potatoes. On his very own plate. With his name on it."

"Oh, boy," I said, handing him over. "First adventures in a lifelong career as a gourmet."

Sheila put Noah over her shoulder and began patting his back. "You're sure you won't stay? If you don't want to try Blackie's ham and beans, we can open a jar of peas and carrots."

I was still smiling as I got into my car and headed home, where a certain mournful basset, scruffy tomcat, and impudent parrot were waiting for their suppers, too.

Which of course was the first order of business after I carried Olivia's boxes from the car into the living room. Winchester gave me one of his doleful "I-expected-more-from-life-than-this" looks when I dished out his usual dry kibble, but I hardened my heart.

"That's it, Winnie my friend," I said firmly. "You heard the vet. You need to keep the weight off." Howard Cosell showed us that bassets are prone to obesity, so we keep a close watch on Winchester's calories.

Mr. P, on the other hand, is a scrawny old tomcat with no weight worries. With an anticipatory flick of his tail, he settled down to his favorite chopped liver mixed with dry kitty food topped with a generous spoonful of leftover chicken gravy.

And Spock thanked me with a gleeful "Bacon. Oh, boy!" when I offered him an appetizing helping of seeds, nuts, Cheerios, and a few of the seedless green grapes I'd brought from the shop. He ate to the accompaniment of loud kissing noises, punctuated by whistles and coos.

While the animals were busying themselves with their suppers, I went upstairs, stripped off my sweaty clothes, and took a shower. Back downstairs in clean shorts, tank top, and sandals, I set the kitchen table for one and poured myself a cold Chardonnay. My own tasty supper—cold cucumber soup, chicken salad on croissant, and strawberry-and-watermelon topped with yogurt—was made even more delicious by the fact that somebody else had prepared the whole darned thing. And that when I was finished, all I had to do was rinse my plate, fork, and glass, and my kitchen chores were done.

Then, while my after-dinner espresso was brewing, I went out to check on Caitie's chickens, who have names like Alberta Eggstein, Egg Nog, Dixie Chick, and Extra Crispy, and are collectively known as the Brood. They live in a coop with a thirty-foot fenced run beside the garden and daily produce more eggs than we can use. Caitie sells them to the Banners, our neighbors, earning enough to pay for the Brood's chicken feed and add a little to her college savings account. Today, they had left me a half-dozen large brown eggs—enough for a quiche, when McQuaid came home from Midland.

Back in the living room with my coffee, it was time to get to work. I sat down on the sofa with my laptop and opened a new folder. I was ready to start going through those boxes, but I needed to make some notes on what I had seen on Purgatory Bend Road that afternoon and what Rita Kidder and Gloria Tanner had told me. I opened a Word document and began making entries based on the current police report as well as what I had seen and heard that afternoon, starting with details of the scene and adding the Tanner interview. It didn't take long. When it was finished, I was satisfied that I had a complete record of everything that was currently known about Olivia's death.

That done, I sketched out the twenty-year-old story of Eleanor Kelly's death, based on Olivia's notes in the folder Zelda had given me and on my later forays into the newspaper and FindLaw accounts of James Kelly's trial and appeal. For good measure, I added notes from my conversation with Charlie Lipman—only a few, because he hadn't told me much of anything. Which could mean that he didn't know anything or that he knew plenty but didn't intend to tell me what it was. That was Charlie for you. The master of duplicity, as always.

Then, for the sake of completeness, I added what I knew about Darwin Neely, who had been suing Olivia, and Jeremy Kellogg, who had threatened to sue. Both had reasonable chances of winning their lawsuit against Olivia, Charlie had said, so given their druthers, both would prefer her alive. Neely was not a candidate for the current identity of James Kelly, though, according to Sheila. Which left Kellogg.

Then, out of curiosity, I went online and googled Jeremy Kellogg. I turned up LinkedIn and Facebook profiles, plus the usual contact information lists as well as Olivia's offending blog post, the one that apparently upset Kellogg and resulted in his threat to sue. Her post outlined Kellogg's alleged sins at a Dallas megachurch, the crimes for which he'd gotten his walking papers: inappropriate sexual relations with at least one parishioner (charges filed, later dropped) and a substantial amount of money said to be missing from the church's fundraising program (investigation closed). No mention of missionary service. There was, however, a mention of his new church, Truth Seekers, right here in Pecan Springs.

I was about to click away from Olivia's post when I noticed something interesting. In her lead sentence, Olivia mentioned the name and address of the Truth Seekers church and Kellogg's name: Jeremy Q. Kellogg. I was reminded that Charlie had mentioned it also, and somebody else—Sheila, maybe, or Jessica? The Reverend Jeremy Q. Kellogg.

And there it was, right in front of me.

James Q-for-Quincy Kelly. Jeremy Q. Kellogg.

JQK and JQK.

Some math geek could probably tell me the improbability of those three initials occurring together. I didn't have any idea what Kellogg's Q-name might be, and it didn't matter, really. But it was intriguing, wasn't it? An odd little bit of randomness calling attention to itself. Or as Ruby might say, the Universe pointing a finger at something. Or someone. And wanting somebody—me?—to notice.

That just about wrapped it up. I had put down as much as I knew about this complicated situation. I saved the file to my cloud, where I could access it from my cellphone or the computer at the shop. Then I tackled Olivia's boxes, opening all five of them and peeking inside each. To start with, I chose the one that contained a dozen or so green hanging folders that looked like Zelda had lifted them right out of her sister's filing cabinet. But while they were full of interesting stuff—background materials for Olivia's two previous books, meticulously compiled and ordered—none of it was relevant to the James Kelly story, at least as far as I could see. And it was the Kelly story I was focused on.

That first box was as far as I got, though. I was about to open the second when Caitie called from the ranch to tell me all about the new horse, who came with the name Comanche and was *totally awesome*. She missed Mr. P and Winnie and Spock and of course the Brood most of all. I was taking good care of the chickens for her, wasn't I? How many eggs had they laid that day? Did Extra Crispy miss her? (He is a handsome black Cubalaya rooster with a splendid orange-red feather shawl and an elegant black plume of a tail.) Had Alberta Eggstein started to molt? Was Egg Nog's foot better? (She had been treating her for bumblefoot.)

To which I answered truthfully, *yes*, *six*, and *of course*, *no*, and *yes*, happy that my teenage girl cared more about horses, chickens, a cat, a dog, and a parrot than about boys. The parrot, perched companionably on my shoulder while we were talking, sent kisses, which made Caitie giggle.

Then Leatha came on the phone and updated me on her husband's health, which has steadily improved since his heart attack some months ago. Sam is a sweet guy who has been very good for my mother—and for me and Brian and Caitie. I love him dearly, so I was glad to hear that he'd been out riding with Caitie and Comanche and was able to do some work in the stable. Leatha and Sam had to shelve their plan to open their ranch as a birdwatcher's B&B when he was stricken last fall, but it was beginning to look like they might be able to move forward on that scheme later this summer.*

I had just said goodbye to Caitie and Leatha when the phone dinged again. It was McQuaid, I thought as I reached for it, calling to let me know he'd arrived safely and gotten checked into his motel. But it wasn't.

"Hey, China," Jessica said. "Am I calling too late?"

I glanced at the clock and was surprised to see that it was almost ten. "Not at all," I said. "What's going on?"

---

* There's more about Leatha and Sam and their Uvalde County ranch in *Bittersweet* (China Bayles #23).

"I was going to ask you the same thing," she replied. "Sorry I couldn't make it this afternoon. Something came up on another story." I heard what sounded like a shoe hitting the bare floor. "Just got home. My feet hurt." A second shoe dropped. Those red heels? Gorgeous, but I'd never be able to wear them all day. She let out her breath in a long whoosh. "You went to the site, right? Did you get anything new out of Rita?"

I hesitated. I like Jessica. We've been friends for several years and I admire her investigative work at the newspaper, and her writing. She broke a serial killer story last year that had baffled all the pros. But how much should I tell her? What would she do with the information? Would she keep it to herself or be tempted to turn it into a newspaper story?*

On the other hand, she had already agreed to look into the background of the Kelly story, and I had asked her to go with Rita and me that afternoon. If another assignment hadn't gotten in the way, she would have heard everything I heard, would have seen everything I saw. So why was I hesitating?

Jessica picked up on my reluctance and her voice became edged. "Hey. I don't want to butt in on whatever you and Rita have going with this thing. I'm not a pushy broad, you know. I don't—"

That made me laugh. "But you *are*," I said. "And pushy broads are fine by me. You can have what I have so far. But please keep it out of print until I tell you."

"Scout's honor," she said without hesitation. "Give me a minute to boot up my computer. If you don't mind, I want to take notes."

It took a while, and when I was done with my report, Jessica was

---

* Jessica's serial killer story is reported in *Out of Body*, book 3 in the Crystal Cave trilogy.

silent for a moment. "I interviewed Gloria Tanner," she said finally. "She didn't say a thing to me about that vehicle stopping long enough for the driver to get out and maybe search his victim for her cellphone. I wonder why."

"Memory is tricky," I said. "And in this case, the emphasis is on '*maybe* search.' It's possible that the driver stopped to see if there was anything he could do to help the woman he struck. When he saw she was dead, he panicked and drove off. Classic hit-and-run."

"Yeah, sure." Her voice was impatient. "But if you go that route, we still have to ask, where is the cellphone? And what happened to the laptop? One of these going missing is weird. Both going missing is *beyond* weird. Who runs without her cell? Every writer has to have a computer. So where are they?"

"Good questions. I wish we had answers." I paused. "When we talked last night, you were going to do some background work on the Kelly case. Did you find anything interesting?"

"Didn't have time," she said apologetically. "I was just settling down to work when Mark called. He was in town and . . ."

She didn't have to finish her sentence. I could fill in the blanks. Mark Hemming is a professor at A&M, where the Texas A&M Forest Service is located. He does research and teaches courses in forest management and fire science, as well as helping coordinate the Forest Service wildfire fighting program. Jessica met him when she covered several Bastrop County wildfires that Mark was managing. Their relationship flamed into one of those full-blown, heated things not long after, and they're still seeing one another—an affair that is understandably hard to manage, since College Station is about 120 miles from

Pecan Springs and both Jessica and Mark are fully invested in careers they love.*

"I was planning to work on the Kelly research this morning," she added, "but something came up at the newspaper and I had to tend to that. And then there was that wreck on the interstate, and—"

"It's okay," I said. "Really, Jessica, not a problem." I was about to add that I fully understood why she would drop everything for a chance to spend the evening with Mark. But I was looking at my laptop, open on the sofa beside me.

On the screen were the notes I'd been making.

And in the notes were those oddly matching initials.

James Quincy Kelly and Jeremy Q-something Kellogg. JQK and JQK.

I frowned. And if that wasn't enough, there was that other bit of information I had picked up from Sheila, which all of a sudden bumped into my mind.

"I wonder," I said. "Have you heard that Jeremy Kellogg was a missionary before he came to Pecan Springs?"

"Kellogg?" Jessica sounded puzzled. "No. I saw in Olivia's blog that he came here from Dallas, where he got into trouble with a church. What's this about his being a missionary?"

"Sheila mentioned it. Somewhere in Mexico or South America." I was also remembering something that Zelda had told me: that after Kelly's conviction was vacated, he was rumored to have disappeared— to have gone to Latin America, she'd said. And that McQuaid had once had a case where someone committed pseudocide in Costa Rica.

---

* The relationship begins in *Fire Lines*, the third novella in the *Enterprise* trilogy: *Deadlines*, *Fault Lines*, *Fire Lines*.

Had Kelly gone south of the border, changed his name and resurrected himself as a missionary? It was possible. Was it probable? Likely?

There was a silence on Jessica's end. "Okay," she said. "So what's your interest in Kellogg—other than his being an avocado snatcher?"

That made me laugh. "It may be a silly reason, actually," I confessed. "I'm looking at my notes and I just noticed that Kellogg's initials are the same as James Q. Kelly's initials. JQK, both of them. And that the names Kelly and Kellogg have a certain similarity."

"Kellogg," she said slowly. And then, "Kelly. Yes, similar." She hesitated, sounding dubious. "I remember that Kellogg has Q for a middle initial. You're telling me that Kelly did, too?"

"Right. James Quincy Kelly. I have no idea what Jeremy's middle name is."

"JQK," Jessica said. There was a silence. "A weird coincidence, if you ask me."

Yes, weird. But there are certainly stranger coincidences involving names. Like the ten-year-old British girl named Laura Buxton who released a red balloon on which she had written her address and the request, "Please return to Laura Buxton." It was found 140 miles to the south and returned by another ten-year-old girl named . . . wait for it . . . Laura Buxton. And the remarkable "Jim Twins," who were said to have been separated at birth and raised by different families. When they finally met, thirty-nine years later, they discovered that they had both been named James, that both had married twice (first to a pair of Lindas, second to two Bettys), and both had just one child each, sons they had named James Allen. If I asked Ruby for her explanation of these bizarre happenstances, she'd probably tell me that the Universe had created a secret code to the Meaning of Everything and was challenging us to decrypt it.

But maybe this weird business of the three initials and the similar-sounding last names was neither a weird coincidence nor the Universe having a last laugh. Maybe the explanation was much simpler. If I were going to change my name, I might want to preserve some remnant of my previous identity, mightn't I? Especially if I believed that I was the only person who would ever connect my previous identity to my current self.

"JQK," Jessica repeated thoughtfully. "Imagine that." A pause. "How about if I see what I can dig up about our Reverend Kellogg? If that guy really was a missionary—which I doubt—there's bound to be some kind of record of his service."

"Good idea," I said. "Where, when, what, how long—whatever you can find. Not that I believe there's a definite connection between him and Kelly. More a matter of curiosity, really."

"Well, maybe. He's a bad actor, though. Have you read Olivia's blog posts about him?"

"One, I think. Are there more?"

"A couple. They're tagged. You know he was charged with sexual assault, don't you? The charge was dropped, but . . ." She paused for a moment. "Just letting you know that Hark has warned me to stay away from stories about that man unless there's indisputable evidence. Preferably an indictment. Even better, a conviction."

"Hark respects the *Enterprise*'s duty to the facts," I replied. He also keeps a tight rein on all his reporters but especially on Jessica, who has a history of getting deeply involved with her stories. Personally involved—sometimes when it isn't smart.

"Well, where Kellogg is concerned, Hark has the right idea," Jessica said. "As an owner of a newspaper, he doesn't want a lawsuit. But I want Kellogg's backstory. I'll get to work on this."

"Do that," I said. "But be careful. And don't do anything more tonight. You've had a long day already."

She chuckled. "No doubt about that. So where are you going from here?"

I glanced at the stack of boxes and then at the clock. After ten. "Bed. I've had a long day, too."

But she wasn't ready to quit. "What about tomorrow? This Olivia thing. You *are* pursuing it, aren't you?"

"Yes, I'm pursuing it," I replied, thinking. Let's see—tomorrow was Thursday. And Friday—"I have to spend tomorrow at the shop. I'm driving down to Fredericksburg on Friday."

"What's happening in Fredericksburg?"

"I'm giving a talk on herbs at the Native Plant Society." And maybe—" I hesitated. "Olivia left a note that Eleanor Kelly's cousin Margaret Greer lives in Fredericksburg. If I can locate her and she's available, I'll try to see her. If that works out, would you like to go? It would mean staying over until I've given my talk. We'd probably be back here by dinner time."

I was a bit hesitant, not sure it was a good idea for two of us to gang up on the cousin. But Jessica is a reporter with a good nose for a story. She's never intimidating. And she's smart. She might pick up something I miss.

"Love to go," she said promptly. "I'll have to clear it with Hark, but count me in. What time will we leave?"

"Let me see what I can set up with Margaret Greer. I'll check back with you to confirm."

"Works for me," Jessica said. "Talk to you later."

Chapter Nine

Sometimes, the traditional reputation of an herb just doesn't hold up to modern scrutiny. In China, *Ginkgo biloba* is called the "fountain of youth" and is believed to have powerful anti-aging properties. It's likely that people formed that idea by association, knowing that ginkgo trees live, literally, for thousands of years. The reasoning goes something like, If the tree can live that long, just think what it will do for us!

But the longevity of the trees doesn't appear to translate to humans. Scientists have learned that ginkgo trees live as long as they do because they produce protective chemicals that fend off disease and because they lack the genetic programming that determines short-span lives for plants and mammals. But multiple studies have failed to find any conclusive evidence that consuming parts of the tree will increase the lives of humans and keep us functioning, mentally, longer.

China Bayles
"What Am I Forgetting? Herbs to Improve Your Memory"
Pecan Springs Enterprise

Hark Hibler wanted more than a few details. He wanted the whole backstory. And he came to the shop on a drizzly Thursday morning to get it.

"Actually, I'm here on a couple of errands," he said, standing in front of the counter. His shoulders were wet and there were raindrops in his dark, tousled hair. "I want to ask you about—"

"But it *wasn't* late," I protested. "I didn't forget! I sent it yesterday."

It is an unfortunate fact that I often miss the deadline for my garden column. This time, though, I was early. So what was he—

"Don't get your knickers in a twist." He held up a hand "I got your column. 'What Am I Forgetting?' or something like that. I read it. Clever piece, maybe a little long." He made a rueful face. "Listen, China, if you've got some magic pills that will improve memory, I'll be glad to buy a bottle. Or two or three, if that's what it takes. Things are getting out of hand at the *Enterprise* these days. Since Jeff Dixon came on board it's hard to keep up with all the new stuff. I'll be the first to admit that I'm running on overload."

I'll bet. Not long ago, the *Enterprise* suffered yet another financial crisis. These are tough times for local newspapers and Hark Hibler, the editor, publisher, and owner, had to go looking for help. He found it in Jeff Dixon, scion of the Dixon political family and heir to the multinational Dixon beer and wine distributorship. Dixon not only has the money to keep the newspaper going and the willingness to part with some of it, but also a longtime interest in newspaper production and management. In return for backing the paper, he asked for a hefty share of it, plus the title of copublisher and a slot beside Hark at the top of the editorial staff.*

I've known Hark since I came to Pecan Springs. I know that he has put his heart and soul into the *Enterprise* and that parting with even a splinter of it must have been like pulling out his fingernails one at a time. But Pecan Springs is growing at warp speed and the newspaper is either going to grow or be gobbled up by the larger, better-financed Austin or San Antonio newspapers. So, with as much grace as he could muster, Hark did what had to be done: he met Jeff Dixon's demands.

---

* The changes at the newspaper are reported in the *Enterprise* trilogy: *Deadlines, Fault Lines, Fire Lines.*

For the most part, it has worked out. The two share the belief that a strong community needs a strong newspaper and they seem to agree on the basic principles of how to make that happen.

But Jeff is a dynamo charged with energy and visionary ideas, while Hark is . . . well, not so much. He is slower and shaggier, with sloping shoulders, soft speech, a shambling gait. For a while, he and Ruby had a thing. They saw one another pretty steadily, but that's tapered off. I'm afraid he's had to resign himself to Ruby's inconstant heart. For better or worse, she prefers come-and-go cowboys and men who never stay around more than a few months. She and Hark are still friends, but I think his torch has finally flamed out.

I cocked my head. "Well, if you're not here to nag me about my column, what brings you to my door?"

He hefted his camera. "I want to take a couple of photos of your guerrilla library. I'm writing an editorial about this fanatical book banning frenzy that's sweeping Texas. I've already got photos of a couple of curbside libraries that offer banned books. Yours is a variation."

"So glad you're interested," I said, and pointed over his shoulder. "Against that wall. The banned book nook. If you see something you haven't read, take it with you. You don't have to return it here—you can drop it off at the diner. Lila put up her banned book shelf yesterday." Lila's Diner is next door to the Enterprise building, so it would be convenient for him. "We'd like to see these books traveling all over town," I added. "So people will know there's nothing to be afraid of—and maybe even something to learn."

"I'll do that." Hark gave me one of his lopsided grins. "You're living dangerously, you know. What's after banned books? You and Ruby planning a drag show?"

"If we are, she hasn't mentioned it yet," I said. "But we've got a psychic fair coming up at the end of the month. Tarot, rune stones, astrological readings, pendulum alignment, astral music."

"I saw your ad in the paper." He sounded vaguely wistful. "I figured Ruby was behind it."

"Make that Ramona," I muttered. "It's her baby."

"Uh-oh." He rolled his eyes. "You really *are* living dangerously." He hesitated, then got to the real reason for his visit. "Listen, China. Jessica Nelson emailed me late last night about a story idea she's got going. She didn't say much, just that it has something to do with Olivia Andrews. And you. She says that the two of you are going to Fredericksburg on an investigation." He leaned forward, frowning. "Want to let me in on it?"

"As it happens," I said uncomfortably, "this is connected to what I said in that email the other morning—talking to you about somebody we both knew. Olivia Andrews."

I was involving one of Hark's reporters in this affair. As an editor, he's got a right to know what we're up to. And as I said, the two of us go back a long way. So I gave him the condensed version of Zelda's visit, my trip with Rita to the site on Purgatory Bend Road and then to the storage unit, and the troubling fact that both cellphone and computer were missing. I also gave him a capsule version of Kelly's conviction, the appellate ruling that had vacated it, and Olivia's idea that the man was living here, in Pecan Springs. Which brought us back once again to Zelda and her theory of her sister's death: that Kelly, whoever he was now, didn't want that story told and had staged the hit-and-run that ensured Olivia's silence.

Hark listened thoughtfully. And then he surprised me.

"I've heard part of this before," he said, and told me that just a couple of days before Olivia was killed, she showed up in his office asking for her old job back. "It sounded wacko to me, but she was totally up-front, no apologies, no beating around the bush. She said she wasn't looking for the work or the money. She was looking for journalistic cover to shelter her from the threat of a lawsuit over stories related to her new project, which involved that old River Oaks murder case and somebody here in town—somebody important."

"Did she tell you who, or how she got the information?"

"No. I grilled her about it, but she wouldn't budge. She would only say that this guy is somebody I know—a guy *everybody* knows—and that his past will knock our socks off because it's so out of line with who he is now. She was pitching it as a story that people need to know because they need to be asking questions about his character, his integrity. If I rehired her, she'd fill me in on the details. I would know everything she knew. The *Enterprise* would have first rights—she'd blog and podcast it only after the newspaper published first."

"I see," I said. "So what did you think? More to the point, what did you do?"

He shrugged. "Knowing Olivia, I thought she might be onto something. She likes to look under rocks and her instinct for stories—especially the more sensational ones—has always been pretty good, far as I know. But in this case . . . well, I just didn't trust her. Of course I was curious. Oh, you bet. I wanted to have what she had come up with. Who the guy was, what he'd done, why all this matters now." He shrugged.

"But?" I prompted.

Another of those lopsided grins. "The woman was a loose cannon. She could write us into a bad corner. So I reminded her of the reasons I let her go in the first place—missed deadlines, too much fast-and-loose with the facts. I may even have mentioned Neely's lawsuit." He turned down his mouth. "But I told her I'd think about it. I was still thinking when she got killed."

"I see." I frowned. "Did it maybe cross your mind that the two things might be related? Her death and the story she was pitching?"

He sighed. "Yeah, that did occur to me, when it happened. I sent Jessica out to cover the story because she has a damned good eye. If there was anything to see, I figured she'd see it. And I got a copy of Kidder's accident report. Have you had a look at it?"

I nodded.

"It's pretty straightforward. Nothing in it triggered any questions for me. And really, China, there was nowhere to go if it did. You know as well as I do that hit-and-runs are the worst crimes to clear. It's entirely likely that the cops will never know who was driving that vehicle."

"You could be right," I agreed. "I was out at the site with Rita Kidder. We talked to the witness who got a glimpse of the truck. Nothing new—at least not enough. On that end, yes. Nowhere to go."

He eyed me. "This thing you're looking at. That old murder in River Oaks. That's the other end?"

"Could be. Tomorrow, I'm going to try to connect with somebody in Fredericksburg who might be able to tell us something. Jessica wants to ride along." I wasn't exactly asking his permission, just letting him know. But he *is* Jessica's boss.

"Oh, yeah?" He perked up. "Somebody who?"

I smiled. "Ms. Nelson will be glad to fill in a few blanks when she gets back. But if somebody calls you from Fredericksburg and wants to know if Jessie really *is* a reporter, please speak for her."

He put on a stern face. "You and Jessica are two of a kind," he growled. "Don't get yourselves in trouble. The newspaper might bail her out but McQuaid would have to take care of you."

"We'll be good," I promised.

"That's what I'm afraid of." He turned to glance around the shop. "Where are those books? I understand that *They Called Themselves the KKK* is on the banned list up in Granbury. I guess our good-doing school boards don't want kids to know the history of one of our longest-running American terrorist groups. But I'm interested in the history of the Klan. Got a copy of that one?"

"We did," I said. "Somebody took it yesterday. But you might be interested in Shirley Jackson's *The Lottery*. Some of the pages are a little dog-eared, but it's perfectly readable."

"*The Lottery*?" Hark asked, raising his eyebrows. "You're not telling me *that's* on the list? Hell, it's a freakin' *classic*! I read it in Mrs. Wilson's eighth-grade English class."

"Yes. Somebody doesn't want Texas students to know that people can be cruel and violent."

"Huh," Hark grunted. "Like their kids don't watch *The Hunger Games*?" He gave me a look. "Well, I'll go take a couple of photos. And you remember what I said. Don't you and Jessica go getting into trouble down in Fredericksburg. You hear?"

"I hear," I repeated obediently.

"And don't let her dive into any rabbit holes. She's bad about rabbit holes."

"No rabbit holes." I chuckled. "If I can help it."

He nodded. "Oh, and before I forget. I've read that some herb called the fountain of youth—ginkee or gonko or something like that—is supposed to be good for the memory. Keeps you young, too. Got any of that stuff?"

"You're thinking of *Ginkgo biloba*, probably. I have it, but when somebody asks, I tell them that the current research doesn't support

157

those claims. I sell it to people who insist, but I always say it probably won't give you what you're looking for. Whistle when you're through taking photos and I'll show you something that's more likely to help."

"I'll do it," Hark said.

He left muddy footprints as he walked across the floor to the banned book nook. But that was okay. The garden needed the rain, and other customers would be coming in with muddy feet, too.

It was going to be that kind of day.

I always feel a little uncertain about giving a talk at the Native Plant Society of Texas. Those folks know their native plants and most are expert plantswomen and men. But they welcome people to their meetings who are just getting interested in gardening, so I content myself with the knowledge that what I have to say will be news to a few people, at least. And I always invite those in the audience who are growing a plant or have a specialized knowledge of it to share what they know with the rest of us. This keeps people awake, if nothing else, and sometimes we can have an energetic discussion with lots of different ideas tossed in.

My Friday talk was titled "The Mysteries of Herbs." Getting it together had been mostly a matter of reviewing my dozen slides on the computer, with a few important points in readable font beside each photo. I also had to make sure they were in the right order and that I knew what I wanted to say about each of them. I was scheduled to begin at two in the afternoon. After answering questions and social-izing with folks over punch and cookies, I'd be finished by four. I was hoping to connect with Margaret Greer either in the morning, before my talk, or after, in the late afternoon.

Reaching Ms. Greer was easy. The phone number I'd found in Olivia's notes was current, and she picked up on the third ring. I gave my name and asked if I had reached Eleanor Blakely Kelly's cousin.

There was a long pause. "Eleanor has been dead for decades. Do I know you?" There was a sharply suspicious edge to her voice. It had a distinct quaver, too. I remembered that Eleanor had been fifty or so when she died a couple of decades ago. Her cousin could be in her seventies, eighties, maybe.

"I don't think we've met," I replied. "I own the herb shop, Thyme and Seasons, in Pecan Springs. Maybe you've heard of it?"

The world suddenly became a little smaller. Or as Ruby would say, the Universe had taken a hand in this affair.

"Now, isn't that a coincidence?" she exclaimed. "I had a very nice lunch in your tearoom—a lavender quiche and the very best tomato soup. You and I have met, but you must meet hundreds of little old ladies. You won't remember me." A shorter pause. "The lady I was having lunch with told me you used to be a lawyer." And once again, that edge of suspicion, although a little blunted now. "Why are you asking about my cousin?"

I am fully capable of deviousness when it's necessary, but I had already decided I wouldn't pull any punches. We would do this thing straight up or not at all.

"I'm asking because I was a friend of a writer named Olivia Andrews," I said. "I believe she may have talked with you about a project she was working on, involving your cousin. I'll be in Fredericksburg tomorrow to give a two o'clock talk at the Native Plant Society. Might it be convenient for us to sit down together for an hour or so, either in the morning or late afternoon?"

A television was loud in the background. It suddenly went off.

"Ms. Andrews came to see me some time ago, and promised to be in touch," Margaret Greer said. "I've been expecting to hear from her. Do you happen to know whether she's still working on that . . . that project?"

"I'm sorry," I said carefully, "but Olivia Andrews is dead. I understand that it happened just a few days after she came to see you. She was out running on the road near her house early one morning, when she was struck and killed."

A gasp. A silence. Then a tremulous, "Olivia Andrews is . . . *dead*?"

"I'm terribly sorry. Yes, she apparently died instantly."

Another silence. "You say it was an accident?" She sounded stunned. And then, immediately, suspicious. "Wait a minute. How did you know she visited me? Where did you get my number?"

I answered more softly now. "Olivia's sister Zelda came to see me the other day. She gave me Olivia's file on the project and asked me to see what I could find out about what her sister might have been working on. Olivia had jotted down your name and phone number and noted that you and Eleanor Kelly were cousins and that she had talked with you."

This time, the silence went on for so long that I thought I might have lost her. "Ms. Greer?" I asked. "Are you still there?"

"I'm here," she said, and took a breath. "Yes, Olivia and I talked." The quaver was accentuated, now, perhaps by anxiety. "Did you say . . . do you know . . . have the police found out who hit her? Have they put him in jail?"

"I'm afraid they still don't have any suspects," I said. "I've read the police report and talked to the investigating officer and a witness. I'll be glad to fill you in on what I know about the current situation.

Would tomorrow work for you? Ten o'clock? Or would four-thirty be better?"

"Ten," she said, with no hesitation. "Unless you'd like to come over this afternoon. I have something you should—" She hesitated. The suspicion was gone from her voice, but it had been replaced by something else, perhaps the shock of hearing that the woman with whom she had talked was dead.

Or apprehension, maybe. Or even fear.

Fear. Was that it? Was this woman afraid of putting herself in jeopardy if she talked to me? Or was she afraid that she might be in jeopardy *now*?

"I'm afraid it'll have to be tomorrow," I said. "I'd like to bring someone with me—Jessica Nelson, from our local newspaper." I was uncertain about mentioning Jessica, but I didn't want to put this elderly woman on her guard by showing up with a reporter in tow. Better to have all the cards on the table. "If you'd like to verify Ms. Nelson's employment," I added, "I'll be glad to give you her editor's phone number so you can call him directly. His name is Hark Hibler. He can speak for me, too."

And then Margaret Greer surprised me. Until now, she had seemed uneasy, disturbed, perhaps even afraid, especially after she learned that Olivia Andrews was dead. Now, all that changed. I had used the magic word.

"The newspaper!" she exclaimed. "Of course. Olivia told me she thought this could be a very big story—this thing she was working on, I mean. She said she was going to talk to Mr. Hibler at the newspaper about it. I've been wondering and wondering and *wondering* whether she'd done that and whether I was going to hear from him, but I didn't know who to ask." She sounded relieved. "Yes, I'll call him. And yes, by all means, bring your reporter! I'm glad to tell you both what I know."

And there it was. We were going to be friends.

I thought.

Chapter Ten

The fragrance of coffee (its bouquet, which may range from herbal to fruity to caramelized) is made up of over eight hundred known aromatics. Generally, the darker the roast, the more of these compounds are changed and the easier it is to detect them by scent. And since our senses of smell and flavor are related, we're likely to find that the more aroma, the stronger the flavor.

Light roast coffee tends to have a more subtle, complex fragrance because it preserves more of the original flavors of the coffee bean: fruit, floral, and other organic notes. The nuanced fragrance is often described as brighter or more vibrant.

Dark roast coffee, on the other hand, undergoes a longer roasting process, bringing out the deeper, more robust flavors: chocolate, caramel, and nuts. The fragrance of dark roast coffee can be quite strong and rich.

China Bayles
"What Am I Forgetting? Herbs to Improve Your Memory"
Pecan Springs Enterprise

Fredericksburg, Texas, may be a bit more cluttered with tourists than some folks like, but the food, the friendly people, and the unique architecture are worth braving the traffic—not to mention the wineries and Wildseed Farm, some two hundred acres of wildflowers, cultivated for their seed and best seen in April and May, when they are a spectacle of rainbows.

Fredericksburg has a unique past that persists in its unique present—and especially in those lovely architectural relics of an earlier era, the Sunday houses. The town was settled in 1846, about the same time as Pecan Springs and by a similar (but better organized and funded) company of German immigrants. They arrived by ship at Galveston and trekked overland by wagon across the Texas wilderness to New Braunfels, on the raw edge of the frontier. From there, it was a sixty-mile, sixteen-day journey northwest across the rugged plateau, their wagon train accompanied by an eight-man armed escort hired to fend off the unfriendly Comanche.

The new town was laid out at the confluence of two streams four miles above the Pedernales River, where the settlers found the raw materials of their new lives: water, timber, and stone. They built their first houses simply, of post oak logs planted upright in the ground. Those who survived the cholera and malaria that plagued the town's first years replaced those makeshift dwellings with more permanent *fachwerk* or half-timbered houses, built of upright timbers with the spaces between filled with rocks and plastered.

Each family's toehold in the vast New World included a half-acre village lot and 10 acres of farmland just outside of town. Additionally, single men were allotted 160 acres farther out in the country, married men 320 acres. It was set up in this way because it was imagined that the settlers would live in the unsettled New World as they had in the settled and civilized Old. They would farm by day and go home to eat and sleep in the village at night.

But things didn't go as planned. Frontier farming was challenged by topography, climate, and the Comanche, and often-impassable trails made daily commutes between countryside and village impossible. Most of the settlers moved out to their ten-acre farm allotments and made weekend visits to town, where they could shop on Saturday, socialize on Saturday night, and worship on Sunday. Which meant that they needed a place to eat and sleep in walking distance of the general store, the *bierhalle*, and the church.

So many of the settlers built what they called Sunday houses on their town lots, usually log or stone houses just large enough to sleep the whole family: one or two downstairs rooms with a lean-to kitchen and a loft for the children, reached via an outside stair. A fireplace served for heating and cooking, and water came from nearby Town Creek. It wasn't long until there were over a hundred of these weekend retreats.

As time went on, the Sunday houses served many other purposes. They became a place where the older children could live while they were going to school in town or a mother could stay in the weeks before childbirth, close to the doctor or midwife. Or where a newly married son or daughter could call home while they saved enough money to build one of their own. But in the 1920s, when the automobile and paved roads made it easier to get from home to town and back, they were used less often. Many were razed and replaced by modern buildings, residential and commercial.

And then fame came to town. President Lyndon Johnson was born on the family ranch outside of Stonewall, just eighteen miles east of Fredericksburg. When he became president in 1963, the road-weary journalists who followed him to the ranch needed a bed, a telephone, and a desk for their portable typewriters. So the Sunday houses still standing were hurriedly renovated. In 1970, the Johnson ranch became a National Historical Park, Fredericksburg became an attractive tourist destination, and the Sunday houses, with their unique history and architecture, became chic B&Bs. But one—the Weber Sunday House— is still standing, on the grounds of the Gillespie County Historical Society's Pioneer Museum. It was built in 1904 by August Weber (no electricity or plumbing, of course) for the family's weekly trips into town, a seven-mile, three-plus-hour wagon trip each way.

Our drive to Fredericksburg was ten times longer and two-thirds shorter than that. I picked Jessica up at seven-forty on Friday morning—a little early, because I was looking forward to an outstanding cup of coffee at a place in Fredericksburg that roasts its own—and we stopped for gas as we drove out of town. The day was a pretty one, still pleasantly cool, the morning sun slanting off the pale green mesquite and the darker cedar. Red-tailed and Cooper's hawks sailed overhead, and a great blue heron rose effortlessly out of a hidden pool. Our route took us northwest across Devil's Backbone, a rugged limestone ridge that slices northwest to southeast across the rolling Hill Country. The landscape was beautiful, with sprawling patches of purple prairie verbena, mealy blue sage, and lovely Texas bluebells. Clumps of staghorn milkweed and mountain pinks grew in the gravel along the road, with a few late orangey-red paintbrush and wine-cups the color of a rich Burgundy. Live oak mottes were scattered across the pastures, which were punctuated as we went farther west by statuesque yucca and undisciplined patches of prickly pear cactus, covered with translucent yellow and peach blooms. At Blanco, we took Ranch-to-Market 1623 northwest through the wine country, heading toward Route 290 at Stonewall.

On the way, I told Jessica about the phone conversation with Margaret Greer. "I don't know what I was expecting," I said, summing up. "But it wasn't quite that. Until she knew who I was, she sounded . . . well, apprehensive, suspicious, maybe even a little frightened. But she warmed up after it emerged that we had met—and especially when she heard that you were coming. In fact, she seemed positively eager.

She has a story to tell and she wants to talk to a reporter. She was just waiting for one to show up."

"I talked to Hark this morning," Jessica said. "She called him yesterday to check me out. Apparently, they had a nice little chat, and she ended up asking for his mailing address at the newspaper. He wondered whether she was going to send him a fan letter." She frowned. "You said she sounded frightened. Frightened about what?"

"I don't know. But Olivia was killed just a few days after their interview. It crossed my mind that Margaret might have given Olivia a clue that led her to uncover Kelly's current identity—or maybe Margaret even told her who he was. When she heard about Olivia, maybe it frightened her. She wondered . . ." I let my voice trail off.

"Whether somebody might target her next," Jessica said. There was a moment's silence while both of us thought about that. Then she added, "What are you thinking we might learn from her?"

"Some of the backstory," I said. "More about Eleanor, what Eleanor's relationship with Kelly was like, what happened to him after he left prison. But mostly who Kelly is *now*—if Margaret knows."

"Do you suppose she gave Olivia any useful information?"

"If she did, it's not in the notes I've reviewed so far. There might be something on Olivia's laptop—if we could find it. Or maybe she didn't. Could be she just wanted to be sure that her cousin isn't forgotten. Maybe she had stories about when they were kids and would like to see them written down."

But that, too, would have interested Olivia, who was always hungry for stories. The victim's story, the family's story, the story of the crime. She, too, would have wanted to make sure that Eleanor, long dead, was not forgotten and would have listened for the details that would bring her to life again. How she had looked, how she dressed, what her hobbies might have been, her passions, her worries, her fears. Eleanor Blakely had been a wealthy widow when she married James Kelly. But was she an elegant River Oaks socialite or an athletic cowgirl or a professional woman or a business owner?

But we were focused on another crime—on Olivia's murder, if that's what it was. Was Eleanor Kelly's story even relevant? How could it help us now?

"Margaret and Eleanor were cousins," Jessica said. "Did Margaret inherit anything?"

"Some mineral rights, I understand. Kelly got the bulk of the property, and he got to keep it after his conviction was vacated. I was wondering if she—Margaret—had kept in touch with him."

"Do you know where Olivia got the idea that Kelly is living in Pecan Springs? Did Margaret tell her that?"

"I don't know what Margaret told her. I went through all but the last couple of Olivia's boxes last evening and didn't find anything even tangentially related to James Q. Kelly, in his past or present incarnation. Actually, I have no idea how reliable any of Olivia's information was," I added. "Could be it was all just dead wrong."

"But Olivia is *dead*," Jessica reminded me. "Mysteriously dead. And somebody seems to have taken her phone and laptop. Which suggests that she might have been dead *right*."

"Agreed." I gave her a wry look. "You have a way with words."

"That's my business," Jessica said. "Speaking of people with the initial Q, I've been doing a little research on our friend, Jeremy Q. Kellogg. I haven't tracked down his origins yet, but I have traced him back to what he was doing before he became pastor of that Dallas megachurch. That scandal wasn't his first. A dozen years ago, he got into trouble at a church in Arkansas, where he was accused of violating a morality clause in his contract. The church board defrocked him for pastoral abuse and sexual misconduct, but the woman he was involved with—a deacon's wife—confessed that the adultery was consensual. So the case was swept under the church carpet. No reason to report it to the police."

"That happened under his current name?"

"Yes. After his Dallas difficulty, he seems to have gone to Mexico and taken up the life of a missionary. But not for very long—only a year or so. Pecan Springs was his next stop."

"Eleanor Kelly was murdered twenty years ago. You haven't gotten back that far with Kellogg?"

"Right," Jessica said. "I'm still looking. And I don't know where in Mexico he went—I need to check that out."

When we reached Stonewall, heading west on 290, Fredericksburg was only about fifteen miles. Once in town, I stayed on Main Street, past the Nimitz Naval Museum, straight to the Caliche Coffee Bar & Ranch Road Roasters, known for roasting fair-trade coffees in small batches right there at the shop. The minute we walked through the door, the rich aroma of freshly roasted coffee—so difficult to describe but so utterly unforgettable—wrapped us in a warm blanket of cara-mel, toasted nuts, cocoa, and vanilla pipe smoke.

"Ah, wonderful!" Jessica said, rolling her eyes. "It was worth driving all the way here just for that *aroma*!"

I ordered a cortado, which is like a latte but with a one-to-one ratio of espresso to steamed milk (latte is one-third to two-thirds) and less sweet. Jessica got a cappuccino. And both of us had the avocado toast: poached egg on kale on a warm, crusty sourdough, topped with mashed avocado, pickled onions, and roasted grape tomatoes chopped and tossed with olive oil, thyme, garlic, pepitas, and red pepper flakes.

The sourdough comes from Joju Bakery, which makes its bread with Texas-grown grain and a sourdough starter that is reputed to be four or five years old—whatever, it was perfect. Breakfast was fine and the coffee was just the treat I'd been looking forward to.

Well fed, fully caffeinated, and ready for our conversation with Margaret Greer, we pulled up in front of the address she had given me. It turned out to be one of Fredericksburg's renovated Sunday houses, a block or so off West San Antonio in a pleasant residential neighborhood of flowerbeds, neatly kept green lawns, and arching pecan trees. The houses on either side probably dated from the 1950s, and the little white cottage—one story and a loft tucked under a green metal roof—would have thrilled the heart of any tiny-house fan. From the street, it looked as it might have at the end of the nineteenth century. Sunny yellow lantana lined both sides of the stepping-stone path to the front porch, which featured a white wooden rocker, green shutters at the single window to the left of the green-painted door, and several terracotta pots of marigolds. There was a large orange tabby cat on the doormat, paws tucked under a white bib, and a small boxy package on the porch floor. As we came up the step, the cat got up, stretched, and waited expectantly for the door to open.

"Hello, pretty kitty," Jessica crooned, and bent over to pet him. "You look just like my tabby back home."

The cat meowed amiably. I rang the doorbell. After a moment, I rang it again. And then again.

Jessica took out her phone. "Two minutes past ten. We've come to the right place?"

I glanced down at the package. Margaret Greer's name and address. "This is it," I said, ringing again. The doorbell was working, because we could hear it chiming inside.

I stepped to the window beside the door. Between a pair of white ruffled curtains, I could see into a cozy parlor, brightened by a spill of sunlight from another window. There was a brightly colored latch hook rug on the polished wood floor, a brown sofa piled with crocheted pillows, and a wall of framed photographs—family members, I guessed. In one corner, a comfortable chintz-covered chair with a white shawl draped over one arm. On the chair's matching ottoman, a cup and saucer and a half-open book, turned face down. Beside the ottoman, a pair of fuzzy pink house slippers. The table lamp was on.

What I saw was troublesome. I turned uneasily and picked up the package. "Come on, Jessie," I said. "Let's try the back door."

The tabby, glad that we'd finally gotten the idea, leaped lightly down the steps to the gravel path between the house and a head-high green privet hedge, a thick green mat of variegated vinca on either side. We followed him single file, through a white-painted wooden gate into a deep but narrow back yard bordered with flower beds. To our left, a trumpet vine covered with bright orange blossoms climbed the trellis at one side of three wooden steps up to the back door.

The cat darted up the steps and waited for me to open the door. I followed him up the steps and knocked. The door opened without resistance beneath my hand and the cat squirted inside.

The skin was prickling on the back of my neck. Not touching the knob, I put my head through the half-open door and called "Ms. Greer? It's China Bayles, here for our meeting. Ms. Greer?"

But there was no point in my calling. Margaret Greer, eyes wide and unseeing, lay on the floor of her small kitchen, some two yards away from the door. She was wearing a paisley-print housecoat. Her feet were bare. There were two neat round holes in the front of her housecoat. She was lying in a puddle of dark red blood.

Chapter Eleven

Modern researchers know that the high antioxidant and antimicrobial properties of rosemary make it an effective food preservative. But this practical knowledge goes back to the time of the ancient Greeks, who used rosemary to slow spoilage in raw and cooked meat. About the same time, over in Egypt, embalmers were using rosemary to preserve human bodies in the form of mummies, so that the dead could live on, eternally.

These demonstrations of the herb's powers of preservation led people to believe that rosemary might also preserve human memory. Which is why Greek students wore garlands of rosemary when they studied for exams. And why funeral wreaths always included rosemary. It was a sign and an assurance that the dead would never be forgotten. They would endure, always, in the memory of the living.

China Bayles
"What Am I Forgetting? Herbs to Improve Your Memory"
Pecan Springs Enterprise

Sweet Jesus." Behind me, standing on tiptoes to peer over my shoulder, Jessica let out her breath. "Is she . . . dead?"

"Yes," I said. "Hours ago." From the door, I could see that the margins of puddled blood had already dried to a crust, and there was what looked like a dried-blood shoeprint in front of the door. My mouth was suddenly dry and it was hard to get my breath. *What happened here? Why? Who?* I put a steadying hand on the doorframe. "Maybe since last night."

Jessica went back down the stairs, pulling out her phone. "I'll call 9-1-1."

"Wait," I said, turning. "Let's decide what we're going to tell the police. About why we're here, I mean."

"Right." Jessica looked up at me, eyes wide. "It probably doesn't have anything at all to do with—" She swallowed. "With us. Or what we came here for. This . . . it might just as well have been a robbery, you know. Or a neighbor with a grudge."

I shuddered at the thought of trying to tell an investigating officer why we were here. Jessica was right. What had happened here might have nothing at all to do with our reason for coming this morning. It was tempting to think that, and make up a story that would avoid all the complications involved with our visit. On the other hand . . .

I led the way back down the steps. "But it might. And while I'm not a practicing lawyer, I'm still licensed, which means I'm an officer of the court—off duty and out of uniform, sort of, but still an officer. I have to give the cops any information that might help them figure out who killed Margaret Greer. You're a journalist. You do, too."

She made a face. "You're right, damn it. But you know what this means."

"It means we're not concealing anything. That we're telling the same story. The truth."

"It means that Pam Clark, at the *Fredericksburg Standard*, will be all over the story. The Olivia story. *My* story."

I gestured toward the house. "She would be all over this, anyway. It's her turf. But you were here first. You discovered the body. And if Ms. Greer's murder has anything to do with our visit, it's also a Pecan Springs story. This is only the Fredericksburg chapter."

Jessica sighed. "Hark will have to know what's happened. And what I'm going to tell the police."

I knew what he would tell her to say. Cooperate, even if it means letting somebody else in on the Olivia story. I took out my phone. "I'll call 9-1-1."

The cops, bless them, did just what they were supposed to do. A pair of them—and a team of skilled medics—got to the house in under six minutes. The first officers surveyed the situation, confirmed that Margaret Greer had been dead for some hours, taped the scene, and began making phone calls. They separated Jessica and me, asked us the usual who, when, and why questions, parked me in my car and Jessie in a squad car and told us politely that someone would be right with us.

Their hearts were in the right place, but I knew better than to believe them. I was right. Which gave me time to sit for a while with my eyes closed and think about the utter finality of death and wonder who would mourn Margaret Greer. Did she have friends who would remember her kindness, her generosity, her lilting laugh, the Valentines she never failed to send? Children who would vow to remember her to their own dying days? Grandchildren and great-grands who would look for her on Ancestry.com or 23andMe when they were building their family trees?

But friends and children and grandchildren lead busy lives, with people and events competing for their attention. Unless they were reminded, how long would they remember? How quickly would Margaret Greer be forgotten? And now that she was gone, who would remember her cousin?

But those somber thoughts were interrupted by a couple of phone calls and a text. It started with an irritated call from Hark Hibler, who demanded to know what the *hell* was going on and why I couldn't keep his reporter out of trouble. And when I had explained (as Jessica no doubt had), added, "Well, screw it. Just keep her out of jail, would you? And don't go there yourself."

Then from my mother, who reported that Caitie had fallen off Comanche but not to worry because the doctor said her wrist was just sprained, not broken. She would have to wear the brace for only a couple of days and then she'd be good as new.

And a text from Ruby, minding the shop back home, letting me know that she had just confirmed the tent and table rentals for the Warrens' barbeque and that Ramona was proceeding with her plans for the psychic fair. She was already collecting RSVPs for her talk about dreams.

With all that, I was pretty well occupied for the forty minutes it took for a sturdy, fair-haired woman in a dark skirt and jacket and a red blouse to get down to me on her morning to-do list. She rapped on my car window, opened the door, and sat down in the passenger seat, giving me a pro forma apology for the delay and flashing a badge wallet that identified her as Detective Carla Baker from the Fredericksburg Criminal Investigation Division. Taking a notebook and ballpoint from her jacket pocket, she asked me to tell her who I am and what I do. When I got to the part where my husband is a retired Houston homicide detective and a licensed PI, her eyebrows went up.

They went up higher when I added that I am currently a shopkeeper and out-of-practice lawyer. "What kind of law?" she asked.

"Criminal defense. Big firm, long time ago."

"So you know the ropes." She clicked her ballpoint with her thumb. "You here on business?"

"Not that kind. I'm here to give a talk." I handed her one of my

Thyme and Seasons business cards, with my personal contact information penciled on the back. "But there's more," I said, and began
with my telephone conversation with Margaret Greer and the story
behind it, including Olivia Andrews' investigation of the murder of
Eleanor Kelly—Margaret Greer's cousin—and Olivia's recent hit-and-
run death.

Detective Baker's pen was busy. When I stopped, her pen stopped.
After a moment, she said, "You drove here from Pecan Springs this
morning? What time did you arrive?"

"Yes, this morning. We left at seven-forty and got here about
nine. We had coffee and avocado toast at the Caliche Coffee Bar.
Great coffee."

"Best in town." She glanced at the time-stamped receipts I pro-
duced, one for the gas when we started out, the other for our breakfast,
made another note, and handed them back. "You and a reporter drove
all the way from Pecan Springs just to talk to Margaret Greer. Why?"

"Jessica Nelson—the reporter—covered the Andrews hit-and-run,
which hasn't been cleared yet. She came with me because she's doing
a follow-up story for the *Enterprise*. And I didn't make a special trip
to Fredericksburg just to see Ms. Greer. As I said, I'm here to give a
talk. I'll be at the Native Plant Society this afternoon. You can check
with Rebecca Lewis there. She'll tell you it's been on their calendar
for a couple of months. I thought I could kill two birds with one
stone—the talk and . . ." I made a face. "Sorry," I muttered. "Poor
choice of metaphors."

"Right," Baker said. "So you planned to talk to Ms. Greer about
what she knew about her cousin's murder?"

"That, and her conversation with Olivia Andrews."

"And you hoped to learn—what?"

"Whatever she knew. Whatever she was willing to tell, which might not be the same thing. Whether she would be helpful or not, I had no way of knowing. Could be she just wanted to be sure her cousin's murder wasn't forgotten."

Baker studied her notebook. "This shooting. Do you think it might have anything to do with your reason for coming? With that hit-and-run accident?" She was looking directly at me now, her steady gray eyes probing. "With that Kelly business from twenty years ago?"

"It might," I said. "On the phone, when we first started talking, Ms. Greer seemed nervous, apprehensive. As she began to feel more comfortable, that lessened." Baker was writing again. I waited, letting her catch up.

The pen paused. "Apprehensive? Like how?"

"When I said I wanted to talk about her cousin, she said, 'Do I know you?' She sounded suspicious, maybe even . . . well, afraid."

"Or maybe just careful," Baker said. "After all, she was an elderly woman, living alone. Somebody she doesn't know calls her up out of the blue, asks about a long-dead cousin—for all she knows, it's a scam of some kind." She clicked her ballpoint impatiently. "Somebody wanting money. Seniors can't be too careful these days."

"Could be," I conceded. "But I need to correct something you said a moment ago. It's true that the police report originally described Olivia Andrews' death as an accident. It happened in the dark, before dawn. She was running with the traffic, on a narrow road with almost no shoulder—a good setup for an accident. But a closer look at the scene and an interview with a witness have suggested that the driver may have hit Andrews on purpose, then stopped to retrieve her cellphone and house key. When I last spoke with the investigating officer, she was planning to amend her report." I gave Rita Kidder's name, and spelled it. "Chief Dawson will be aware of the amended report if it's been filed," I added. "You can contact her if you want the latest update. Tell her we've talked." I rattled off Sheila's direct phone number.

"Sheila Dawson?" Baker smiled. "I met her at a conference of the Women of Law Enforcement up in Fort Worth last fall. Gotta take my cap off to her. That cop shop in Pecan Springs was known to be one of the most exclusive boys' clubs in the state. She is one brave lady to take it on. She had that baby okay? She's back at work?"

I wanted to laugh. Sheila's name and phone number had been the secret password. Detective Baker and I were besties now, fellow card-carrying members of the Old Girls' Network, sharing news about a mutual friend's baby.

"Noah was born in November," I said, "and they're both well and healthy, although the baby's teething and Sheila says she could use a little more sleep. I'll be talking with her when Jessica and I get back to Pecan Springs. But do give her a call—she'll be interested in hearing about your investigation. She can send you both reports on Andrews, if the update is available." I paused, giving her time to think about this. "I didn't go into the kitchen, but from the doorway, it looked like Ms. Greer died from a couple of gunshots. Is that right? Any idea when it happened?"

She considered, hesitated, and then decided. After all, we were both on the same side now. "Shot twice in the chest. Small caliber, 9mm. Probably last night. Looks like she had been reading in the living room."

I remembered the teacup, the book, the shawl. I pushed my luck. "Shell casings? Prints?"

"Two casings. One partial print."

"Ah," I said. Casings left behind? With a print? The killer must be somebody who didn't watch true-crime shows.

All business again, she closed her notebook. "You and Ms. Nelson are free to go. Before you get out of town, though, you'll need to stop by the police station and leave your prints. And a statement. I'm sure you know how to do that."

"You'll find my prints on the door, the doorframe, and the stair rail. Neither Jessica nor I went into the kitchen."

"Wherever they are," Baker said, sliding her notebook into her jacket pocket, "we'll find them."

And that was that. The police station is on the eastern edge of town, and what with traffic and a lengthy delay in getting set up to take our prints and make our statements, that little job took the better part of two hours. That left just enough time for a quick fast-food lunch. And then it was on to my afternoon gig.

The Native Plant Society meets at St. Joseph's Halle, a charming, century-old mission-style stone building only a few blocks away on West San Antonio. As usual, the meeting was well attended, with a mix of regulars and new folks, all of them passionately interested in the incredible variety of Texas wild plants. The slide show worked just fine, the talk went without a hitch, and there were plenty of intelligent questions and discussion. I even learned several new things about a couple of plants I didn't know very well. And some new things about a plant—the yaupon holly—that I thought I knew very well. It pays to ask people what *they* know instead of telling them everything *you* know. I enjoyed the afternoon and agreed to come back another time.

But after what we had seen in Margaret Greer's kitchen, the afternoon—however pleasant and instructive it might have been—was definitely an anticlimax. Jessica and I talked about it as we headed home. We were still talking about it when we got to the Devil's Backbone Tavern, where we had decided we would have supper.

179

The Backbone prides itself on being the "oldest dive bar" in Texas, which it no doubt is. Built on the site of an Indian campground and said to be haunted, its history dates back to the 1890s, when the stone building served as a blacksmith shop and stagecoach stop at the foot of a treacherous hill on what is now Route 32. At the end of Prohibition, it began selling legal booze and added a dancehall, its location—on the Comal side of the Comal–Hays County line—making it the most popular hangout for miles. Hays was dry until well after the turn of the twenty-first century, while Comal was proudly (and profitably) wet from the get-go.

Ghosts or not, thirsty Hays County folks made the Backbone a rip-roarin' success. Now, it features live country music and offers itself as a dive bar wedding venue. The web page boasts: "Studies show that couples who get hitched in the 'Oldest Dive Bar in Texas' with Conway on the Jukebox and Pearl Beer in the icebox, are happier, richer and cooler than the rest. (It may not be exactly what your in-laws had in mind, but then again, neither were you.)"

We weren't thirsty but it was suppertime, so we ordered chili-cheese fries and burgers slathered with melted cheese and hangry sauce: a tongue-toasting red sauce made with jalapeños, serranos, habaneros, cayenne, and a few other unidentified incendiary peppers. It was Friday night, so there would be live music later. Robyn & Lunchmeat Hootenanny tonight and tomorrow night, according to the sign behind the bar, and I made a mental note to tell Ruby. She likes Hootenanny. And she loves to come out to the Backbone to dance and talk to cowboys.

No live music for Jessie and me. Instead, we enjoyed our burgers to the tune of classic country on the jukebox, accompanied by the *click-click-jingle-jangle* of a pinball machine and gleeful shouts of "That's off the board, baby!" from the shuffleboard table. And I do

180

mean classic country. Johnny Cash, "I Walk the Line." Dolly Parton, "Jolene." Tammy Wynette, "Stand by Your Man." And my all-time favorite, George Strait's "Amarillo by Morning."

Marinated in hangry sauce and country music, we were just driving into Pecan Springs when Jessica got a phone call from Hark. They spoke briefly and when she clicked off, she turned to me. "Hark says he wants us to stop at the newspaper. He's got something for us."

"Tonight?" I frowned, irritated. "*Both* of us? Can't it wait until tomorrow? I've got a houseful of animals at home and I'm late with their supper."

And then I had to chuckle. McQuaid and Caitie were gone, I didn't have to cook for the family, and I was planning to use the evening to sort through the remaining two boxes of Olivia's notes and old drafts. But first I had to feed the dog, the cat, the chickens, and the parrot. Ah, life with a menagerie.

"Yes, both of us," Jessica replied. "He was being mysterious about it. But insistent." She sighed. "I'd rather go home and climb into a hot bubble bath. But I think we'd better find out what he wants, China. If we don't, he'll let me have it tomorrow. Anyway, it's probably nothing. It won't take very long."

"I doubt that," I grumped, but I was resigned. "As long as it helps to keep the peace between you and your boss."

I swung off the highway at West Alamo Street and headed for the newspaper.

THE OLD SQUARE-CUT LIMESTONE BUILDING that houses the *Enterprise* is just a block off the courthouse square, but it was after hours and there was plenty of room to park on the street. It was pushing eight o'clock, and on the second floor, the newsroom was dim except for a light in one of the two rows of cubicles that fill the high-ceilinged space. And empty except for Reggie Watkins, who was monitoring the phone at the night desk while he stared at a computer screen. It was unusually silent, too, absent the daytime mutter of voices and the trio of TVs on the wall, tuned to the cable channels.

Reggie raised his eyes over the top of his monitor as we came in and gave us a grin and a thumbs-up when Jessica pointed to Hark's office at the far end of the newsroom. He was probably used to seeing her in the newsroom after everyone else has gone home for the day. As the cops-and-crime reporter for the paper, she is on the job 24-7, on standby to cover meth busts, oil property thefts, migrant smuggling, and cattle rustling (yes, still a thing in Texas). She has a scanner app on her phone that enables her to pick up live law enforcement feeds from the city police and the Adams County sheriff's office and she keeps an eye on both police blotters. Pecan Springs may be a small town, but it's on a busy interstate corridor that funnels drugs and crime right past our gate and, too often, right into town.

I followed Jessica up the three steps to Hark's office, which has a large glass window overlooking the newsroom below. Through the window, I could see Hark hunched over his computer, scowling through nerdy black-rimmed glasses and running his hand through his dark, shaggy hair.

"Probably looking at financial reports," Jessica said to me, sotto voce. "Things are better since Dixon bought into the *Enterprise*, but they're not great."

"Should the rest of us be worried?" I'm just a lowly columnist, but I'm a reader and a citizen of Pecan Springs. I'd hate to lose the paper.

"Of course you should be worried," Jessica said, raising her hand to knock. "Newspapers are going under all across the country—little ones, big ones, all sizes. The Dixon money helps, but it's not the only answer. And it's not a guarantee."

On the other side of the door, Hark growled, "Stop that chattering and come in, damn it."

We went in. "I'm really glad that China already knows that your bark is worse than your bite," Jessica said casually. "Otherwise, she'd probably think you were pissed off at her because of something she's done. Missed a deadline or something like that. She might even think you'd called her here tonight to fire her."

"I haven't missed a deadline in . . . a while," I protested. "A couple of months, at least."

"Then you've broken some other rule," Jessica said. "There's no telling what he'll come up with to—"

"Shut up and sit down," Hark snapped.

"We'd better not argue with him," Jessica advised me. "He doesn't like people who argue. He might even fire both of us."

"He can't fire me," I said. "I'm not an employee. I trade my columns for ad space."

Ignoring both of us, Hark leaned over and picked something up off the floor. A package, wrapped in brown paper, like the bags you used to get in your grocery store, inexpertly sealed with crisscrossing strips of silvery duct tape and double-wrapped with twine.

He handed the package to me. "For you. From the woman who called me yesterday. And who got herself killed last night."

The flat package was about a foot square and a few inches thick and weighed a couple of pounds. It was addressed to me, care of Harkness Hibler, Editor, *Pecan Springs Enterprise*. The return address was Margaret Greer's. Both addresses were printed with a black Sharpie in a shaky hand. The package was stamped *Priority Mail* and bore a galaxy of stamps.

I pulled in a deep breath. I had last seen the woman who sent this lying on her kitchen floor in a puddle of dark blood. I felt suddenly cold. Life is short. Death can be sudden. And brutal. Had it taken Margaret Greer by surprise? Or had she seen it coming? Had she thought about it before it arrived? Had she thought about it long enough to be afraid? And, being very afraid, had she sent *this*?

Hark took a pair of scissors out of a drawer. "We won't know what's in it until you open it," he said. Like all newsmen, he has a thick skin and a jaundiced eye. But I heard what might have been sympathy in his voice.

I steadied myself, snipped the duct tape and twine, sliced the paper, and took out an album.

"A scrapbook!" Jessica exclaimed. "Is there a note?"

I looked quickly through the packaging. "No note," I said. "Just . . . this."

The gray linen cover was embossed with the words "Never Forgotten" in a large, ornate gilt script. On the inside front cover, in a sloping hand, was written *Eleanor Blakely Kelly.* The stiff pages were covered with transparent self-adhesive film on both sides and filled with photographs.

"There's quite a lot of stuff here," I said, turning pages. "Looks like it's all about Margaret's cousin." To Hark, I said, "The woman who died in River Oaks."

The thirty or so pages were filled with pictures, newspaper clippings, pressed flowers, theater programs, handwritten notes, graduation announcements, concert ticket stubs, scraps of fabric—the sort of thing you find in a thousand keepsake albums. All of it compiled by Margaret Greer's dead cousin.

Hark was leaning over the arm of his chair, curious. Jessica got up and was peering over my shoulder.

"Baby pictures," she said, half under her breath. She reached down to turn a page. "Family photos. Birthdays. Off to school."

"School and college," I said, and flipped forward a few pages, to a college cap-and-gown commencement photo. The young woman accepting her diploma was dark-haired, slender, attractive, proudly stepping into her new life. *Eleanor*, I thought.

"Keep going," Jessica said. "Maybe there will be some pictures of her husband. That's what we need, you know. If we could see what James Kelly looked like *then*, we could probably recognize him now."

I turned more pages. We were now into Eleanor's post-college life. There were photos of her with several young men, and then only one. And then an engagement announcement, to a man named Eugene Blakely. An engagement photo clipped from a newspaper—a dark-haired, vibrant young Eleanor and her solemn, self-impressed fiancé, older by at least a decade, perhaps more. Wedding and reception photos, honeymoon photos, Mr. and Mrs. Blakely starting a life together. Snapshots of formal dinners in evening dress, an oil field and drilling rigs, skiing vacations, a beach home, a sailboat, a champagne breakfast. Abruptly then, Blakely's obituary, framed in black. It was long and extensive, listing college degrees, professional achievements, and experience in the oil and gas industry. With it, a photo of an engraved granite marker banked with flowers in a neatly kept cemetery.

Then a blank page, as if to mark a hiatus. And then I turned a page to another chapter of Eleanor's life. "Look, Jess," I said eagerly. "A wedding photo. It must be James Kelly! But—"

"Uh-oh," Jessica said, and both of us bent closer. It was the usual wedding party, in color. The bride—Eleanor, older now but still attractive, dark-haired, vivacious—in a smartly stylish silver-gray gown, holding a bouquet of trailing purple orchids. Four bridesmaids in similar dresses, all an elegant silvery gray, a shade darker than the bride's. Was Margaret one of them? A small flower girl in a twirl of purple tulle, a little page boy in a gray suit and purple tie. The groom and four groomsmen in black tie, all sporting purple orchid boutonnieres. The entire party, flanked by flowers, posed under a wide flower arch. There was only one . . . oddity.

The groom's face had been cut out.

"James Kelly," Jessica breathed. "He's been defaced."

Hark leaned forward to look. "Well, *hell*," he said. "But maybe not every photo?"

"Maybe not." I leafed rapidly through the remaining pages. Photos of Eleanor with a pair of cute Corgis. Eleanor on a horse, watching a horse race at the new (then) Sam Houston Race Park, Eleanor in her palatial new River Oaks home. With her in many of them was a male. In khakis, a suit, jeans, cargo shorts, bike shorts, swim trunks. A faceless male.

"Margaret must have cut up these photos," Jessica said, thoughtful. "He killed her cousin and she didn't want to look at him. But he was a part of Eleanor's life and these are Eleanor's photographs, so she left him in. Without a face." She looked at Hark. "Did she tell you she was sending this?"

He shook his head. "Not this, specifically. Just said she was thinking of sending something to the person who had called her—to China." He looked at me. "She wanted your mailing address, but I didn't have it, so I gave her mine. I told her I'd make sure you got it."

"But *why?*" Jessica wondered "She was planning to see you today, China. She was expecting us."

"Yeah," Hark said. "Why not just give it to you when you met instead of going to the trouble of wrapping it and taking it to the post office?"

"Your guess is as good as mine," I said. To Hark: "I gave her your number so she could verify Jessica's status. Was that all she asked, or was there something more?"

"It began with Jessica. When I told her that she's our crime-and-cops reporter, she seemed fine with that. She also asked about you." Hark's grin was only slightly malicious. "I told her you're a nosy ex-lawyer who likes to poke around in other people's private business and dig up their old dirty secrets. So she could expect you to ask all kinds of personal questions. No offense, of course."

"Of course." I rolled my eyes. "What else?"

"She asked about Olivia—kept pushing me on what I knew about the hit-and-run. I gather that she hadn't known about it until you told her. She said the Fredericksburg paper didn't cover it. No reason they should," he added. "We're out of their readership area."

I nodded. "She didn't know Olivia was dead. She'd been waiting to hear from her. Or from you. Olivia apparently dropped your name."

"Yeah, that's what she told me. She seemed worried that they haven't arrested the driver. Said she was afraid if they didn't catch him soon, he was going to get away with it." He sat back in his chair. "She's right, of course. Too many hit-and-runs go unsolved."

"Did she seem afraid?" Jessica asked. "Did she say she was worried about her safety?"

Hark shook his head. "Not in so many words. But when she said she might have something to send, I asked her what—sort of joking, you know. I said that the mailroom looks pretty carefully at everything. We always call the police when we get any bombs or envelopes with white powder. She laughed and said it wasn't exactly a bomb. But it crossed my mind that whatever she was sending, it might be something she'd be glad to get out of the house. She didn't want to wait any longer."

"And in a few hours she would be dead," I said soberly.

"She was afraid of *him*," Jessica said, pointing at the album. "Of Kelly. China, it has to be that. She knew Kelly killed her cousin. She knew that Olivia had figured out who he is now and planned to blow his cover. When you told her that Olivia was dead and *how* she died, it had to have frightened her—especially when she learned that you had found her phone number in Olivia's notes. After she talked to Hark, she thought about it some more. After all, she had known Kelly. He had been married to her cousin. She might be the only one still alive who could identify him. She got scared. She began to think he might show up on her doorstep."

"And she was afraid that if he got to her before we did," I said, "the album wouldn't be found. And if it was, that nobody would understand its real significance—even if they wondered about all those mutilated photos. So she wrapped it up and took it to the post office."

"And there's this." Hark turned back to his computer monitor, scrolled through a screen list of emails, marked one, brought up an attachment, and hit the print button. On the floor beside his desk, a printer turned itself on, cleared its throat, and got to work. A moment later, he handed me a document.

"From the chief's office," he said. "Came this afternoon."

It was an amended police report of the hit-and-run on Purgatory Bend Road, updated with the information Rita Kidder and I had uncovered when we went to the site and talked to Gloria Tanner. Rita had done what she'd said she would. It was still an unsolved hit-and-run, but at least the report was complete.

"So it's now clear that we have one killer and two murders," Jessica said, half under her breath. "Olivia Andrews in April. Margaret Greer, last night."

"Make that three." I held up the album. "Except that this one happened twenty years ago."

One plus one plus one equals three.

A matter of simple addition, right?

It would be a while before we found out which of us was wrong.

Chapter Twelve

Yaupon holly (*Ilex vomitoria*) is native to southern North America, as far west as the Texas Hill Country. A small evergreen tree that tolerates heat and drought and produces pretty red berries in winter, yaupon is North America's only indigenous caffeinated plant. One of its historical uses is reflected in its species name: *vomitoria*—so called because some Native American tribes consumed it (in quantity) as a purgative in purification rituals.

Yaupon's caffeine content (around 60 mg per cup) is about a third lower than that of coffee or tea, and its theobromine and theophylline help to boost mental clarity without jitters or stomach upset. During the 1700s, yaupon was grown for export on colonial plantations in the Southeast and marketed across Europe as "Appalachian tea." During the Civil War, it replaced unavailable tea and coffee. In the 1930s and 40s, the federal government included the plant in its Green Belt program, encouraging Southern farmers to plant it as a cash crop alternative to cotton and tobacco. But cheap coffee and tea imports muscled yaupon out of the market and the program never got off the ground.

That's changing. Thanks in part to the internet, demand has soared. Growers are harvesting, roasting, and distributing more than ten thousand pounds of yaupon holly each year.

Look around. You may find your next cuppa growing right outside your door.

China Bayles
"What Am I Forgetting? Herbs to Improve Your Memory"
Pecan Springs Enterprise

S aturdays are always busy at the shop. This one was more so because I was teaching a mini-class on yaupon holly, one in a series of ninety-minute Saturday classes on different herbs. A dozen people had signed up—a manageable size for an enjoyable morning of sharing something useful.

I took my group out to the garden and introduced them to the two yaupon trees growing there so everyone could take a good look, consider how they can be used as landscape plants, and harvest enough leaves for a brew.

Then we trooped over to Thyme Cottage, where we settled down in the great room to talk about the fascinating history of this plant's use by Native Americans, colonialists, and modern growers, as well as the recent scientific interest in its chief bioactive compounds—theobromine and theophylline. We discussed the problematic claims about yaupon as a "detox tea" (not all that different, in intention, from the Native American use of yaupon in purification rituals), and I gave them a handout on both yaupon and its South American cousin, *yerba mate*, with references they could study later.

Then I demonstrated how to roast the fresh leaves and alternatively, dry them for longer storage. We brewed both fresh and dried leaves, drank, and discussed. For comparison, I also brewed a large pot of *yerba mate* so we could taste the difference (which is minor, at least for me). Those who didn't have a yaupon tree in the backyard and wanted to try the tea at home—or try *yerba mate*—could choose from commercial products in the shop.

And then it was time to help Ruby with the Saturday lunch bunch, which kept us busy for the next hour and a half. Finally, when the tearoom had cleared out and the shop traffic had slowed, I grabbed a glass of hibiscus tea and a slice of quiche (today: tomato, basil, and caramelized onions) and sat down behind the counter to catch up on my phone messages.

I called Sheila's office, feeling guilty for not letting her know about what had happened in Fredericksburg. But I would have to feel guilty a while longer, because she was at a conference at the university and wouldn't be out until late afternoon. I connected with Caitie and learned that the wrist was still sore but improving and she planned to be back on Comanche that afternoon. I answered a couple of customers' questions about herbs and fielded an inquiry about the upcoming psychic fair from someone who said that she and a carload of friends planned to drive over from College Station. She had seen a notice of it on social media and mentioned that quite a few people had said they were planning to come. They especially wanted to RSVP for Ashling's talk. They had heard she was totally *awesome*. I had to think for a moment before I remembered that Ashling was Ramona, in her incarnation as a dream coach.

I also talked to McQuaid, who was still on the job out in Midland and not sure when he'd be home. "How's it going there? Any developments on that hit-and-run you were looking into?"

"Jessica and I went to Fredericksburg yesterday," I said. "To see Margaret Greer. The cousin Olivia mentions in her notes."

"Jessica went with you, huh?" I heard the *click-click* of keys. He was doing something on his computer while we talked. "That sounds good. Nice drive? How'd your talk go? Many people?"

"The talk was fine," I said. "It was what we found *before* the talk that wasn't."

"Oh, yeah?" *Click-click.* "What was that?"

"Margaret Greer was dead. We found her body. In the kitchen."

The *click-click* stopped. There was a silence. Then, "Uh-oh," very softly. I had his full attention now. "So tell me."

When I finished my thumbnail sketch of events, he gave an accusing whistle. "I thought I told you to stay out of trouble."

"I would if I could," I said crossly. "Do you think I ordered up a murder just for the heck of it? What happened wasn't my idea, you know."

Wisely, he moved on. "Do you think the woman's murder had anything to do with Olivia's hit-and-run?"

"I do, and with Eleanor Kelly's murder, as well." I told him about the album Margaret Greer had mailed to Hark at the newspaper. "Every single one of the photos of James Kelly has been defaced. Looks like Margaret took the scissors to him, maybe at the point when she inherited the album, after Eleanor's death."

"*O*-kay," he said slowly, making two long syllables of it. "So now you've got two murders. Any idea what's next?"

"Three murders," I said. "Eleanor Kelly."

"Ah," he said. "That one."

"Which brings us to Chuck Loomis," I said. "The former partner of yours at the Houston PD, who might have worked the Kelly murder. Did you ever get in touch with him?"

"Chuck?" He sounded perplexed. "Why? Was I supposed to?"

He had forgotten. I stifled a sigh. "You said you could call," I replied patiently. "If you do connect with him, please ask if he had anything to do with the case and if he did, what he remembers. What kind of evidence did they have against Kelly, for instance? And anything he knows about the vacatur."

"I can do that," McQuaid said slowly. "But when you think about it, does it really seem likely that somebody would kill two people just to keep a vacated conviction a secret? After all, far as the law is concerned, he's clean."

"Yes, he's clean. Unless he's a fugitive. Or thinks he is."

"Thinks he is?"

"Sure. Maybe the DA didn't retry because Kelly fled to Mexico or somewhere and came back with a new identity. If that's the case, he may be afraid that if his real identity and his whereabouts became a matter of public knowledge, the current DA might decide to retry. After all, there's no statute of limitations on murder. Maybe when Olivia threatened to spill the beans, he got scared and killed her to keep her quiet. And then discovered that she had been in contact with his former cousin-in-law. He had to kill *her*—Margaret—because she could identify him."

McQuaid considered that. "But how did Kelly learn about Margaret? And how did he know how to find her?"

"If our theory is correct, he has Olivia's cell phone and maybe her computer. She undoubtedly had notes on her computer—I have several pages of printout. And no doubt used her phone to set up a visit with Margaret."

There was another silence. "Yeah. I can see how that works. Okay, China. It might take a little while to track Loomis down. I haven't talked to him in four or five years. For all I know, he's sunning himself on a beach in Tahiti. But I'll give it a try." He paused. "When I get home, let's dress up and go out to dinner somewhere . . . romantic. Somewhere with tablecloths and candles. We haven't done that in a long time."

"Dress up?" I asked incredulously. "As in a *dress*? And a suit and tie?"

"It does sound a little improbable," he admitted. "When you put it like that."

"If we want a tablecloth and candles, we'll have to drive to Austin. It's hard to find that kind of romance in Pecan Springs."

"You know how I feel about Austin traffic," McQuaid said. "Maybe we should just go to Bean's." Bean's—short for Judge Roy Bean's Bar and Grill—is where we go when we're in the mood for cabrito fajita and nachos loaded to the max.

"We could do that," I agreed. "Besides, I'm not sure I have a dress that would go with a tablecloth and candles. Heels are definitely out. And when was the last time you wore a tie?"

McQuaid laughed. "Okay, Bean's it is, then. See you when I see you."

Still smiling, I put my phone in my pocket and went to wait on Betty Sue Cameron, a friend from our local Myra Merryweather Herb Guild who wanted to create a gift basket of culinary herbs for a June bride.

"It's for my niece," Betty Sue confided. "She's just got her MA in economics and now she's getting married—to a man with two kids in middle school. I don't think the poor thing has ever done more than scramble an egg or maybe pop a frozen pizza in the oven, and now she's going to cook for a family?" She handed me a penciled list. "I was thinking she should start with the basic herbs, along with a copy of the herb society's *Essential Guide to Growing and Cooking with Herbs*. I hope you have that book. Oh, and a couple of little pots of chives for me."

"The book is on the bottom rack in the corner. If I have any chives left, they'll be on the stand just outside the door." I scanned her list.

Rosemary, basil, dill, coriander, mint, parsley, oregano, thyme, sage, garlic. A more than adequate starter set. "I'll get these for you."

I collected the herbs, added packets of parsley and dill seeds and a Thyme and Seasons gift certificate as a get-acquainted present from the shop, and Betty Sue went on her way, happy, with her niece's wedding present and two pots of chives tucked into her tote bag.

I had gone back to the counter to check on some orders when my phone dinged. It was the call I had been waiting for, from my former law firm colleague, Aaron Brooks. I'd been thinking of him off and on all week and had phoned him the evening before, leaving a message and asking him to call me.

Ah, Aaron. It was good, as astonishingly good as it's always been, to hear his deep, resonant voice, the little catch in it when he said "China, is that really *you*? Feels like forever, babe." I could pick his voice out of a crowd's clamor, instantly recognizable, even when we haven't spoken for months. And on the rare occasions when we've managed to spend some time together, it's as if we haven't been apart for more than, oh, an hour or two. There's an instant and almost electric connectivity, the warmth of it essentially unchanged from the last time we connected.

The last time? Aaron almost never gets this far west, and my most recent trip to Houston was almost two years ago. I flushed, remembering. I had gone to his office to get a look at some files that might help explain a mystery I was involved in. Aaron had kissed me, quite effectively, and then said, "Now that we've got that out of the way, we can get on with what you came for." After that, it was business as usual—but I hadn't forgotten. My heart belongs to McQuaid, but I have to confess that it's hard to forget Aaron.*

---

* China saw Aaron most recently when she was investigating a friend's mugging in *Death Come Quickly* (China Bayles #22).

I cleared my throat. "Yes, it's me," I said lightly. "A voice from your dimly remembered criminal past."

Aaron's chuckle was as warm as the brush of his fingers on my cheek. "Dimly remembered? Come on, get real. *Never forgotten* criminal past is more like it. And wasn't it *your* criminal past, too? Whatever we got up to, we got up to together." The springs of a chair squeaked and I pictured him leaning back. "Good to hear from you, love. What's going on out there in the wild Texas boonies? Any chance you're coming my way? It'd be wonderful to see you."

"I wish I were," I said, and in that moment, I really meant it. It's strange how a voice—a sound, a few words, a sentence—can conjure up hours and days and months of experience, experience so suddenly, powerfully real that I was breathless.

Get a grip, I thought, which was exactly what I'd always had to tell myself when this man was around. *Get a grip.*

"But I'm not." I took a breath. "It's a usual Saturday and I'm here at the shop, waiting on customers and wondering about an appellate case our pal Johnnie argued a couple of decades ago. It happened before my time at the firm, before you guys left to hang up your shingle together."

Aaron and Johnnie had moved into an office on University Boulevard, a few blocks from the Rice University campus. They'd asked me to go with them, too—we could be Brooks, Carlson, and Bayles, they said. I liked the sound of it and I was tempted, if only by the prospect of working full-time with Aaron. But I had just enough good sense to know that what the two of us had together was likely to change, which in a partnership environment could turn a romance into a serious problem. There's nothing worse than the on-the-job havoc that is almost unavoidable when you have to work with an ex-lover. Anyway,

I had another dream—the dream I was living now—and Aaron and Johnnie and the law weren't part of it.

"Before we left?" Aaron laughed shortly. "That would be ancient history. What's the case?"

"It *is* ancient history." In a few sentences, I sketched out the details of Eleanor Kelly's death and James Kelly's conviction and subsequent appeal—his successful appeal. "Does that ring a bell?"

"A tinkle, yes." There was a moment's silence, as if he were thinking. Then: "I remember Johnnie talking about it. He hadn't handled all that many appeals at that time—this was one of the early ones. It was an arson case. He seemed to think the guy got a raw deal."

"Johnnie thought everybody got a raw deal," I replied. "That's what made him so good. He had a passion for appellate work. And a gift." Johnnie had been a talented storyteller. He understood the importance of creating a storyline for every case and not straying from the narrative.

"Yeah, that's what he wanted all his clients to think," Aaron said drily. "But I'm talking *really* raw, as in a serious injustice. If I'm remembering right, that is. I may have that case mixed up with something else." He paused. "Too long ago. A couple of centuries at least. So tell me—what's your interest in this prehistoric matter?"

"A current situation here that might involve James Kelly. The vacatur seems to have been a matter of prosecutorial misconduct, so you'd think the DA would be primed for a quick retrial, if only to clean up his image. But that apparently didn't happen. I'd like to know why. Case load? Laziness? Human error? Weak case?"

Aaron joined in the litany. "Missing evidence? Compromised expert witness? Or maybe the DA who won the original conviction was voted out of office and the new guy had different fish to fry."

"Or the DA actually did go after Kelly," I said, "but Kelly couldn't be found. Like, maybe he took off for Mexico or someplace where he could hang out incognito for a few years. Maybe there's still a fugitive warrant out for him." Arrest warrants generally don't expire, and they'll show up on a background check—another good reason, from Kelly's point of view, for some kind of identity swap.

"And you're asking me to find out for you."

"Yes. And I'd love to see a photo of this guy if you can round one up."

"That's a tall order." Aaron's voice became teasingly seductive. "What's in it for me, sweetheart?"

I laughed, remembering how many times he had asked me that question, in just that tone of voice. But that had been a billion years ago, and I'd given him a different answer. Now, with exaggerated primness, I said, "How about dinner? McQuaid and I will have you over for barbeque the next time you're in Pecan Springs. Feel free to bring the current wife. Or the girlfriend. Or come solo. Give us a few days, though. McQuaid's on a case in Midland."

The invitation was sort of a joke, since Aaron rarely ventures out of Houston. And since he's on wife number three, Paula, if I remembered correctly. Apparently he didn't take it that way, though. As a joke.

"Well, dang," he said. "I was hoping maybe we could . . . You know. Like old times." He sounded wistful. "Remember how I'd show up at your door, uninvited, with a bucket of Kentucky Fried and that cheap wine you liked. What was it? An Italian Prosecco? We must've drunk gallons of the stuff."

"Nino Franco Rustico Superiore Valdobbiadene." I laughed. "I'm surprised that you remember. I haven't thought of it in years. I wonder if I could find a bottle here in Pecan Springs."

"Of course I haven't forgotten." His voice dropped. "Good times, weren't they?"

"They were," I said lightly. "But nothing lasts forever."

"That's what Paula says, too." There was a moment's silence. "Actually, our conversation is timely, China. I need to be in Austin next week. I don't think I can manage dinner, but how about lunch? I can drive down to Pecan Springs."

"Of course. It will be good to see you again." I said it as if I meant it, which I did. They *were* good times. And McQuaid would likely be home.

"It will." He was emphatic. "And there's no longer a wife. Paula and I have split. The divorce is in the works. An expensive divorce, I regret to say."

"Oh, sorry," I said, but without a lot of conviction. I hadn't been a fan of Paula. She was a stunning, mega-smart assistant DA, formidable in the courtroom and probably in bed, too—none of which had anything to do with the way I felt about her, I reminded myself hastily. I wasn't terribly surprised to hear about the divorce. In the high-powered, torqued-up planet on which Aaron and Paula lived and worked, a long-term relationship had a brutally short half-life. I remembered this uncomfortable fact all too well, because I had lived on that planet once. Punishing schedules, competing interests, nerves like frayed electrical wires, ready to short out and spark a fire. And always the queasy feeling that we were like trains passing on parallel tracks, briefly side by side but heading in opposite directions.

"Sorry?" Aaron chuckled ironically. "Hey, don't be. It'll all work out, you know. And it's not unexpected. The kind of work we do is hard on a marriage."

"Tell me about it," I said. "My father was a career lawyer. My mother was a career alcoholic."

"And you and I—" There was a sharp *ding* in the background. "A call on the other phone," he said. "Gotta take this one, sweetheart. I'll see what I can dig up on your Kelly business. Don't forget—we're doing lunch. I'll call you soonest. Until then, consider yourself kissed all over."

Click. He was gone.

I was standing there with my phone in my hand, slightly flushed and tingling from my involuntary consideration of his last few words, when Ruby came in from her shop, frowning. She was cool today in shades of green, from her lime sandals and leggings to her leaf-green print tunic and the grass-green silk scarf tied around her orangey-red hair. She looked terrific. But she didn't look happy.

"Uh-oh," I said. "What's wrong?"

She rolled her eyes. "Guess."

"Bigger than a breadbox?" I despise guessing games. "Tell me," I commanded.

"Well, it's a couple of things." Ruby held up her phone. "The first one is Mrs. Pickle. I just got off the phone with her and she said—"

"Pickle. On the other side of Crockett, right? Just east of the restaurant parking lot?"

"That's her. Almira Pickle."

I shuddered. The Universe must be putting some special synergy to work here. Almira Pickle bears a strikingly distinct physical resemblance to Almira Gulch (aka the Wicked Witch of the West, voted one of the fifty best movie villains of all time) in *The Wizard of Oz*, which Caitie insists on watching a couple of times a year. And there's more to the similarity than just appearance. While most of our neighbors are tolerant, live-and-let-live types, Almira (like the Wicked Witch) feels she has received a special mandate to impose her beliefs on her neighbors. This has resulted in several unpleasant encounters. During the last months of the pandemic, for instance, when we were still asking all our customers to mask, Almira refused. She wore a big anti-vax button, too, making her position even clearer.

I didn't want to ask, but I had to. "Why did Almira Pickle phone you?"

"To tell me that she's joined that new church—Truth Seekers, it's called."

Truth Seekers. That would be the Reverend Jeremy Kellogg's latest church. But what did that have to do with anything? "And she was calling about—"

Ruby looked pained. "About the psychic fair. She says it's the work of the devil—fortune telling and tarot and astrology and it can't be allowed to happen in our neighborhood. She says her pastor agrees with her. Reverend Kellogg."

"Really?" I raised both eyebrows. "Has Mrs. Pickle or Jeremy Kellogg ever stepped foot in your shop? Do they know what goes on *there*? Fortune telling, tarot, astrology, rune stones, pendulums. All sorts of devil-raising activities. You're in the neighborhood, too. And you happen. Every day."

Ruby made a face. "She doesn't like that, either. But she says she's never objected to what I do so long as I do it behind closed doors. The psychic fair is different, out in public where everybody can see, with costumes and things that might entice the children to be curious about tarot and astrology—'deviltry,' she called it, among other things. She's organizing a group of the church members who live around here. They're going to file a complaint at the city planning department, saying that the fair will create a neighborhood nuisance." Her voice was apprehensive. "And Reverend Kellogg is encouraging her to protest. In front of our shops, the way they did at Dos Amigas last June."

"Oh, yes. The Dos Amigas protest." The restaurant had hosted a Pride drag event that the protesters didn't like. Ruby and I had watched with growing concern as more and more protesters gathered, booing and shouting and carrying the kind of ugly signs you see on TV, signs you hope will never show up in your town. They kept people away from the restaurant, and kept our customers away, too. One even called us to ask that we let her know when things settled down so she could come and buy what she needed. This tense and scary situation went on for a couple of hours and promised to continue for the rest of the day.

But finally a group of people attending the event—choir members from a different church—went out on the patio, linked arms, and started singing "We Are the World," louder and louder. They knew all the verses, too, bless them. Confronted by that peaceful, heartfelt demonstration, the protesters finally just melted away.

"Kellogg was behind that episode, too," Ruby added with a sigh. "I don't think he's a very nice man."

Kellogg again. He wasn't content with pinching avocados. I patted Ruby's arm reassuringly.

"Don't worry about it, Ruby. The complaint isn't going to be a problem. We've got our permit. Mrs. Baggett is pretty strict about things, but I don't think she'll do anything more than tell us to keep the noise down, or make us close at six. As for the protests—well, I wouldn't worry. If you ask me, they'll probably attract attention. Make people curious."

"I suppose it could even increase the attendance," Ruby said. "It could be like telling folks there's something really evil about a drag show. But everybody thinks of Mrs. Doubtfire or Tony Curtis and Jack Lemmon in *Some Like It Hot*. They want to know what's so bad about drag."

I frowned. "Wait a minute. You said 'a couple of things.' The protest is one. What's the other?"

Ruby cleared her throat. "The permit. It seems . . .well, we've run into a bit of a problem."

"A problem with the permit?" That didn't sound good. "What kind of problem?"

"Well, we don't have one. A permit, I mean. At least, not yet."

"We don't have one?" My voice went up a notch. "*Why* don't we have one?"

"Because Ramona didn't do what she was supposed to do," Ruby confessed. "She said she went online and got the form she needed and started to fill it out and then . . . well, she didn't. Submit it, I mean."

"Or pay the fee?"

"Or pay the fee."

"Then we'd better not trust Ramona to do it. Maybe you'd better go to the planning department first thing Monday morning. We need to be sure it gets done." I knew I wasn't being very gracious, but *really*. I straightened my shoulders. "What's the city's deadline for a June event?"

"Um . . ." Ruby closed her eyes. "Friday."

"Good." I was relieved. "Next Friday. We've got almost a week to get it done."

"No." Ruby opened her eyes. "Last Friday. Yesterday."

"Last Friday? Oh, *no!*" I shook my head in dismay. "And Mrs.

Baggett is such a stickler when it comes to deadlines. She won't want to cut us any slack on this."

"I am so sorry, China. I tried to impress the importance of this on Ramona but she doesn't always listen." She gave me a small smile, meant to be helpful. "How about if we tell Ramona that she has to reschedule the fair? Put it off for a week or two, until mid-July, maybe. We're pretty busy right now, anyway, with Lori's weaving guild show coming up and another catering event, as well as the barbeque out at Cassidy Warren's ranch next weekend. What would you think of rescheduling?"

"That might work as far as the permitting is concerned," I said. "And it's certainly true that we have plenty on our plates. But our advertising is already out there. It's on our website and on social media, and we're already getting calls from people who are planning to come. All that will have to be changed. And if Mrs. Pickle goes to the planning department on Monday and registers a big complaint, she will poison the well. Mrs. Baggett will tell her we have no permit. Then Mrs. Pickle will complain that we're having a fair *without* a permit and probably show her our advertising. Mrs. Baggett will then get the city's rent-a-lawyer to send us a cease-and-desist letter, threaten to impose a fine, and flag us as nasty, careless people who can't be trusted to follow the rules—unworthy of future permits."

Ruby heaved a resigned sigh. "Well, I guess Ramona and I had better be at Mrs. Baggett's door when she unlocks it on Monday morning. We'll explain the whole thing and throw ourselves on her mercy. I'll also get Ramona to finish the paperwork and write a check so we'll be ready if Mrs. Baggett lets us go ahead with the original date—or even if she makes us reschedule."

"I wouldn't take Ramona, if I were you," I said. "You know what happens when your sister gets frustrated. Her inner poltergeist comes out. Things . . . happen." I could picture Ramona losing her cool, papers flying, pencils dancing across the desk, the computer monitor flashing, the office printer spitting out reams of paper.

I didn't have to spell it out. Ruby shuddered. "You're right. Ramona might not behave herself. I'll go. By myself. First thing Monday."

"And be sure and tell Mrs. Baggett that Mrs. Pickle and Reverend Kellogg are planning to see her," I said. "I don't think she'll buy their argument that Satan is running the show. That's just a personal belief—and a weak argument. But she might ask you about parking. And noise. And traffic and crowd control."

"I'll be prepared," Ruby said. "I'm sorry, China."

Impulsively, I hugged her. "I'm sorry, too, Ruby. I wasn't very nice. I apologize."

And then both our phones rang at once. The Castle Oaks Nursing Home was calling Ruby about her mother. She waggled a goodbye to me and turned to go back to her shop, phone to her ear.

My call was from Chuck Loomis. "Miz McQuaid?" he asked.

"That's me," I said. It's not a name I use but it's technically correct. And sometimes it's just easier to skip the explanation. "But please, call me China. So Mike was able to reach you?"

"China? Now, that's a weird name. People must ask you about that all the time." His voice was gravelly but relaxed and pleasant. "Yeah, Mike caught me out here on Brays Bayou with a fishing rod in my hand. Best place to be on a June afternoon in Houston. There's even a little breeze."

"Brays Bayou?" I was surprised. It's an urban waterway, channelized and cemented, running down the middle of a thirty-one-mile-long green strip park, right through one of the busiest cities on the continent. In the background, I could hear the roar of traffic. "You can actually *fish* in Brays Bayou?"

"Oh, you bet. I'm in my boat just west of the 610 Loop today. Over the years, I've caught a dozen different kinds of fish out of this water. Largemouth bass, crappie, catfish, sunfish, Rio Grande perch, longnose gar, spotted gar. You never know what you're going to get, which is part of the fun of it. And you have to be good—these fish spook easy."

"I don't suppose you actually eat them," I said warily.

"Nah. Mercury, PCBs, dioxin. But I'm good with catch and release. That way, you don't have to clean 'em." He chuckled. "You ever skin a catfish? Not my idea of a way to spend an hour."

I cleared my throat. "Did McQuaid tell you that I'm curious about a case you might have worked on? A woman named Eleanor Kelly, in River Oaks. Murder one, arson." I gave him the date.

"Yeah, that's what he said. Long time ago—hard to remember details. How come you're asking?"

"A friend has an interest," I replied evasively. "I told her I'd look into it. Am I talking to the right guy?"

"Yep. That was my—" There was a loud *splash* and a muffled "*What the devil?*" then "Hang on a minute. Something weird goin' on here." The phone was dropped, followed by a series of mysterious scuffling, scraping, banging noises, a few muttered curses, and another *splash*.

"Sorry," he said. "Had to get a snapping turtle off the hook. Jeez. That sucker must've weighed thirty pounds. Lose a damn finger if you're not careful." A couple of metallic clanks, maybe the lid of a bait can. "Where were we?"

"You were saying you worked on the Kelly case."

"Yeah, I did." His voice took on a gritty edge. "The fire marshal and I were sore as hell when that SOB lawyer got the conviction vacated. 'Prosecutorial misconduct.'" He snorted contemptuously. "We got it right. Kelly was guilty as sin, and the jury agreed. Put that guy away for life. But the damn prosecutor had to go and screw it up."

I wanted to say *Screw-ups happen. That's what appeals are all about.* But I held my tongue. "It was an arson fire, I understand. Do you remember the details?"

"Yeah. Unusual, a fire in that ritzy neighborhood." He rattled off items, fast. "Burn patterns on the floor and walls, puddle configurations, pour patterns, crazed glass in the bedroom window—all classic indicators. The victim was in bed, doped up on Quaaludes and alcohol. The autopsy also showed Percodan, Demerol, some other stuff I don't remember. Died of smoke inhalation."

All circumstantial. "What evidence did you have tying the husband to the crime?"

This answer came a little slower. "Well, he bought the Quaaludes, which you could still get back then, if you knew where to look. Plus, he was a much younger guy involved in a homosexual relationship with a male dancer. The motive was money. *Her* money, of course," he added. "That what you're looking for?"

I didn't want to rub it in, but I had to ask. "That's it for direct evidence?"

There was a brief silence. "It was enough," he said. "Didn't take the jury long to come back with a verdict. Four hours, as I remember. *They* got the picture."

"Hmm." I paused. "Four hours is a strong jury response. And the appeal was decided only on the prosecutor's error—right?" And then the crucial question for me. "I'm wondering why the DA didn't retry right away."

"I wondered too," Loomis said. "Like I said, we put together a good case. I kept expecting to hear something—like maybe the prosecutor's office asking for new evidence or taking another look at what we already had. Or maybe a plea deal in the works. But then a new DA came in and things . . ." He exhaled noisily. "Who knows what the hell goes on in that office when nobody's looking? Anyway, I was done. And plenty busy with other stuff."

That didn't surprise me. A cop's job on a case is finished when he steps out of the witness box after redirect and recross. What happens after that—it's not his innings. He's done what he can. He's out. He moves on.

"And then, of course," he added, "it didn't matter."

I frowned. "What do you mean, 'it didn't matter'?"

"What I said. Case closed. End of story. Nothing more to see here. Guy's dead."

"Dead? Who's dead?" My jaw dropped. My heart skipped a couple of beats, stopped, started again. "Kelly? Kelly's *dead*?"

"Yeah, Kelly." He was wryly amused. "That's who we've been talkin' about, ain't it?"

I gulped a breath. "When? Where?" Another breath. "How do you know?"

"You mean, *you* didn't?" Loomis chuckled. "Well, shit. Pardon my French, but I could have told you that up front. I figured you knew and just wanted to hear about the way the case got worked, maybe about the vacatur. Yeah, sure. He's dead."

"When?" I repeated incredulously. "Where?"

"Oh, two, maybe three years after the vacatur. Mexico someplace, couldn't say for sure. The guy wasn't under travel restrictions. He was free as a bird, could go wherever he wanted. And I wasn't keeping an eye on him. Somebody happened to mention it in a briefing, then I saw it in the newspaper."

"In the *Houston Chronicle*?"

"Yeah, probably. But there wasn't much detail, just something about an auto accident, car off the road, over a cliff, a fire." A chuckle. "Ironic, wouldn't you say? Kills his wife in an arson fire, dies in a fire when his car goes over a cliff. Justice served."

"I suppose the body was burned beyond recognition." Heavy snark. "So no photos."

"Probably. I don't remember." He paused. "Hey. Where'd you get that? Thought you said you didn't know anything about this."

I shook my head. Well, that little detail—Kelly's death—explained why the DA didn't retry, appeal, drop the charges, or get to work on a plea deal. Kelly was dead. Or to rephrase: the DA *believed* that Kelly was dead, which (true or not) amounted to pretty much the same thing, as far as the case was concerned.

But Olivia didn't think so. Somewhere, somehow, she had come across something that convinced her that James Kelly was alive. And living comfortably under a new identity in Pecan Springs, safe in the assumption that nobody would ever know who he had been before he became who he was now. Was she *right*?

The bait can lid rattled again. "Hey," Loomis said. "You still there?"

"Still here," I said. "But I should let you get back to your fishing. And thanks. You've been very helpful. Very. I really appreciate it."

"No problem. Listen, you tell that hubby of yours to pack his rod and come on down. I'll show him some good spots. Maybe he'll pull in a six-foot alligator gar. Some guy did that a while back, down at the eastern end of the bayou. Hundred and thirty pounds. Hundred and thirty! Whale of a fish story, but he's got a photo to prove it."

"I'll tell him," I promised insincerely. But if I did, McQuaid would probably still prefer Canyon Lake, where the interstate is twenty miles away and the only sound is the clamor of ducks and geese and the quiet lapping of waves against the boat. Where you can eat the fish you catch—at least, that's what I would have said last week.

Except that just the day before yesterday, I read a warning from Texas Parks and Wildlife against eating striped bass from Canyon Lake more than once a month. Mercury, they say. Can you believe that? Mercury, in Canyon Lake? It's everywhere.

And James Kelly is dead. A whale of a fish story—if only there were a photo to prove it.

Chapter Thirteen

Queso Dip with Chorizo

1 tablespoon vegetable oil
4 ounces fresh chorizo, cooked and drained
2 cloves garlic, minced
1/2 sweet onion, diced
1 poblano chile, minced
2 tablespoons all-purpose flour
1 1/4 cups whole milk
1 Roma tomato, diced
1 8-ounce package shredded Monterey Jack cheese
1 8-ounce package shredded Pepper Jack cheese
Salt, pepper to taste

Heat oil in a large skillet over medium heat. Add chorizo and cook until browned, 5–8 minutes. Drain excess fat; transfer to a paper towel–lined plate. Add garlic, onion, and poblano to the skillet. Sauté until onions are translucent, 3–4 minutes. Stir in flour until lightly browned, about 1 minute. Reduce heat. Gradually stir in milk and tomato. Cook, stirring constantly, until thickened, 4–5 minutes. Gradually add cheeses and stir until smooth. Add cooked chorizo. Season with salt and pepper.

J essica had a similar reaction.

"Dead?" she yelped. She stared at me over her glass of wine. "You're saying that Kelly is *dead*?"

We were sharing happy hour munchies—a basket of Maria Lopez' warm blue corn tortilla chips, and queso with chorizo sausage—on the Dos Amigas patio, across the street from the shops. To the muted accompaniment of mariachi music on the garden loudspeaker, I had given Jessie an abbreviated play-by-play of my conversations with Aaron Brooks and Chuck Loomis, omitting the lurid details of my once-upon-a-time romance with Aaron and Loomis' thirty-pound snapping turtle.

"No, I am *not* saying he's dead," I replied emphatically. "What I'm saying is that the report of his death would have been more or less welcome in the DA's office. The delay in going to retrial suggests that they were worried they might have an iffy case, primarily circumstantial, and arson science has been constantly evolving. My guess: when word of the Mexican car wreck reached Houston, the DA was glad to close the case. And that was the end of James Kelly, as far as they were concerned."

She put down her wine and picked up a chip. "So you're saying he's alive."

"I'm saying we don't know. The *Chronicle* article Loomis mentioned might be a good place to start. With luck, it could give us a date and a place where we could—maybe—find a Mexican death certificate."

"But even if we do, it might not tell us much," Jessica observed. She dipped her chip in the queso. "This stuff is yummy. I wonder how hard it is to make."

"Not hard at all," I said. "Remind me, and I'll give you a recipe. And you're right. A death certificate won't tell us for sure whether the dead body in the fiery car crash at the bottom of a Mexican cliff actually belonged to James Kelly, even if it was carrying Kelly's wallet and identification papers."

I sipped my wine, thinking of McQuaid's story about the Costa Rican pseudocide. "And it won't tell us—as a for-instance—whether the real Kelly might have died six months later of too much tequila. Or whether he's still alive and living in Pecan Springs, where Olivia discovered his identity and threatened to tell his story. All of it. Including his death. Which might, at the least, be embarrassing. At the worst, it could raise a whole flock of new questions. *Somebody* died in that car, apparently. If not Kelly, who?"

Jessica brushed chip crumbs off her red blazer. "You haven't found anything in Olivia's papers? The boxes her sister stashed in the storage unit—you took them home to look through, didn't you?"

"Yes, I took them home. And no, I didn't find anything in them— anything related to her Kelly investigation, I mean. Nothing related to Margaret Greer, either. I went through the remaining two boxes last night after I got home from our visit with Hark. Nothing but a couple of old manuscripts, notebooks on different writing projects. To-do lists, tax records, credit card statements, that kind of thing. They're out in the car right now. The boxes, I mean. I'm taking them back to the Store-It-Rite when we're done here."

Jessica's hand hovered over the last tortilla chip. "Mine?" she asked. When I nodded, she took it. "We don't have Olivia's computer. But how about flash drives, memory sticks, maybe even floppy disks or SD cards? Or maybe she saved her files in the cloud?"

"Nada." I shook my head. "I was hoping I'd find some storage devices. A flash drive tucked into an envelope, maybe, or just floating around loose in one of the boxes somewhere. But there was nothing like that. It was all *paper*. And not a scrap of it related to James Kelly. Or to Eleanor Kelly, or to an arson murder in Houston or to Margaret Greer." I paused. "I haven't gotten around to cloud storage, though. I wonder if Zelda knows anything about that."

"But even if there's cloud storage," Jessica pointed out, "we probably can't access it unless we have Olivia's computer."

"Not even then. There are laws about that. But Zelda is Olivia's executor. I'm planning to call her tomorrow and update her on what's been going on. I'll ask her to see what she can figure out for us. She may need a court order."

"I have online access to the *Houston Chronicle* digital archives," Jessica said. "Tomorrow, I'll spend some time looking for that article. The archives aren't a hundred percent complete, but it might be worth the effort. With luck, maybe I'll find a photo."

"Good," I said. "Any details you can dredge up would be welcome. A photo, especially. We really need a photo—full face, if possible. It's pretty hard for a guy to change his facial structure. And if he believes he's safe because he's dead, maybe he hasn't bothered." I thought of something else. "What about Jeremy Kellogg? Jeremy *Q.* Kellogg. Making any progress with—"

Someone came up behind me and put a warm hand on my shoulder. A woman said, "Hey, China. And hello, Jessica. Nice to see you both."

I looked up. "Oh, hi, Janie." It was one of the restaurant's pair of owners, Janie and Janet, who look so much alike (long auburn hair parted in the middle, bright smiles, dark eyes and dimples) that people regularly confuse them. Ruby, Cass, and I have gotten to know the pair pretty well over the past several years. They invited us to plant and maintain their restaurant herb garden (in return for free advertising on their menu). And we sometimes ask them to partner with us on large catering events, like Cassidy Warren's barbeque, coming up next weekend. They were lending us a couple of servers.

Usually, Janie is all smiles, a gracious host. Today, though, she looked concerned. She bent closer and lowered her voice, speaking just to me. "Excuse me for interrupting. I won't take a minute. I just wanted to tell you that I overheard one of our neighbors—Almira Pickle, who lives on the other side of the parking lot—talking about you and Ruby."

I made a face. "She probably didn't have anything good to say."

"She didn't, and she said it so loud, I couldn't help overhearing. I was parking my car in the shade of the big pecan on that side of our lot. She was talking . . . well, plotting is more like it . . . with somebody from her church. They were sitting in Almira's backyard, discussing ways to cause trouble at an event you and Ruby are planning. A psychic fair, something like that. Almira says you're committing child abuse."

"We probably are," I agreed. "We're showing the kids a few different ways to think about the Universe. But that's not in Almira's playbook. In her view, she's protecting the neighborhood children from the devil's vile influence. I understand that she intends to file a complaint with Mrs. Baggett at the city planning department."

"She's also organizing a protest," Janie said. "She says that the fair is all about grooming kids to become astrologers and fortune tellers—worshippers of Satan." She lowered her voice again. "And they're not just planning to picket your shops, either. They're going to boycott you. Worse yet, they're planning to *bomb* you."

"Bomb us?" I scoffed. "That's crazy."

"Not that kind of bombing," Janie said. "Review bombing. People do it on the internet, when there's something they don't like. She dreamed that an angel told her how to do it on Facebook and Yelp. She says she *has* to do it, because the message came from an angel."

A dream? Almira was unhappy with us because we're featuring astrologers and palm readers and she's following an angelic operating manual that was delivered to her in a freaking *dream*?

216

"But review bombing can be really bad, too." Jessica leaned across the table to join the conversation. "That happened to a beauty salon in San Antonio last year. The owner was involved in a local hot-button political issue and people posted hundreds of one-star reviews to her Yelp page. She went out of business."

"Yelp tries to stay on top of that," I said. "When they see a blizzard of reviews that look phony they post an alert on your page. But their filters sometimes miss the activity—and when they do, it may be too late." I looked at Janie. "Did Almira sound like she was serious about weaponizing Yelp?"

"Oh, you bet, China," Janie said fervently. "That minister of theirs—Kellogg, his name is—he's involved as well. He's been telling them it's their duty to protest in any way they can. And when they do, he wants them to cause as much trouble as they can—without actually getting arrested, of course. Remember the group that boycotted us during Pride Month last year? This is the same bunch. If they had their way, they would have closed us down for good, just because of who we are."

"I remember," I said grimly. Ruby and I had watched nervously as the anti-LGBTQ protests had gathered steam across the street. But it hadn't occurred to either of us that a simple psychic fair would be accused of child abuse. Or that something so innocent might evoke deviltry—of the human kind.

"It's that avocado pincher again," Jessica said. "I'm thinking that the *Enterprise* ought to do a story on this thing. On the protest they're planning."

"Oh, don't," Janie said. "That's exactly what they want. Media attention. For their cause. And we don't want to encourage anybody to join them."

"It depends on the media attention," I said. "I'm sure Jessica's story would *discourage* protest."

"But you can't tell in advance who will show up," Janie said. "When they picketed us, we were lucky that the choir was here—the group that came out on the patio and started singing. Otherwise, it could have gotten really ugly." She looked at me, her expression dark. "If they picket your event, it's going to cause traffic problems and bring the police to the neighborhood. And of course there's always the threat of violence. Almira said they are planning to recruit protesters on social media, and I'm sure some of them will be carrying guns. Janet and I would love it if you could do something to *stop* them."

She was right about the guns. Texas is open carry, no license required. "I'm afraid we can't stop them," I said. "The sidewalk is a public space and they have a First Amendment right to express their views. But we'll certainly do our best to defuse the situation." I glanced across the table. "And if the *Enterprise* wants to cover the fair, of course we would love it. We can always use publicity."

"I'll talk to Hark about it." Jessica shouldered her bag and pushed back her chair. "China, I need to be on my way. I'll call you with an update on that archive research." She pushed some money across the table. "My share of the happy hour tab."

"Put that away," Janie said. "You two are on the house." She turned to me. "China, we're doing an event together next weekend, I understand. Out at the Warren ranch."

"I'm looking forward to it," I said enthusiastically. "And I'm very glad your folks will be helping us out, Janie. Fifty is really too big an event for our team to handle on our own."

Janie smiled. "I'm sure it'll be a huge success."

"So am I," I replied.

Little did we know.

The traffic on King Road was manageable, the drive was almost pleasant, and by the time I got to Olivia's Store-It-Rite unit 126, the evening air was cool. I parked out in front, punched the code into the lock on the roll-up door, and turned on the overhead fluorescents.

In the doorway, I stood still, looking around, frowning a little. Something seemed . . . different, not quite the way I remembered it. What was it? After a moment, I realized that the heavy mustiness that had greeted me on my first visit was lightened now by a faintly lingering, almost ghostly fragrance. Jasmine, was it, and nutmeg? But the outdoor air that flooded through the open door was heavily scented with the exhaust of a truck with the motor running across the way, and the fugitive fragrance was overtaken by the kerosene-stink of diesel before I got more than a brief whiff of it. All I could smell was the diesel. If there had been anything else, it was entirely possible that I had imagined it.

I shook my head and got to work, toting the five boxes from my car to the front corner of the unit where I had originally found them, stacked just inside the door. I was glad when the job was finished, although disappointed that I hadn't found what I had been looking for—what Zelda had been so confident I would find. Something that would take me deeper into the James Kelly story, give me a clue to where to look next. If Olivia had left a paper trail behind, it wasn't in those boxes.

I pulled out my phone to check the time. Pushing eight o'clock. The animals would be waiting for their dinners. I was thinking that it was time I locked up and headed home when my glance was caught by the glint of a small silvery scrap, like the torn corner of a foil gum wrapper. It was lying on a dried footprint—a footprint that had once been *muddy*—on the cement floor of the narrow center aisle.

A footprint? I blinked. A *muddy* footprint?

Then I saw that there were several other muddy footprints, a chain of them, leading toward the rear of the unit. They were too smudged to tell much about shape and size, but I knew they weren't mine. It had been hot and dusty-dry when I was here on Wednesday. These footprints had to have been made on Thursday, when it had rained hard enough that customers tracked mud into my shop. When it had rained hard enough to create mud in front of this unit. Which meant . . .

I stood there for a moment, sorting this out. Then I went to my car and retrieved the flashlight I keep under the driver's seat. The overhead fluorescents didn't throw enough light on the situation. I needed more. For a closer look.

On Wednesday, all I had done was pick up the five boxes Zelda had stacked just inside the door and leave again. I hadn't bothered to examine anything else stored in the unit. Now, I poked my nose and my flashlight into everything—the boxes, laundry baskets, furniture. The china cabinet, the loveseat, the side tables, the desk.

After a half hour, I was a lot dustier and a little bit wiser. From the footprints on the floor and the disturbed dust on the furniture, I concluded that sometime on Thursday, when it was raining, someone had entered Olivia's storage unit. Someone who had walked up the narrow central aisle from the front all the way to the back. Someone who had made a thorough search, going through the boxes, looking into the china cabinet, pulling out the drawers in the tables, opening the rolltop desk.

Someone who knew the gate code and the code to the lock on the door.

Someone compelled to search through Olivia's stored possessions.

Why? Looking for what? For the same thing I was? For papers, journals, diaries, notes? For clues Olivia might have left to James Kelly's past and current identities? Clues he had to destroy before someone else found them and learned what he had done, who he had been, who he was now?

I took a deep breath. Had he found what he came for? If he had, it was gone, like Olivia's computer and the phone—where he'd likely found the address and codes that he used to unlock the doors. I looked around. The pale fluorescents cast a ghostly blue glow across the boxes and the furniture, the sad leavings of a life that was taken, of other lives that were gone. The tables, the tall china cabinet, the velvet loveseat, Olivia's vintage rolltop desk.

The desk. I stood still, staring at it. My grandmother China Bayles, my New Orleans grandmother, who taught me to love gardens and had planted the seeds of my present life—*she* had had a desk like that. For me, it had been a delicious, delightful place of mysteries. A desk with half-a-dozen secret spaces, little cubbies hidden behind a shelf, under a drawer, inside a secret panel. When I was a girl, I loved to play at her desk, exploring all the secret spaces she had shown me, and leaving little trinkets and notes to myself, treasures to be rediscovered on my next visit. Zelda had said that her sister used this desk regularly. What if she—

I slid the desk lid open and shined my flashlight across its drawers and panels. This one was very like my grandmother's, and in the next few minutes, I had located three of the secret hiding places I had found when I was a kid. One was under a false drawer bottom. Another was behind a panel behind a shelf. Still another was at the back of a drawer. It was the fourth space, behind the carved rosette in the center panel, that held what I was looking for—what *he* had missed.

A thumb drive.

Chapter Fourteen

Since the days of the Greeks and Romans, rosemary has been recognized as a memory booster, and its usefulness has been demonstrated in a number of scientific studies in the past half-century.

- A study at the University of Northumbria showed that the scent of rosemary helped to enhance what is called prospective memory: for instance, remembering to fetch that book from the shelf in the hall.
- Other research has looked at the effect on cognition of the scent of rosemary. In one study, students were asked to recall images and numbers. The stronger the scent, the better the participants' speed and accuracy.
- A study published in *Psychogeriatrics* tested the effects of rosemary oil aromatherapy on twenty-eight elderly dementia and Alzheimer's patients and found evidence to suggest that its properties can prevent or perhaps slow Alzheimer's disease.

China Bayles
"What Am I Forgetting? Herbs to Improve Your Memory"
Pecan Springs Enterprise

Whatever you do," McQuaid commanded, "do *not* plug that drive into your computer." There was a pause. "You haven't, have you?" he added warily.

I dropped the thumb drive on the WWI wooden artillery case that serves as our coffee table and sat down in my recliner. "Not yet," I said into my phone, "but I was about to."

"Set phasers on stun," Spock shouted from his perch in the corner of the living room. "Engage."

McQuaid breathed an audible sigh of relief. "Well, *don't*. The damn thing could be loaded with malware. Our computers are net-worked. If you infect yours, you'll infect mine. Which will infect the office, which—"

"But I really need to see what's on that drive," I protested. "And it came out of Olivia's desk. I'm sure it doesn't have any—"

"The only thing you can be sure about where malware is concerned is that you can never be sure." His voice became measured. "Do. Not. Plug. That. Thing. In."

"But if I can't plug it in, how am I supposed to find out what's on it?" I asked, trying to keep my voice level. "I'm running out of places to look for information, McQuaid. I am *sure* there's something important on this, or Olivia wouldn't have taken the trouble to conceal it. And the only way to read it is to plug it in and—"

"Boldly go," Spock squawked cheerfully, but McQuaid didn't agree.

"Wait, China. How do you know it was Olivia Andrews who hid that drive?"

"How do I—" Silly question. "Well, for starters, it was in Olivia's desk, in her locked storage unit, where her sister had put it. What's more, somebody else was there looking for it, too. James Kelly, I mean—whoever he is now. But Olivia was the one who hid it and I was the one who found it."

"Dor-sho-gha!" Spock urged, fluttering his wings. *Dor-sho-gha*, Brian tells me, is Klingon for "Get on with it, damn it!"

"Maybe not," McQuaid replied, in that coolly logical, masculine tone that is calculated to drive me absolutely nuts. "Maybe *he* was the one who hid it. The muddy footprints guy, I mean."

"But that's *crazy!*" I objected. "Why would he go to the trouble of—"

"Happens all the time. It's what keeps security professionals up at night."

"I am the Borg," Spock announced. "Resistance is futile!"

I raised the recliner footrest. I had opened the door to one of my husband's favorite rants: cybersecurity. We were going to be here a while.

"In fact," he went on, "the Department of Homeland Security did a security penetration test a year or two ago. They had DHS staff plant data disks and USB flash drives in federal agency and contractor parking lots. Sixty percent of the drops were picked up by employees and plugged into company and agency computers. Sixty percent!"

"But why would James Kelly go to the trouble of—"

"And when the disk or drives had a company logo on it, fully *ninety* percent of the pickups got plugged in. People want to be helpful to their employer. And they're curious. They don't stop to think that they might be infecting the company computers. That was probably how the Stuxnet worm got into that Iranian nuclear plant a few years ago. And then escaped into the wild. It infected networks all over the world. It was a huge hot mess."

I tried reason. "All that may be true, McQuaid, but it's beside the point. What I'm saying is that James Kelly would have no reason to put malware on a USB drive and hide it in that desk. He could have no idea that anybody—"

Spock executed a neat three-sixty on his perch. "Look under the hood, Scotty," he cried triumphantly.

"He might be doing it to throw you off the track," McQuaid said. "To deflect your investigation. Or to steal data from you, monitor your screen, listen in on your keyboard, encrypt your files, spread infections across the network. *Our* network."

"But he doesn't know I exist. That I'm looking for him, I mean."

"Margaret Greer didn't know he was looking for her, either." McQuaid's tone was ominous. "And she's dead."

"That hardly follows," I objected. "For one thing—"

"China, you need to take this seriously. Here's what I want you to do. Call Blackie. Tell him to put you in touch with the guy who did the malware work on the Foster case for us. Jerry something, in computer science at the university. I can't remember his last name, but Blackie will. Talk to Jerry. He'll figure it out for you."

"But it's Saturday night," I said. "I probably can't get this Jerry guy until next week!"

"Then you'll just have to wait, won't you." His voice softened. "I'm looking forward to getting home, hon. Probably Monday. We can talk about it then."

There was no point in arguing with this man. I sighed. "Okay. Miss you. Love you." Meaning that whatever little tiff we might be having at the moment, life was going on and so were we.

"Miss you and love you too," he said.

"Miss miss miss." Spock scratched himself enthusiastically. "Love love love."

I clicked off and sat, staring in frustration at the thumb drive on the coffee table in front of me. Was it full of the information I needed? Full of nasty code? Both? Or something else—what, I had no idea.

"Fascinating," Spock said, sounding exactly like his namesake.

"Oh, will you just *shut up*?" I snapped.

I CAUGHT BLACKIE, WITH SHEILA and Noah, in their neighbors' backyard, enjoying barbequed ribs and potato salad. He answered the call on the second ring and knew immediately who McQuaid wanted me to talk to.

"Jerry Nathan. In the computer science department. He's a real whiz when it comes to computers, especially all this new AI stuff that everybody's talking about. I'll text you his number."

"Thanks," I said. "I'll look for it. Enjoy your ribs."

"You bet." Voices in the background. Then, "Hey, don't go. Sheila wants to talk to you. Hang on."

The next voice was Sheila's. "I heard from Detective Baker, over in Fredericksburg. She tells me you have been one busy lady."

"I had nothing to do with it," I said defensively. "I just happened to have an appointment to talk with a woman who might know something about James Kelly, and when I got there, she happened to be dead." I immediately felt guilty. "Sorry," I muttered. "I should have called you last night and let you know what was going on. But this has been a little frustrating."

"I get that," she said. "Anything I can do?"

"Not at the moment. Better late than never, here's where we are." I told her about the album Margaret Greer had sent to me at the *Enterprise*, with all its faceless photos of Kelly. And about the thumb drive I had found. "Too many blind alleys, one after the other. And now McQuaid won't let me plug that drive into our computers. I suppose he's right, but it's sort of the last straw, you know?"

"I know," she said sympathetically. "Blind alley at my end, too. Kidder has turned in her amended report, so it's likely that instead of having an open accident investigation, it'll be an open homicide. We'll get Hark to run another story in the *Enterprise*. Maybe that will turn up something. And they're just getting started over in Fredericksburg. Connie faxed Kidder's report to Detective Baker. Who is high on you, by the way. You gave her the only live lead she's got. She said she'd keep us updated on whatever she picks up."

"What about the print on the casing left at the scene?"

"No match on IAFIS."

IAFIS is the national fingerprint database. It's been in operation for only a couple of decades. I'd be surprised if Kelly's prints were in it.

"That would have been too easy," I said. I added, "I'm hoping Jerry Nathan can let me into that thumb drive without infecting my computer. It may have something to tell us."

"Good luck," Sheila said. "Oh, and I also wanted to tell you that Noah and I used the stuff in your basket and both of us slept all night. Pure heaven, China. I can't thank you enough."

"Best news I've had all day," I said, meaning it.

Sheila *tsk-tsked.* "You mustn't have had much of a day."

I hated to admit it, but she was right. It didn't get any better a few minutes later when Jerry Nathan's voicemail jauntily informed me that Dr. Nathan wasn't available and would return my call as soon as he finished doing whatever he was doing now. But it was a summer Saturday night and I didn't expect much. He might not be in town. Or if he was, he was probably already out on the lakes and wouldn't be back until Monday.

So I was surprised when Nathan called Sunday morning around eleven, while I was making the bed. He listened to my tale of the thumb drive, chuckled, and said, "Well, it doesn't sound like much of a threat to me. But McQuaid's right, you never can tell about these things, so let's take it seriously. Have you got an air-gapped PC?"

I blinked. "A what?"

"A PC that's physically segregated and incapable of connecting wirelessly with other computers or network devices."

228

"Um, I don't think so," I said slowly, mentally inventorying the various computers around our house.

"Right. You're out on Limekiln Road, aren't you?"

"We are," I replied. Guessing what was coming next, I added hastily, "But really, you don't have to—"

"No problem." He was brisk. "I'm heading out to do a loop around Canyon Lake and you're on my way. Won't take but a minute to check it out. If you're going to be home for a while, I could stop by with the sandbox machine I use for situations like this. Look for me in twenty."

He was there in fifteen. Dressed in riding gear and boots in spite of the warm, sunshiny June morning, Jerry Nathan arrived with a roar, astride a large black Harley-Davidson lavished with shiny chrome. He skidded to a stop with a spray of gravel.

The thumb drive in my pocket, I went out to the driveway. Winchester, always curious about visitors, went with me and sniffed his way around the Harley while I offered its rider a cold drink in the kitchen or wherever he wanted to do his work.

He took off his helmet and rubbed his sleeve across his forehead. In spite of his sweaty red beard and his PhD, the young man didn't look much older than Brian. He gave me an engaging grin. "We can do this out here," he said. "It'll be super quick." Without getting off his motorcycle, he pulled what looked like an ordinary laptop out of a leather saddlebag—his "sandbox machine," I guessed—and plugged the thumb drive into it while Winchester gave his boots a comprehensive sniffing. He pronounced his verdict a few moments later.

"Clean," he said, handing it to me. "You're good to go."

"Clean?" I stared at the thing in the palm of my hand. "What does that mean?"

"It means clean." He gave me a slightly pitying look. "There's no malware on it. No files, either. Stripped. Nothing on it. Blank, empty, nada. You can use it if you want."

"Nothing on it? But I was hoping for—" I stopped. I had been hoping to see a couple of folders full of files containing details about James Kelly, whoever the man was now. Maybe some images, too. "Clean" was okay if it meant no malware. "Stripped" wasn't.

I tried to swallow my disappointment. The thumb drive and whatever was on it had been pretty much my last hope. "Thanks," I muttered, pocketing the drive. "Sorry you had to come all this way for nothing."

"Don't think of it that way," Jerry said cheerfully, putting the laptop back in the saddlebag. "Nothing is good. Nothing is exactly what you want to hear when you've got something like this. Nothing is the best."

"Thanks," I muttered, not very graciously. "Can I pay you? Or would you rather invoice McQuaid?"

"Nah. Forget it. Just tell the boss I said hey." He put his helmet on, threw me a wave, and was gone in a cloud of exhaust.

Winchester had ambled off in lazy pursuit of a giant swallow-tail, leaving me alone. I stood still at the edge of the driveway for a moment, feeling disheartened. Stripped. Nada. Nothing. I had meant what I said to Sheila. Too many blind alleys here. And this really *was* the last straw.

I crossed to the stone wall on the other side to pick a few fronds of lady fern and a handful of June wildflowers—purple coneflowers, red and yellow gaillardia, brown-eyed Susans, some lavender-colored monarda, a few gorgeous Texas bluebells. Maybe the flowers would cheer me up, make me feel better.

And they did, but not enough. I might as well admit it. I didn't know who Kelly was—who he was *now*, that is—and there wasn't anywhere else I could go with this. I had worked as far as I could through Olivia's papers. She was dead, and the police investigation into her hit-and-run was as good as dead, too. Her computer and phone were gone, and there was nothing relevant in the boxes I'd found in the storage unit. Margaret Greer was gone, too, murdered before she could share what she knew. And even though the album she had managed to send had offered plenty of Kelly's photos, the man himself was frustratingly faceless. Nada. Nothing. As empty as that damned thumb drive.

And there was more. For all I knew, the real Kelly was probably already dead. Had died years ago, as Chuck Loomis insisted, in that fiery car crash at the foot of a Mexican cliff. Which would mean that Olivia had been barking up the wrong tree altogether. That Zelda was mistaken. That her sister's death was purely accidental or occurred in a brief moment of road rage. And that Margaret Greer's murder was merely a coincidence, a robbery gone wrong, a payback for a neighbor's grudge.

Did I believe all that? *Could* I?

But what other options were there? There were no more accident sites to investigate, no witnesses to interview, no storage units to search, no secret drawers, no memory sticks. There simply were no more *facts*—and even the greenest first-year law student knows that you can't build a case without facts. I had to face it. This mystery—if that's what it was—might never be solved. And maybe it wasn't a mystery at all, just a string of coincidences, a little game played by the Universe like some baffling Wordle that had no meaning at all.

I had stopped beside a rosemary bush to pick a couple of sprigs when I got a call from Jessica. She sounded as discouraged as I felt, especially after I told her my bad news.

"Nothing on it?" Jessica asked. "Then why was it hidden?"

"No idea," I said. "Anyway, it's empty. No help to us at all."

"Well, *phooey.*" She blew out a breath. "I'm afraid my news isn't any better."

"What news?" I asked, but I thought I knew. I was right.

"Loomis told you the truth. I spent an hour digging around in the *Houston Chronicle* archive this morning and found the article on Kelly. It goes into some detail, probably because the trial and his release from prison got him some local attention. According to the paper, his car went off a cliff near Chihuahua, Mexico, a year after he was released. The article includes an interview with the woman—an American on a hiking trip—who spotted the car and called the police. The body was so badly burned that it couldn't be identified. Kelly's car was still registered in Texas, so that's apparently how the identification was made. I'll forward the clip." She hesitated. "Do you suppose it's worth my time to look for a death certificate?"

I added one last sprig of rosemary to my wildflower bouquet. "I don't think it would prove anything, one way or the other, Jess. If he's dead, he's dead. If he isn't . . . Well, somebody who went to that much trouble to fake a death—including collecting a corpse to go over the cliff with the car—isn't going to mind paying a little extra for a death certificate."

"I suppose you're right." Jessica paused. "But there's something else—something weird. Could be a coincidence, but maybe not. You know that our buddy Kellogg was in Mexico, too."

"That's not news, is it?"

"No. But what *is* news is that he lived in Chihuahua—the same town near where Kelly's car was found burned."

"Huh," I said. "When did he live there? Same time as Kelly's accident?"

"No. I mean, I don't know. The record I found is fairly recent, just a couple of years ago—right after he left the Dallas church, that is. He went there to work for the Tarahumara Tribal Christian Outreach in one of their Indian missions. But he *could* have been there earlier. He could have been there at the time of the accident." She paused. "It just seems . . . well, pretty coincidental to me. What do you think?"

"What do I think?" I went up the back steps to the kitchen. "I think that Mexico is a big country. And that it's pretty coincidental that the two American guys we're looking at are both hanging around that one town."

"Yeah," Jessica said. "And there are those initials. JQK and JQK. What are the chances of *that*?" She paused. "So what's next, China? Where are we?"

I had to be honest, given that the thumb drive had just turned up empty, "As far as Olivia is concerned, I think we've gone about as far as we can go—unless Baker comes up with something over in Fredericksburg. Maybe she'll find somebody in the neighborhood who saw something. A vehicle, maybe."

"Well, I've got my eye on Kellogg." Jessica let out a long breath. "I have the feeling that he's our guy, China. I should dig deeper into *him*. I wonder if anybody has checked to see whether he has an alibi for the night Margaret Greer was killed."

"Sheila might be willing to look into that," I said. "But it's the weekend. Let's table Kellogg for now. There's always tomorrow." I put a smile in my voice. "And I certainly hope you have pleasant plans for the rest of *today*."

"Oh, you bet!" Jessica's voice lightened. "Mark will be here in a few minutes. We're going tubing on the river. The water isn't very high, so it should be a lazy ride."

I opened the cupboard beside the sink to look for a vase. "Haven't done that in years," I said. "You guys have fun. And be safe."

"You and Mike should come and join us this afternoon," Jessica said. "And bring Caitie—she'll love it. We'll make it a party."

"Rain check," I said, looking into another cupboard. "McQuaid won't be back from Midland for another couple of days. And Caitie is still in Utopia, at the ranch. I'm batching it."

"Then *you* come. We'll make it a threesome. And maybe we'll figure out something on the Kellogg business. Have you talked to Detective Baker since Friday? Any new developments there?"

"I haven't talked to her, but the chief has, and Connie faxed her Rita's amended report. Baker hasn't turned up anything, either, but she promised to keep Sheila in the loop." I found what I was looking for—a white ceramic vase—and took it down. "And thanks for the river invite. It's cooler today, so I'm going to spend some time in the garden. The weeds are waiting. They'll get ahead of me if I let them."

"Oh, hey, there's Mark," Jessica said. "Gotta go. Enjoy your weeds. And let's keep thinking about Kellogg. We'll come up with something. I want to *nail* that rat."

I was chuckling as we traded goodbyes. I filled the vase with water, added a spoonful of sugar to help the flowers stay fresh, and arranged them. I had just finished when I heard the sound of an automobile and looked out to see a silver Lexus stopping in the drive. The driver's door opened and a blond, strikingly attractive man got out. Still carrying the flowers, I opened the back door and went out onto the deck, where he saw me and waved.

And yes, he still looked like Robert Redford. Not the rough-hewn young Redford of *Jeremiah Johnson* nor the older, time-worn Redford of *Havana*, but the charming, suave, half-baffled Redford of *The Way We Were.* When I hear Streisand sing the title song, I always think of Aaron and how *we* were, while I remind myself that it's the laughter I want to remember and not the pain—just who we were and what we were, together, before everything got so terribly complicated. It was that kind of love affair.

But at this moment, all I could do was stare as he came up the path to the deck. "Aaron? What are you doing here? I didn't expect—"

"Old times." He held up a bucket of Kentucky Fried Chicken and a bottle of wine as he came up the steps. "Apologies for inviting myself for lunch. But I was coming to Austin for a meeting tomorrow, so I thought I'd just drop in. Anyway, I've brought you something I think you'll want to see. About the Kelly case." He put the bucket and the bottle on the table, glanced over his shoulder. "Mike's still in Midland, I suppose."

"Yes," I said, irritated. I put the vase of flowers on the table. "If you had bothered to call, I could have—"

"Well, then," he said. He reached for me, pulled me close against him, and kissed me, quite thoroughly, just as he had the last time we saw one another. As I did then, I pushed back, hard—until I . . . well, until I didn't. And I was just as breathless as I'd been then, and my heart was beating just as fast.

"There," he said with satisfaction, letting me go. "Isn't that great? Everything between us is exactly the way it's always been. Old times, old friends. Don't you find that comforting? I do."

Actually, I did. But I also found it annoying. I heard myself saying, exasperated, "I wish you wouldn't do that."

"No, you don't. Not really." His confidence was annoying,

in part because he was right. He picked up the bottle. "Where's your corkscrew?"

It was beyond strange, sitting with Aaron at the picnic table on the shady deck behind the house, with Spock keeping up his end of the conversation from his patio cage, Mr. P purring from his end of the table, Winchester snoring under our feet, and assorted crowings and cacklings from the direction of Caitie's chicken coop. At first, I'd been uncomfortably aware that Aaron was nicely dressed in pressed khakis and a silky blue shirt the color of his eyes while I was wearing the denim shorts and red tank I'd jumped into when I showered after my morning run. I was also uneasily remembering that I had told Aaron that McQuaid would be gone. Had he thought that was an invitation? But I tried not to think of that. Anyway, he had said this was about Kelly.

"So what have you found about Kelly?" I asked, handing him the corkscrew and a pair of wine glasses.

"First we eat," he answered. "On the deck. You can tell me all about your place and your shop and I can tell you all about my life. Then we review Kelly."

"Yes, Counselor," I muttered. But he was calling the shots, so I put the chicken on a platter and set out plates and cutlery and paisley napkins. I added some leftovers: a dish of rice pilaf hot from the micro-wave, a three-bean salad perked up with a citrus dressing, some cheese, and the last of the grapes from the shop.

With all that food on the table and the vase of wildflowers in the center, it looked like a real party, and when we both sat down, we found that we were hungry. We chattered and drank and stuffed ourselves. I was burning with curiosity about the reason for his visit but managed to stifle it until he was ready to open the subject. We talked about people we had known and cases we had worked on and places we had gone together—the summer we went tarpon fishing at South Padre Island, the winter we went skiing at his parents' lodge at Angel Fire. He talked about his current wife and the marriage that had gone wrong. I talked about McQuaid and the marriage that was going right, feeling a little smug, yes, and grateful for the life I was living.

But sorry for Aaron at the same time. In the best of circumstances, marriage is hard. It was much, much harder in the world he lived in. We—Aaron and I—would never have made it if we were both living and working there.

And then he went out to the car to get his briefcase and we took cheese and grapes and coffee to the living room where it was cooler. We sat on the sofa and he put his briefcase on the floor beside the coffee table. He opened it and took out a legal-sized brown accordion file pocket filled with documents.

"I dug around in the file cabinets," he said. "It took a while, but I finally located the Kelly case. Since I don't know why it's of interest to you, I brought the whole thing. It's all there, trial court record with Johnnie's notes on errors and issues for appeal, notice of appeal, appellate briefs, court orders, rulings, transcripts, and so forth. I'll leave it with you. Make all the copies you like. Mail it back when you're done." He slanted a suggestive smile at me. "Or bring it the next time you're in Houston. We'll go out to dinner, make an evening of it. No strings, of course."

"Thank you," I said, taking the file pocket. Given the dead end I was facing, I wasn't sure how I could use it. But it wouldn't hurt to review it. I might find something of interest.

Aaron closed the briefcase, leaned back against the sofa arm, and swung his feet—L.L. Bean deck shoes, the ones he always wore—onto the coffee table. Totally Aaron, making himself completely at home.

"Before you dig into that, China, there are a couple of things you should know. First, I was a little more involved with that appeal than I was ready to talk about on the phone. Johnnie took the case because he saw the prosecutor's stupid error and recognized it as a slam dunk. But once he started digging into the trial record, he began to see that it was more than that. Kelly had gotten the worst kind of raw deal. Johnnie was convinced—totally, completely convinced—that he was innocent. I'm not sure I'd go quite that far. But I can say that this conviction was based on nothing but disreputable junk science, an outdated mythology based on an obsolete theory of cause and effect. I'm not saying that's why the DA didn't retry. But that's why he didn't retry right away."

I raised my eyebrows. "Ah," I said. I had read the media reports that came out when Texas executed a man convicted of setting a fire that killed his three children. On appeal, experts had discredited the prosecution's arson claims, leaving no scientific evidence that a crime had occurred, but the appeals were denied. I knew what Aaron was talking about.

"Yes. A classic example. Johnnie talked to a number of experts in the fast-developing science of arson investigation. They told him that the prosecution's so-called evidence of arson—the crazed glass in Eleanor Kelly's bedroom windows, the puddle configurations and burn pattern on the floor and walls—none of that was evidence of an accelerant or of a fire intentionally set. Instead, it was evidence of something that these more up-to-date scientists were calling a flashover. That's when flames and gases get hot enough to ignite everything in an entire room, all at once. For years, fire investigators had been mistaking the patterns created by flashover for signs that a room had been doused with an accelerant. But when the National Fire Protection Association put out a new fire investigation guide, that changed. Which meant . . . But you know what it meant. A great many court cases might have to be reevaluated."

"So Kelly was *innocent*," I said softly. And if Kellogg were Kelly, he was innocent, too.

Aaron frowned. "Well, that can still be debated, I suppose. But the evidence that was used to convict him could be challenged. The DA who convicted him was out of the picture, and the newly elected DA wasn't eager to stake a reputation on retrying a case he might lose. All of which explains—at least to my mind—why he wasn't retried."

I nodded. It doesn't speak well of the justice system, but there it is.

Aaron smiled, reminiscing. "Johnnie was a lot of things, as you know. He was a drinker and a womanizer and his courtroom high jinks sometimes got him into trouble. But he was an expert judge of character—the best I've ever known. He believed Kelly was innocent, not just based on the evidence, but on the man's character. He was working to get the DA to officially close the case, but there were all kinds of political games—you know the drill. And then Kelly took matters into his own hands. He left town—went to Mexico, people said. Next thing you know, we heard—"

"That Kelly was dead," I said.

He cocked his head. "How did you find out?"

"McQuaid knows the lead investigator on the case. After I talked to you, I reached him. Caught him with a rod and reel in his boat, out on Brays Bayou. He told me that Kelly had died. In a car crash."

"Brays?" He shook his head incredulously. "You've got to be kidding. People actually fish in that bayou?"

"What can I say? The man's retired. He likes to fish. And he has a good memory. It was his investigation, so he paid attention when he saw the story in the *Chronicle*. A car wreck in Mexico, body burned beyond recognition, etcetera. A reporter friend got into the *Chronicle* archive this morning. She confirmed it for me. The story, I mean." I met his eyes. "Not the death. Could've been anybody in that car." And Kelly could have been resurrected as Kellogg, with a new identity and a full set of newly purchased papers. Kelly might even have worked that transformative magic through the Tribal Christian Outreach, where Kellogg showed up a decade or more later as a missionary.

"Probably not worth looking for a death certificate," Aaron said. "They're easily bought down there. No telling who was in that car. And if Kelly's alive, he's going under another name." Aaron paused. "Unless you've got a clue . . ."

"Who, me?" I shrugged. "As usual, I'm clueless."

Aaron snorted. "You are one of the least clueless people I've ever met." He leaned forward and pulled the file pocket toward him. "As I remember our phone conversation, you said you were interested in a current situation here in Pecan Springs that might involve James Kelly. Anything new on that?"

Nothing but a pair of unsolved homicides, I thought. "Nothing that can be directly attributed to him," I said aloud. I frowned. "You mentioned that there were a couple of things I might want to know before I go through the case file. You've given me one. What's the other?"

"This." Aaron reached into the back of the file pocket and took out a black and white glossy photo of a good-looking young man dressed in slacks and an open-necked white shirt, leaning against a sleek,

240

racy-looking sports car. It was parked in the driveway of a porticoed white house. He held it out to me.

"James Kelly," he said, "taken a few weeks before his wife died. That's a Ferrari 250," he added, with a hint of envy. "It's not the car that went over the cliff, of course."

I stared at the photo, stunned. "*This* is Kelly?"

And then it began to fall into place. All of it, one piece after the other, until I could see what Olivia had seen, what Margaret Greer had known. I could also see that the vacatur of Kelly's conviction was entirely irrelevant. The man might or might not be innocent, but both of the women had assumed, as had the jury, that he was guilty. And that was why—despite the fact that their killer was officially dead—the two of them were no longer alive.

Aaron was watching me. "You actually recognize this guy?"

I nodded mutely.

"And he's alive?" He was interested. "He's hanging out somewhere around here?"

I nodded again. My mouth felt dry.

"Are you going to tell me who he is—and why it matters?"

I put the photo on the table. "Not yet. Maybe after I get it sorted out. And figure out what to do." The first was hard enough. Given what I knew about the two women's deaths, the second was going to be much harder.

"Interesting." Aaron glanced at his Rolex—yes, he still wore one— and stood. "Well, as I said, make all the copies you want and mail the file back when you're finished. Or bring it, preferably, the next time you come to Houston. I'd love to stay longer, but I promised a friend in Austin that I'd take her to one of those mystery dinner theater performances tonight. You know, the ones that feature a dead body just inside the door—and one of the dinner guests is the 'killer.'" He made a face. "My friend thinks it's *fun* to solve a murder mystery."

I shuddered. Fun to solve a murder mystery? I could think of a few other words for it—*fun* was not one of them. At a dinner theater, once you've identified the bad guy, you go on to dessert and after-dinner coffee. I had identified the bad guy. What did I do now?

I stood too. Aaron put a hand on my shoulder and bent in for a quick brotherly kiss, on my cheek this time.

"Good luck with this thing, whatever it is," he murmured against my ear. "And watch yourself. Stay out of trouble." He stepped back. "If I can help, you'll let me know?"

Why did all these men think they had to warn me to stay out of trouble? "Count on it," I said. I held up the photo. "Thank you for this. And the file. And the Kentucky Fried and the Prosecco. It was perfect."

"Yes," he said. "Yes, it was." He picked up his briefcase. "A road not taken. But I haven't forgotten where it went and how good it was. I hope you haven't either. I wonder if you sometimes wish . . ."

But that, thankfully, was as far as he got. He straightened with one of those hundred-watt smiles of his. "I just hope McQuaid knows how lucky he is."

"If he forgets," I said, "I'll be sure to remind him." I looked down at the photo. "And thanks. Much appreciated."

It wasn't Kellogg.

Chapter Fifteen

Lemon balm (*Melissa officinalis*) is a perennial herb with a distinctive lemon scent. The fourteenth-century nuns of the French Carmelite Abbey of St. Just used it with other herbs to make their celebrated Carmelite water, a "miracle water" that was considered a restorative panacea. While its original recipe was a closely guarded secret (patented by a series of fifteenth- and sixteenth-century French kings), it was said to have been made of lemon balm, chamomile, sage, angelica root, mugwort, fennel, cinnamon, and cloves. Also known as *Eau de Melisse*, it was carried by ladies of the court of Charles V of France. It was in such demand that the nuns marketed it in a bottle with a red wax seal embossed with an image of Mount Carmel.

More recently, a study reported in the journal *Neuropsychopharmacology* (October 28, 2003) reports that lemon balm extract produces significant, demonstrable improvements in mood and cognitive performance in healthy young adults, suggesting potential benefits for attention, memory, and alertness. Once again, science has confirmed a traditional remedy.

China Bayles
"What Am I Forgetting? Herbs to Improve Your Memory"
Pecan Springs Enterprise

After Aaron left, I brewed an espresso for myself, and—still grappling with my surprise and shock at what the photo had shown me—sat down with my laptop. I had intended to write an email to Zelda. I'd agreed to keep her updated on the situation, and

I had been thinking I should tell her about Margaret Greer's murder and how it might be connected to her sister's death.

But I didn't get very far. The operational word here, of course, was *might* be connected. There was no direct evidence linking the two deaths, aside from the facts that Margaret and Olivia had talked about Eleanor on the phone and planned to meet, and that Jessica and I had arranged to talk with Margaret about her cousin. There wasn't much point in sharing this part of the story with Zelda. It would just stir up a flurry of questions for which I had no answers. I could tell her about my visit to the hit-and-run site and the interview with Gloria Tanner. But then she would inevitably ask if there were any new leads, and what could I say to that? I couldn't tell her that I now knew who Kelly was, because I had no idea what I should do—or even what I *could* do—with this information. The photo proved who Kelly was now, but that was only one aspect of this complicated situation. It didn't prove that Kelly was driving the truck that struck and killed Olivia. Or that he caught up with Margaret Greer and killed *her*.

I needed more evidence. And when I had it, Sheila was going to hear it first. And after her, Detective Baker.

But I didn't want to tell either until I had some sort of plan. I needed to know more. Better yet, I needed to come up with enough probable cause for Sheila to obtain a search warrant. Given the local politics, a tip simply wouldn't be sufficient. I needed evidence. And that would be hard to get without showing my hand or compromising the ensuing police investigation. Tainted evidence—evidence obtained illegally—is generally inadmissible at trial. I couldn't risk that for Sheila.

So I had nothing to tell Zelda. She would just have to get in line. But what about McQuaid? Maybe he would have some ideas. I picked up my phone to call him—and then had second thoughts. Yes, I could definitely count on him for advice. After all, he'd been involved in hundreds of homicide investigations and knew the drill far better than I did. But I also knew that his first response would be something like "Stay out of trouble, wife!" And that his second response would be to step in and take charge of the entire situation.

Yes, I could talk to McQuaid. But not before I told Sheila. Which brought me back to that question. How could I learn more without tipping my hand?

I was turning this question over in my mind when Ruby called. I wasn't ready to talk to her about what I'd learned, but I did have something to tell her: the Yelp bomb thing that Almira Pickle was cooking up. "She said an angel brought her the how-to instructions in a dream," I concluded. "Would you believe?"

"In a *dream*?" Ruby laughed. "That's ironic, wouldn't you say? But it makes me wonder . . ." Her voice trailed away as if she were thinking. "I'll talk to Ramona about it," she said after a moment. "She's into dreams and dream counseling. Maybe she can come up with a way to handle this."

"That's dangerous," I said. "Almira's bad enough. Ramona might go off the rails, too."

"Well, then, maybe *you* have an idea," she retorted.

"Afraid not," I sighed. "Yeah, I guess. Talk to Ramona."

I put my phone in my pocket, closed the laptop, and went out to the garden.

At least I knew what to do with the weeds.

WHEN I WENT BACK INDOORS at the end of the afternoon, the garden was cleaner and neater and the compost bin was topped off with limp green stuff. As for me, I was warmer, sweatier, dirtier, and sadly, no wiser. But I slept on the matter overnight, waking often to consider the problem from yet another angle. When I got up the next morning for my run, I had come to a conclusion. It was time to stop stalling and get on with it. I knew what I was going to do.

Today was Monday and the shop was closed, so I went in a little later. On the way, I put in a call to Fredericksburg to see if Baker and her team had turned up anything new on Margaret Greer's murder.

Either they hadn't or the detective was playing her cards close to the chest. All she would tell me was that her officers had learned nothing of any consequence in their door-to-door survey of the neighbors, and that she was currently collecting doorbell video from several houses on either side of and across the street from the Greer house. She planned to start reviewing it that afternoon. If she saw anything useful on the tapes—or anywhere else, for that matter—she'd call Sheila and let her know.

"But remember that it's still early days," she said, wanting to reassure me. "We've barely gotten started. I'm confident that we'll find Greer's killer."

I hadn't expected to learn much from Baker, so I wasn't disappointed. That determinedly cheerful tone didn't fool me, either. She had no leads, she knew it, I knew it. I started to tell her about the album Margaret had mailed to the *Enterprise*, figuring that was something she ought to know. But she was in a hurry to get to a meeting—that's what she said, anyway—and she cut me off. Which was okay. I understood. She had a job to do, she needed to get on with it, and the album wasn't immediately relevant. I thanked her and hung up.

But I held onto the phone. Sometime in the depths of the wakeful night, I had concluded that it was time for me to call Sheila, tell her what I had learned so far, and text her the two-decades-old photo of James Kelly and his racy Ferrari that was now in my phone. After I did my part by filling in the details she didn't already know, she could figure out what was best to do with the information. She had the resources to handle the investigation—I didn't. She could do it much more adeptly than I could. And she could deal with the political fallout in the mayor's office. I would let Zelda know I was turning everything over to the police and get on with my very lovely life: my husband, my daughter, my business—the things that, after all was said and done, mattered most to me.

I called Sheila's office and told Connie I'd like to talk to the boss.

"Afraid you'll have to get in line, China," Connie said. "She and the mayor drove to Austin for a ceremony honoring citizen participation in community policing. I hope it can wait. She likely won't be back before early afternoon."

Well, yes, it could wait. In the meantime, I would treat myself to something pleasantly productive for a couple of hours, out of doors. The forecast was for possible rain when a front slid through around noon, but the morning was bright and pretty. I found my trowel, the clippers, and a five-gallon bucket in the storage shed behind the shops and went out to the Apothecary Garden, where I set about restraining the lemon balm that had gone rogue and shoved its way into the corner occupied by its peppermint cousin.

Lemon balm may look like a fragile green plant, but like all the mints, it loves nothing better than to reseed itself generously among its friends. Turn your back on it for a few weeks and you'll find it in your garden, your lawn, your neighbor's lawn, and the park down the street. But I could forgive its bad manners. This morning, it was lovely, with tiny blossoms of the palest lavender and pink arranged tidily around the stems. And not just lovely, but tasty. If I found a few minutes later today, I would strip the leaves from the plants I was pulling and dry them for tea.

Now that I had decided to dump the Kelly business in Sheila's lap, I intended to spend the morning thinking of other things. Like finding a way to thwart Almira Pickle's threatened protest against the psychic fair. Or collecting additional copies for my shelves of banned books. Or seeing if McQuaid could manage a few days off for a beach trip to South Padre Island. Now *that* was an enticing idea. Caitie would love it. Winchester too. Maybe Brian and Casey could also join us, so we could all get better acquainted. That would give me a chance to find out what kind of wedding the kids were planning. When, where, how formal—little details I should probably know.

But sometimes my mind just refuses to let loose of a subject. While I pulled plants and dropped them into the bucket, I was remembering that I had puzzled over Charlie Lipman's decision to send Zelda to me with her theory. Now, knowing who Kelly was, I understood why. The man was one of Charlie's clients. Charlie may have known his backstory long before Olivia discovered it and threatened to take it public. He might even have been involved in giving Kelly advice on how to cover up a past crime—his assumption of that false identity, for instance. Charlie is a canny old fox. When Zelda showed up with her theory of her sister's death, he may have begun to wonder whether the lid was about to come off Kelly's past. He might have seized the opportunity to involve me, with the idea that I might come up with answers to questions he didn't want to ask himself.

And while I had already decided to turn the matter over to Sheila, I couldn't help mentally screening various scenarios that might produce enough probable cause to justify a warrant to search Kelly's premises for that truck, as well as Olivia's computer and her cell phone. Of course, if this were one of Sue Grafton's wonderful mysteries (no doubt titled *H is for Hit-and-Run*), Kinsey would sneak onto the premises and start searching, using her handy-dandy pocket lock-pick set. Even Lucas Davenport and Virgil Flowers, McQuaid's favorite detectives, are not above a little breaking and entering when they feel compelled.

But Kinsey and Lucas and Virgil are fictional. They can get away with things that won't work for me. If I entered Kelly's property uninvited, whatever information I might produce would be inadmissible in court. The evidence might be so badly tainted that it could never be used. Kelly could get away with murder—with multiple murders. I could lose my law license, and Sheila's friendship, which would be worse.

Of course, if I had an invitation . . .

I frowned. Yes, that would be a different story. If I had a legitimate reason to go on the property, I could look for that truck. With any luck, it hadn't been scrapped or sold across the border and—

No, I thought firmly. I was *not* going there. I was going to do exactly what I'd planned: turn this whole business over to Sheila as soon as she got back from Austin this afternoon. I picked up my bucket, full of outlaw lemon balm, and turned around to see Ruby on the deck outside the tearoom, watching me. It took just one glance to tell me that she was the bearer of bad news.

She waited until I was standing beside her. "Mrs. Baggett lowered the boom," she said tersely.

"Uh-oh." I put my bucket down. "What happened?"

"When I went to the city office to get the permit, I ran into trouble. It turns out that Mrs. Baggett goes to the same church as Almira Pickle—you know, the lady who thinks we're doing the devil's work over here. Drag queens, child abuse, banned books, herbs that cause abortions. You name it, we've got it."

"Mrs. Baggett goes to *Kellogg's* church?"

"She said that a friend invited her, so she went as a guest. After the service, Mrs. Pickle recognized who she was and made her listen for ten minutes while she complained about the psychic fair. It caught Mrs. Baggett off guard because she carries her office in her head and knew perfectly well that she hadn't seen a permit application for a psychic fair. Then I showed up at her desk just as she opened for business this morning." Ruby turned down her mouth. "She let me have it. At point-blank range. Like a flame thrower."

"Oh, too bad," I said fervently. "I hope you weren't scorched."

"I'm sure my eyebrows are singed. Long story short, after she got home from church yesterday, she went online and looked at our website and of course she saw our ad for the fair. With vendor photos and games for the kids and costumes and everything. I tried to explain about Ramona and the bad timing, but she wasn't interested. She just kept saying that rules are made for a reason and that everybody has to follow them."

"Or civilization will descend into anarchy, I suppose. And it might," I added, and told her what Janie had overheard in the Dos Amigas parking lot: Almira Pickle plotting to disrupt the psychic fair—by foul means. "And it's not just street protesting. She and her friends are also organizing some serious social media harassment on Facebook and Instagram. And Yelp."

"Yelp? Uh-oh." Ruby looked troubled. "That is seriously bad news, China. The Crystal Cave gets a lot of traffic from Yelp. And so does the tearoom."

"Thyme and Seasons does, too." I frowned. "So what's our next step? As far as the permit is concerned, I mean."

"We wait. I called Ramona and told her about the problem. We looked at some dates and chose one—the second Saturday in July. I went ahead and filed for a permit for that date and paid the fee. Ramona is going to call all the vendors and let them know. And notify her RSVPs for her talk on dreams. We'll get it done."

"Well, the date isn't bad," I said. "In fact, it's probably better. You've been saying that the June calendar is too crowded. I'll go ahead and change it on the website."

"It's not that simple." Ruby pulled down her mouth. "Mrs. Baggett says that the permit won't be approved until all the complaints are settled. Now that I've filed it properly, Almira Pickle will have a week to make a formal complaint. And then a committee will review it and let us know."

"Remember what I said," I muttered. "If there's a way to stop that woman—"

"I'll go on our Facebook page and let people know," Ruby said, ignoring me. "I'll say something like 'tentative date' and 'scheduling difficulties.'"

"You could say 'the devil is in the details,'" I replied. "And let everybody use their imagination."

Ruby turned to go, then turned back. "Oh, speaking of details. I got a text from Cassidy Warren this morning. She wants somebody to go out to the Blind Penny to meet her, take a look in the party barn and get her sketch of the setup for Saturday's barbeque, as well as take a few photos, both indoors and out. I told her I couldn't do it. Mom has a bad eye infection and I have to take her to the eye doctor this morning. So she asked if you could come."

"Me?" I asked, startled.

"Yeah. If you can, please take plenty of photos, especially of that party barn. Neither Cass nor I have ever been out there. Things will go a lot more smoothly if we know the kind of setup we'll be working in, where we can put the grills and the serving tables. You know, the usual."

I stared at her. *Could I go out to the ranch?* Was this just an extremely fortunate coincidence or . . . something else?

"Ruby," I said, "Did you *arrange* this?"

She gave me a blank look. "Arrange it? What are you talking about? I'm asking, that's all. I mean, if you've got something else to do today, I can text Cass and see if she's available. But whoever goes probably needs to get going fairly early. It's a lovely morning right now, but the weather guy on KXAN-TV says there's a storm front coming through in an hour or two. The weather service will probably issue a severe thunderstorm warning. Heavy rain, wind, maybe even hail."

When the Universe presents you with a coincidence that is stranger than fiction, do not ask questions. Just say *thank you* and run with it.

"Glad to do it," I said. I picked up my bucket. "And just to confirm—Mrs. Warren specifically told you to ask *me*? She mentioned me by name?"

"Yes." Ruby gave me an odd look, took out her phone, and pulled up a text. "If you can't make it, ask China," she read aloud. "Tell her I'll leave the main gate unlocked." She pocketed her phone with a frown. "But I don't understand. Why in the world are you—"

"Never mind," I said quickly, turning to go. "I'm on my way." I paused and added, "But don't delete that text."

"Wait a minute," Ruby said. "I don't understand. What is—"

And then she was staring at me, fixing me with an intent,

concentrating look that made me feel suddenly shivery—the kind of feeling you get when you hear the dentist starting his drill, you know what's coming, and you'd leave the chair if you could but you can't.

I couldn't leave, either. I couldn't *move*. All I could do was stand still, very still, while Ruby probed my intentions.

And then she understood. She released me and both of us relaxed, like tautly strung wires coming unstrung. "China, I don't think you ought to do this," she said. "That truck. You're going to look for—"

She stopped and closed her eyes for another moment, then put her hand on my arm. "But you're going to do it anyway, aren't you." It wasn't a question. "No matter what I say."

Her fingers were like ice and I covered them with my hand. "I have to," I replied. "It's the best way." No, that was wrong. It was the *only* way. "And there's nothing to worry about," I added. "Honestly, it'll be easy. I promise you. All I'm going to do is use my eyes and take a few photos. No problem at all."

"No." She shook her head. "No. Believe me, please. I wish I knew what's going to happen but I don't. I just know it's not going to happen the way you think." Her voice became urgent. "You should take some-body with you, China. *I* should go with you."

I should have listened to her. I didn't. "But you have to take your mom to the eye doctor," I reminded her, and let go of her hand. "Anyway, I'm *telling* you. There's nothing to worry about. I'm going to look around for that truck, that's all. If I spot it, Sheila can get a warrant to seize it and search for Olivia's computer and her phone. And it'll just be Cassidy Warren and me. Her husband is in Oklahoma City this week."

"You're sure about that?" She frowned. "How do you know?"

"Because I read it in the *Enterprise*. He's getting some kind of award from the National Petroleum Institute."

"Have you told Sheila what you know? That you're going to look for the truck?"

"Not yet. I'll tell her when she gets back from Austin."

"Well, I'm glad *he* won't be there," she said. She frowned. "But I can't help feeling . . ." Her frown deepened.

Remember that photo Aaron pulled out of Johnnie Carlson's decades-old file? The good-looking young James Q. Kelly leaning against his racy Ferrari? It was a photo of a much younger Palmer Warren.

Yes. That would be Palmer Warren, the George Clooney hottie with the salt-and-pepper hair and beard and alligator Luccheses, who had been convicted of killing his first wife and had killed two women to keep that conviction secret.

Palmer Warren, former city councilman, president of the hospital board, major sponsor of minority college scholarships, energetic organizer of such community charity events as the annual Pennington Bass Fishing Tourney and Back the Blue on the Green, and (not least) close personal friend of the mayor.

Palmer Warren, wealthy in his own right (or maybe in Eleanor's), married to Cassidy Pennington Warren, the nearest thing to Pecan Springs royalty.

Palmer Warren. Which is why, after a night-long debate with myself, I had decided to hand the entire matter over to Sheila. I had gone as far as I could go with this. I had no badge, no authority, no legitimate cover, no desire to go any further. Palmer Warren was unreachable, out of bounds, hands off, way above my paygrade.

But Cassidy Warren's message to Ruby completely changed the calculus. Her texted invitation to visit the ranch gave me explicit written permission to enter the property and take photos. If I saw the truck, I could report it to Sheila, along with probable cause for believing it to be a murder weapon. If I were a *cop* and saw that suspicious truck, I could search and seize it without a warrant, under the "plain view doctrine." As a civilian, I couldn't do that, but when the chief went out to the ranch, she'd be taking a search warrant. If the truck was there, it was entirely possible that Olivia's computer and her cell phone were there, too. And if Palmer Warren could be tagged for her death, he would certainly become the prime person of interest in Margaret Greer's murder.

We had a very good shot at holding the man accountable for *both* his crimes.

Chapter Sixteen

In medieval Europe, forget-me-nots (once called scorpion-grass), were thought to be an antidote for insect and scorpion stings, hence useful as a relief from pain. An old common name *herba-clavorum*, from the Latin for "plant" and "nail," came from blacksmiths' practice of twining [forget-me-nots] through horses' manes to reduce their pain while shoeing them.

Plant Lore, Legends, and Lyrics: Embracing the Myths, Traditions, Superstitions, and Folk-Lore of the Plant Kingdom (1914)
Richard Folkard

The Warrens divide their time between two residences. They spend the week in a large, luxurious house in an upscale neighborhood of Pecan Springs. They spend weekends and holidays at the old Pennington family Blind Penny Ranch, some ten thousand acres of Hill Country wilderness on the Guadalupe River west of Canyon Lake. If Palmer Warren still had that white pickup, I'd bet my bottom dollar that it was a dinged-up ranch truck, not a vehicle the socially aware couple would park in the driveway at their town house. He'd keep it at the ranch, where it was probably used to tow a horse trailer.

I had a general idea where the ranch was, but I'd never been out there so I had to ask my phone for directions. And when I pulled up the map, I was in for an informative surprise that confirmed my suspicions. It turns out that the ranch is on Remington Road, which intersects Purgatory Bend about twenty-five miles outside of town. In fact, the quickest way to the ranch takes you past the very spot where Olivia was struck and killed—convenient for the killer, if he happened to be on his way back to the Blind Penny.

Of course, I reminded myself as I got in my car and drove away from Thyme and Seasons, this might be a very wild goose chase. I knew I was right: that James Kelly had reincarnated himself as Palmer Warren, stablished himself in Pecan Springs, and married Cassidy Pennington. I was only guessing that he was at the wheel of the hit-and-run truck. But with any luck, I might be able to find the truck that he had used as a murder weapon. And with a little more luck, the forensics guys would find the traces of DNA that would identify the truck as the vehicle that killed Olivia.

Guessing, yes. But as I swung onto Purgatory Bend, I couldn't help congratulating myself for putting it all together, for solving Olivia's murder, for coming up with the right answer. It had taken a while, some head-scratching, and a lot of luck, but I was finally there.

I had no way of knowing how wrong I was.

FOR THE NEXT COUPLE OF hours, it would be a lovely day in the Hill Country. After that, though, there might be trouble. Before I put my phone away, I brought up the radar and saw that the front was moving faster than the forecast had predicted. The leading edge was a nasty line of bright red and yellow storm clouds, trailing a wide swath of green. And as the westbound highway lifted to the rim of the Edwards Plateau, there it was in front of me: a line of gray clouds with a dark blue underbelly, lying on the western horizon. Usually, these threats were over and done with by June, when a dome of high pressure sets up shop over central Texas and summer guarantees us weeklong strings of hundred-degree days.

But this wasn't all bad. The long, dry summer was just a thought away. Those clouds might bring us the last chance of rain we'd see in weeks. And while weather that slips in from the northwest can bring downpours and hail, it usually lasts only a couple of hours. It's nothing like the tropical storms and hurricanes that fling themselves across the coast and then loaf around the inland plains for a couple of days. Nearby Williamson County once got drenched with nine months' worth of rain—twenty-four inches—in forty-eight hours, courtesy of a hurricane. While the sky overhead was clear and vividly blue and the line of dark blue clouds was too far away to be ominous, I was glad to be on my way early.

It had been hot but the annual summer bakeoff hadn't begun and the Hill Country was at its loveliest. The spring grasses hadn't yet been toasted brown, the live oak leaves were still shiny as green buttons, and there were a few late-blooming paintbrush. A pale Cooper's hawk sailed off from the top of a silver-leaved cottonwood tree, a pair of high-flying scissortail swallows freewheeled somersaults in the empty sky, and jaunty red cardinals, quick and bright as dancing flames, flared along the barbed wire fence. The road was bordered with flame acanthus and yellow sneezeweed, red yucca, sprawling white-blooming jimson weeds, clumps of wild green-gold grasses. And beyond all this cacophony of color, the hills folded themselves into the darkening distance, draped with sedate blue-green cedar.

The junction of Purgatory Bend and Remington was not well marked when I reached it a half hour later, and if the map on my phone hadn't told me to watch, I might have driven past it. But there it was, marked by a large white wooden sign with the outline of a horse and the words Blind Penny Ranch, 3 miles. Breeding Top Quarter Horses for 80 years. The road was a narrow asphalt two-lane that followed fast-running Penny Creek through a series of rugged hills and across a couple of low-water crossings. There had been some recent rain and both crossings were six inches deep in clear, rippling water that fountained up from my tires as I drove across. Tall white flood gauges were posted at each of the crossings, marked off at one-foot intervals to a height of five feet, a reminder that this was flash-flood country.

In addition to its reputation for quarter horses, the Blind Penny is known as one of the finest hunting ranches in Adams County, with nearly ten thousand acres of cedar-topped ridges, cottonwood and sycamore bottoms, live oak and shin oak mottes, and fields of native seasonal grasses. This was Indian country once, part of the wide homeland of the Comanche and Tonkawa. It's high-fenced now and stocked with game—axis deer, antelope, wild pigs, Rio Grande turkeys, and native white-tailed deer—for the hunts Palmer likes to offer his friends. Not commercial hunts, just friendly sallies out to the hunting camps he's built in the wilderness, with the host himself as guide. He often brought kids from the community out here, too, to shoot on the archery range and fish in the lake. I couldn't help thinking regretfully about that and Palmer's many other civic projects and wondering what would happen to them after he'd been convicted of two murders—assuming I found what I was looking for, of course.

There was one last low-water crossing and the road dead-ended at the ranch gate, which was closed but unlatched, as Cassidy Warren had promised. I got out of the car, opened the gate, drove through, and closed it behind me—ranch country etiquette, which you violate at your peril. Leaving a gate open can cause all kinds of trouble.

The ranch lane was a graveled two-track with a grassy center strip, leading along Penny Creek to the top of a low ridge. There, I slowed to a stop and looked down on the ranch compound: a sprawling old-style stone-and-cedar ranch house that looked large enough to sleep a dozen or more, an attached multicar garage, a large corral, and several metal-roofed sheds around a couple of barn-like structures, maybe the party barn and a stable. On the near side of the compound, a tennis court, an archery range, and what might be a horseshoe pitch. On the far side, Penny Creek was dammed to form a lake of six or eight acres or so, with a wooden dock where a rowboat, a canoe, and a paddle boat were moored. A silver Mercedes-Benz was parked in front of the house—probably Cassidy's car—but there were no other vehicles in view. I felt a tug of disappointment. If there *was* a ranch truck, it must be under cover. Okay, but where? In that multicar garage attached to the house? In a barn, under a shed, somewhere off-site? At a remote hunting camp, for instance, where I had no mandate to go.

And now that I was actually here, looking down on this serenely pastoral setting, I wasn't quite as sure as I had been. This felt too lovely, too normal, too perfect to be the ranch home of a two-time, perhaps even three-time killer. But I was here now. I had a job to do, and it was time to get started.

In remote rural Texas, whether you're expected or not, you don't go straight up to the door of somebody's ranch house and knock. The customary greeting protocol is to park out front, toot your horn two or three times and yell out a loud "Hey howdy, folks—anybody home?" You toot and you yell until somebody opens the front door and demands, "What the *hail* you doin' out there? Come on in here and stop that hollerin'." Or some more civil version of that invitation.

But my job and Mrs. Warren's texted invitation to take photos gave me an excuse to skip the standard greeting—for a few moments, at least. I could start with a quick, private look around those outbuildings, where I was supposed to visit and photograph the party barn. What I was looking for was much bigger than a breadbox. If the truck was here, it shouldn't be hard to find. The likeliest place was in one of the sheds that were clustered around the barns.

So when I drove off the ridge and down to the ranch compound, I followed the circle drive away from the house, between the tennis court and the archery range, toward the barn and what looked like a stable, located on opposite sides of the corral. As I got closer, it was easy to see which was the party barn, so that's where I parked. It was also easy to see that the shed sheltered no pickups, so I was focused on the barn. I left my shoulder bag in the car and took my phone, for photos.

It was a large structure with a peaked roof and vertical barnwood siding that looked as if it might be a century old, a pair of barn doors at one end, and a roofed flagstone patio to one side, where the entry door was situated. Inside, the high open space was crisscrossed with massive wooden beams, floored with wide pine planks, and lit with huge deer-antler chandeliers, faux antlers, I hoped. I took a dozen quick photos of the exterior and interior and its well-equipped kitchen, featuring a party-size refrigerator, cooktop, and ovens—photos for Cass and Ruby, to help them with their planning. They could park Big Red Mama, our shop van, at the back of the barn, set up the barbeque grills on the patio, have the tent pitched adjacent to it, and locate the serving stations and dining tables in the tent. If it was a very rainy day, the tables could be moved inside the barn, where the Devil's Rib would likely set up, too.

But I took care of the picture-taking task expeditiously, for there wasn't a lot of time. Cassidy might have seen or heard me drive in and

I wanted to grab a quick look into the stable on the other side of the corral. I let myself out of the party barn by a side door and walked quickly around the corral. The sky was an ominous pewter now, and thunder echoed against the hills. I could smell the rain.

The stable was constructed of the same barnwood as the party barn, but smaller. I opened the smaller door and peered inside. The double doors at both ends were closed and the place was dark, with just enough light to make out the wide, dirt-floored central aisle and stalls for ten horses, five stalls on each side. They were empty. The horses must all be out in the pasture.

But as my eyes got accustomed to the dim light, I saw a couple of vehicles parked side by side at the far end. One was a bright yellow amphibious all-terrain vehicle, like the four-wheel ATV that Leatha and Sam keep at their Utopia ranch so they can cross the Sabinal River without driving into town to cross at the bridge.

More interestingly, the other vehicle was a pickup. And even in the dimness I could see that it was light-colored.

A light-colored pickup! My heart skipped a couple of beats and, without stopping to think, I hurried down the aisle toward the truck. As I got close, I saw that it was a Dodge Ram, a big pickup, a muscle truck. But it was a four-door crew-cab model, and Gloria had been very clear: the truck she saw *wasn't* a crew cab. There was no row of lights on the cab roof. And the truck wasn't white—it was gray.

The wrong truck. *Damn.*

But if it had been the right truck, I reminded myself, there would be a problem. It wasn't in plain sight. It might have been tricky to explain that I had just accidentally happened to notice the hit-and-run truck inside a closed building into which I had not been invited. It was time to leave, and the back door was right in front of me.

Outside, I stood for a moment, considering. The skies overhead were an ominous gray and looked as if they might open in a deluge at any moment. To the west, a flash of lightning and quickly, a loud clap of thunder. If I didn't get moving, Cassidy Warren and I would be doing whatever we had to do in the rain. It was time to drive around to the front of the house and let her know I was there. I walked around the end of the corral toward the party barn and looked up—and that's when I saw it.

A white pickup, out in plain sight.

Well, almost. Still hitched to a two-horse trailer, it was parked behind the party barn, in a graveled parking area a few feet away from the back of the building. The trailer was blazoned with BLIND PENNY RANCH. BREEDING TOP QUARTER HORSES FOR 80 YEARS in bright red letters. The pickup was an F-150, ten or fifteen years old and showing its age. The bed held the usual jumble of ranch gear: a heavy roll of barbed wire, three or four metal fence posts, a post pounder, heavy fencing pliers and a pair of leather work gloves, a machete, a dirty saddle blanket, and a wooden box of horseshoeing gear: horseshoes, horseshoe nails, hoof nippers, a hoof rasp. A working truck, a ranch truck that carried enough essential tools to get the job done. A rifle hung in the gun rack in the rear window—another essential tool, out here in ranch country.

I walked forward along the passenger side. With mounting excitement, I saw that the truck was a two-door cab, like the one Gloria Tanner had seen. There was a row of five lights across the top of the cab, but the amber cover on the middle one was missing, and the socket was empty. And then the clinchers. There was a long scratch across the lower passenger-side door. And the towing mirror on that side was broken. I had found the truck that killed Olivia. And I knew who the killer was.

I raised my phone and took a couple of quick photos of the cab roof lights and the mirror, I was bending over to get a photo of the scratch when I heard the crunch of footsteps on the gravel behind me.

"Who are you?" a woman's voice demanded. "And just what the devil do you think you're *doing*?"

Startled, I straightened up and turned around. Cassidy Warren was standing a dozen paces from me, at the corner of the party barn. She was wearing scuffed boots, jeans, and a plaid cowboy shirt. She was holding a shotgun. And it was pointed straight at me.

Chapter Seventeen

You may have heard the old story that rubbing garlic on a bullet ensures that it will do its job. There is a similar legend about the magical powers of *Myosotis*. It is said that the flowers of forget-me-nots were an ingredient in the secret formula that the bladesmiths of Toledo, Spain, used to quench and harden their forged blades. It was also thought to protect people from witches.

China Bayles
"What Am I Forgetting? Herbs to Improve Your Memory"
Pecan Springs Enterprise

The next moment was silent and . . . well, uncomfortable. And then, to make matters even worse, there was a sudden flash of lightning, a loud clap of thunder, and it began to rain.

"China?" Cassidy lowered her shotgun. "Well, my goodness. I didn't recognize you, bent over like that. What are you doing back here? Why didn't you come to the house when you drove in?" She noticed the phone in my hand and frowned. "You're taking pictures? Why are you taking photos of my ranch truck?"

I may draw the line at breaking and entering but I am as willing as the next lawyer to lie my way out of a difficult situation. To tell the truth, if I had been quick-witted enough to come up with a lie, I would have. I might have told her that Ruby had asked for photos of a vehicle we might use if we had to get around on the ranch. Or that my hobby was collecting images of trucks hitched to horse trailers and loaded with ranch junk. Or—

But her question had stopped me. Why was I taking photos of her truck? *Her* ranch truck?

Wait a minute. Ever since the day before, when Aaron handed me the photo of James Kelly with his Ferrari and I understood that Kelly and Palmer Warren were the same guy, I'd been assuming it was Palmer who had struck Olivia with his truck.

His truck, which he expected to leave out here, safely hidden away on the ranch. He hadn't even bothered to replace that broken mirror or get that scratch repaired. But why should he? He probably didn't know that the truck had been spotted.

Cassidy's mouth tightened. Her voice was lower and darker now. "Why are you taking photos of the truck?"

The same question again, almost. But not quite. It wasn't *the truck*. It wasn't *his truck*, either. The first time, she had said it was *her truck*. Her ranch, the Pennington family ranch. *Her* ranch truck, which she used to do ranch work and tow the trailer that hauled her quarter horses. Her husband might not have been driving it when it struck Olivia. *She* might.

Seen in that way, it made a certain sense. Charlie had said that Cassidy Warren had a spine of steel and the teeth of a piranha, especially when it came to anything having to do with the Pennington family. Everybody who knew Cassidy Warren knew that the Pennington legend was her most precious possession. If she had learned that Olivia planned to broadcast the truth about her husband's past, she would see it as a threat to him, to herself, and to the Pennington reputation. *Cassidy* could have killed Olivia. She could have killed Margaret, too.

But so could Palmer.

I still didn't know. Was he the killer? Or was she?

And confronted with these chilling possibilities, I couldn't think of a lie. I looked straight at her and heard myself telling the naked truth.

"Because it's the truck that killed Olivia Andrews."

Another silence. Then, "Oh, *dammit*," she said, under her breath. The shotgun came up again. And the rain came down harder.

I weighed my options. I could lunge for the gun, Kinsey-like, but I didn't think that was smart. You don't want to be reaching for a shotgun when it goes off. You get dead that way. The truck window was open, but the rifle in the gun rack was not within easy reach. Ditto for that lethal-looking machete in the back of the truck. She could blast me before I could arm myself.

I couldn't think of any other options.

But I did manage to think of a lie. "Just so you know," I said quietly, "Ruby Wilcox is aware that I'm here, and *why*. I've told her my suspicions. She knows I intended to have a look at your truck. And if I don't make it back to town within a certain amount of time, she will alert the police." In a more judicious tone, I added, "Of course, the truck isn't going to tell us who was driving it. Or whether it was an accident or . . ." I let my voice trail off.

This gave her something to think about, and I saw her chewing on it as we both stood there in the rain. If Palmer had done it, she could throw him under the bus. After all, he was only a Pennington by marriage. She could always claim she didn't know anything about his past or present crimes. Local sympathy—and the local prosecutor—would likely be with her. *She* was a Pennington by blood.

If she had done it, she could claim that it was an accident. I hadn't mentioned Margaret Greer's murder. She would have no way of knowing that I knew about it.

There was another possibility. Either one of them—Cassidy or her husband—might have hired somebody else to kill Olivia and Margaret. Cassidy had plenty of Pennington money. Palmer was wealthy in his own right.

But while she thought about what this meant going forward, she had to be trying to decide what to do with me, *now*. She could shoot me and dispose of my body out there in the vast Hill Country somewhere—not a terribly difficult job, although the county's cadaver dogs would probably find me in pretty short order. There was also my car to dispose of, which would be something of a challenge in these days of search and rescue drones. And there was my story about Ruby and the call to the police. When the cavalry showed up, she would have to explain the missing me. Mine would be the third murder potentially tied to the Warrens, for Margaret Greer would inevitably come up.

Alternatively, she could let me go and take her chances with the legal system—the alternative I definitely favored. I pointed her in that direction.

"A word of advice," I said. "You've been in tight places before. You know how to get yourself out. You're quite well known around here. Your family has a great many friends and you have the resources to hire a first-rate defense—" I was about to say that she could afford a lawyer who could construct a believable defense, but my phone rang.

I have an old-fashioned telephone ringtone, which I like because the commanding *brrring!* cuts through whatever other distractions I'm dealing with. I was still holding it in my right hand. I looked down at it, then back up at Cassidy.

"I have to answer this," I said. "It's the Fredericksburg police. Detective Baker, returning the call I made just now. She's expecting me to pick up. If I don't—"

It was a flimsy lie and an even flimsier threat. But I said it commandingly. And it worked.

She flinched at the word *Fredericksburg*. "I guess you have to answer it, then, dammit," she said thinly. It was raining hard now, the drops bouncing like hail off the ground. "But watch what you say."

I nodded. "China Bayles here," I said.

I lied. It wasn't Baker. It was Connie Page. She sounded urgent. "China, Detective Baker called. She has doorbell video on a white pickup truck that turned around in a neighbor's driveway. License number FX1 23DM. The vehicle is registered to Cassidy Warren and appears to have been driven by a woman. I notified the chief, who asked me to let you know. I phoned the shop, but Ruby says you're out at the ranch, meeting with Mrs. Warren. Are you okay?"

"Doorbell video," I repeated. "White F-150. Driven by a woman." I was hoping Connie would understand what I couldn't say.

"That's it," Connie said. Then, even more urgently, "What have you got there, China? The truck? Mrs. Warren?"

"Both," I said, and trusted her to understand what I meant when I added, "The boss will need the paperwork."

"A search warrant. I'll tell her. Do you need help out there? I can—"

"That would be a very good idea," I said.

I clicked off and looked at Cassidy. "According to the Fredericksburg police, they have a white F-150 on video, license plate FX1 23DM, on the block where Margaret Greer was killed. The driver was a woman."

The driver was a woman. Which let Palmer Warren—James Kelly— off the hook, at least for Margaret Greer's death.

I was standing where I couldn't see the license plate, but Cassidy's eyes flicked in that direction, saw the number, then came back to me.

She stood still for a long moment, the rain pelting down on both of us. She didn't ask me how I had come to be involved with the Fredericksburg police or with Margaret Greer or who the boss was. She was just trying to make sense of what was happening and not doing a bang-up job of it.

"Oh, hell," she said at last. Her shoulders slumped and she lowered the shotgun. "There's been enough killing. I'm sick of it. Go on. Get out of here. And tell Ruby I'm canceling the barbeque. We're done."

I didn't wait for her to change her mind. I didn't exactly run for my car, but I walked very fast.

I DROVE AS FAR AS the intersection of the ranch road and the main road and parked there, waiting while the lightning flashed, the thunder rumbled, and rain and dime-sized hail pounded on the roof. It was like being parked under a waterfall. The rain was coming down so hard that the windshield wipers couldn't manage and I turned them off. My hair was dripping wet and I was soaked through and shivering, so cold that I turned the heater on. I found Caitie's pink sweatshirt on the back seat and used it for a towel, wishing desperately for a strong, hot espresso.

But I did have a cell phone signal, which isn't always a given, out here in the hills, especially in bad weather. I phoned the chief's office again and gave the whole story to Connie—no shorthand this time. I also sent her the photo of James Kelly. She would relay it to Sheila, who had just gotten back from Austin.

The police arrived a half hour later: three squad cars, Sheila, Rita Kidder, and four other officers. The chief stopped the caravan, got out of her squad, and ran through the rain to my car.

"You left Mrs. Warren at the ranch?" No hello, just the question. That's Sheila's working style.

My answer was just as straightforward. "No choice. She had a shotgun. She told me to go. I went."

"She's still there?"

"Far as I know. She hasn't driven out this way. And this road only goes as far as the ranch."

"Connie says you located the truck that killed Andrews."

"Yes. Behind the big party barn, opposite the corral from the stables. It matches Gloria Tanner's description down to the scratch on the door panel. And it's wearing the license plate Baker got from that doorbell camera. Two deaths, one truck. You've got a search warrant?"

"Rita will have it on her iPad by the time we get there." She paused. "The photo you sent—it's pretty clear. Palmer Warren *is* James Kelly. Why do you think it was Cassidy Warren who killed those women?"

I hesitated. "To tell the truth, I'm not sure she killed Olivia. Gloria Tanner didn't get a look at the driver. Far as I can tell, either she or her husband could have done that."

"Wonder what kind of alibi they have."

"Shouldn't be hard to find out," I said. "You might also want to ask where he was the night Margaret Greer was killed, too. According to Baker, it was a woman who was driving the truck in Fredericksburg. But Palmer might have been with her."

"So we don't know whether the same person killed both Olivia and Margaret. Could be one or the other." She wrinkled her forehead. "Or both."

"Right. Each has a motive." I smiled crookedly. "But Olivia's phone should help resolve some of these issues, if you can find it. She must have been in touch with her killer."

"We'll do our best." Sheila reached for the door handle. "Now go home and get dry. I'll call you when I've got news."

"No way." I turned the key in the ignition and started the car. "I'm coming with you."

"No, you're not," Sheila said firmly. "This is police business, China. You're going back to town. I'll call you when it's done."

"But you need me to show you where—"

She held up a hand. "You've done all you can do and then some. I'm grateful. Very grateful. But you're going back to town. And don't try to mess with me or I'll arrest you for contempt of cop." A smile ghosted across her mouth. She opened the door and got out, then paused. "That oil you gave me for Noah's gums is miraculous. The little guy slept all night again. And so did we. Thanks."

She slammed the door and ran back to her squad, ducking through the rain. A few moments later, the caravan drove up the road toward the Blind Penny.

"WELL, *PHOOEY*," RUBY SAID WHEN I got back to the shops and told her about the cancellation. "We were going to make a nice little profit off that barbecue. You don't think she'll change her mind?"

"I don't think she'll be in any position to host her friends," I said. "Things are going to be dicey for the Warrens for a while." I told her the rest of it.

"Ai-ai-ii!" Ruby said, wide-eyed. She shook her head. "I *knew* I should have gone with you! She might have fired that shotgun!"

"I don't think so," I said. "Just think of the mess she'd have to clean up. And murder number three is bound to get some attention.

Anyway, it's all over now. Sheila will see that Cassidy owns up to whatever she has done."

It didn't quite happen that way, though.

It rained steadily in Pecan Springs until the middle of the afternoon, and the TV weather guy reported that it was persisting in the Hill Country to the west. Low-water crossings over four counties were closed, and there had already been several rescues. One driver didn't make it. He drowned when he drove around a barrier and his car was swept away. People don't realize how little it takes to push you off the road. Twenty-four inches of fast-moving floodwater can carry away most vehicles, including SUVs and pickups. And you can't tell how deep the water is until it's too late. I couldn't help wondering how things were going out on the ranch but I had to admit to being glad to be out of harm's way.

At home, I made an early night of it. Winchester and I were tucked into bed by ten, I with a book and Winchester with his favorite cuddle monkey. Mr. P was dozing on McQuaid's pillow, his paws folded neatly under his white bib. His rumbling purr and Winchester's wheezy snore were comfortable sounds in the quiet room. I had finished my book and was about to turn out the light when Sheila called from her squad car. She was driving home.

"You're keeping late hours," I said. "How'd it go?" Hearing me talking, Winchester opened one gloomy basset eye to make sure he wasn't supposed to do something about an intruder, and shut it again.

"You got off the ranch just in time," Sheila said.

"Yeah?" I asked. "What does that mean?"

"We got stopped at one of those low-water crossings on our way into the ranch. The water came up to the two-foot mark on the flood gauge and stayed there. It was almost six by the time it was low enough to make the attempt. You know what flash floods are like out there in that country. Too dangerous to cross. Nothing we could do but sit there and wait until it went down."

"Uh-oh," I said. "But you got across okay? You found the truck? You executed the warrant?"

"Got across. Found the truck. It's on its way to the impound lot. Forensics will start on it in the morning." She paused. "And yes. We found what we think is Andrews' computer. And her phone. We'll start work on both tomorrow."

"Fantastic," I exclaimed. "That's wonderful, Sheila! You've found everything!"

"Not quite. We didn't find Cassidy Warren."

"What?" Startled, I sat up straight. Winchester opened both eyes. "She wasn't at the ranch?"

"Nope. We looked until it was too dark to keep looking."

"She didn't drive out to the main road while I was there," I said. "And the road you took dead-ends at the ranch. Where *is* she?"

"Palmer Warren showed up while we were waiting to cross. He—"

"I thought Palmer Warren was in Oklahoma City."

"He was. He got back this afternoon. When we got onto the property and couldn't locate his wife, he checked the vehicles. Her Mercedes was there, as well as the white Ford pickup you found behind the party barn and a Dodge pickup in the stable. But a TerraScout was missing. *Is* missing. And so is she."

"A TerraWhat?" Then I remembered. "Oh, the amphibious ATV. I saw it. Bright yellow."

"You saw it? *You* were in the stable?"

Stupid. "Of course not. Forget I said that."

Sheila grunted. "Palmer thinks Cassidy might have taken it to check on her horses. They're in a pasture several miles on the other side of the lake—a rugged area, hard to get to. She had to cross a creek."

"She tried to take it across when it was flooding?" I shuddered. "That's crazy! She's lived on that ranch her whole life. Surely she wouldn't try a trick like that."

Sheila's voice was matter-of-fact. "Her husband says those horses mean more to her than he does. That storm was pretty fierce. We saw hail the size of golf balls—large enough to injure an animal out in the open. She'd be worried about them. And Palmer says he refuses to ride in that ATV. Says the center of gravity is too high. He was in a rollover with it last year and was lucky to get out of it without injury."

Palmer Warren. I thought of my conundrum. Who was driving the truck that killed Olivia? Was it Cassidy or her husband?

"Did you interview him?" I asked. "Does he have an alibi for Olivia's death?"

"Yes and yes. I spent more than an hour with him. The week Olivia was killed, he says he was in Albuquerque, looking at some property. We'll check it out."

"And the night Margaret was killed?"

"The guy gets around. That night, he was in Omaha. Again, it sounds pretty tight."

"I guess that settles it, then. It was Cassidy. She must have chosen dates when her husband was out of town, so she'd be free to move around. Have you fingerprinted the phone and the computer?"

"That's in the works. When we find her, we'll print her."

When we find her. I remembered the flash floods I had seen and the wreckage they had left in their wake. It wasn't a pretty thought.

Sheila yawned noisily. "Excuse me. Long day."

"You sound tired," I said, wondering as I often do how in the world Sheila keeps going the way she does.

"Bone-weary. I am ready to crash. I have to be out there again in the morning. We're bringing in additional assets at dawn. Texas Parks and Wildlife is sending a drone search and rescue team. We'll find her."

I was about to say *I hope she's okay*, but the words suddenly seemed so ridiculously ironic that I bit them back. If Sheila's and Baker's investigations went the way they were headed, Cassidy Warren would be charged with the murders of two women. If convicted, life without parole. I finally settled for "Not a good outcome all around."

"You got that right." Sheila was silent for a moment. "I owe you an apology, China. When you came into the office with that story from Andrews' sister, I thought you were way off the mark."

"I didn't pick up on that."

"Well, I did. I was humoring you, just because we're friends. I kept thinking you must have something better to do. But I have to tell you that if you hadn't put your head down and got to work on it, we'd still be treating Andrews' death as just another hit-and-run. And if you hadn't made the connection between Andrews and the victim in Fredericksburg, Baker would be nowhere on that case. Chalk up two for you. Thank you."

"You're welcome. But you ought to consider thanking Charlie, you know. He's the one who sicced Zelda on me."

"Yeah, well, I'm sure he had his reasons."

"I am, too. In fact, I think it's likely that he's known all along about the connection between James Kelly and Palmer Warren. He may even have had his suspicions, either about Palmer or Cassidy and Olivia. As their attorney, though, he knew he didn't want to know. Charlie is devious."

"All you lawyers are. Devious as the night is long."

"I'm not a lawyer," I said. "And there's not a devious bone in my body. Now, go home and get some *sleep*."

"I'm there," Sheila said. "I'm pulling into our driveway at this very moment. Good night. And thanks again."

"Good night." I clicked off the phone, wishing I could feel better about what had happened that day.

Chapter Eighteen

Since ancient times dreams have been important in the life of many traditional populations and the basis not only of spiritual and religious development but also of intellectual development, permitting a direct contact with the realm of the supernatural. Dream-inducing plants are considered sacred; they are the source of divinity manifesting in the human body and acting on the mind.

Drugs of the Dreaming. Oneirogens:
Salvia divinorum *and Other Dream-Enhancing Plants*
Gianluca Toro and Benjamin Thomas

One species highly valued in Mexican traditional medicine is *Calea ternifolia* Kunth (*Asteraceae*), the "dream herb," an endemic species of Mexico and Central America, traditionally used by the Chontal Indigenous Peoples for divination due to its oneirogenic [dream enhancement] properties.

"*Calea ternifolia* Kunth, the Mexican
'dream herb,' a concise review"
Canadian Science Publishing
https://cdnsciencepub.com/doi/10.1139/cjb-2021-0063

There are more things in heaven and earth, Horatio, than are dreamt of in your philosophy.

Hamlet, Act 1
William Shakespeare

They found the ATV first. It was lodged against a tree just below a crossing on Penny Creek, several miles west of the lake. It was another day before Cassidy Warren was found, hung up in a barbed wire fence a half mile downstream. Somebody from Parks and Wildlife located her body with a drone equipped with a thermal camera—if not for that, it might have been a week before she was found. Her husband was planning to give her the kind of funeral a Pennington deserved. She would be buried next to her parents in the Pennington family plot.

"It's probably just as well," McQuaid said when he got home from Midland late Thursday night and heard the terse recap of my misadventures. We had taken our wine glasses out onto the front porch, where Winchester blundered through the rosemary bushes, on the trail of the armadillo that regularly eludes him. We sat in the swing and listened to the crickets in concert, their melody occasionally accompanied by the booming *who-who-whooo* of a great horned owl and the harsh, percussive *skeow* of a green heron down at the creek.

"I don't mean to sound dismissive," McQuaid added thoughtfully. "But after all, she died doing what she'd done all her life—taking care of her horses. She had to know that she was facing indictment and trial with a strong possibility of conviction. It would have been a catastrophe for her. She was always so proud of being a Pennington. And since there's no trial, many of her Pecan Springs friends may never have to know the whole story."

I held up two fingers. "She's avoided two trials. One in Adams County, for Olivia's murder. The other in Gillespie County, for Margaret's. But people *are* going to know the full story, just as soon as Jessica pulls it together. She and Hark both feel that it isn't fair to Olivia to let her life and death—or Margaret's—be forgotten. The story is going to get out there."

"Sounds like the truck is the strongest piece of evidence they've got in the hit-and-run. The broken mirror, the missing cab light. Any chance of finding the victim's DNA on the truck somewhere?"

"It was sitting out in the rain. There was nothing visible, but they're still working on that. However, Detective Baker says they matched a partial print on the shell casing in Margaret Greer's kitchen to Cassidy. And Cassidy's prints are on Olivia's cell phone and her computer."

"Sounds tight." McQuaid finished his wine. "Palmer Warren wasn't involved?"

"If he was, Sheila's team will figure it out and charge him. But his alibis for both murders seem to be pretty solid. And judging from what's been found on the phone and the computer, it looks to me like Cassidy decided that this was *her* responsibility—not so much on her husband's behalf but to shield the Pennington family reputation. I've talked to Palmer. He's pretty broken up about Cassidy's death. He blames himself."

"It would be hard not to. Cassidy may have done it to keep her family out of the news, but it was *his* criminal past she was trying to hide. Palmer may be innocent, but he was never completely cleared. How is he going to feel about Jessica splashing the details of his criminal history for everybody to read?"

"He says he's ready to come clean. He's tired of hiding behind an assumed name—a false front, he called it. Ironically, he told me that he had agreed to cooperate with Olivia on the story. But he knew he had to tell his wife first. He couldn't let her read about it on Olivia's blog or hear it on her podcast. He had no idea that Cassidy would see it as a threat to the Pennington reputation, and then go out and kill a couple of people."

"She must have thought that a simple hit-and-run job would

get them out of it, with very little risk." He glanced at me. "And it might've, if you hadn't stuck your nose in."

I corrected him. "If Zelda hadn't gotten suspicious about the missing phone and computer. And if Charlie hadn't sent Zelda to me with her wacky story, hoping I would get curious and start digging. Charlie *used* me." I had contacted Zelda as soon as I learned about Cassidy's death. She now knew as much as I did. And Charlie and I had had an overdue conversation about laying all the cards on the table.

"Charlie." McQuaid chuckled wryly. "Trust that guy to be playing with pocket aces." He paused. "That vacated murder conviction over in Houston. What's going to happen there?"

"Charlie is talking to the DA about a dismissal. I think he'll get it. I suspect that the Houston DA won't want to be bothered with a retrial of a dicey twenty-year-old arson homicide. No idea how they'll handle that phony death down in Mexico, though. It's complicated."

McQuaid agreed. "There's always another story behind the story." He stood and held out his hand. "Speaking of stories, come on, wife. We have an unfinished chapter. Upstairs."

And as it always does, our chapter came to a remarkably satisfying conclusion.

I KEPT AN ANXIOUS EYE on Facebook and Instagram, alert for the review bombing that Almira Pickle had dreamed up. But as the weeks passed, our permit was approved, and everything seemed pretty normal, my apprehension level climbed into the red zone. Almira and her friends must be saving it all up for the day of the fair. This only added to my growing catalog of nail-biting worries about the event. Would Ramona behave herself? What would we do if the vendors failed to show up?

This was a first-of-a-kind for Pecan Springs—what if *nobody* showed up? And it was hotter than blue blazes. Would we all simply melt?

There was one thing, though, that made me feel better every time I thought about it. Jessica called one afternoon to say that she'd just gotten verification of a story she'd been working on. "It's about the Reverend Kellogg," she said. "Your avocado thief."

"Kellogg?" I was wary. "What about him?

"A federal grand jury in Dallas has apparently been investigating him for that mess at the megachurch. The indictment came out this morning. Nine counts of mail fraud, three counts of wire fraud, and one count of conspiracy. There's more, and plenty juicy. You can read all about it in my story. It'll be out tomorrow."

"Wow," I said. "Jessica, that's . . . wild."

"Yep." She sounded smug. "Couldn't happen to a nicer guy."

When Ruby heard the news, she laughed. "You see?" she said. "It may take a while, but the Universe gets its man. It's called karma."

I WAS RIGHT TO WORRY about the weather, but not the way I thought. When I woke before dawn on the Saturday morning of the fair, I heard something rattling against the window. I sat up. "Don't tell me," I said incredulously. "It can't be."

"It is," McQuaid said. "Rain." He got out of bed. "Stay where you are. I'll start the coffee."

Well, *rats*. I lay back down and pulled the sheet over my face. I mean, for cryin' out loud, this is *July*. July is brown and scorching. July is blowing dust and burn bans and pavement hot enough to fry bare feet. It never rains in July. Ever.

But it did. To be fair, after the first twenty minutes, it subsided to a drizzle. Still, it was raining hard enough to keep sensible folks indoors. It rained, off and on, until nearly eleven, while dozens of people called the shops, wondering if the fair had been rained out.

And then, just when Ruby and I were within five minutes of leaving a POSTPONED note on Facebook and texting Ramona that we were rescheduling, the rain stopped. A cheerful sun came out, a brisk breeze began drying things off, and the temperature was a good fifteen degrees cooler than the day before. We were in business.

As planned, the first vendors arrived at noon to set up their booths. From that point on, the day went astonishingly well. Oh, there were a few problems, but they were manageable, like the circuit breaker that tripped when the sound equipment was plugged in and the vendor table that collapsed when somebody leaned against it, spilling crystals and candles onto the grass. As the afternoon went on, there were plenty of people and they all seemed to be enjoying themselves.

Still, I couldn't help worrying. Remembering Janie's reminder of the protest that had effectively closed down Dos Amigas, I left Laurel in charge of the shop and hung around outside to keep a wary eye out for Almira Pickle and her friends. I expected to see them marching down the street at any moment, brandishing ugly signs and chanting and maybe even threatening people. Or maybe they would infiltrate the crowd and at some point, begin to raise a ruckus. I had my phone in my pocket and I was on the lookout for anybody acting out of line. I had even alerted Sheila to my concerns, in case things got out of hand and we needed to call the cops.

But I seemed to be the only person who wasn't carefree and high-spirited. Ramona had done an excellent job of rounding up vendors. She and her team of psychics set up shop at the back of the garden, near the alley. She had arranged an online signup, so clients could make appointments ahead of time. The women were constantly busy and there was even a lineup of people hoping for a cancellation. In addition to Ramona's talk on dreamwork, I had asked my friends Jeanne Guy and Stephanie Raffelock, both from Austin, to present their popular Story Circle writing workshop, *You've Got This! Claiming Your Creative Spirit*, and Ruby invited Dr. Melissa Scott, her mentor from the university's psychology department, to give a talk on current research in parapsychology and dreams. The RSVP lists for the workshop and the two talks had been filled almost as soon as we posted them online.*

In addition to Ramona's team of psychics, there were a dozen other vendors and energy workers with a wide range of offerings: crystals, candles, jewelry, nutrition, books and CDs, and more. A woman came up from San Antonio to interpret tarot cards, another was throwing coins out of a polished turtle shell for the I Ching, while yet another, dressed as a priestess of Freyja, was reading runes. A pair of astrologists had brought laptops and were casting birth charts, a young man was skrying with a black obsidian bowl, and a past life reader had set up an attractive booth screened with silk curtains, explaining that things sometimes got a little intense and that she and her clients needed privacy. The guy who did the aura photography and the readings was kept busy. While I heard one man sniff "Good art, bad science," I had to admit that the pictures I saw were fascinating. To keep things lively for the children, there was face painting, palm reading, astrology games, and a crystal ball. And of course, there were the costumes. What would a psychic fair be if it weren't for the wizards, witches, fairies, fortune tellers, and surprising visitors from other galaxies?

---

* For Ruby's adventures at the parapsychology lab: *Somebody Else*, book 2 in the Crystal Cave trilogy.

But for me, the biggest, most stunning surprise of the day came when I dropped in on Ramona's talk on dream interpretation. I came in through the side door and stood where I could see the audience as well as the speaker. Every RSVP had shown up and the room was crowded—so crowded that I hoped the fire marshal was busy elsewhere. Ramona was near the end of her presentation, talking about the potential importance of lucid dreaming to understand ourselves. She was excited and animated as she urged everyone to keep a dream journal and share their dreams with their friends. I am not Ramona's biggest fan, but I have to admit that the woman is a passionate and compelling speaker, especially when she's talking about something that interests her deeply. She was on her best behavior, too. I watched her for almost ten minutes and I didn't see a single sign of her poltergeist.

And then, as I turned to go, I was shocked—*stunned*, really—to see Almira Pickle on the far side of the room, in the very front row. Almira Pickle! The woman who had been instructed by a dream angel to review-bomb us into oblivion, who had threatened to call out the pickets, who was planning a boycott, and who was inalterably convinced that we were all practicing Satanists intending to convert little kids to our wicked ways. Clearly mesmerized, she was leaning forward, a half-smile on her face, her eyes fixed with a zealot's burning intensity on Ramona.

I had to blink. Was that really Almira? Why was she here, in this room, on the front row? What was that hypnotic look? Why wasn't she out front with a sign and a squad of pickets?

What in the devil was happening here? Immediately suspicious, I went looking for Ruby, who (at six-feet-something in her wedgies) stands out in a crowd. She wasn't in her shop. Or in the tearoom, where a few clusters of people were enjoying a snack break.

I found her in the kitchen behind the tearoom, munching on what Cass was calling a cosmic cookie. It is made of three kinds of seeds, two kinds of berries, chocolate chips, coconut, nuts, and oats—everything in the cookie galaxy, Cass says. Cosmically wholesome.

"Isn't it going *well*?" she crowed happily, lifting her cookie in salute. "Everybody tells me they're having a fantastic time! They say we just have to do it again—only do it bigger. And more often."

I was not going to be distracted. "What have you *done*?" I demanded. "And just how in the hell did you *do* it?"

"Do what?" She took another cookie off the rack and held it out. "Here. Nibble on a cosmic cookie. Cass has sold four dozen of these today—everybody loves them. There's flaxseed. It'll help you calm down."

"No thank you," I said, not very graciously. "I don't want to calm down. I just saw something I can scarcely believe. Almira Pickle, on the front row of Ramona's audience. I expected that she and her crew would be out front picketing, but there she sat, looking like she had just found her guru and signed on for a life of utter devotion. Do you have any idea what's going on?" I gave her a narrow look. "Did *you* do something to convert her? Have you been playing any of your spooky mind games with her?"

"I did *not*," Ruby said emphatically. She munched her cookie. "Ramona did."

I stared at her. "Ramona? Ramona did *what*? What did Ramona do?"

"She did some dream telepathy."

"Dream telepathy?" I stared at her. "Is that a thing? I've never heard of it."

"Dr. Scott says it happens in other cultures, where dreaming is more a part of people's lives than it is here. She says that some people—

people who do a lot of dreamwork, for instance—can communicate telepathically with another person while they are dreaming. Ramona has been working with Dr. Scott for the past six months. She experimented on Almira."

"Experimented? On Almira? Just how did *that* work?"

"When I heard that Almira got the idea for the Yelp interference in a dream, I thought it sounded like she might be a receiver—somebody who is especially receptive to dream communication. As I said, Ramona has been working in the parapsychology lab with Dr. Scott. So she experimented with sending dream messages. Not threatening, of course, just . . . discouraging." Ruby's smile was almost smug. "Ramona also sent her a special invitation to this afternoon's talk and followed it up with a personal email. Almira seems to have turned into a *fan*."

I was appalled. "You mean, Ramona meddled with Almira's *head*?" I am rabid on the subject of our right to privacy, and there's nothing more private than somebody's dreams.

Ruby finished her cookie. "Would you rather be dealing with a crowd of screaming pickets out front? And a ton of negative Yelps and bad reviews on our Facebook page?"

"Of course not. But—"

"Exactly. We had to do *something*." Ruby adopted the reasonable tone she likes to use when she is explaining something I should have already thought of. "Dream messages aren't a lot different from what advertisers do with their subliminal prompts to buy this and that. How many tubes of toothpaste have you bought because you saw a commercial about whiter teeth on TV?"

I frowned. "The end doesn't always justify the means."

"Maybe not. But you've got to admit that Almira's means were pretty unjustified too. Ramona didn't fight fire with fire. She fought fire with dreams. And it worked. You can't argue with that."

I altered my strategy. "We don't *know* that's why she's here. Maybe Almira got a cold and she didn't want to picket. Or she figured it wasn't smart to cause trouble in the neighborhood. Or decided—all by herself, no help from Ramona—to give the event a chance before she called out her storm troopers."

"Maybe," Ruby said lightly. "Or maybe she dreamed that she could learn something about dreaming if she came to our event—without an armed guard." She took a cookie off the rack and turned to go. "Next time you talk to Ramona, you might want to say thank you."

I was still thinking about that when I heard a commotion on the flagstone patio outside the kitchen, where the astral photographer had set up shop for the afternoon. I opened the door just in time to hear somebody say, "Uh-oh, here come the cops! Are we making too much noise? Somebody complained?"

It was the cops, all right, but just one. The chief, in uniform, her blond hair scooped into a bun at the back of her head. I was glad to see that she was looking better—more rested, I thought.

"You've got a nice crowd," she said, glancing around. "I didn't see any pickets out front. Have you had any trouble?"

I wasn't eager to share the details of Ramona's dream experiment, which I was viewing as something akin to home invasion. "Looks like we dodged that bullet, at least for today," I said. "Did you come to get your astral photo taken? Or your fortune told? I'm sure we can find somebody to cast a birth chart for you."

Sheila laughed. "No, but I might want to ask Ruby to cast one for Noah. I understand that he's a Scorpio. I think I need to know more."

She lowered her voice. "Actually, I have some news that may interest you. How about if we step inside?"

"Sure. Let's sit down with a drink and a cosmic cookie."

"A *cosmic* cookie?" Sheila's eyebrows went up. "Should I go out to the squad and get my ticket book?"

I grinned. "Not that kind of cosmic. But this has everything *else* a cookie lover's heart could desire—nuts, seeds, berries, coconut, chocolate chips. We've been selling them all afternoon. Cass gave me the recipe. I can email it to you."

"Please do. Sounds like Blackie's kind of cookie."

Back in the kitchen, I poured tea for both of us and we took our glasses and a plate of cookies into the nearly empty tearoom, where we sat at a table in the back corner.

"What's up?" I asked. "News about what?"

"A couple of things," Sheila said. "Remember when our forensic team disassembled the passenger-side door of Cassidy's pickup?"

"Yeah. They found blood inside the door, on the glass and on the window regulator."

Forensics had already tied Olivia's cell phone and computer to Cassidy Warren. Both had been found in the bottom drawer of her bedroom dresser, with her underwear. Both were covered with Cassidy's fingerprints. So they began looking for anything that would tie the truck—the alleged murder weapon—to Cassidy's victim. To Olivia. The impact had resulted in a blood spray across the passenger window and door. The visible blood had all been cleaned up, by one of the ranch employees, as it turned out. Cassidy told him—and Palmer, too—that she had hit a deer. But she hadn't realized that blood might run down *inside* the door. It was still there when forensics went looking.

"We finally got that DNA report," Sheila said. "But I can't blame the DPS lab for being late. We had to put a couple of more urgent requests ahead of this one. After all, this wasn't a rush job."

I understood. Cassidy was dead. But I had been wondering.

"So?" I asked. "What did they say?"

"It was a DNA match," Sheila said. "Olivia's blood. Inside the door."

I let out my breath in a rush.

"We've finished checking Palmer out, too," she went on. "He was out of town on both occasions, and he denies that Cassidy told him what she was planning. He's been cleared of both murders—here and in Fredericksburg. And he's pretty devastated by the whole thing."

I shook my head. "So this was entirely Cassidy's doing."

"Right." Sheila looked grim. "I'm only sorry we won't see her in the courtroom. No case is ever a slam dunk, but this one would come pretty close. Baker feels the same way, over in Fredericksburg. She's glad to be able to close the case, but she would have liked to see the killer go to trial."

"Maybe so," I said. "But Cassidy's death saved both counties a ton of money and time." I added, "And deprived a team of defense attorneys of their legitimate livelihood."

"Well, there's certainly that." Sheila finished her cookie. "You know I'm always glad to deprive a few defense attorneys of *anything*. And you're definitely right about saving county money and time. If we had arrested Cassidy the minute we got the DNA report, her trial would still be a year away and appeals another few years after that. Justice takes a very long time."

A very long time. I thought of Eleanor, long dead—perhaps accidentally. Of Palmer, who had been hiding from her death and its tragic consequences for the past two decades.

And of Olivia and Margaret, whose lives had been taken to conceal Eleanor's death and Palmer's conviction.

And of Cassidy. Had the Universe stepped in to see that justice was served more swiftly in her case?

And I felt suddenly grateful to Jessica, whose job it is to make sure that the stories of these women will not be forgotten, that the voices of the dead will linger in the hearts of her readers.

Surely there is justice in that.

About the Author

Growing up on a farm on the Illinois prairie, Susan Wittig Albert learned that books could take her anywhere. She earned an undergraduate degree in English from the University of Illinois at Urbana and a PhD in medieval studies from the University of California at Berkeley. After fifteen years of faculty and administrative appointments at the University of Texas, Tulane University, and Texas State University, she left her academic career to write full time. She is the founder of the Story Circle Network, a nonprofit organization for women writers, and a member of Sisters in Crime, Women Writing the West, Mystery Writers of America, and the Texas Institute of Letters. She and her husband and co-author Bill Albert live in the Texas Hill Country.

www.susanalbert.com and *www.susanwittigalbert.substack.com*

Resources

You can find background material for this book, including recipes and suggestions for further reading, at:

www.susanalbert.com/forget-me-never-book-29

Books by Susan Wittig Albert

For a detailed list, including the latest additions,
visit *www.susanalbert.com*

MYSTERY SERIES

The Crystal Cave Novella Trilogy (China Bayles Mysteries)
The *Pecan Springs Enterprise* Novella Trilogy (China Bayles Mysteries)
The Darling Dahlias Mysteries
The Cottage Tales of Beatrix Potter
The Robin Paige Victorian-Edwardian Mysteries
(with Bill Albert, writing as Robin Paige)

THE HIDDEN WOMEN SERIES: HISTORICAL/BIOGRAPHICAL FICTION

Loving Eleanor
A Wilder Rose
The General's Women
Someone Always Nearby

MEMOIR

An Extraordinary Year of Ordinary Days
Together, Alone: A Memoir of Marriage and Place

NONFICTION

Writing from Life: Telling the Soul's Story
Work of Her Own

EDITED VOLUMES

What Wildness Is This: Women Write about the Southwest